PENGUIN BOOKS

THE MARRAKESH ONE-TWO

Raised in Brookline, Massachusetts, Richard Grenier attended Harvard before winning an appointment to the U.S. Naval Academy. After serving as a deck and gunnery officer in the navy, he returned to Harvard, but left the university once again on winning a Fulbright scholarship that enabled him to study in Paris, where he became a student at both the Sorbonne and the Institut d'Etudes Politiques. He later embarked on a career as a peripatetic journalist, working for the French, British, and American press; for news agencies; and for newspapers, radio, and television. In 1967 his first novel, *Yes and Back Again*, was published to considerable critical acclaim. Richard Grenier now divides his time among Los Angeles, New York, and Paris.

Richard Grenier

The Marrakesh One-Two

Penguin Books

For Pat and Liz

PENGUIN BOOKS
Viking Penguin Inc., 40 West 23rd Street,
New York, New York 10010, U.S.A.
Penguin Books Ltd, Harmondsworth,
Middlesex, England
Penguin Books Australia Ltd, Ringwood,
Victoria, Australia
Penguin Books Canada Limited, 2801 John Street,
Markham, Ontario, Canada L3R 1B4
Penguin Books (N.Z.) Ltd, 182-190 Wairau Road,
Auckland 10, New Zealand

First published in the United States of America by
Houghton Mifflin Company 1983
Published by Viking Penguin Inc. 1984

LIBRARY OF CONGRESS CATALOGING IN PUBLICATION DATA
Grenier, Richard, 1926–
    The Marrakesh one-two.
    Reprint. Originally published: Boston: Houghton
Mifflin, 1983.
    I. Title.
[PS3557.R439M3 1984] 813'.54 84-1206
ISBN 0 14 00.7372 8

Printed in the United States of America by
R. R. Donnelley & Sons Company, Harrisonburg, Virginia
Set in Primer

And when it was told him that she asked his head of King Arthur, he went to her straight and said, Evil be you found. You would have my head, and therefore ye shall lose yours. And with his sword lightly he smote off her head before King Arthur. Alas, for shame! said Arthur, why have ye done so? Ye have shamed me and all my court, for this was a lady that I was beholden to, and hither she came under my safe-conduct. I shall never forgive you that trespass. Sir, said Balin, me forthynketh of your displeasure, but this same lady was the untruest lady living, and by enchantment and sorcery she hath been the destroyer of many good knights. Then Balin took up the head of the lady, and bare it with him to his hostelry, and there he met with his squire. Now, said Balin, we must depart. Take thou this head and bear it to my friends, and tell them how I have sped, and tell my friends in Northumberland that my most foe is dead. I will hie me in all the haste that I may to meet with King Rience and destroy him. Either else to die therefore. And if it may hap me to win him, then again will King Arthur be my good and gracious lord. Where shall I meet with you? said the squire. Said Balin, in King Arthur's court.

SIR THOMAS MALORY,
Le Morte d'Arthur

I

I COULD HEAR the muezzin calling the faithful to prayer but I didn't hear nobody pray, man. No, I didn't. And it's a pretty miserable call too, let me tell you. GWAWAWAWA-WAWAWAWK. FNUHUHUHUHUHUH — glottal stop. On and on, five times a day. And I didn't *see* nobody pray either. Never, never, never. Not once. Omar says it doesn't mean they're bad Moslems, they only pray in mosques or at home and you can group your prayers. Like one in the morning before you go to work, and then when you get back home at night the other four, ping, ping, ping, ping, right like that. But what does he know he's a crazy Lebanese Christian.

I'm lying there on my bed in the Marrakesh Hilton with the fan on me and a wet towel on me for evaporation, and the temperature is somewhere between 110 and 120, and I don't care if I live or die. Because the Moroccans and the Hilton people got into a fight and the Hilton people said *You can't do that to us* and the Moroccans expropriated the hotel, which is why the air conditioning doesn't work, so the Hilton people are suing before the International Court of Justice in The Hague. And on this private matter I am rooting like mad for the Hiltons, while placing my trust in the justice of Allah of course, on which I am meditating day and night. For justice will come, for the poor, the needy, and the hot. Allah is great.

The telephone beside the bed rings and a voice says, "Is this Opal?" And I say, "Now do I sound as if my name's

1

Opal?" And he hangs up and I give the switchboard operator a number and it rings but no answer. And I give her the number again and it rings and rings and rings, and still no answer. So I chew her out a little and ask her is she sure she's getting the number right and she swears, *Oui, Monsieur, absolument!* and it rings some more and I give up. Is this Opal.

Omar, my Beverly Hills Arab, comes charging into the room in his Brooks Brothers shirt, his blue eyes all intent and nervous. This blue-eyed Arab.

"What are you doing lying in bed? How about Hamza, the Prophet's uncle! Where's the scene where Hind eats his liver? Al Azzar says it's okay. They gave us the absolute green light. Get it written, Burt, for God's sake. We might have to shoot it next week!"

"They're not going to like it in Shawnee, Oklahoma," I said.

"How about Salome, for Christ sake!" Omar said, indignant. "Didn't she get the head of that John the Baptist?"

"But she didn't eat it."

"But every Arab knows the story! Little Arab kids sing the song: rata rata rata rata, *and Hind ate Honda's liver.*"

"Hamza. Honda's a Japanese automobile. It doesn't have a liver."

"Don't give me any arguments! It goes in!"

"Okay, okay. It goes in."

We're making this pro-Mohammed movie to show Islam in a good light to religious-type people in the West and he wants Salome to eat the head of John the Baptist. We're going to give Islam a fair shake, you get it? We're taking on Christianity, Voltaire, and B'nai B'rith. Money is no object. Arab oil is paying for it. If they want Jeanne Moreau to eat Hamza's liver it's all right with me.

"In it goes!" I declared emphatically and started to rise from the bed, and Omar scurried out to take a dip in the swimming pool. You sure didn't see *him* praying. And I lay back on the bed again.

Because you don't know what the problems were. We're

2

making the life of Mohammed, right? It's going to be like *The Mohammed Story*, or *The Second Greatest Story Ever Told*, like *Mohammed Superstar*. But Islam, a little detail, has this ferocious hostility to the graven image, rather well known in historical circles, and they don't like tri-acetate images either. There is no show business in Saudi Arabia, you can believe me. The Egyptians are backsliders to the point of having a film industry of sorts, but never deal with sacred subjects. There are places where they'd kill you in a spirit of devoted piety for daring to represent the image of the Prophet. They take these things seriously. No one had ever even thought of doing the life of Mohammed until Omar except for Moustapha Akkad, and you know what happened to him. So Omar had to go about it very cautiously so that we didn't get ourselves assassinated by some fanatic. After conferring with the doctors of Al Azzar in Cairo he tells me we've got to cut out Mohammed. We're doing *The Mohammed Story*, you understand, but Mohammed's got to go. Too holy to be portrayed. We've got to "shoot around" Mohammed. But also all his immediate family has to go: This wealthy widow he married who gave him his start in life. All his ten or so other wives. His children, all the daughters. His famous sons-in-law. Ali goes. Omar goes. The four first caliphs go. Mohammed's mother and father go. The ten Companions of Mohammed go. That's the ten apostles right there. Talk of Hamlet without the prince. This was Hamlet without the prince, king, queen, Ophelia, Polonius, Horatio, Laertes, Rosencrantz, and Guildenstern. It was going to be Hamlet with the gravediggers and Fortinbras. The only thing they would give me was that I could have P.V. Mohammed. That is I could script shots from Mohammed's Point of View, subjective camera. I could have faces reacting and people talking *to* Mohammed. But Mohammed couldn't answer them because his voice would be too holy. I got to work it all in by hearsay. And Mohammed couldn't cast a shadow. He was too holy to cast a shadow. That would be sacrilege too. Mohammed seems to have been about five foot four but when people speak to him in our movie they look up to him as if he's the size of Bill Walton. But it is still the Mohammed story, you understand, and the working title is *Mohammed, Man of Mecca*, because confusingly enough the Moslems are quite proud of the fact that Mohammed isn't set up to be any kind of a supernatural being but just a man like you or me, give or take a little. I mean there's no abracadabra about Son of God, on the third day ascended into heaven where he sitteth on the right hand of God the Father from whence he shall come to judge the quick and the dead sort of stuff. Just an ordinary mortal prophet. The Koran only is a miracle, which Mohammed dictated by bits and pieces here and there when he was in his states, and which I will leave you to read for yourself and you can come to your own conclusion.

The phone rang and a voice said, "Celia?" And I said, "Celia? There's no Celia here." And I had the switchboard operator try a number three times with no answer. Celia. What a bunch of goofs.

When Omar laid the project on me I first read the Koran, of course. And there are reams and reams of *Allah is great. Allah is one. Allah is supreme. Allah is merciful.* And suddenly you run into, *You are also forbidden to take in marriage married women, except captives whom you own as slaves.* And then more Allah is great and Allah is merciful until you come to, *Men have authority over women because Allah has made the one superior to the other and because they spend their wealth upon them. Good women are obedient. As for those from whom you fear disobedience, admonish them and send them to beds apart and beat them. Then if they obey you, take no further action against them. Allah is high, supreme.* Which was pretty moderate, I guess. Then there were sexy parts. *If any of your women commit fornication, call in four witnesses from among yourselves against them: if they testify to their guilt confine them to their houses till death overtake them. If two men among you commit indecency punish them both. If they repent and mend their ways, let them be. Allah is forgiving and merciful.* Which was pretty equitable really. I mean what's sauce for the goose was sauce for the goose. And there was a lot of good solid stuff, like, *Those of you who divorce their wives by declaring them to be their mothers should know that they are not their mothers. Their mothers are those who gave birth to them. The words they utter are unjust and false: but Allah is forgiving and merciful.* Which was a good point to clear up. I mean I was sure it had led to a lot of misunderstanding until Mohammed cleared it up. Then I read a whole bunch of biographies of Mohammed, the life of Mohammed and the life of the Prophet, and on to *The Meaning of Islam* and *Islam Today* and *Islam in the Modern World*, whose authors explained that when Mohammed talked about slavery he didn't really mean slavery, and in any case it was all very advanced for his time. And Omar breathing down my neck every day saying, "Dramatize, Burt, dramatize. We've got to have a good dramatization." Not that there wasn't material, but up to then I'd been a Christianity and Judaism man and Mohammed struck me as kind of a gamey figure for a religious leader, I mean for a man God spoke to personally. I didn't know what to make of him really, sort of a blend of Saint Teresa of Avila, Jane Addams of Hull House, William the Conqueror, and Casanova. I mean actually he had a very interesting life. Here he was this orphan, and he gets a job with this rich widow in the camel business, and although she's so old she's virtually half-dead by the standards of the times, about forty-something, fifteen years older than Mohammed, she proposes to him and he marries her, the devil, which would have given us a lot of sex-for-the-aging-woman stuff, very topical. Then they have these four girls, but the boy dies, and if you didn't have a male offspring the Arabs called you "the mutilated one," because boys are valued more highly than girls, it would seem. And so when he has his midlife crisis Mohammed gets the Call, and has visions, and goes into a trance and Allah dictates all these *Suras* to him, which together make up the Koran. And either Mohammed is plagiarizing the Bible like mad and is a hysterical plagiarist or it's one hell of a coincidence. Or maybe Jehovah and Allah are the same

5

Person and they were all getting it really from the same Source, but which still leaves you with the problem of a lot of signal interference. Because there are a lot of discrepancies between what Jehovah says and Allah says. According to Allah the Jews aren't so special anymore and have to follow all these weird dietary laws as *punishment*, although they don't even know it, they're so dumb. And the Christians are dumb too for having been taken in by such a gimmick as the Ascension and this three-in-one nonsense, which is just a load of gobbledygook. Although Jesus still makes it as a Moslem prophet and the movie *Jesus Christ Superstar* is banned in the Arab Republic of Egypt as sacrilegious. Then there's the whole *Hegira* business, and Mohammed goes to Medina, and there's politicking and ins and outs. And he expels one tribe of Jews, but they can take a little property. And then he expels another tribe of Jews, but they can't take any property. And then he gets sore and figures they've really driven him too far, and when the last tribe of Jews surrenders he has all the men slaughtered and the women and children taken as slaves. Allah is merciful, but not necessarily Mohammed, I guess. And he's got really no sense of humor when it comes to satirical lady poets, and has Asmā bint Marwān run through with a sword right in her bed. When an old adversary in intellectual jousts who'd kidded him some is thrown on his knees before the conquering Mohammed and pleads, "But who will care for my sons, Mohammed?" Mohammed cries, "The Devil!" and lops off his head. He didn't like to be kidded. Meanwhile Mrs. Mohammed has died and Mohammed is marrying a new girl every time you turn around. He catches a glimpse of the flesh of his stepson's daughter and is very disturbed, and prays to Allah and Allah tells him it's okay, he can marry her. And he's very disturbed about attacking the Meccan caravan, because killing is bad, but on the other hand the Meccans are very wicked, and he prays to Allah and Allah tells him, "Go get 'em," more or less. He's always praying to Allah for guidance and if Mohammed really

6

wants something bad enough you get the impression Allah is going to tell him it's okay. I mean Allah can't seem to say no to him. Mohammed also has these terrific visions of the past in which he prophesies himself. I mean, it's as if Richard Nixon got up in the morning and he told the Cabinet, "Boys, I had this fantastic vision last night of George Washington. George Washington was addressing the Continental Congress and he said, *In nigh onto two hundred years will appear among you a man of peace from Whittier, California. Trust him. Listen to his words. He will lead the people out of the vale of permissiveness.* No kidding, boys, that's exactly what George Washington said in this vision." Ah, Nixon. Life was empty without him.

So I was tooling up for Mohammed with considerable eagerness thinking he was juicier than a lot of characters you get in the religious-movie business when Omar comes back from Cairo with the word: no physical incorporation of the Prophet, no Gertrude, no Claudius, nobody. Fortinbras and the gravediggers. And also he had an armload of stuff from five Egyptian writers which was supposed to give me new material, translated from Arabic. Well, what can I say? It proceeded from the abstract to the general, and from the general to the abstract. We weren't exactly going to do the life story of Mohammed anymore, you see, but rather the story of the beginning of Islam. And since they were taking away my cast of characters they were giving me some principles to replace them with. Like Islam was humane. Islam was tolerant. There was no coercion in Islam. Islam was against slavery. Islam believed in the equality of women. Islam preached kindness to the poor, widows, and orphans. They were very strong on Mohammed's Jane Addams side. And I was supposed to take these ethical canons and work up an almost entirely new cast and invent a string of little playlets which would illustrate Islam's principles. And we were going to have the nerve to still call this *Mohammed, Man of Mecca.* But there were going to be a lot of camels and camel charges and great shots of the

7

desert, which had been our intention from the start naturally. It was going to be an Arabian Western. A kind of ethical Western disguised as the birth of Islam.

The phone rang again and a voice said, "Is Pearl there?" Well, you'll never believe it but there was no Pearl and I asked the operator for a number and this time someone answered.

"Hello," said a girl's voice.

"Who's this?" I said.

"Suzanne," she said. "Who's this?"

"Jerry."

"How are you, Jerry. How have you been?"

"Okay. How have you been?"

"Okay. I just got back from my vacation. How's business?"

"Okay. Kind of slow."

"When do you think business is going to pick up, Jerry?"

"I don't know. When do *you* think business is going to pick up?"

"October. Round about October."

"October? I'm glad to hear that. What makes you think October, though?"

"I've just got a feeling, Jerry."

"Well, it's been nice talking to you, Suzanne. Give my love to everybody."

"Give my love to everybody too," she said, and hung up.

My room was on the ground floor and I'd left the door open and the full-length window on the court side to get what air there was, and now Omar came charging in the window from the swimming pool in his blue bathing trunks, all buzzed up about something. I was still lying down and mumbled, "I think I found a way of handling that liver-eating scene discreetly . . ." But Omar threw himself into the chair by the desk and cried:

"She's going to ruin me! I've got to call her mother. What time is it in California? Why did they invent the telephone? She *knows* I hate to call on the telephone when I'm working.

8

There's something unnatural about it. I've explained it to her a million times but she won't understand. The whole thing's ruined!"

He fixed me with his feverish eyes, in a state of utmost agitation, communicating urgency and the need for understanding through the eyes, but groping desperately for the words.

"The disembodied voice!" he appealed to me. "What good does it do? She won't understand! If I don't call her it's because I'm busy, absorbed in my work! If I called it would only . . ."

And then the words stopped coming. He'd jammed. Still looking at me agitatedly, cravingly, but no words. An unqualified "she" with Omar was usually his wife, Chloe. He felt around his bare chest as if he expected to find a pack of cigarettes Scotch-taped to the skin, discovered a pack on the desk he'd left there earlier, and lit one fumblingly, gradually becoming more relaxed.

"You know I'd have had her here if it weren't for the air conditioning," he declared. "I'm going to call her mother, maybe she can dissuade her."

"Dissuade her from what?"

"Taking the kids out of Sunday school!" he exploded. "I'll be disgraced if the word gets out! What will they think of me in Bahrain and Abu Dhabi, let alone Saudi Arabia! What kind of a Muslim can't keep his kids in Muslim Sunday school!"

"Why Sunday?" I said. "I thought Friday was the holy day in Islam."

"What do you want me to do in L.A.?" he asked in exasperation. "Send them to Friday school? In L.A. Friday school is on Sunday! We've got this Center."

He leaned back and took a long drag on his cigarette, slowly blowing the smoke out into the air.

"Maybe you call her," he said. "Explain to her that I'm busy, overworked. Tell her I'm monogamous. You know how devoted I am to her. Tell her. Fix it up."

9

Mind you, this guy was our producer, our fearless leader, the chief. But he was a coward with women.

"Eight hours' time difference," he said reasonably. "You could call her right now. Explain to her how it upsets me to telephone. Convey to her tactfully that I am not screwing around with starlets because it's an all-male cast and Jeanne Moreau hasn't gotten here yet."

"How about Mouna?"

"Mouna raped me," he said. "I was a reluctant coconspirator. I entered into the relationship against my own better judgment." And then bitterly: "That's right, you crazy fuckhead! Tell her all about Mouna! Be serious. Tell her I'm under great nervous strain. Make her put the kids back in Sunday school. Here. Here's the number."

He scribbled it down.

"I'll be right in the next room. Let me know as soon as the call's over. It'll be a big load off my mind."

This was going too fast.

"Wait a minute, Ome. I don't know if I'm really qualified here. Maybe she's got some religious objections. How do I know? What religion did she use to be anyway?"

"Mormon."

"Christ."

"On both sides," he added solemnly.

"Is she from Salt Lake City?"

"Idaho."

"But what if she starts talking to me about Joseph Smith, Ome? I don't know anything about that stuff. If she were a Methodist it would be something else."

"For God's sake it's got nothing to do with Joseph Smith," Omar promised irascibly. "Can't you see she's just putting the screws to me?"

"Did she convert, by the way? Is she supposed to be a Moslem now?"

"She kind of halfway converted," Omar said absentmindedly. "She took instruction. She's nothing but a troublemaker. You see the way we get along. Now that we're almost broken up, tell me the truth."

10

He looked at me, his eyes intent, at the same time excited and dependent.

"When I first met Chloe, when we weren't married yet, what did you think of her?"

"I thought she was crazy."

"What kind of crazy?"

"A malicious malcontent."

He seemed stupefied.

"And you didn't tell me!" He got to his feet. *"You son of a bitch!"*

"Now wait a minute, Ome." I tried to calm him down. "You mean if I'd told you, you'd have dropped her? You'd have told her, *I'd really like to marry you, Chloe, but my friend Burt says you're a malicious malcontent?"*

"I guess not," he said on reflection, and sat down again. "Just call and tell her I'm under a tremendous strain, and that I'm in a big conference with the money guys and the King of Morocco, and that I promise to call her more often when I have the time. And put the kids back into Sunday school."

He went into the next room, still in his swimming trunks, the back of his thighs marked from the chair, and I tried his number in Los Angeles. No one answered. Omar came back in and sat down despondently, saying he wished he'd married a woman who was more stable, had more sense of responsibility.

"I think I'll type out some pink sheets with Jeanne Moreau eating Hamza's liver," I said, getting up and putting on my trousers, and Omar rose lightheartedly, seemingly quite sanguine now, the dark cloud having passed, although you really might wonder why since his circumstances remained completely unchanged.

"Don't worry, m'boy," he said jauntily. "We've got plenty of time. Rest. Relax. Life is more than work. It is written." And he sauntered back out toward the pool. Perhaps he felt I was helping him bear his burden.

As soon as he was out of the room I checked my watch, finished dressing, and got a brown attaché case down off the shelf of the wardrobe. Locked inside the bathroom, I snapped open the cover and counted the hundred-dirham bills.

The streets were like an oven, pinkish orange buildings shimmering in the heat, the air stifling. As soon as I started walking I could feel the sweat dripping down my back. Djemaa el Fna, the great central square of the Medina, was the usual madhouse, crowded with Moroccans in native dress gathered to disport themselves and shop a bit at the end of the day. The whole square throbbed and wove to whining Arab music played by dozens of competing groups of street entertainers. Fortunetellers told fortunes. Snake charmers charmed snakes. A group of illiterates listened in rapt fascination to a professional tale teller, the latest installment of an Arabic Mary Tyler Moore Show, no doubt. Acrobats did balancing acts with bicycles. Sidewalk peddlers squatted beside their wares set out on a small blanket: local handicraft assorted with ballpoint pens, flashlight batteries, ancient alarm clocks. Behind were the more successful merchants in their rows of *souks*, street stalls, selling native robes, handmade leather goods, T-shirts. Thousands of people milled about in the square, clustering in circles to watch sidewalk magicians, moving on, chatting with acquaintances. The men were mostly in their djellabas, women in variants of the kaftan, most of them veiled. Girls with pretensions to modernity wore a combination of veils and platform soles. The Berber women's faces were bare, marked with discreet blue tattoos on the forehead and chin. Water sellers jangled in elaborate bemedaled costumes with red-tasseled sombreros, carrying great coin-decorated leather water satchels over their shoulders. Every minute or so someone would give them a small coin, swig down a cup of tepid water from a common brass cup, catch syphilis maybe, go away happy. No one seemed to mind the heat but me.

From a distance I kept my eyes on a *souk* selling goatskin handbags until I saw Driss stroll by in a red polo shirt. He circled about until he spotted me and then, certain I was tracking him, moved off toward the center of the square. I followed many yards behind. He joined a dense crowd watching a Berber woman with a combination snake-and-child act and I edged in beside him. Two children and three snakes were all having fun together while a slightly larger child played snake-type music on a native pipe and the mother strode about bossily, ordering a kid to do this, a snake to do that. She brusquely snatched a ten-foot snake away from a two-year-old toddler and he started bawling like hell, arms outstretched. *Gimme back my snake!* I felt my attaché case lighten as Driss took hold of it, and I reached down with barely a glance and grasped the handle of his identical case. In another minute or so he moved on, but I stayed on watching the show. The bold-faced Berber woman had a lot of style, strutting back and forth. She could get those snakes and kids to do anything. *Nothing in my hands. Nothing up my sleeves*, she seemed to be crying, tugging up the sleeves of her dress. *Now watch this!* It was a pretty good act, really, if you liked kids and snakes.

2

I'LL LEVEL with you. This was going to be a shitty movie.
But there was a market for it. There were half a billion
Moslems in the world, right? If we had our Bible epics, why
couldn't they have their Koran epics? Money talks. Oil talks.
But the Koran is an inferior literary work, you will say. All
hysterical and repetitious. No story line. And some fanatic
is going to assassinate us if we show the Prophet. Which is
exactly why they needed me, author of *The Song of Jesus*,
which raked in all those shekels, because of the knack I
have with that kind of thing, an indefinable touch, that certain *etwas*. Yes, sir. Like when the camera vertical-panned
down from Christ on the cross and there was Jimmy Stewart
dressed as a Roman centurion and we were going to have
him say, *Surely this is the Son of God*. And suddenly it came
to me, no by God. He should say VERILY, *this is the Son of
God*. And frankly I think that "verily" made the picture.
My, yes. I also wrote *The Song of Paul*, a new twist on the
thing, you see, showing it from Paul's P.V. as it were, the
Road to Damascus, all that. It didn't turn out to be as strong
at the box office because Paul turns out to have not as much
sex appeal as Jesus, through no fault of mine, but it was a
cute idea and I'm still loyal to that picture even if it wasn't
so successful and I tell everyone it's an unrecognized masterpiece and they should catch it if it ever plays at a nearby
drive-in. I mean if they like Christian movies.

Because I can talk not only Spanish, French, and German,

I can talk Authorized Version. I can even say things in Arabic, which dazzles even me. I mean if you say something to me in Arabic I can say it right back at you, with all the funny throat sounds and everything, without understanding what it means, of course. It's a gift. I can improvise Authorized Version by the hour on any subject: *Every man also to whom Rockefeller hath given riches and wealth, and hath given him power to eat thereof, and to take his portion, and to rejoice in his labour; this is the gift of Rockefeller. For he shall not much remember the days of his life; because Rockefeller answereth him in the joy of his heart.* How many people can really handle their *answereths*? And they got Sandor to direct because he'd shot *Song*'s big chariot race. And Serge Greenberg was doing the music because he'd won an Academy Award for *Noah*.

These Arabs came to us because they recognized in all humility that they didn't know shit from shinola about making big religious epics and they wanted the best. That money could buy. Steve Garfein was doing the sets and Esther O'Neal was doing the costumes. In fact I was the only *goy* in the bunch, which was kind of a disgrace for somebody, maybe us Christians, but which shows you another reason why these Arabs felt they needed me, why I was doubly important. Their secret ambition was to have this movie a boffola not only in Egypt and Bangladesh, where everybody is dying of starvation anyway, but in the West, Goysville, White-Bread America, so that when Arab oil money starts buying up not only Fifth Avenue but Exxon, General Motors, U.S. Steel, IBM, Du Pont, Boeing, General Electric, General Mills, and Proctor and Gamble, people won't worry because they'll realize the Arabs share a kindred culture with us, the same humane values, because they'll have seen this movie. And I was their blue-eyed boy with access to the hearts and minds of this white-bread world. I mean I literally have these blue eyes, and real dirty blond hair, and though between you and me I have my flakey side I *looked* like the kind of American these Arabs wanted on their team, or at least not to worry. The Arabs have nothing against

15

Jews. I mean nothing that would get in the way of business. They really don't. If a Jew has talent, something they want, and the two sides can get together on price, it's a deal. No prejudice.

But I had more going for me than my fancy footwork with *answereth*s and *yea, verily*s. I had a mystic fascination for these Arabs. They had only to look at me and you could see them thinking, *This guy is for us. This guy has the key to the hearts and minds of White-Bread America.* And I must say I threw myself wholeheartedly into the work, learning the Koran and Mohammed biogs and early commentaries off almost by heart. Try me. Who was *'Abd ar-Rahmān ibn 'Awf*? The early Companion of Mohammed who was so good at business. Who was *'Ali ibn Abi Tālib*? A cousin of Mohammed's who married his daughter Fatima and became the fourth Caliph. What did Mohammed do at the battle of the Badr Wells? Like a good general he remained in a hut at the rear and prayed and came out once to fling a handful of pebbles in the enemy's direction. *Māriya* was an Egyptian slave of Mohammed's and mother of his son Ibrāhim. Not to be confused with *Maryam*, which is what the Arabs call the Virgin Mary who Mohammed thought was the sister of Moses. *Rayhāna bint Zayd* was a beautiful Jewish concubine Mohammed took after he slaughtered her husband and all the other male Jews of the Qurayza tribe. Not to be confused with *Zaynab*, a beautiful Jewish concubine who tried to poison him after he had killed her husband, father, and uncle. In turn not to be confused with *Safiyya*, the beautiful seventeen-year-old Jewish wife he took after killing her husband for concealing his goods up in Khaybar, the one who caused all the ruckus because Mohammed violated his own commandments by having sex with her that very night, whereas he'd ordered his followers most severely to wait until the beginning of the next menstrual cycle before putting the boot to women captives. *'Ā'isha bint Abi Bakr* was the beautiful six-year-old Mohammed married but the wedding wasn't celebrated until she was nine. They gave her the good news when she was playing on her swing and let her bring along all her dolls and toys. Sometimes Mohammed played little games with her. *Ka'b ibn al-Ashraf* was the Medina poet who was punished for writing verses against Mohammed by having his head cut off to devout cries. The *Omayyads* were the powerful Mecca family that was punished for so ferociously opposing Mohammed by being allowed to establish the dynasty that ruled the Moslem world from Poitiers to the Indus. I'm telling you, I knew my onions on Islam. Actually I was even thinking of converting myself for the experience and so I could go to Mecca but they told me there was a three-year wait between when you convert and they let you go on the pilgrimage. They want to make sure you're on the up and up. With all the phonies and opportunists around you can see their point.

What Omar Hammoud was doing on the movie is a little freakier to explain, but logical too in its own way. Allah is wise. Allah foresees all. Omar wasn't working for me, you know, I was working for Omar. He was the producer, and theoretically even the director, because of Sandor being Jewish. On the credits Sandor was going to be called the "executive production consultant." I first knew Omar from high school in Beverly Hills, believe it or not, although "knew" is overstating it a little. He looked familiar to me. I remembered his face. I thought he was Jewish, actually. I don't know. He just looked kind of Jewish, a blue-eyed, Jewish-type person. In those days how many Arabs did you expect to find in Beverly Hills? I could almost swear to you he went under the name of Marvin then. He was a Native Son of the Golden West, as opposed to his folks, who were Native Sons of the Golden East, meaning Lebanon, and he seemed to me like just another Marvin in a blazer, until I ran into him in front of the Castellana Hilton in Madrid a zillion years later and it turned out his name was Omar and we were great buddies because we'd spent our boyhood together.

Mind you, at this time I was, all things considered, comparatively successful in life, what with the discovery of cinema gold in Spain, the Bible-movie business charging along, and Christian piety rampant. I'd broken up with my wife but it was a minor failure. I'm sure she was happier with this securities analyst in Zurich. Whereas Omar wasn't successful at all. He was deeply unsuccessful, marked for deep failure, deep unsuccess. After Dartmouth he'd been gnawing away at the fringes of the film industry all those years without getting anywhere. Really pitiable. And then oil happened. Whereupon it was suddenly revealed unto Omar that he was not only this crazy Arab but that he spoke Arabic — kid-Arabic, but Arabic. Also, he said, he was this Moslem. Now I will tell you my darkest suspicions. I think Omar was born a Lebanese Christian. I think he was converted to Islam by seeing *Lawrence of Arabia*, brought around by Peter O'Toole and Alec Guinness, those well-known Moslems. He was always very vague about his Moslem childhood, and I personally think it was the phonus bolonus. The blue eyes and fair skin could have come from Circassian blood, as he claimed, or they could have come from some Christian kind of blood, like say French. But he really could speak Arabic, and when he went around raising money in Bahrain, Kuwait, Libya, and Dubai, not to mention Abu Dhabi, these Bedouins in Rolls-Royces thought he was *one of their own*. While at the same time representing the Best of Hollywood, get it? From the people who gave you *Gone With the Wind, Ben Hur, The Ten Commandments*. He had a lethal, unbeatable, razzmatazz, Judaeo-Moslem one-two. One: he was a Moslem; he spoke Arabic; he was one of their own; they trusted him. Two: he was real Hollywood, the adopted son of John Wayne out of Gary Cooper. He could tap the best Judaeo-Christians in Hollywood to come make this Judaeo-Moslem movie of theirs. When he laid it out for me there in Madrid I could see the grandiose possibilities. We did up a contract, with me getting a decent share of the action because I was in on it right from the speculative stages and I worked up a hundred-page treatment for him, and he took it around to these sheiks. And the next thing you know he had millions. It turned out the sheiks had been crying into their camel milk all these years because the West didn't give Islam a fair shake, with Voltaire saying Mohammed was an impostor and all, and now their time had come. Oh, yes, oh, yes. And we had one theologico-artistic supervisor with us for each sheik who'd kicked in money. One sheik, one supervisor. All come to watch us make the big movie. Of course right now no one could watch anything because Sandor, the director, was getting a bunch of one- and two-shots out of the way, doing meaty dialogue scenes with camera, lights, and fifteen people jammed into a crazy mud hut, temperature 120 degrees. While I worked at the hotel in refreshing 110-degree comfort.

Hamza was the closest relative to Mohammed that they let me keep in the scenario, and I was just finishing up this scene where Jeanne Moreau eats his liver when Sandor burst into my room at the end of shooting the next day, his gray hair soaked with sweat, fanning himself with a big straw hat with a red-white-and-green ribbon.

"What is this *God is great*?" he stormed. "A thousand times in the scenario you have *Allah is great*, and now Omar tells me it's got to be *God is great*. It'll kill us on lip synch! What is this God? We were all agreed on Allah! It'll sound idiotic. *God is great, God is great, God is great*. Every time anyone turns around, *God is great*. What's the matter with Allah? As long as we stick with Allah, people think, they're a bunch of crazy Arabs, what business of mine is it what they say, they can say what they like. But 'God'! Why, so much, all the time God? Are we making a *couscous* Western or aren't we?"

He slumped into a chair, putting his hands over his face.

"I'm trying to make this movie in plain Hungarian," he moaned. "And crazy people they give me to work with. Where did he get this God?" he pleaded. "Weren't we agreed on Allah?"

"Must have been one of the advisers," I said. "A couple of months ago they even wanted Ulluh."

"Who?"

"Ulluh. That's the way they pronounce it. Listen to them. *Inshulluh*. If God wills it."

"Oy yoy yoy," moaned Sandor. "Not only my friends won't speak to me, now people are going to laugh at us." He shuddered at the horror of it.

"Aw, come on, Sandor. You'll get used to it. Say it a few times. God is great, God is great, God is great, God is great. It comes tripping right off your tongue once you get used to it."

"Why?" he said.

"That's what it means," I said. "'Allah' is just Arabic for 'God.' In Arabic, Abraham prays to Allah. Moses gets the Ten Commandments on Mount Sinai from Allah. Allah forbade Joseph to fool around with Potiphar's wife. Allah sends down his Holy Spirit to produce Jesus, one of Islam's top prophets. They even go along with the virgin birth, although Jesus still isn't the son of Allah somehow, *Sura* nineteen."

"Sura shmura!" Sandor barked angrily. "What do they know from *suras* in America? We're going to be a laughingstock! Explain to the advisers!"

"I've explained it to them already. But they *want* people to know they're saying God is great. They think it's a strong point. They want to proselytize a little."

The door was open. Mouna walked in, all in white. A tight sweater with no bra, miniskirt. Dark. Good looking. Hostile, but wasn't she always. She had this English-type accent because she'd been to the American University in Beirut. She was like the joke at Pinewood. *Oh, my dear, are you English?* American actress: *No, just affected.* But Mouna was an Arab.

"Is Omar back?" she asked. She had a courtesy smile which served to enhance her general impression of belligerence.

"He rode back with those Persian Gulf people," said Sandor.

"Sandor, may I speak to you?" asked Mouna evenly.

"Sure," said Sandor.

There was a moment of silence during which no one moved.

"Speak to me here," Sandor said. "Why so private? Burt doesn't own points in the picture?"

Mouna smiled icily to demonstrate that her composure was unruffled.

"Sandor, I want you to be nice to the Libyan. If the Kuwaitis pull out the Libyans will take up the slack."

"All right, all right. I'm nice to everyone. Why shouldn't I be nice to a Libyan?"

"I want you to be especially nice to him. And you too, Burt Nelson."

Why the last name? How many other Burts were there around? I didn't see why I had to answer. I looked down at my typewriter and folded my arms. Mouna turned abruptly and walked out of the room.

"How do you like those knockers?" said Sandor, acting as if he was hefting two lead-filled basketballs on his chest. Seventy years old and taking sixteen kinds of pills a day to stay alive and still all he thought about was girls' boobs. "What do you care?" he said. "So she's a secretary with delusions of grandeur because Omar's *shtooping* her. Humor her!" He shrugged. "Hey, Mouna! Come back!" he cried, bounding up out of his chair and lumbering after her out into the corridor. "Burt invites you to have a drink!"

She returned rather promptly, it seemed to me, and sat in a leather armchair, regally relaxed, as if she'd won a point, while I gave her a vodka and tonic out of the refrigerator. I tried to catch Sandor's eye but failed.

"I can handle these people," he said gaily to Mouna. "Don't worry. I'm a Hungarian. I understand the way they think. You know the story. You go into a Budapest restaurant. The menu says: *No changes! No substitutions! This is it!* The Hungarian says: *I didn't have the soup. Can I make a telephone call?* The Orient begins where people want you to come, they go like this."

He made a downward gesture with his hand. Centuries

ago it must have been the start of a downward sweeping motion toward the signaler, but now only the vertical part remains, enigmatic when unfamiliar.

"You know the first person I ever saw do that in America?" asked Sandor. "David Selznick." He made the gesture agitatedly. *"Sandor! Sandor! Sandor! Come quick!"*

"What are these colors you always wear, Sandor?" asked Mouna melodiously, nodding at his red-white-and-green hat ribbon.

He leaned back and spread his arms.

"Hungary!" he announced expansively.

"Ah, so you're a patriot too," Mouna said with satisfaction.

"Say, listen," said Sandor. "A Hungarian I am when it suits me. Look." He took up the hat and presented it first right side up, then upside down, then backward, then backward and upside down together. "This way it's Hungary. This way Italy. This way Iran. And this way?" he asked Mouna eagerly.

"Mexico," I said.

"Who's asking you?" said Sandor.

"I never heard that Italy and Hungary had the same colors," said Mouna almost as if the fact she hadn't heard of it placed the matter in doubt.

"Don't use that argument," said Sandor. "There are a lot of things you haven't heard of. Listen, Mouna, what do you think it should be, *Allah is great*, or *God is great*?"

"What does Omar say?" asked Mouna as if who were we to speculate on such a question when it had probably been decided by Higher Authorities.

"Never mind Omar," said Sandor. "What do *you* think?"

"I think we should allow a consensus to emerge among the Arabs on the production," Mouna said coolly. "They understand Islam best, you can be certain of that."

"They understand Islam all right," said Sandor. "But what do they know from Nashville, Tennessee? Don't we want to make this movie a hit in America?"

"We Arabs have a deep sense of honor about religion,"

she said severely. "Nothing must be allowed to compromise its fundamental essence."

"Who's talking fundamental essence?" asked Sandor good-humoredly. "We're talking box office! Film rentals!"

"Commercial success is completely secondary," said Mouna coldly. "No Muslim would ever allow his religion to be misrepresented at any price. There is Muslim pride. Money is of no importance whatever."

Which certainly wasn't the way Omar felt.

"What do you know about it?" I said. "You're a Christian."

She looked at me with sheer hatred.

"I'm an Arab first and a Christian second!" she spat out, her eyes raging. "We Arabs all understand Islam! Which has been demeaned and debased and vilified by Europe for a thousand years!"

I didn't even like the way she said "Arab." With a hard "r." It sounded like "Adab." When she left, Sandor held his head in his hands.

"You did a lot of good," he said. "Very diplomatic. Very delicate. Forget it. You think who is this secretary. But she's a secretary who's *shtooping* the producer! You don't know how it works?" He slid down in his chair into a roughly copulatory position, imitating Mouna, her pelvis rotating periodically to meet Omar on top. "They're *shtooping* to-night upstairs. They *shtoop* a little." He stops. "*Darling, I've been thinking. Don't you think Allah would be better than God?*" Omar's voice: "*Don't bother me. Let's shtoop.*" Sandor makes copulating motions again, stops again. Mouna's voice: "*But really, darling. Don't you think Allah would be more Arab?* And he gives in! That's how women get their way! It pays to be in with the women! You don't know this? Don't you care about the movie?"

He was disgusted with me.

"You're young," he said. "Good flat stomach. But you could learn about women from an old race defiler like me. Yuh, *Rassenschänder*." He brightened. "That's what the Nazis called a Jew who had sex with gentile women. You didn't

23

know this? You see, these little Hungarian Jewish sperms, the white stuff that comes out, every one circumcised and barmitzvahed. When these little Hungarian Jewish sperms got to the end of this nice gentile girl's vatsis, even with no baby, these sperms keep burrowing, burrowing, burrowing, and they get into the gentile girl's *bloodstream*. Then later when this nice gentile girl has a baby even with a nice gentile boy, some of these Hungarian Jewish sperms get into the baby and pollute him! His racial purity is ruined! They were crazy, those Nazis. They believed this. Turn fifty Hungarian Jews like me loose and we're going to pollute the whole Aryan race." He roared like a lion. "The whole race, *kaputt!* I remember I went to Berlin in 1933 . . . 1934? . . . to get a print of a film I made. I was a Hungarian so I could go in and out still. And this girl I knew leans out of the window of the old UFA studios when she sees me in the street and yells, *'Hallo, Sandor, du alter Rassenschänder du!' Hey, Sandor! You old race defiler!*"

His tone became sadder.

"It was that trip I was in the office at UFA when in for the first time comes Rolf Fischer in his Nazi uniform, brown shirt, cap, the S.A. He'd been in the Red Front, same as me. And we all say to him, 'Rolf! *You?*' 'Don't worry, don't worry,' he says. 'I'm a roast beef Nazi.' Roast beef? What is this roast beef? 'Sure,' he says, 'brown on the outside, red on the inside!' A lovely man, big healthy fella, skied, climbed the Alps with me. So first there's the blood purge. The S.S. and the S.A. hated each other! Then Rolf goes in the army." Sandor took a breath. "Fell in Russia. *Gefallen.* You speak German. A lousy bad joke about Jewish sperms defiling Aryan women and millions of men die. Your friends die. Your whole family dies." He turned and stared bleakly at the wall of the room of the Hilton Hotel for about a minute, lost in the somber past, then shrugged stoically. "As if I'm the only one."

After a time he turned back to me, his mood lighter.

"Hey, listen. Burt. Be a good kid. Don't get into arguments

with this Mouna. What do you care she's pretentious? You're so smart? Be smarter than her. We got enough troubles already. You want this to be a happy set? Don't talk politics with her! You know why the Israelis won in '67, according to Mouna? Because the U.S. Sixth Fleet destroyed the Egyptian and Syrian Air Force. She believes what she wants to believe. Listen, Burt, she's a fanatic-type girl. You don't argue with this kind. You joke with her a little. You kid around with her a little. You talk about the movie with her maybe, very practical. Listen, I've had good times with her, in Benghazi, Tripoli, Algiers, while you were back in Madrid. We went to the Minister's house in Tripoli, her with a skirt split up to her ass, all the Minister's women locked in the cellar. She was the only woman, five men, she had the time of her life. We danced, laughed, out on the terrace under the stars. Beautiful. She had a nice sense of humor."

Sandor paused and said, seemingly with no connection: "Hey, Burt, you ever hear of the King David Hotel?"

"Sure, the Israelis blew it up under the British Mandate."

"Kids read stuff in college history books, think they know as much as you do," said Sandor. "You know the survivors of the camps were making their way to Palestine? Whatever way they could? And the fucking British were blockading the beaches? Dragging our poor Jews back and putting them behind barbed wire on Cyprus? Well, in those days I belonged to a committee called Americans for a Free Palestine. Palestine meant Jews then. And I gave them a lot of money. And what did these Jews do with this money?" He gestured matter-of-factly. "They blow up the King David Hotel. A paragraph in a history book to you. Not to me."

He paused, staring at me, his face expressionless.

"Or to Mouna," he said.

"Mouna?"

"They killed a lot of people at the King David Hotel. Including her brother."

There was silence.

"So you see the barrel of dynamite I'm sitting on here,"

said Sandor, one corner of his mouth drawn in. "I hope you can keep your mouth shut."

"Don't worry."

"I mean it," said Sandor, looking at me hard. "Can I trust you?"

"You can trust me," I said.

3

DRISS NEVER WANTED to go to bed. Once he got two drinks in him he was good for the night. Now he was brooding about something, turning it around, getting sullen. You took what you could get sometimes. We were alone in a bare room. Not his room, not my room. Just a room, a couple of blocks in from Boulevard Moulay Rachid. It could have been anywhere in the French provinces: four chairs with metal frames strung with yellowing white plastic; a square dark-wood table, its top covered with glass to protect the surface; two dinky lamps with forty-watt bulbs. It was authentic French tat. A radio was blaring Arab music, squawks and glottal stops. The room had been swept electronically, just in case.

We'd come separately through the dark streets. No one had followed me, I don't know about him. Driss was a heavily muscled man, black-bearded, dressed in civilian clothes, a beige suit, too tight around the shoulders. He spoke good French, which was what we were talking, and he laughed now, boisterously but with a resentful edge, a man who took slights to his honor ill.

"Old Walter!" he said, punching me on the shoulder. "We could stop corruption in this country like *that!*"

"I suppose."

"Why 'suppose'?" he said, his hackles rising.

"Well, you never know for certain, do you?" I said, not having any instructions on what to say to this.

"The whole fabric of society of this country is rotten," he declared angrily. "Pan American. The scandals never stop. There's not a minister in the government that hasn't taken millions in bribes. The government is rotten from top to bottom. And the King."

Driss brooded, his eyes hooded. It was freezing in the room. The air conditioning was merciless.

"What about the King?"

"It's not the King!" he snapped suddenly, seeming to reverse himself. "It's capitalism! There's the rot. It's in the very nature of capitalism. Greed."

Sometimes I wondered why this guy worked for us.

"The most important thing is Morocco," I said neutrally. "You have to think of what's best for Morocco."

Driss looked at me, his eyes bloodshot.

"I know you're an American, Walter," he said. "But with the Americans we're free to do what we like. I have my opinions but we're still friends, you and me, aren't we?"

"Certainly."

"The Istiqlâl are just feathering their nests. They only pretend to be in the opposition. The pro-Moscow people would just deliver us into the hands of the Russians. Only the Army can save the country."

"Are there a lot of people who feel like you?" I asked.

"No," said Driss darkly. "It's just my private opinion."

"You'll tell me if there's any development in that direction in the military," I said clearly.

"Don't worry," he said with a surly shrug. "The Army's loyal. And the King is right about the Sahara. I know you've got bases in Spain, Walter, but will you support us on that?"

"We'll do what we can."

Driss seemed deaf to the music, which whined on. Was it a love song? A call to patriotism? Was it Om Kalsoum?

"And we don't have oil, just phosphates," said Driss bitterly, then lapsed into silence, sitting forward, his elbows on his knees, knees wide apart, hands hanging down. He slipped a flask out of his pocket and took a swig. Moslems weren't supposed to even drink. He'd been very important

28

for us when he commanded the military district around Rabat. Now he was less important.

"You better go now," I said.

He went first. I waited a quarter of an hour then went. Did a little counter-surveillance. No one followed me. This was my hobby. Why not? It was more fun than backgammon.

A few days later I was sitting in another room, also swept, also very secure, even more secure, a Safe House, in short, this time up in Rabat near the Oudaïa Kasba, an isolated, rundown villa with a majestic view of the bay from the garden. They had a hospital-like feeling, those rooms. Not that they looked like hospitals, with their old-fashioned lamp shades and shabby furniture, but they gave you an intensive-care-unit feeling, no germs allowed. Across the desk from me in front of a discolored wall sat Bob Fitz-William, my control officer, although he might have been known by other names in his time. You're probably thinking, now that you know my secret life, that between Fitz-William and me there was this sacred bond, brothers in arms, that kind of stuff. But it didn't feel that way somehow. In front of me I had this large, ungainly, J. Press–dressed American with thick eyeglasses and a Social Register accent. They say the idea that the Company was run by eastern preppies was a myth, but all the case officers I ever drew had these lockjaw Groton and St. Mark's accents. And I should make clear right away that a cultivated career officer with this organization was one thing and a sleazy covert operator was quite another, the line between the two being very sharp, a distinction awkward and even obnoxious to the popcorn crowd. On FitzWilliam's side of the desk you had a man who knew lots, ran operations, but did everything by remote control, was unexposed, totally insulated from the old rough and tumble. On my side you had a different type article entirely, kept in ignorance as much as possible by the very logic of the way the business was organized, the compartmentalization, the restricting of information to the barest minimum of what you needed. Half the

29

time I didn't know fuck-all about what I was doing. But in actual contact with the warp and woof, you see. On my side you had a man who did other things for a living, of course, got out into the real world, otherwise no cover. No warp. No woof. FitzWilliam lived discreetly among kindred spirits, went home every night to a wife and kids in a secure house, called Langley on the scrambler every day for all I knew, to hold hands with the DCI. I was out there all by myself, lying day and night, deceiving my best friends, packing a weapon and I might have to use it. If something went wrong I ended up in a ditch with a bullet in my head, unclaimed. If something went wrong with FitzWilliam he had diplomatic immunity. My, yes. Although when Company people got taken hostage in Teheran later I confess it gratified me a bit. No diplomatic immunity there, no sir. Let them see what it was like for us. Tough it out, boys! "Animals" they called us sometimes. Jokingly, of course.

So you see, Bob FitzWilliam looked down on me socially from the heights of New Canaan, Connecticut, and St. Mark's and Harvard. Whereas in his book I was a military lout from Heartland America, which was pretty funny considering Beverly Hills. And he looked down on me because he had a fancier education, with a Ph.D. from Harvard for a dissertation on Kwame Nkrumah. I was a low, vulgar, risk-taking type while he was a cerebral, sit-behind-a-desk type. But I actually went out and ran these Drisses and Mohammeds and Fouads, talked to them and touched them, things FitzWilliam only heard about second-hand. And for an animal I was very smart, a very superior-type animal. And who the hell was FitzWilliam to look down on me anyway? I was in the movies. I was glamorous. I knew Elizabeth Taylor. And I'll tell you something else, *amigo*. If FitzWilliam looked down on me, I looked down on him. And if I were really to tell the truth it was because he was soft. He looked soft. All intellectual warrior and education and no *cojones*. Because beneath my reedy long hair, man, parted in the middle like Our Lord, and beneath my faded jeans, and above all beneath my hippie Hindu shirt, man, beat the heart of a fighter jock. Fly a fighter plane a few years and you've got one chance in four of getting killed just in an accident, not even counting combat. This covert operation shit was safe compared to that. And FitzWilliam knew all this. Oh, yes, he did. I bet it was right there in his control book: *Nelson, Burt. Heart of fighter jock.* So we looked down on each other mutually, which was all right by me.

And I sat there across the desk from FitzWilliam in this bare room with its stained walls in this tacky safe house and summarized the conversation with BULLMOOSE, which was Driss's code name: hostility to the King, hostility to the Istiqlâl opposition, hostility to capitalism, hostility to Moscow, a lot of hostilities there, a broad, comprehensive range. Faith in the Army though, the Salvation of the Moroccan Nation. Looked like the recipe for a military coup to me. Attitude toward ODYOKE? Subject to evaluation.

"Well, what do you think?" asked FitzWilliam, peering up uncertainly through his glasses, bewildered despite his immaculate Glen Urquhart suit. He had been taking notes.

"You're asking me for a sensitive evaluation?" I said. "I'm the cut-out here. I tell you what BULLMOOSE says. You do the evaluating. You're the *tête pensante*.

"Talk English, for Christsake, Nelson," he said, and glowered at me, the eyes large behind the glasses. He was waiting for an answer. It must be humbling for a man of FitzWilliam's breeding to ask an animal like me what he thought. Do him good, though.

"Well, Fitz, old buddy," I said. "What do you want me to tell you? He hates capitalism. He hates communism. He hates the King. Also he was drunk."

"But which does he hate the most?" asked FitzWilliam, as if there was an answer in the back of the book and we ought to be able to look it up. "And how many senior officers are there like this? We support the King after all. What are we doing with a character like this on our payroll? Should we continue the operation?"

"You mean a real operation appraisal? A risk-benefits

analysis? That's for you to figure out, old Fitz," I said. "You ask all those other creeps of yours. And you put all the dope together in the great cocktail shaker in the sky. And it'll tell you just what to do, sure as shootin'."

"Stop kidding around," he said gravely. "What's your gut feeling?"

"Well, I think I'm going beyond my brief a little bit, Fitz. But if you really want my *gut feeling*, it's that we have to look at the Larger Picture, Fitz, which is what you should be doing, not me. They're always complaining we don't have contacts with the real opposition. Here we've got a terrific contact with the opposition. Figure it this way. We support the King. BULLMOOSE is on our payroll. He knows where the money's coming from. It should make him just that much more loyal to the King, all other things being equal."

"When are all other things equal?"

"Shut up," I said. "What are the possibilities? Either the money makes BULLMOOSE loyal to the King, in which case terrific. Or BULLMOOSE and some pals overthrow the King, in which case we have a friend in the new regime, like contributing to both Republicans and Democrats because you don't know who's going to win. Or it doesn't influence policy at all, but somehow BULLMOOSE tips us off to something. My theory is that a guy who takes our money is a true friend since he's going to be looking to do something for us because he wants to keep the money coming. That's my deeply held theory. Anyway, what have we got to lose? What's he costing you? A few thousand dollars?"

"Of all the operatives I've ever had," said FitzWilliam, "why are you the biggest pain in the ass?"

"Because I make more money," I said. "Because I know Elizabeth Taylor."

"What do you do it for then, Nelson, if you don't need the money?" said FitzWilliam, glaring angrily. "It goes against your own theory."

Which was really insulting, as if I was some corrupt local.

"Because within my bosom burns the sacred flame of love

of country!" I said. "Because I am an undying foe of godless atheism!" I laughed. Fitz didn't laugh.

"Fuck you, Nelson," he said.

"Fuck you, too," I said. "But tell me something, old Fitz. If I'm such a pain in the ass, why do you guys use me? How about that?"

He kind of strangled a little and didn't even answer.

I knew why they used me and he did too. I had great contacts. I spoke strange tongues. I had a hell of a cover, could go anyplace. I was a little unprincipled, a little calloused, a little idealistic, a little cynical, not squeamish, just right for the job, you know, and I was a beautiful liar. There was no flickering shadow in the eye, no hesitancy. If you didn't know I was lying you could never tell. It was beautiful. But most of all, to be practical, it wasn't everybody who was cut out for this kind of work. Frankly, it wasn't everybody who had the nerves. They knew a fighter jock when they saw one.

So this was the other part of my hobby. Was I reckless? Was BULLMOOSE a valuable asset? Well, the heavy thinkers and heavy computers would decide all that in Langley, Virginia. I was just a button-man, really, a simple soldier in the Army of Freedom. It didn't have much to do with the rest of my life. I had two lives. In my real life I was this movie-business character. And then I had this very minor, secret life as a part-time whatever. And the twain didn't really meet much. You've heard of Sunday drivers? Or Sunday painters? I was a Sunday patriot. No more, no less. It was much less interesting than you'd think.

Back in Marrakesh, Sandor hailed me as I crossed the lobby of the Hilton.

"How's the fossil business?" he called.

"Okay," I said.

I had this fossil business in Rabat. I exported fossils embedded in stone. It was a sideline.

"Omar's looking for you," said Sandor. "He's at Moulay's."

33

4

"SHE'S GOING TO RUIN me!" Omar cried as soon as he saw me approaching his table. "She's going to turn the Arabs against me. I won't have a leg to stand on. I always knew she'd do me in."

Moulay's was a fly-blown café halfway between the Medina and the Mellah that served mint tea and little cups of coffee. Omar claimed it was the best Arab coffee in town. Made him feel close to his roots, you know. A few old men sat against the walls, staring rheumy-eyed at life.

"She should see a shrink!" Omar declared angrily. "She's completely neurotic. Okay, I'm neurotic, you're neurotic, everybody's neurotic. But she's *very* neurotic. She could really do harm to somebody. Me, for example. I tried to make an appointment for her, but she wouldn't go."

"Where?" I said.

"To see the shrink. She's going to goddamn fucking ruin me. I should have known as soon as I met her father. I thought he was going to be sore as hell at me, seducing his daughter, but he was tickled pink, and now I know why! I took her off his hands! Ha, ha. What a sucker. Look, you speak to her. She likes you. You can bring her around. Go talk to her."

"On the telephone."

"No, back at the hotel," Omar said, as if why piddle around. Direct action.

"Back at what hotel?"

34

"*Our* hotel," he said, slightly baffled. "She's in the suite."

"Who are you talking about?" I said.

"Mouna," he answered, and then without missing a beat, "You can get around her. I know you can. Women always take advantage of me. They get me all mixed up. I turn to mush. You know how to be tough with 'em. Anyway she likes you."

Well, you can see why I thought he was talking about his wife.

"Mouna likes me?"

"Listen, sweetheart, none of that. If there's anyone who can talk her into going to a shrink it's you."

I was running the whole thing through again in my head. A female was going to do him in, get him in bad with the Arabs, but it wasn't his Mormon wife, it was his Arab girl friend, Mouna, and she should see a shrink.

"Why should she see a shrink?"

"Because she needs psychiatric help!" he said impatiently. "She's completely unstable. She's siding with these Arabs against me."

"But you're supposed to be an Arab."

Omar groaned.

"I mean these nig-nog Arabs. That Libyan! I'm a pacifist, right? Islam is a pacifist religion, right? We've got this nice pacifist camel Western, right? Now he wants to put in all that eye-for-an-eye, tooth-for-a-tooth stuff! Cutting off the right hand of thieves! It'd make you throw up all over the table. And *she's siding with him!*"

"Well, they do cut off the right hand of thieves in Libya," I said. "And Saudi Arabia."

Omar looked at me, incredulous, although he certainly knew it as well as I did.

"It's in the Koran," I offered.

"*You too?*" he exclaimed in horror. "What do I care what's in the Koran! Who's the Muslim, you or me? What's it going to look like in America? They'll think Arabs are blood-thirsty animals!"

"No, no, Ome," I mollified him. "Take it easy. I'll do what-

35

ever you say." I spoke slowly. "But you want me. To tell Mouna. To see a shrink. Because you and she. Have a difference of view on the movie's story line. Is that it?"

"Just tell her that eye-for-an-eye stuff has to stay *out*," Omar said, sweeping the whole psychiatrist proposal off the table. "Israel is none of our business. I don't care if she *is* a Palestinian. And tell that Libyan to go fuck himself."

"I tell *Mouna* to tell the Libyan to go fuck himself."

"Right."

"And you think Mouna is going to do this for me," I said. "She won't do it for you, but she'll do it for me."

"Right," he said again, his attention beginning to wander.

"And I've got to do this right now," I said.

"Okay," he said, as if it was my proposal. "I'll take you back, and then I'll leave you two alone."

"You realize that I don't have a snowball's chance in hell," I said. "I'm the worst person on this production to try to ask her to do anything."

"Okay, m'boy," Omar said, rising. "Tell me what she says as soon as you're finished with her. You'll explain it to her much better than me."

He was standing by the table, waiting for me to get up. The old men along the wall stared at us fatalistically, as if it was all in the hands of Ulluh.

"This is insane," I said. "I have no influence with her at all. And what difference does it make what Mouna says anyway? You're the producer."

"Do it out of friendship," said Omar, and we rode back to the hotel in a production car and went up together in the elevator. A few yards from the suite he shared with Mouna, Omar pointed to the door and sort of ran away.

"Oh, Burt Nelson," said Mouna when she opened the door, less hostile than you might have thought.

"Omar wants me to talk to you about something," I said.

"Sit down," she said, her eyes evasive. There was little active animosity. It was as if her mind was elsewhere. She had on another one of her tight jerseys, pink this time.

Women in most Arab countries wore bedsheets and veils but Mouna wore slit skirts and no bra. A real representative of Arab womanhood. A girl who didn't wear bras because they demeaned women by pandering to prurient male interest but wore jerseys so tight and sheer you could see not only her nipples standing out like ballpoint pens, but every single grain around the areola — I don't know, I didn't think a girl that did that was sincere.

"Omar tells me to tell you that he thinks the eye-for-an-eye stuff should stay out," I said.

I wasn't taking any responsibility for it. I was just a conduit. Mouna didn't seem very interested. It was a waste of time anyway. Why should the scenario writer of a movie have to go argue with the producer's secretary just because the producer let women bully him?

"And what's your opinion?" Mouna asked, somewhat warily.

"I don't think I'm really entitled to an opinion," I answered briskly. "I think a consensus should emerge among the Arab members of the production."

Why not? Suck her out of position. It was too broad though. She looked suspicious.

"Is that what you really think?"

"That's largely what I think. That's what I think in large measure."

"Let's talk about it tomorrow," she said, looking tired, her dark skin even darker under the eyes. "It's getting late. We'll talk about it while Omar's out on the set." She still seemed to be thinking about something else.

"How did she take it? What did she say?" asked Omar, waiting on pins and needles down in the bar.

"It didn't go as bad as I thought, I must admit," I said. "We're going to talk about it tomorrow while you're out on the set."

"Oh, great! I knew you could handle her. You really work on her tomorrow. Have a drink."

"I'm not making any promises."

37

Afterwards I went by Sandor's room. He was sitting up in bed, writing in the margins on his copy of the shooting script.

"You think in general I should be nice to Mouna so she'll intercede in our favor with Omar, isn't that the idea?" I asked him. "Isn't that what you said the other day?"

"Sure," answered Sandor, but as if he didn't attach much importance to the point.

"But now Omar wants me to be nice to Mouna so she'll intercede in his favor with these shieklings."

Sandor shrugged. "It's their money," he said.

"But why Mouna? Why does everything on this movie have to go through Mouna?"

"Ah," said Sandor philosophically. "A beautiful girl. Nice *zaftig* girl."

"What's *zaftig* got to do with it?"

Sandor cast his eyes up to the heavens as if there was a lot about life that I didn't know yet, but added, "Arab women. Power mad. They run things from behind the scenes. Like the Shah's twin sister."

Because the Shah was still there. Oh, yes. Very much so.

"What are you talking about? The Iranians aren't even Arabs. I'm the only Westerner on this crazy set who can tell one Arab from another Arab."

"What's a Kurd?" challenged Sandor, trying to catch me.

"Something you eat with whey," I answered, and left him baffled. But he came lumbering out after me.

"Hey, Burt! Come back!" he called, and when I was back inside his room, said in a hushed voice: "You know what I heard over the weekend? You know where Kerkorian got the money to take over Metro? From the Arabs! It's Arab money! And we all thought it was the Mafia. What kind of a world. I have to talk to some Arab from *The Sheik of Araby* to find out where the money came from to take over MGM?"

The next morning after breakfast I looked for Mouna in the hotel rooms that served as the movie's production office, and then in Omar's suite, but she was in neither

38

place. A quarter of an hour after I'd settled over my type-writer in my own room she came to the door, still open in the wan hope of a breeze, and looked in guardedly.

"Oh, Mouna. Hi," I said.

She came in without saying anything, no smile, no salutation, and sat on the sofa. She was a little spooky. As so often, her face had a blank, dead look, but through the superficial calm you could see rage, hatred. She made me a little uneasy.

"I hear it was Arab money Kerkorian took over Metro with," I said.

Mouna said nothing. Suddenly she began laughing loudly. Mouth wide open, lots of teeth. Made her look more Arab. It wasn't the most natural laugh you ever heard.

"You're afraid of me, aren't you?" she said, laughing uncontagiously. "I can tell. What are you afraid of? Are you afraid I'll *vamp* you?"

Frankly this was the last idea in the world that would have crossed my mind, but Mouna seemed to fancy it, putting on an embarrassing sultry look, eyes narrowed and smoky, waving her arms bewitchingly in the air. Beirut's Theda Bara.

"He's afraid I'll vamp him," she sneered, and rose, approaching my chair, arms undulating in a mysterious pattern I couldn't figure out, still doing her Theda Bara routine. When her hand touched my neck it was like a lizard. It had the chill of death.

"He's afraid of me," she said, weaving her face in front of mine, slithering both arms around my neck now, and panic seized me.

She meant it.

Now she was sitting on my lap. I was stunned. I couldn't think. I'd misjudged her. I'd made a mistake somewhere. Her face was just an inch or so from mine, eyes narrowed. Pola Negri. It was supposed to be a joke. But she wouldn't like it if I brushed her off. Then it wouldn't be a joke anymore.

"Afraid?" she asked mockingly.

"Omar's my best friend," I bleated out, which was a crazy lie but the best I could do.

"Omar's married," she said coldly.

"But I'd still feel bad about it. The two of you have this relationship, don't you? You and him?"

She looked at me contemptuously for a moment and then moved to the arm of the chair and slid her hand onto kind of my private parts.

What was I supposed to do now? Unhand me, young woman? Indignation? I'm not the kind of a boy you think I am? This was ridiculous. And she was kind of rubbing, but still so hostile, I wasn't enjoying it at all. I was hating it.

"Afraid of Omar?" she said, taunting.

"Well, it wouldn't make a happy set," I said. "It would create a lot of ill will."

"Do you think so?" Mouna asked, pausing, smiling. "I don't think so. I think Omar would take anything from me."

"You're a real mean woman, Mouna," I said.

She looked blank.

"You mean he'd take it from you," I said. "He'd just turn on me."

She laughed. Presumably I wasn't showing enough resolution because she got up and shut and bolted the door, then shut the floor-length window on the court side, lowering the venetian blinds. It had been hot in the room before. Now it was like a sauna.

"I'm not going to do it!" I said, but she laughed again and started taking off her clothes.

"Stop! Put your jersey back on!" I told her. "I'm not going to do it, I'm telling you!"

But she stripped right down and lay down on the bed, her arms folded beneath her head, glowering at me. I don't know where Sandor got this notion that she had a nice sense of humor. I didn't think she had any sense of humor at all. It was broad daylight despite the venetian blinds and she looked real naked. There was lots of pubic hair.

40

"You're afraid of sexually independent women, aren't you?" she said defiantly.

I thought: no, it's just you I'm afraid of, dearie. But I didn't know what to say out loud.

"I know the kind," she said scornfully.

I don't know what made her so confident she was going to get her way. I'd as soon have slept with an alligator. And I didn't like fooling around with a friend's girl friend either. It made me feel creepy. But she was taking kind of a long lead and it was going to be a little awkward getting out of it without making her lose face. She might not take it well. She might be vindictive. What was she doing this for? Because I had blond hair? I think it was because I had blond hair.

She suddenly spread her legs and parted the hairy part so you could see bright pink and, glaring at me, began rubbing herself. Mind you, I don't say she was enjoying it. It was kind of a mating call. But it got embarrassing and I went over to the bed to get her to lay off, humor her out of it.

"Ah haaaaah," she said gloatingly, her face lighting up with the joy of conquest, and she sat up and got out my thing.

"We shouldn't be doing this," I said.

I was a little weak, I think.

I started rubbing her too a bit, out of politeness. There was no kissing at all. We had a strictly genital relationship. Suddenly she got very wet, and, breathing heavily, looking at me with steamy eyes, whispered hoarsely, "Can't you see you're driving me wild?" Which frankly I thought was a very corny line. But we cleared the decks for action, like, me on top, both of us slathered in sweat by now. We were two salty kids. Mouna spread herself out as if she was preparing for union with the Rain God. I started in stiff as a ramrod, pushed in an inch or two, and then it started to go, deflate, and the next thing you knew it was limp spaghetti. And there we were.

She made a rasping, sputtering noise, like speechless. I

41

mean I guess she had a point. But she got all riled up and angry. It wasn't my fault, was it? What could I do? But she mastered herself.

"Don't be nervous!" she commanded, which kind of made me nervous.

"What do you want?" she said, all tensed up, pressing for immediate results. "I'll do anything. Do you want to see anything?"

"Nothing in particular, really. Couldn't we just lie here awhile? See what happens?"

She lay back for a few seconds, her eyes darting around resentfully, then started to work on me again, letting her wet tongue trail all over my chest. It must have been pretty salty. Still nothing.

"What is it?" she burst out heatedly, as if I had to have a gilt-edged reason. If I didn't have a good enough reason it was the end. All deals were off. Go to jail.

"Nothing really," I said helplessly. "I'm really very sorry. Can't we just take it easy for a while?"

I was sincerely ashamed of myself and thought she was justified in feeling a little impatient with me, but she was so recriminatory. After all it wasn't deliberate. I was doing my best.

"That's all right," she said, as if she'd suddenly recalled something. Probably read it in a book.

"This happens to everybody," she said bitterly. "Don't worry about it."

We lay comparatively quiet for five minutes, maybe six minutes, but with Mouna conveying internal agitation somehow. She never seemed really relaxed. We started kissing a little, believe it or not, her with a desperate undercurrent. Her mascara had run all over her face as if she'd been crying. It gave you an *in extremis* feeling as if we were suffering some great ordeal, rounding Cape Horn, man against the elements. Mouna was building up steam again. She pulled away just a millimeter and suddenly I knew it. I knew what she was going to do. It was as if I could read it in flashing lights on her forehead. She abruptly flipped her-

42

self topsy-turvy, head to toe, slid herself to the right level and raised a leg in case I should care to partake, and she was at it. In a few seconds it was stiff and she let out a triumphant *Aaaah!* Then, quick, quick, she flipped around again, sat astride me this time, grabbed this crowbar with both hands, fitted it in with fierce concentration to let herself down on it. When it started to go soft. Like a balloon when you take your thumb off the neck. Limp spaghetti again.

She looked at me with real hatred. I always knew she hated me.

"I've done everything!" she cried in a rage, her fists clenched. "I've kissed you and embraced you! I've embraced your penis with my mouth! What else can I do!"

"Take it easy," I said.

"What can I do! I've done everything! What's wrong!"

She was still sitting astride me, seething, her knuckles white. She was pretty well built actually, the breasts really nice seen from this angle, the nipples kind of purple-color because of the dark skin. It didn't do any good though. She was too hostile. She climbed off and threw herself down beside me on the bed, glaring ferociously at the ceiling, occasionally glancing at me with a death-ray look. I snuggled up to her, making as if, you know. I mean there are other ways of giving a girl satisfaction.

"No!" she barked. "I want you inside me!"

She really was opinionated. No give at all.

Well, I felt it was all my fault. What the hell. This well-built, good-looking girl, ravenous for humping, and I wash out. But it began to come over me that she felt it reflected on her, suggested she wasn't sexy enough to provide me with a reliable erection. And what could I do to reassure her, to relieve her insecurities? She wanted only one thing. It was unnegotiable.

The muezzin called the faithful to prayer. *Wawk, wawk, wawk.* Frankly it could have been a hot day in Topanga Canyon. Fortunately we got talking about other things.

"I think infidelity is good for a marriage," she said belligerently. "The change stimulates."

43

We were sitting face to face on the bed now, like two kids in the last stage of strip poker, and she reached across and grabbed my thing and it got stiff as a poker. And I reached across and grabbed her thing and she was really quite wet. So like a flash I pushed her back and got her legs untangled and got on top of her and jammed it in. A couple of inches. And then it kind of stuck, too much friction. And again: spaghetti. The trouble was she got wet outside and I didn't have time to get the wetness inside. I should nudge in bit by bit, bringing the slippery stuff in with me as I went, except I had this haste problem. Maybe we should hang her upside down so it would run in faster. Unless maybe it just wasn't in the cards. Maybe Allah knew best.

Well, yes, she was looking at me as if she could kill me. "Did you come?" she asked to my surprise, as if this would be a consolation. Nothing in it for her, of course, but it would at least prove she was sexy.

"No," I said. I didn't think fast enough. What was a little faked orgasm? There would have been a section on it in her book: Premature Ejaculation.

She gave a cry of burbling rage. She was a real crazy, I was beginning to think. Recrimination, recrimination. The whole thing was getting to be a goddamn nightmare. She pulled away from me on the bed.

"I'm sorry," she said sardonically, "but I don't enjoy being 'lovingly intertwined.' Certainly not in this weather."

She drew over to the very edge of the bed and lay there with her eyes closed. Time passed. Was she asleep? Actually I liked her better inert than active, and I started fooling around with her a little.

"No!" she spat out, ripping my hand from between her legs and shaking herself angrily as if to get rid of a disagreeable presence. "You had your chance."

What kind of an attitude was that? You had to perform on demand right that minute? Maybe her feelings were hurt.

I think she snoozed there a little. I was dripping with perspiration and went in the bathroom and took a shower, and when I got out she was awake and wanted a shower too.

44

She really looked nice all soapy and slippery. I liked the look of the soapsuds on her pubic hair, as if it proved it was real hair, and I reached into the shower and started fooling around with her again. Soapy breasts are great. She squealed. I got into the shower with her and we played some games. Made her laugh some, I did. With girls that have big breasts you do like this. You soap them up like mad so they're all slippery. Then you put your arms around the girl and hold her tight, and slowly slide down along her front, your chest flattening her breasts. And when you get to the point where the top part of your chest moves lower than the center of gravity of her breasts, suddenly the breasts squeeze slipping and slithering up on top of your shoulders as if of their own accord. It's pretty good fun. Then I helped her dry off, including between her legs, which was all soft and furry now, and we got back on the bed, and I thought I'd have another go at her. I felt I could really do it this time. The current was really running.

"No," she snapped. "I'm already showered."

What kind of priorities was that?

"So you'll take another shower," I said.

"No," she said grittily. "It's too hot. Take your hands off me."

She wouldn't do it. She was a grudge holder. In a while she started putting her clothes on again, such clothes as she'd come in, a light jersey and miniskirt, no underpants.

"Oh, yuh, Omar wanted me to talk to you about this eye-for-an-eye stuff," I said. "Can't we leave that out? They'd really hate that in America."

Mouna snickered.

"No, really. In an American picture you can *act* as if you believe in an eye for an eye. But you can't say it right out, *We believe in an eye for an eye.* It sounds barbarous."

Mouna was opening the doors and windows. I'd gotten dressed too.

"We'll see about that with Omar," she said aloofly, and moved to pick up her bag. It looked as if she was going. I felt as if I could punch a hole in a solid oak plank now, but she was going. I'd been right from the start, she had a very disagreeable personality.

"Hey, wait a minute," I said. "Where are you rushing to? Don't you want to sit down for a couple of minutes? Talk about old times or something?"

"Well, well, well, tender feelings," she said with this kind of sneer. "Very sentimental. Very sentimental for CIA man."

"CIA man? So that's what you've been thinking!" I laughed. "How ridiculous."

5

IT WAS RIDICULOUS. Some people see CIA men behind every bush. Simone Signoret once kept pulling people at a dinner party into the kitchen to warn them I was a CIA man. And Roman Polanski told me once in Poland, "Hey, they tell me you're a CIA man," which showed he had a healthy skepticism about such yarns and I left Poland. And several other times when I was in some place like Chile or Greece or Guatemala on completely legitimate film business some local would take me aside and say breathlessly, "Betsy Lausfelder tells me you're a CIA man." Other Americans were *warning these people off me* as if I was Typhoid Mary or something. Once these paranoid Americans found out I was a graduate of the U.S. Air Force Academy and had been a career officer for a while, back when my hair was shorter and I was cleaner cut, and that the Air Force had sent me to school again and I spoke these funny languages, they put two and two together and got twenty-two. You can't change a leopard's spots, you know. Once a military type always a military type. You can take the boy out of the military but you can't take the paramilitary out of the boy. And the longer my hair and the more hippified my clothes, the more it proved it all for some of these people. I was obviously General Westmoreland in drag. One Radical Chiclet girl even said, "You can tell he's a CIA man because he always hangs around with people from the Movement." I couldn't win. It wasn't even true I always hung around with people from the Movement. I knew conservatives. I'd drop in now and then at the U.S. Embassy wherever I happened to be to renew old acquaintances with the Air Attaché, Military Attaché, people like that. I didn't see why I had to turn my back on old friends. They were always glad to see me. I'm a loyal American. The vanity of some of these people! Why should the CIA give a royal fuck what Simone Signoret says to Brigitte Bardot at a dinner party? They're not even stars anymore. They don't know the difference between the CIA and the DIA. What's the 40 Committee? They don't know. They don't know frigging anything. The whole thing was ridiculous. It was hypothetically ridiculous. I mean, someone like me *automatically* gets suspected of working for KUBARK. But it can't be true of everybody. If you had to turn in your suit the first time anyone ever said you were a spook you'd be out of business before you started. Anyway, Mouna was a *provocatrice*. She said things just to get you riled up. It was my measured judgment that she knew absolutely nothing and was talking through her hat. Well, I never said it was a risk-free business, but I measured it all out with an eyedropper and that was my measured judgment.

I was on deck in front of the hotel when the cars started coming back at the end of the day, all dusty from the drive back from that mock-up Mecca they had out there in the desert. Sandor and Omar had that safari look as they climbed out, Omar talking to some Arab I'd never seen before.

"Moroccan police," whispered Sandor, nodding his head back in the direction of the Arab, dressed in a light gray business suit, standing aside with Omar.

"What does he want?"

"Ha! Ha!" said Sandor enigmatically, drawing me with him into the lobby, and, once inside, in a hushed voice: "It's the Saudis! They're bringing pressure on the Moroccans!"

"To do what?"

"To stop the film!"

"Why?"

" 'Why,' " said Sandor disparagingly. "You a grown boy, an Islamic scholar, and I got to explain to you orthodox Arabs don't like pictures yet?"

"I thought it was okay with them as long as we didn't show Mohammed."

"Hah, hah," said Sandor. "We *say* we don't show Mohammed. But back in Arabia they hear we *do* show Mohammed. And who is playing Mohammed? Peter O'Toole!"

"They don't believe us? How about all these other Arab supervisors we got around here? What the hell good are they if they can't even report back that we don't have Peter O'Toole? Won't the Saudis believe the other Arabs?"

"Hmph, Arabs," said Sandor, wagging his head back and forth as if he had some doubts about Arab brotherhood. "Listen, *you* they believe ahead of another Arab."

Omar came into the lobby with a deep scowl on his face, alone now.

"Very tough, very tough," he said, coming up to us. "I think it'll go to the King."

"For Christsake, tell him we don't have Peter O'Toole," I said. "No O'Toole, no Mohammed. Can't he see for himself?"

Omar raised his hands as if it was much more complicated than that.

"Look," said Sandor, holding up a copy of *Maroc Soir*, from a nearby newsstand. Five pictures of the King on the front page. Half the page-one stories were about Spanish Sahara, or rather "Moroccan Sahara under Spanish domination." The headline: WILL RIYADH USE THE OIL WEAPON FOR OUR SAHARA?

"Oil," said Sandor portentously. "Loans."

"And all endangered by little us?" I said. "You mean an Arab brother would use that kind of pressure on another Arab brother? Just to stop a movie?"

"The Saudis say we're a sacrilege," said Omar gloomily. "And here we're doing our best to rehabilitate Islam. Give them the best PR they've had in a thousand years, aren't we, Burt? And I could bring a multi-million-dollar film

49

industry into Morocco. This could be a new Almería! I could do for Morocco what Samuel Bronson did for Spain!"

"He went bankrupt, actually," I said.

This new development was giving me a sinking feeling because the one thing you might not know about me is that I sincerely hate the idea of being poor. It's the Beverly Hills in me. The truth is that I am oddly breezy about physical danger. I knew that theoretically bad things might happen to me someday with all the shenanigans I was up to but in a peculiar kind of way the danger of it made my blood race, gave me some kind of psychic lift. I was an adrenalin freak. But the idea of poverty gave me no psychic lift at all. It made me all morbid, and listless, and depressed. I mean, here I was living from one hundred-thousand-dollar screenplay to another, virtually from hand to mouth, but on this movie I had a chance of breaking out of the vicious circle. If we brought in a winner Omar of course would be rich as Croesus, but I had two points of the gross and with any kind of luck that could mean millions, removing forever the specter of being independently poor. And I will tell you my secret plan. With a few million I could go back to my old home town as a writer-producer, because in my opinion all this stuff is hogwash about directors, who are nothing but glorified cameramen and the movies are a writer's game, the only trouble being that in Hollywood they shit on writers. Unless you pull off the hat trick and turn yourself into a writer-producer. And I had an even *more* secret plan, which was to incorporate myself in Liechtenstein, because I was getting sick and tired of sand and heat and Arabs and I wanted to go sit on top of a mountain of white snow in the Alps and write movies about William Tell, or John Calvin, or Admiral Byrd, or anybody who did interesting things in a cold climate. Calvin, for example, was a much sexier subject than most people realize, and the fight he had with Luther over the Lord's Supper was really very dramatic, and it was my reading of Calvin's *Institutes of the Christian Religion* that convinced me of the godliness of making money, and and of how horrible and really wrong it was to be poor. So if people took pot shots at me with a magnum .357 I felt it was all in good fun, no hard feelings, but I had a morbid dread of assaults against my bank account, which was both sacred and holy. This was an idea which I had internalized from my Christian upbringing, and I had internalized it real deep.

Mouna suddenly appeared on the periphery of my vision.

"May I speak to you, Omar?" she said, and took him off somewhere, her striding ahead, him following abstractedly to the rear.

"He's lucky he's got a girl like that," said Sandor approvingly. "With all the ups and downs in this business, the women need to be tough."

Sandor didn't ask my opinion and I didn't give it.

An hour later the four of us were sitting together on the terrace of a French restaurant with red-and-white-checked tablecloths. The air was cooling as the light faded rapidly from the sky. It was like landing a plane at sunset. In the air, all brilliant and luminous. But a few seconds later, touching down on the landing strip between the glowing markers: night. Sandor, earthbound, was eating a mushroom omelette, Omar steak and salad, and Mouna grilled fish. I was the only one who was eating Arab food, a pastilla, but with a knife and fork, not with my hands like a real Arab. I'm not that crazy. Some of the Arab actors would come walking by on the way to another table from time to time, and we'd all salute each other ceremoniously, lots of smiles, bowing. The Arabs usually spoke French or English to each other, since "yes" in Egyptian is *iwah*, while in Moroccan, for example, it's *naam*.

"They're very mean with their horses," Sandor said. "The stunt men told me. They break their jaws to make them sensitive. Pftooey. The SPCA would be after us in a minute if we tried that in Hollywood."

"You didn't get any calls from London during the day?" Omar asked Mouna. "They said they'd call this morning."

"I wouldn't know about the morning," said Mouna. "But they certainly didn't call in the afternoon."

"Why wouldn't you know about the morning?" Omar asked, puzzled at the punctiliousness.

"I was in bed," answered Mouna, smiling into her grilled fish.

"Sick?" asked Omar, still adrift. She looked perfectly all right.

"No," Mouna said melodiously.

"What were you doing in bed then?"

"Mr. Nelson and I were in bed," she said.

I felt a chill in my spine.

"You mean you were in bed and Burt was in bed," Omar pressed her nervously. "Different beds."

"No," said Mouna liltingly. "The same bed."

I didn't look at anyone. I didn't see anything at all. My inner eye was closed. I could just hear the voices.

"We had this wild erotic experience," Mouna continued. "But just physical. It doesn't affect what we have between us, darling." She laughed.

I didn't want to ever open my inner eye again, but felt I had to make some kind of move. I couldn't sit there without moving a muscle. I glanced gingerly at Sandor, who was bug-eyed. Then at Mouna, who was still smiling into her plate. Then at Omar, who was staring at me rather intensely, his eyes all bloodshot, his head turned straight toward me.

"Is this true?" he asked.

"No, don't be silly," I said shrugging. "It's Mouna's idea of a joke."

But she didn't back me up. Just kept smiling at her plate.

"You have your Chloe," Mouna said musically. "And I have my lovely Mr. Nelson. Who's a very ardent lover, I must say."

Well, that at least was a lie. But Omar was staring at me quite horribly.

"Cut it out, Mouna," I said. "He's believing you. It's not funny."

"But it's not supposed to be funny. My darling," she said, pursing her lips and blowing me a kiss across the table, which was ludicrously out of character and really would give people the wrong idea about us.

Omar turned back to me, pushing his chair back in agitation, clutching his napkin in a crumpled ball on the table.

"I want to know if this is the truth!" he declared, his face white beneath the tan. But why was he asking me? Why didn't he ask her?

"Of course not," I reassured him. "What an idea."

He swiveled back to Mouna, who was smiling smugly at the table.

"*You son of a bitch!*" Omar raged at me hoarsely, then abruptly stood up, upsetting his chair, and stormed off the terrace and down the street, leaving his steak unfinished.

What did he take *her* word for? Why didn't he believe me? There was a bit of a stir among people at nearby tables, but not as much as you might think. It all happened very fast and Omar was known among our people, at least, to be on the excessive side. Sandor bent over and picked up Omar's chair, wheezing a little, then stood, slightly alarmed.

"Well, I think I'll leave the two of you," he said, leaving his meal unfinished too.

"Oh, no, you don't. Sandor! Stay!" I said. "I'm not going to be left alone here with Mouna." It was unflattering but to hell with her. "Mouna and I have nothing to say to each other that we can't say in front of you. Think of the movie. Do we, Mouna."

Sandor sat down apprehensively.

"Now what did you want to go and say that for?" I asked Mouna.

"Because it's true, my darling," she said, preening herself. Everybody was darling now.

"She's hopeless," I said to Sandor, whose face looked as if he had nothing to do with all this. He had no connection with it whatever.

"You really shouldn't have done it, Mouna," I said. "I think you caused Omar a lot of psychic pain."

Mouna flared up.

"What business is it of yours whether I cause him psychic

53

pain or not!" she seethed, furious, standing. "You filthy pig!"
Then she stormed out too. Everybody was so excitable.

Sandor's eyes were darting around as if he was wondering
what was going to happen next. But he adjusted soon
enough and walking back to the hotel along Boulevard
Mohamed Zerktouni he was humming merrily, bursting into
what I suppose you could call song. *Ich bin die fesche Lola.
Der Liebling der Saison. Ich habe eine Pianola. Zu Hause in
mein'm Salon.* "I'm the hot-stuff Lola. The darling of the
year. I have a pianola. That I keep in my living room." It
doesn't translate very good.

"For God's sake, Sandor, I hope you don't think I've been
fooling around with Mouna. Do you think I'm crazy?"

"No, no," said Sandor, humming jauntily again, casting
his eyes up to the starry heavens as we walked, essaying a
dance step or two.

"Well, if you believe her you've got really bad judgment.
Didn't you see how she flew off the handle? Don't you recognize a vindictive female when you see one?"

"Vindictive, ha, ha," said Sandor.

"Oh, come on. Do you think I'd be so irresponsible as to
jeopardize the working harmony of the whole production?"

This seemed so logical and I felt so sincere while saying
it that it took quite a while after I'd gotten back to my
room for me to remember that it wasn't true. I don't know.
It felt true.

It was suffocatingly hot and the door and windows were
open, and I was lying under a wet towel trying to get cool
when it started to come home to me that this had turned
into a really nasty movie. How could I work with Omar
now? How could he work with me? It was flesh-crawly. Did
I have a chance of getting myself believed if I stuck to my
story? It was just Mouna's word against mine after all. She
couldn't prove anything, could she? But having Mouna in
such a state of active malice made me nervous and got me
worrying about money, which as I explained to you is my
weak point. If Mouna really went on a rampage, could
Omar take away my points of the gross? Would my contract

hold up? Or what if she just fucked everything up and the picture never even got made! All that money lost! It made me feel really sick. I am very cowardly about money. And there was even the KUBARK thing. She was all-around bad news, that woman. She made me worry, and I hate to worry.

I didn't want to close the door because it would cut off the cross draft, afraid I couldn't sleep in the heat, and as I lay there in the half-darkness in the room I could occasionally hear people walk down the corridor outside, chatting in French, English, Arabic. *This bloke was riding with his hands back like this, didn't even have the reins in his hands,* a voice said. *But the horse just followed the other horses.* It must have been one of the English stunt men. During a lull I could hear people drinking out by the swimming pool.

All at once someone very large walked rapidly into my room and plumped down on the chair by the desk, snapping on the desk light. He got smaller. It was Omar, who rose again in that fidgety way he had and shut the door, then sat again, in shorts and a red-and-blue sport shirt, staring out the window. He'd changed clothes since dinner.

"We've got to get this settled," he said, still staring off, but his inner motor running fast. "Can you make a socialist scenario out of this or not?"

"What?"

"Why can't he be a socialist?" demanded Omar, turning toward me intently. "He said a lot of socialist things. A lot of it's pretty left-wing."

"Who?"

"Muhammed. You soft-pedal the property rights stuff a little, the blood price," he went on hurriedly. "You bring up the all-men-are-brothers stuff, the universalist side of Islam."

"Why? Why are we doing this?" I was still lying naked on the bed with a wet towel over me. Omar was charging along, assuming his troops were behind him.

"I honestly think Muhammed was very left-wing for his time," he declared earnestly. "I really do. The Koran is filled with left-wing stuff."

"Like if a slave woman commits adultery," I said, "she

55

only gets half the punishment of a free woman who commits adultery."

"Right. Which was very advanced for its time."

. "What's half of death? *Sura* Four."

"Look," he said, catching on, a hint indignant. "You think Algeria is such an egalitarian country? You think nobody drives around in a limousine in Algeria?"

Ah. Algeria. That's the way it was with Omar. You had to wait for the pieces to fit in place. He was no whiz at giving you things in the right order.

"Algeria?"

"Because they'll want story approval," he said impatiently.

"You mean if we move the production from Morocco to Algeria," I said, which Omar ignored as too self-evident.

"They did a beautiful job on *The Battle of Algiers* and *Z*," he said enthusiastically. "But they want a socialist Muhammed. Do you think you can do me a socialist Muhammed? Read all the material over again. I see him as sort of a Fidel Castro figure, an Arabic Castro. A national leader, okay, but anti-colonialist, anti-imperialist.

"Anti which empire? Byzantine or Persian?"

"Either. Both," said Omar as if what was the difference. "No exploitation of man by man. Boumedienne led the revolt against French rule, he'll love it. Put in stuff about fair laws for the workers, collectivism. Do you think you could find something that could be a sort of prefiguration of the French oil companies being nationalized?"

"How about Al Azzah in Cairo?" I said. "Are they going to want a socialist Mohammed? You've got to worry about them too."

"The big thing," said Omar in reply, sighing as if in relief, "is that Algeria has its own oil. The Algerians can tell the Saudis to go stuff it! You don't use any of this strong-arm stuff with the Algerians. No, sir. Not with Boumedienne. Tested in battle! A warrior-leader! The man who led the rebellion against the French!"

"Actually it was Ben Bella who led the rebellion against

the French," I said. "Boumedienne threw him out in a coup after independence."

Omar hadn't heard of Ben Bella, which shows the view of the Islamic world from Beverly Hills isn't unobstructed. It was before Omar discovered his Arab heritage.

"Well, it'll take some rethinking," I said, raising myself on one elbow, then sitting on the edge of the bed.

"That's all I'm asking you to do, m'boy. Rethink. Rethink. Hold yourself in readiness to rewrite the whole damn thing at a moment's notice. In a socialist direction. Or some other direction. Stay flexible."

He rose and strode to the open window, looking out at the lights around the swimming pool, then came back and placed a hand on my sweaty shoulder, looking at me solicitously.

"I just wanted to be sure I had your loyalty," he said gravely.

"Sure you've got my loyalty," I said.

Well, it was true. I was loyal.

6

HE WAS A FUNNY GUY. Like take his scatteredness. You'd never think he could be a successful producer. You'd never think anyone in his right mind would give him money. But these people did. He had a way of pulling himself together when the situation was *in extremis*, when he was right at the brink. I'd been in the office with him when calls came in from ministers of this or that on the Persian Gulf, money men. Before the minister called, Omar's mind would be wandering, he'd be rambling along, unable to get out a coherent sentence. But when Mouna said it was the minister of such and such on the line, you could see him get a grip on himself, breathing heavily. He always took deep breaths in emergencies as if oxygen would do it. Somehow he'd concentrate his mind, give perfectly sensible answers if with a certain agitation, at least until he went ripping off into Arabic, after which it was anybody's guess of course. He wasn't your ordinary, everyday movie producer.

My book was a pretty good book. I was still Public Affairs Officer in the Air Attaché's office in our embassy in Madrid when we dropped those unarmed atomic bombs in Spain by mistake, and I had the genius idea of writing a book showing it was all a commie plot, which was rather audacious of me since anybody who read the *New York Times* knew we'd freely admitted we'd dropped them. But this was for people who didn't read the *New York Times* and thought *The Love Machine* was the real story of James Aubrey of

CBS Television, or *The Carpetbaggers* was the real story of Howard Hughes. The real story, you know, told at last, the inside, intimate, exciting stuff, with just a few insignificant changes in detail to protect the author from a libel suit. The Air Force kept me on full pay and allowances and relieved me of all other duties and the idea was to have the book a best seller, which unfortunately we failed to accomplish, but we made a bold try. A good enough effort so the Pentagon got me onto a defector-type book, about a real Romanian defector priest, my Church of Silence book. It was while working on this one with this real priest that the Pentagon and I discovered the deep religious strain in my personality. And this one sold well, and they made a movie of it, which got me into the religious movie business, and other movie business. It was *la revanche de Beverly Hills*. Or the conquest of heredity over environment. Or early environment over later environment. I mean I'd tried to run off into the military and the Air Force and be a fighter jock, but show business had won out in the end. I worked for a director once who was making a Western in Mexico with real Apaches, but the Mexicans had taken him to see the Maya pyramids in the Yucatan and he wanted me to work the pyramids into the story too, up in Apache country. He explained to me that the important thing wasn't whether or not the Maya pyramids had actually been built up in Apache country, but whether they *could* have been built up in Apache country. You get it? All African rivers flowed toward the sea, but some of them *could* have flowed inward into Lake Victoria as in *The African Queen* with Humphrey Bogart. Queen Christina abdicated the crown of Sweden because she was a screwball and probably a lesbian and quarreled her way overland across Europe for three years before arriving in Rome, but she *could* have abdicated for love of John Bowles and gone there direct on a beautiful boat like Greta Garbo. Cardinal Richelieu was a real cardinal of the Church in both history and Alexandre Dumas's *Three Musketeers*, but he *could* have been just plain Mister Richelieu as in the great Hollywood movie with Gene Kelly.

Embracing this concept was a truly liberating experience. And I realized that in my own humble way I had been feeling my way toward the light in my bomb book. We dropped the bombs, okay, but it *could* have been a commie plot. You just had to use a little common sense about it. Montcalm couldn't have won the Battle of the Plains of Abraham because we'd all be speaking French. A little common sense and the world was yours.

I didn't know which angle to rewrite the scenario from though, and they'd finished their mud-hut scenes, so I drove out in my Peugeot the next morning to Mecca, about three-quarters of an hour from where you left the main road. We'd had to grade the access road ourselves, a dusty, rutted track out through this African hard scrabble land. Before I came it was as green as Ireland, they told me, but it sure looked like the Arabian desert now, all sun-baked and tawny-colored. Halfway down the sandy track, wheels drumming on the ruts and rocks, I came to our Checkpoint Ali, a real armed roadblock with a red-and-white striped boom as at a railroad intersection, to keep out thieves, belligerent strays of one sort or another, fanatics who might want to kill us for desecrating the Prophet, for example. Someone had blown up the chuck wagon a couple of weeks before. It was a hostile country. The villagers where we'd built our Mecca weren't being contaminated by Western decadence, you'll be glad to hear. When our set carpenters were unloading steel tubing from a truck to build the Kaaba the inhabitants of a little mud house next to the truck threw stones at our guys and laid open the head of one of them because, mounted on the back of the truck, they'd been able to look into these Arabs' little court, you see, prying eyes. The carpenter didn't see anything, you realize, but the villagers just had this wonderful sense of privacy. Actually I'm mistranslating by calling them villagers because they called themselves a tribe, which is a little closer to it. And the tribe was divided into opposing clans. We couldn't give the refuse from our meals to the dogs because enraged Arabs would appear shouting why did we give our refuse to these people's dogs and not to their dogs. On the foundation of our Kaaba we thought we'd build them a little school when we left, as a remembrance of our stay. It was a village of perhaps three hundred people. But half the villagers were in a fury because the school would be on the turf of this other clan, why couldn't we build it on the turf of *their* clan — so it looked as if they were going to get no school at all. But it was good that they weren't being corrupted by Western softness, mushy easygoing ways, that contemptible spirit of compromise, stuff like that. Don't you think? They were true to their very own selves, which was what was important after all.

As I came over the last rise I saw Mecca, crenelated, mud-colored, a vision of sun-parched grandeur, both splendid and austere, exactly as it had existed in sixth century Arabia in the imagination of our set designer. Our Kaaba was demonstrably better than the Arabian Kaaba, which is hung with only modern black cloth, while ours had authentic-looking gray and white stripes woven into great rough traditional-looking cloth. In addition to which ours was built on steel tubing giving it lightness as well as strength, whereas the real Kaaba might have strength but I'll bet it didn't have lightness. I drove through the holy city at reduced speed. It was deserted. The costume tent was deserted, a Rolls Royce in the shade at one side. The men's-room trailer was deserted. The segregated dining area under tarpaulins was deserted, none of the usual Moslems on one side, none of the usual Christians, Jews, and Moslems of elevated rank on the other. Nobody on either side of any religion.

"Hey, where is everybody?" I asked a six-year-old girl in a long Moroccan dress, a little citizen of this Allah-forsaken village before we turned it into Mecca.

She didn't speak French. Her face forbidding, she raised her hand in a sign of warning. I wasn't supposed to take her picture. We were making a ten-million-dollar Islamic supermovie in her front yard and I wasn't supposed to take her picture.

61

In the infirmary I found Sister Anne, the English nurse, tending to the day's wounded.

"They're up on the hills behind," she said, waving in that direction. "Thousands of them. It's Mohammed's return to Mecca."

She had in her care three collapsed actors, two passed out from the heat, the third with a bandage around his head.

"They are barbarians, these Moroccans!" the bandaged one declared passionately, lying on a mattress in his Bedouin suit. He was from Beirut and was planning to join the La Mama acting company in New York, to play in what language I never discovered.

"This morning I am leaving Mecca, a persecuted Muslim," he protested, "and they are throwing stones at me from the walls, hard rubber stones. These Moroccan extras, men and women both, these savages, they are throwing from the front, to hurt me devilishly, and I run away! And Sandor explain, *No! Not in the front! In the back! Wait until he pass, and then throw behind!* And they translate for these Moroccans, *Throw to the back of him.* So next time they wait until I pass, and then these devils they *throw me in the back!* They hit me. Back! Head! They fell me completely!"

"They knocked you out."

"Yes, yes! They felled me out!"

"What were you doing leaving Mecca?" I said. "I thought Mohammed was coming back to Mecca."

"This morning he leave," said the actor moodily. "This afternoon he come back."

About a mile behind the village I found them, Sandor, Omar, two camera crews, the script girl, about fifty technicians, cars, the generator truck. As I approached in the Peugeot they all turned and flagged me anxiously to halt, I was going to spoil a shot. Climbing out of the car, I crept forward cautiously. The whole crew was in a slight recession, both cameras pointing toward the crest of a nearby hill, everybody staring intently at the summit. Sandor was very much in command, dashing from one camera to another in his Hungarian straw hat. The sun was high in the sky, the heat stifling. Walkie-talkies were squawking in Arabic. Suddenly, over the ridge line of the hill, we saw the wrapped heads of Bedouins in full desert costume. It was that Heart In Mouth moment. Then their shoulders appeared, the heads of camels, horses. There were dozens. Hundreds. Then the whole hill was swarming with Arabs in desert dress, a thousand of them. It was Mohammed's army returning to Mecca in triumph. When they got to Mecca they would be acclaimed by the multitude. The prodigal Prophet returned. Let there be singing and the clashing of cymbals. In historic fact Mohammed's first return to Mecca was surrounded by all the joy of a tour of the Ku Klux Klan with flaming crosses through the Negro district of a southern town in the old days, with the petrified darkies all hiding indoors, fearing for their lives. The tensions in Mecca only let up bit by bit. But we needed an upbeat end to the movie, to bring out the Horatio Alger aspect of Mohammed, which was legitimate I think, and so I'd played up the triumphant, clashing-of-cymbals side of Mohammed's homecoming. I mean the Meccans didn't actually welcome Mohammed back with clashing cymbals, but they *could* have welcomed him back with clashing cymbals if they'd only had enough foresight to realize what a big success he was going to be in the years to come and how famous he was going to make his old home town. It also gave us a big final scene for the picture. Omar was hurrying like mad so he'd have all his Mecca shots in the can in case the Moroccans closed us down, so we wouldn't have to build Mecca again in Algeria or wherever. Also there were these hundreds of camels we'd brought up from southern Morocco. What if we had to move to Mexico? Where did you get camels in Mexico? Did Mexico have enough oil?

Two Arabs on handsome horses came streaking down the hill toward us, a cloud of dust rising behind them, and galloped straight past the cameras, crying in English, "The Moslems are coming!" — a line I never wrote, but which wouldn't be on the final soundtrack since it would be post-synched. As they reined in their horses I could see that both riders had blue eyes, which they'd kept narrowed to slits as they came by the cameras. They were Englishmen.

"What do you mean, 'The Moslems are coming'?" called a burly man on horseback, our cavalry colonel. "More classical style, Alf! I want some 'forsooths' and 'gadzooks'!"

Standing beside Omar near camera number one was an immensely fat Sidney Greenstreet of a man I'd never seen before. Although the temperature was over 110 he was wearing a pale-green suit, a paler green shirt, a lime-colored tie. Despite his weight he moved with a curious elegance.

"Burt, I'd like you to meet Halil," said Omar. "Burt's our scenario writer."

He didn't tell me who Halil was because I knew already. Halil was our Mr. Fix-it. He was going to fix things for us with the King. At a price. He could fix anything in Morocco, they said. The big mistake the Hilton people made was not being represented by Halil which meant they didn't know who to bribe, very embarrassing. Otherwise we'd have had air conditioning. But could he fix the Saudis? Halil lifted his straw hat and greeted me with a smile of patrician charm. He had blue eyes too, another blue-eyed Arab. Or was he a Berber? A Berber in a Rolls Royce. He greeted me in French. He had greatly admired *The Song of Jesus*, which had been very successful in Morocco, he said. He had much preferred it to *Jesus Christ Superstar*, which had been vulgar, and banned in any case. He'd seen it in Paris. Did I enjoy water-skiing? Sailing? I must be his guest at his beach villa in Tangier, where Niarchos's sister-in-law had recently visited him. I liked water-skiing and sailing too, I told him. Could I do both?

"By all means!" he exclaimed, smiling urbanely. "Would you care for a cigarette?"

Even the fetching out of a package of *Gauloises Bleues* was an exercise of courtly grace.

"No, thanks, I don't smoke."

His eyes flickered.

64

"That's all right. Take the package anyway."

I took the half-empty blue package and put it in the pocket of my shirt.

"I must be getting back," he said, making a serene gesture in the direction of Mecca. Our Mecca.

"I'll drive you back to your car," I offered.

"Can I come too?" asked one of the production assistants, a Moroccan.

The steering wheel of my Peugeot was so hot from the sun I had to hold it with a hand towel I kept in the glove compartment.

"I understand you export fossil stone," said Halil as I drove slowly through the sand and shingle. "Stone with pre-historic fossils embedded in it."

"That's right."

"To museums?"

"No, just decorators. In polished slabs."

"It must be very decorative," said Halil appreciatively. "Are you having any trouble with the new nationalization directives?"

Under new government orders, fifty-one percent of all foreign business ventures in Morocco had to be sold to Moroccan nationals.

"Not yet."

"If you do, let me know," said Halil, smiling warmly. "I have friends."

"I will," I said. "I will."

Halil's chauffeur had seen us coming and was standing by the open limousine door in his visored cap. As Halil stepped in ponderously a Land Rover came barreling down from the location in a cloud of dust and stopped in front of the infirmary. A man in handsome black desert costume came hobbling out, half carried by two assistants. By the time I got there Sister Anne had sent one man running to the new chuck wagon for a bucket and ice and another to our command post to telephone for the doctor. The injured man was the stunt rider Alf who had yelled, "The Moslems are coming," and he was sitting now in a chair as Sister

Anne carefully cut off the boot from his right foot with surgical scissors.

"Seems a shame to ruin them beautiful boots," Alf said, his blue-eyed smile very bright.

"Don't worry, we'll buy you another pair," said Sister Anne, busy snipping.

With the boot off, the rider's ankle was swelling fast, an ugly bluish-white.

"I fell right. The bloody horse fell wrong," he said.

"Move your toes."

The toes moved.

"Well, it can't be broken."

"That's nice," said Alf.

The man with the bucket of ice water arrived and Sister Anne carefully edged Alf's foot into it, and he sat there, dressed like one of Mohammed's generals, the king of the desert, with his foot in a yellow plastic bucket of ice water.

"Does that feel better?" she asked.

"A little," said Alf, his hands tight on the arms of his camp chair, but still smiling. "Yeah."

"Does it hurt much?" I said.

Alf turned his eyes to me and closed them for an instant as he gave the tiniest of all possible nods. The smile didn't leave his lips.

"Just a bit," he said. "Yeah."

Omar arrived in a flurry of agitation.

"It's all covered by the insurance," he proclaimed. "Don't worry. You'll have the best of everything." And then to me, "Where's Halil?"

"Gone back."

Omar grimaced. "The doctor can't come. Can you take him to the hospital?"

In a few minutes we had Alf installed in the back of my Peugeot with his ice bucket, and one of the Moroccan assistants to hold it still for him. It was a long, careful drive back along the dusty track, trying to jolt my passenger as little as possible.

"How you doing back there, Alf?"

66

"Not bad," he said.

I glanced back at him, outlandish-looking now in his antique desert robes. When I looked at him he smiled quickly.

At the hospital a French doctor took him in charge, an orderly wheeling him off on a rolling cot in the direction of the X-ray department.

"Broken," the doctor said when he came out to account to me. "We'll have to put it in a cast. He won't be able to ride for a while."

When he'd finished his report his face lit up.

"So you're making a movie out there, eh? What's it about? Lot of action? A thriller?"

I told him. It seemed to sober him a bit. He seemed to find the subject un-fun, which was worrying. Maybe Mohammed had no sex appeal for Western audiences. This was the first time I'd discussed the film with a representative of the Outside World and it was something of a sneak preview.

"But there's a lot of action," I said, attempting to awaken his enthusiasm. "We're not going to get bogged down in religion. There'll be big battles."

None of this was having the desired effect.

"And we've got a Mecca out there you'd never believe," I said. "Straight out of the seventh century. The pilgrims are going to come to this new Mecca now. They won't need to go to Saudi Arabia."

There was an odd shift to the doctor's face and I said, "You've been to Saudi Arabia."

"As a matter of fact, I have," he said.

"You're not a Moslem."

He didn't look Moslem.

"No," he answered patiently, slightly amused.

"How'd you like it? Was it nice?"

The doctor let his eyes wander around the room for several seconds with a peculiar twist to his mouth. Perhaps it had been a bittersweet experience. He finally stared at me calmly and said:

"They asked me to amputate a man's hand."

There was a moment's silence.

"For what? What was the matter with it?"

He was still staring at me composedly.

"Nothing."

"What did they want you to amputate it for?" I asked, although by now I knew the answer.

"It was going to be on television, for the edification of the masses." The doctor paused. "He was a thief."

I felt a little sick to my stomach.

"What did you do?"

The doctor took a deep breath.

"Well, I refused to do it." He looked away. "It wasn't an easy decision. There were people who said I'd be saving the poor man's life. Without me they might just whack the hand off with a butcher's knife and then plunge the stump in camel's dung."

His composure was gone now and he rubbed the side of his nose nervously.

"But I couldn't amputate the hand of a healthy man," he said as if embarrassed.

I decided not to ask what eventually happened to the thief, whether an Arab doctor took his hand off or did they use the camel-dung system, what was the show's Arabian Nielsen rating. The doctor and I finished the arrangements about Alf, our wounded stunt man, and then we parted.

"Good luck on your movie." The doctor smiled coolly.

Why my movie? It was these Arabs' movie. I was just the screenwriter. Back at the hotel I took the package of cigarettes Halil had given me out of my pocket. It was half full and I dumped the loose cigarettes out onto my desk, then took the paper package apart. On the inner wrapping was penciled lightly: "At the King's garden party Friday." I ripped it up and flushed it down the toilet.

7

"IT'S OUR BIG CHANCE!" trumpeted Omar, charging up to me at the swimming pool at the Hotel Mamounia. "Halil spoke to the King's brother! He's going to save the bacon! The King's going to come out on the set! We're saved by the glamor of the movies! Bette Davis and Joan Crawford! They did it!"

We used to go over to the Mamounia to swim because of the atmosphere. Flowering jasmine perfumed the air, and you could see the snow-capped crests of the Atlas Mountains, which were really awe-inspiring when you were swimming, and also Winston Churchill had slept there. And he'd painted paintings in the garden. The pool itself had lots of aquamarine Islamic tiling; it was like swimming in a mosque. The whole thing was preposterously luxurious and made the pool at the Beverly Hills Hotel look like Skid Row. Omar was so lit up I thought he was going to jump into the water from sheer excitement, but he waited for me to swim to the side and climb up onto the tiled edge.

"Bacon?" I said.

"Okay, wise guy, I don't need you to tell me good Muslims don't eat bacon," he said, still bubbling over with good spirits, sitting beside me on the edge of the pool.

"And you know something else?" he said, lowering his voice confidentially. "You know the King's birthday party?"

"No."

Omar was impatient.

"Well, the King has a birthday party, it's a big deal here. Every year he has some special attraction. Like he has a golf tournament on his private links, he's mad about golf. Or he has a *fantasia*. You know, when a hundred Arabs come galloping at you like crazy, firing their rifles into the air, and the women going, you know —" He imitated the bloodcurdling shriek that Arab women make at celebrations, demonstrations, funerals. Half a dozen people at the pool turned to look at us.

"Ululating," I said.

"Last year he air-dropped a parachute brigade right down on top of the party," Omar recalled. "Real class."

His manner became conspiratorial.

"And you know who the special attraction is going to be this year?"

"No."

"*Us!*" Omar rejoiced. "The King's going to give the party at the Bahia Palace here in Marrakesh while we're shooting a scene from the movie! It was Halil's idea. He's really a genius. You and I would never have thought of that. Never underrate the magic of the movies! We're too blasé. We forget how glamorous the movies are to outside people. Even crowned heads."

"Three days ago he was going to close us down because we were a sacrilege, and now suddenly we're so glamorous he's offering us as entertainment to the guests at his birthday party."

"He doesn't have to be consistent," said Omar.

"And what scene in the Bahia Palace? We don't have any scenes to shoot in the Bahia Palace."

"How about the scene where Muhammed comes down from the mountain and everybody's waiting for him to tell them what the Archangel Gabriel told him. That's a big scene for a Muslim."

"Are you crazy? The set won't match. The architecture's a thousand years off."

"Then make one up," said Omar, undeflated.

"You mean a fake scene?"

"Why not? He'll never know the difference," Omar said breezily.

"You mean you'd waste a full day's shooting on a scene that you know ahead of time can't possibly be in the picture? This film's costing almost a hundred thousand dollars a day."

"Money, money," said Omar derisively. "Haven't you gotten it through your head yet that money is the least of our problems on this movie? These Arabs are made of money! Haven't you heard of petro-dollars? What we need isn't money, it's *wiliness*. Think up a good scene the King will like, I'm telling you." And he went off to get into his swimming trunks.

Well, if it was all right with the money men it was all right with me. We had these actors who were making believe they were seventh century Arabians, now they could make *believe* they were making believe, a little playlet for the entertainment of the King of Morocco, Hollywood by the Sahara, Mohammed at the Movies, Boy Meets Camel. I've never understood it. People meet a religious fanatic or an eagle scout or whatever and they think how pathetic, he really believes this stuff, look how creepy his clothes are. But they see an actor who is only *pretending* to be a religious fanatic, with a camera crew shooting the scene and a guy with a clapstick who runs out and says, *Song of Mohammed. Shot fifty-three. Take two*, and it's glamorous. Since Omar had suggested it himself I chose the scene when Mohammed comes down from the mountain and all his disciples are waiting around anxiously to hear how it went, with a few lines from other scenes thrown in to make it sexier. What the hell. It was just a phony scene. In about a week the King's elder sister came out to the Mecca set to look us over, dressed in a beige Saint Laurent suit. She and Mouna talked about jewelry, fingering each other's necklaces; Mouna's must have been something Omar gave her. "You see what I told you about Mouna?" Omar whispered. "Isn't she loyal to the movie?" When did he tell me that, I wondered. Then he informed me we were going to shoot the

71

scene for the King's birthday party not at the Bahia Palace but at the golf course the King had outside Marrakesh.

"At a *golf* course!"

"Well, it's sort of a palace too," said Omar to mollify me. "There'll be someplace we can shoot. The King's a golfing nut. He's got to have his golf."

"Even the King's going to know this scene's a fake," I said. "Why don't we have Mohammed hit a hole in one? I can see the shot. The faithful surging onto the putting green as the ball plunks in and a voice over says, *Allah is great.* We can do *Sura* Eight on hole eight, *Sura* Nine on hole nine."

"And the King's sister wants to meet Guy Lockley," said Omar. "So write him into the scene. She doesn't know he sucks cock."

"But Guy's only three years old when Mohammed comes down from the mountain," I protested, not that this would cut any ice with Omar.

"Cinematographic license!" he declared gaily.

And of course he was right. If Rita Tushingham is only eighteen years old at the end of *Doctor Zhivago,* which meant that they snipped out twenty years between the Bolshevik Revolution and the Khrushchev Thaw and that the Japanese attacked Pearl Harbor during the presidency of Warren G. Harding, why couldn't Guy Lockley play Mohammed's nephew at the age of three? Guy Lockley, a cut-rate Richard Burton, our star. A ten-million-dollar movie and all we could get was Guy Lockley. But still, bewitching enough for such as the King of Morocco's sister, it seemed.

The big day. My first king. We'd given up any serious pretense that we were doing real shooting and set out with our fleet of cars and trucks and trailer dressing rooms at only about nine, whereas we'd have been on the set already shooting at eight if it had been for real. I didn't see why we even had to put film in the camera. Sure enough, not far outside Marrakesh, in the middle of semi-desert, we came to this eighteen-hole golf course with palm trees and mossy fairways, so lush and green they must have piped water from the Atlas Mountains to keep it wet down, a positive obscenity in those desiccated surroundings, with built-in guilt. Only the sand traps looked authentic. Beside the golf course was a kind of Moorish country club enclosed by a sun-baked pink-earth wall, inside the wall a Florida-style swimming pool and vast patio, at one end an arabesque-covered doorway leading to the King's private apartments. Royal retainers in native dress were setting up great buffet tables and decorative red-and-green tents on the patio, and what looked like musicians were dragging instruments and music stands and chairs into one corner. While we pre-tended to shoot scenes were they going to be playing *music*? Apparently we were just part of the floor show. Plausibility of décor no longer even bothered us. The only empty place we could shoot without getting walked on by guests or waiters was the corner opposite the orchestra so we parked our generator truck outside, and ran our electric cables over the wall, and set up camera and scrims and standby lights and aluminum reflectors to fill in the shadows. The elec-tricians then stopped, puzzled. The light was wrong. We'd be shooting straight into the sun, with everyone's face in deep shadow. But Sandor reassured them, "Don't worry, don't worry. It's just for the King. It's just a rehearsal." Finally we had everybody assembled, the cameramen and sound men and script boy, and first and second and third assistants, and we hauled our actors out of the make-up trailer, and they all stood there in the scorching sun in their costumes by the swimming pool. It really looked like Beverly Hills again, a biblical play at a Hollywood Sunday school, the First Church of Christ, Horticulturist. But where was the King to watch the shooting of this historic movie? Where was the King's sister to get Guy Lockley's autograph?

"We'll go ahead anyway," said Omar. "Make like we're really shooting. The King will come by later." To the chief sound man who pointed at the musicians warming up in the other corner, he said softly, "So record it anyway. What does it cost you?"

You could see the actors felt silly. The scene was supposed

to take place at the foot of a bleak mountain and here they were at a King's birthday party, waiters bustling about. But they grouped themselves obediently under Sandor's instruction. "*Quiet!*" the assistants bawled to widespread indifference in the other corners of the patio, and Omar, pretending to be the director, called, "Camera." A man with the clapstick dashed in front of the camera, banged his clapstick, and sang out, *Mohammed, shot fifty-three, take one.* After which Omar said gravely, "Action."

"*He's been up on the mountain for three days!*" anguished a beautiful white-robed English actor named Timmins. And I drifted off. I can't stand to listen to my own lines. In temperatures like that you don't stay out in the sunlight one minute more than you have to. I wandered over and stood in the shade of the orchestra tent. "Where are you fellas from?" I asked a man with a mustache shuffling some sheet music. "*Le Caire,*" he said. They were Egyptians.

Looking back in the direction of the King's private apartments I saw a man resembling Sal Mineo in Bermuda shorts come through the double doors followed by half a dozen other men, some in polo shirts, some in army uniforms, two young soldiers carrying golf bags. Our Moroccan assistant production manager rushed up and kissed the man's hand while everybody else stood around with greasy smiles. My God, the King. I walked over to get a better look, and as I arrived he was saying, "*Continuez! Continuez!*" waving graciously to the film crew to go on with this terrific movie we were making. Then he trotted across the patio and out the main gate, followed by his retainers and his golf bags, off to play a few holes out on the links. He didn't even stay to watch us.

"Hey, what are we supposed to do now?" asked Omar, hurrying up to me urgently. "We've done this shot five times already. We can't keep doing it all day."

"Who's going to complain?" I said. "The waiters? Move the camera and do it five times from another angle. Then move it back to the first angle again. Who'll know the difference?"

74

"Aw, come on. Pick me out a new scene for variety's sake." Omar offered me a mimeographed copy of the script, bound in orange cardboard, half the pages dog-eared to serve as place markers.

"Where's the King's sister by the way?" I asked.

"She's not coming," he said sourly. "Somebody screwed up. It's a stag party. The King's birthday party's always stag. That's why Mouna couldn't come."

"Guy is going to be very disappointed. Here, do this one, another waiting scene. They're in Medina, waiting for Mohammed to arrive across the desert from Mecca. They can shield their eyes and stare across the swimming pool and say, *No man can survive out there in heat like this.* They can improvise on that one indefinitely."

The orchestra was starting to tune up now, and three great buffet tents were all installed. According to a waiter one had Moroccan food, one French, and one Spanish — presumably in honor of the Spanish part of the old protectorate, up in the north around Tangier. By the main entrance were the *mechouis*, a great barbecue pit with lamb roasting on rotating spits. Moslems aren't supposed to drink so the booze tent was set up outside the gate on the golf course side — not in The King's House, you see. The French buffet was piled high with roast chicken, pâté de foie gras, hors d'oeuvres, smoked salmon; the Moroccan, with giant platters heaped with assorted *couscous*. It looked as if it was going to be a sumptuous spread. The guests were starting to arrive — all men, all in sport shirts and bright colored slacks, many with sunglasses, straw hats because of the sun. The invitations had said to come dressed in *style Saint-Tropez*, and the higher the rank the more Saint-Tropez was the Arab. They were Cabinet ministers, industrialists, bankers, ambassadors, most of them down from Rabat and Casablanca; it seemed very extravagant. Some carried little flight bags and went into a row of beach cabins at the far end of the patio and changed into swim trunks, then came out and plopped into the pool. Others drifted over toward the movie corner and idly watched Guy Lockley declaiming,

No man can survive out there in heat like this, shot forty-three, take thirty-five. To the consternation of our bewildered boom man the orchestra struck up *Strangers in the Night*, with an Egyptian Mario Lanza warbling melodiously. If you've never heard *Strangers in the Night* sung in Arabic you haven't lived. The musical competition finally brought our film unit to a dismayed halt, and Sandor had the crew move the camera for a while. More and more guests kept coming, including a red-headed hairdresser down from Paris who couldn't get enough of the waiters. "I just can't *resist* them when they have a little melanin in the skin," he said. To stay out of the sun I was standing under the buffet tents, looking at the great heaps of expensive food, wondering when we could eat.

There were hundreds of guests now, maybe a thousand, maybe only five hundred but they looked like a thousand, when suddenly there were swirls and eddies at the golf course entrance and it was the King again, back from the links, with greaseballs in sport shirts scurrying up to kiss his hand and the King waving them off, it wasn't necessary, we were being informal, we were very Saint-Tropez today. Two Moroccans standing by the side of the pool were slightly more conservatively dressed than the others, which is to say they had on checked sport coats over their polo shirts, and to tease them for their stuffiness the King merrily pushed them into the swimming pool. What a country needs is a King with a good sense of humor, that's what I say. The second man to get pushed in could even have slid away because he saw what had happened to the first one, but when the King wants to push you into the swimming pool I guess you let him push you into the swimming pool. Oh, Your Majesty, you're such a cutup. Then the King called out something in Arabic, "Let joy be unconstrained," no doubt, making benevolent, delighted gestures to his subjects, then hopped along back toward his private apartments, waving happily to his guests as he went. Out of the corner of my eye I saw that Halil had arrived, grotesquely fat in a cornflower-blue sport shirt, talking suavely to other guests. The or-

76

chestra broke at the end of a set and our movie unit went back to *He's been up on the mountain for three days*, but Halil, who'd set the whole thing up, didn't even come over to watch.

I was a little embarrassed at my connection with these strolling Koranic players over in the corner. Far from being outraged because we were engraving graven images beside the swimming pool of the Protector of the Faith, however, the good Moslem guests didn't even seem very interested. We were hardly getting more attention than the Egyptian Mario Lanza. How anybody could have thought we were shooting real footage in the middle of that nuthouse I can't imagine; I just hoped it was good for PR, that we were worming our way into the King's good graces.

I mingled around with the other guests, eavesdropping on conversations when they were in French. It appeared another party was being planned for the next day, for the women this time. There was going to be a ballet. A guest who'd just arrived by car said he'd been held up by a big military convoy, over fifty trucks. A lot of the Frenchmen seemed to be doctors. I noticed they were eating already at the Moroccan tent and went over and put away some stuffed dates, then was one of the first to dig in at the French tent. When you're the first to spoil a beautiful ornamental display of food you always feel you're doing something wrong, but I liked smoked salmon. Back at our little cinema corner to tell Sandor and Omar we could eat now, I saw a man in dark glasses come rushing by in a state of high excitement. *They're attacking the buffet!* he cried. *His Majesty will be furious!* A few minutes later the King emerged again, scowling darkly. He'd changed his clothes and was wearing matching pink slacks and sport shirt, on his head a straw hat with a band of the same pink. He looked as if he was going to make us all stay after school and write *I will never start eating before the King* one hundred times on the blackboard, but someone scampered up to him with a gold-covered book with the names of all the guests, and people started crying "Happy birthday dear King" or whatever in

Arabic, and guys were kissing his hand, and a couple of them even his feet, and an official photographer was clicking away, and the King relented. "Let joy be unconfined," he waved again to his subjects, and made his way to an empty tent near our film unit. Turning his back on everybody, he sat down at a table all by himself and began to eat. I thought this was rather rude of him but one of our Moroccan assistants explained, "Traditional! Tradition! The King eats by self at birthday party." And so be it. And the best of Moroccan luck to you, King Ahmed III.

I grabbed Omar and dragged him out to the firewater tent by the golf course.

"I think he's great," said Omar. "A really juicy guy. At last he's got this country running. Wouldn't you raise the price of phosphate if it was your only export item? And he's cutting out corruption."

"Oh?"

"That squeeze play on Pan Am is a thing of the past. That's the curse of these countries, *baksheesh*, but he's got the problem licked now. And he loves the movies! None of this oriental folderol. He's a real constitutional monarch, less powerful than the King of Sweden, I'll bet."

"Did you see Halil?"

Omar raised his finger to his lips and mimed secret delight, glancing about him as if as yet unrevealed forces were operating in our favor.

"How about those two actors of ours they're holding in Tangier, flew over from Madrid? Could he at least spring them?"

"He's working on it," Omar whispered.

"I'm glad the King got rid of corruption," I said.

Cairo's finest finished the Egyptian version of *A Foggy Day in London Town* back inside the courtyard, and next I heard the sound of castanets. Good God, were we going to have to compete now with Spanish dancers? Then I knew it wasn't castanets. The sound was faint, half-covered by the noise of the party, but there was an unemotional mechanicalness to it. It wasn't musical.

78

"Hey, Ome," I said. "Is there an army camp around here somewhere out in the *bled*?"

"I don't know," he answered offhandedly, knocking back a vodka and tonic. "Why?"

The staccato noise was a shade louder now.

"You hear those firecrackers in the distance?"

Omar listened.

"Firecrackers!" he crowed. "They're going to have a big fireworks show tonight! It's on the program!"

"Those firecrackers are machine-gun fire," I said.

Omar stared at me.

"Take my word for it."

We bolted out of the tent. We were on high ground dominating a luscious green golf course with rolling fairways, rustling palm trees. A foursome complete with caddies was trudging along the greensward on the far side of the course. Beyond was sand and desert, on its edge a long string of trucks. Making their way across the golf course in extended order were several infantry platoons in battle dress, jump boots, red berets, firing short bursts from submachine guns slung over their necks and shoulders.

"A military exercise!" said Omar. "Terrific. Last year a whole parachute brigade parachuted right down in the middle of the festivities."

"What are they firing?"

"Blanks, of course. What do you think?"

Some golfers closer to us put their golf clubs to their shoulders as if they were rifles, and, pointing them at the advancing soldiers, shouted, *"Bang! Bang! You're dead!"* Beside us outside the refreshment tent an outraged gentleman in a golfing cap declared, *"Marching on the greens in hobnail boots! Wait till the King hears this!"* Down below, the soldiers, slowly advancing onto higher ground, fired some short bursts in the direction of the first foursome and two of the caddies pitched forward, the rest of the party raising their hands.

"The caddies are in on it," said Omar, incredulous. "Isn't that planning for you?"

79

Far over to the right, near the King's living quarters, a detachment of soldiers had already reached the pink walls of the residence and a line of white-dressed bus boys and cooks in big chef's hats filed out with their hands in the air. They were so far away that we could hardly relate the dim sounds to the action but the soldiers were firing bursts over there too. Three of the cooks went down. There was nothing dramatic about the way they fell, no convulsions or extravagant sprawling. They just sat, then lay, little white figures. A whining sound accompanied each machine-gun burst from the soldiers crossing the golf course below.

"The cooks are in on it too, I guess," said Omar, slightly unsettled. "I hope this doesn't spoil dinner."

"They're firing live ammunition, Ome," I said.

"What?" He looked shocked. But he'd heard me.

The parking space was cut off already, crawling with soldiers. And I wasn't going to go down the fairway toward those bastards in red berets I can tell you that.

"Back," I told Omar brusquely. "Back to the pool. Maybe we can get out the other side."

He obeyed me like a child. We dashed back into the pool enclosure, where the party was still in full swing, the Egyptian band playing, people eating, swimming, the King still with his back turned. In a pinch like this you couldn't save everybody, only one or two. Sandor was sitting despondently on an electrician's case, wearing his Hungarian hat.

"It's a coup d'état," I said, breathing heavily. "A battalion of soldiers is coming across the golf course. We're going to try to get away on the other side."

"But they won't bother us, will they?" he asked, puzzled.

"They're shooting the cooks and caddies," I said, and he got to his feet immediately.

The three of us jogged toward the back gate, Sandor having the time of his life.

"It's like Berlin!" He laughed. "Six minutes I had to get away from the S.S.! It makes me young again."

Out the back gate it was a tawny desert wasteland. Perhaps three hundred yards away were trucks, trucks, trucks, disgorging soldiers in red berets, submachine guns.

"Back we go," I said. "Be inconspicuous. Stay away from the gates and the King. They can't kill all of us. If we get through the first few minutes we'll be okay."

Inside the enclosure again I took a .38 I carry and ditched it in a trash can under one of the buffet tables. Guests in garish sport shirts were still chatting, wolfing down *mechoui* and smoked salmon, the Egyptian orchestra playing, *oom pa pa, oom pa pa*. This whole little world was going to come apart in just a few seconds, and no one knew. The King was still eating by himself with his pink back studiously turned. Should I warn him? Who were these soldiers? Were these our guys or somebody else's guys? I didn't have a program. Something said no. Let the Moroccans fight it out among themselves. I should take some evasive action for myself in the few seconds I had left but couldn't decide what. Should I dart back into the King's private quarters? But that was where the King would go, and where they would go after him, and I knew the way assault infantry came into defended buildings, with weapons firing. *Oh. Burt Nelson. Sorry about that.*

"Into the bathing cabins," I said to Sandor and Omar, and we ran the length of the pool and took shelter in the green-and-white wooden structures, me peeking out the door as minute after minute ticked by, the party undisturbed.

"I'm going to go back and get the crew," said Sandor.

"You won't have time," I warned, and as I spoke an explosion sounded out in the court. The music came to a ragged halt in a bonking of drums and clattering of cymbals. A trumpet player sagged forward, draped over his music stand. The next grenade I saw myself — a little black pineapple, lobbed in over the wall, rolled near the King's tent and exploded in a sound of breaking china. The King rose, aghast, facing the pool and the guests now, then, very dignified, cried, "*Pas d'affolement!* Don't panic!" and strode swiftly toward his living quarters.

Soldiers now erupted through the gate on the golf course side. They hadn't slept or eaten for two days and were in a sort of frenzy. They'd been told the King had been debauched by foreigners, was idling in luxury, Western ways, drink forbidden by the Prophet, and I can see that after two days crossing the desert in trucks the scene they saw spread before their eyes must have looked a little decadent to them, the Saint-Tropez sport shirts, the drinking, white-linen covered tables groaning with rare foods. They began shrieking wildly in Arabic, firing bursts at any large group of guests, dumping the food tables onto the ground, running every which way. A panicky stampede of guests started toward the rear gate and reached it just as the first wave of soldiers came in from that side with submachine guns blazing. Thirty people went down right there. I got down onto the floor of the bath hut, the lower the better, but still kept the door open an inch, peeking out. You never knew what might happen out there. The most surprised people of all seemed to be the swimmers who'd been caught in the middle of the pool, their ears filled with water, and who dazedly swam to the side and climbed out, standing at the pool's edge with their hands raised, the water running off them. A gray-haired man in a bathing suit came dashing up to our cabin to take shelter.

"*C'est du sérieux*," he babbled when he saw us hiding inside. "*Il y a des cadavres partout.*"

"What did he say?" asked Omar anxiously.

"He says there are dead bodies everywhere."

"Gack," said Omar, less frightened than I would have thought.

The first frenzy over, the soldiers in the court, firing less, were shouting orders in Arabic and French, making everybody raise his hands, herding people into groups. Dozens of soldiers were tramping into the residential quarters with guns at the ready, no doubt after the King. *Shoot everyone who's armed!* I heard someone cry. *Clean out those cabins.*

The time had come to surrender. We all marched out quickly with our hands very high. A soldier in camouflage battle dress beckoned us onward with his weapon while another one threw a grenade into the cabin next to ours. It exploded. There were groans within. We gathered by the pool, a group of a dozen or so swimmers, party-goers, *bons vivants*. Something about our looks must have displeased a sergeant across the pool because he fired a burst in our direction and I heard the bullets zap through the air. Without thinking, I sank to my knees, fell over sideways, lay motionless on the blue tiling. I wasn't hit but I would play dead with the real corpses. In our group I was the only one to fall down though and our guard kept shouting, *Haut les mains! Haut les mains! Haut les mains!* and I was afraid he might put a bullet in me for not raising my hands and I stood up again. Down the line a man called out, *I'm the Lebanese ambassador*, waving his passport in the air. A soldier grabbed it and threw it into the pool and said, "And I'm Abdelwahab Doukkali!" The red-headed hairdresser from earlier shrilled, "I'm just a *coiffeur* from Paris!" At which a soldier raged, *"Tu aurais mieux fait de rester à Paris plutôt que de venir t'encanailler avec ces porcs!"* so there was no getting out of it that way. Although not shrieking anymore the soldiers still had a wild-eyed, manic look as if they were on speed. In fact I think they were on speed. It was hard to quite take in that they were the same Moroccans we saw every day mopping the floors at the hotel, in the fields and *souks*, idling, begging, bickering. They looked different on the other side of a machine gun.

"*Enlève ton pantalon*," a soldier brusquely ordered Omar, who looked alarmed.

"He says take your pants off," I said.

Omar complied rapidly and the soldier threw the pants into the pool.

To a Frenchman in an orange polo shirt five or six people down the line from us, a soldier said, "Take off your shirt."

"Why my shirt?" the man asked.

The soldier fired a machine gun burst straight into his chest, and he collapsed, making hideous sucking sounds, blood all over. Another man ran to where he lay on the ground, crying, "I'm a doctor," and the soldier plowed a burst into him too.

"*Couchez-vous! Couchez-vous!*" someone shouted. "Everybody lie down!"

We all lay down.

"Up! Stand up!" the call came.

We stood up. Along the line came a search party, feeling under prisoners' arms, in pockets. In the side pocket of a man next to Omar a soldier found a gold cigarette lighter and threw it on the ground and stamped on it, presumably as a symbol of luxury.

"Foreign pigs!" he shouted.

But that didn't stop the next soldier from lifting my wrist watch after he'd patted me down, nor the one after that from lifting Sandor's. But the second soldier was spotted by an officer.

"Give it back!" he ordered, marching up sternly. "We're the army of the people!"

The soldier handed it back to Sandor sheepishly, but the one who took my watch, and who had not been seen, merely gave me a furtive glance. I had noted there were no reprimands for shooting prisoners dead, just for stealing watches, and I was afraid my soldier might double back later and shoot me so he wouldn't have to give my watch back. I sincerely wished I could tell him how welcome he was to the watch, how willing I was to make this small contribution to the people's army, but I didn't want him to shoot me for being a smart ass either. There were more bursts of machine-gun fire, men shot down in far corners of the patio. A man in a black-and-white sport shirt ran across the courtyard crying, *Stop firing! Stop firing!* Who was he, I wondered. Why didn't they shoot him?

"Down!" the call came. "On your stomachs!"

We all lay down again. It was sweltering hot lying flat in the sun. I was pouring sweat, it even running into my eyes. More flurries of machine-gun fire broke out, but muffled now, coming from inside the King's residential quarters. Soldiers were still marching about on the patio, shouting orders in French and Arabic, but with my face pressed against the tiling I couldn't see much. Wounded men were groaning, and as a faint background to the groans and soldiers' shouts I began to hear a low chanting. It was the *chahada*, the Moslem death chant.

"On your backs!" a soldier cried in French.

I rolled over.

"Roll over, Ome," I told him, because people further along were still lying on their stomachs. It would be a shame to get shot in a jurisdictional dispute.

"Arms up! Hands up!" someone shouted.

Still lying on our backs, we raised our arms, as if in some demented gym class. The death chant went on. People were lying in the sun in sports clothes, dying. Someone turned on a transistor radio playing martial music. The music stopped and a voice came on in unemotional Arabic, succeeded after a few minutes by a French voice which appealed to the population to be calm. *The King has been executed*, the radio announced. *The people's army has taken power*. Then martial music again.

"On your feet!" the order came. "Up!"

I stood up, feeling wet and dizzy, still keeping my hands raised. Sandor and Omar looked all right, Omar a little dazed, Sandor flushed from the heat. A man to my left didn't get up at all but just lay there. Another man further along was struggling with a tourniquet around his leg, using his belt, his white slacks all running with blood.

A detail of four soldiers came marching along the edge of the pool, submachine guns across their chests, hardware clinking in their pockets. One of them barked something in Arabic, pointing at me, and then in French, *"Le blond."* They came to a halt.

"Come with us," one of them said curtly.

I lowered my hands and followed them with a strange sense of exhilaration. I don't know why. At least I wouldn't die slowly of wounds. They set a smart pace, two of them marching in front, two behind, cutting over toward the wall on the desert side. The huge patio was strewn with hundreds of bodies in bathing suits and sport shirts, most of them alive, guarded by soldiers, some of the prisoners lying on their backs, some on their stomachs. By the back gate, soldiers were dragging dead bodies into a specific area, corpse after corpse, perhaps forty or fifty of them already. An awkwardly deposited body in a bright-blue sport shirt filtered into my consciousness. Halil. His great bulk horizontal, he seemed less fat, the blue eyes still open. Dead. A chill went over me but we marched on. *Hup, hup.* Our cameras and key lights were still standing where we'd been shooting the Mohammed scene. Where were the crew, the actors? The King's dining tent was empty, ghostly. *Hup, hup.* Through the entrance to the King's private quarters. Across another court. Inside the residence itself the air was icy from the air conditioning, half-dark compared to the searing light outside. The rooms were filled with soldiers, churning about. I was half-blinded at first and they were just shadowy shapes to me, but I had an impression of uncertainty in their movements. I can't explain it. My escort came to a halt in front of a closed door, knocked. Questions were put and answered in Arabic. I was pushed into the room. Behind a desk sat a barrel-chested Moroccan officer. He rose. It was Driss, our BULLMOOSE.

"Ha! Walter!" he declared, his eyes quite mad. "Now you see! Corruption is at an end!" He gestured toward the patio. "Thus die the enemies of the people!"

I couldn't think what to say to this.

"Well?" he asked.

I had no instructions to cover this. It hadn't been in our scenario at all. Whose idea was it to kill the King? For that matter, whose idea was it to carry out a coup d'état? It was something along the lines of a double-cross.

"What will Washington say?" asked Driss eagerly, as if he thought he was going to get a special award for effort. Above and beyond the call.

"I shouldn't think they'd like it," I said.

Driss's face grew dark, then turned away, and he spat out something in Arabic. Two soldiers took me by the arms and led me out of the room, and I was marching again. *Hup, hup.* Down marble hallways. Down a marble staircase into the basement. We halted in front of a door guarded by two other soldiers, bristling with weapons. They opened the door and pushed me in.

It was a men's room, jammed with other prisoners. Large and spacious, walls and floors in veined Carrara marble, it was really a luxury men's room with beautiful white Turkish towels and hairbrushes laid out on a long white marble shelf above set-in washbowls, but still a men's room, a faint odor of antiseptic mixed with perfume, at the end the toilet stalls with metal doors. Some three dozen men, almost all Moroccans dressed for the party, were standing, or sitting on the marble floor, many smoking, gaze abstracted. There was little talking. Were we prisoners or merely being protected? Prisoners. Was this the gratitude I got for the money we gave Driss, being thrown in with the enemies of the people? I looked from face to face among the men, the gravity of their expressions contrasting with the frivolity of their clothing. See where it got you, dressing up like Jean-Paul Belmondo, forgetting the people? Now the people were wroth. But the faces weren't fearful but vacant, fatalistic. The only people talking were gathered in a corner of the room by the toilet stalls around an average-sized man wearing dark eyeglasses, dressed in pink, slacks and sport shirt a perfect match. Good Christ it was the King! He was still alive. He had aplomb, I'll say that for him. He was the most self-possessed man in the room, talking in a low voice in Arabic with the circle of men around him.

"It's the King!" I whispered to a man sitting on the floor with his back against the wall.

He turned his face toward me where I squatted beside him and looked me in the eye. Not a muscle in his face moved. He was right, of course. Why should he answer me? Who was this *ferengi*? I probably didn't look trustworthy to him. I ambled over to the men around the King, but conversation stopped and two grim-faced men turned and stared at me in silence. I didn't feel welcome. The King's expression I couldn't make out under the dark glasses. I walked back and sat down at an empty place against the wall, staring up at the fluorescent lights. Every so often someone would use the toilet. After all it was a men's room. A middle-aged Frenchman near me was whistling absent-mindedly and soon a man in officer's uniform from the King's circle came marching up.

"His Majesty wishes you to stop whistling," he ordered. So it wasn't such a secret.

"Me, whistling?" said the Frenchman.

A few minutes later he was whistling again. I don't like whistling either.

"His Majesty told you not to whistle!" I snapped at him.

He looked resentful but stopped. If by some chance these were to be my last minutes of life I didn't want to spend them listening to some old jerk whistling *La Vie en Rose*. I'd rather listen to the *chahada*.

The door burst open and what looked like a platoon of infantry marched into the room, fully armed, under the command of an officer, and formed in ranks in the middle. The officer had no difficulty locating the King and went straight up to him and said something in Arabic. The King blenched but kept his composure. Everyone with him melted away and in an instant he was standing there by himself. It looked as if they were going to put him up against a wall and shoot the poor bugger right there, right in the men's room. The officer seemed to be asking him to do something, but the King was shaking his head. He wouldn't do it. He wouldn't go with them. It was clear now. He was shaking his head angrily. He wouldn't leave the room. They wanted to take him someplace private and probably execute him. He wasn't going. He was going to make his stand here. He took off his sunglasses and put them in his breast pocket, his face drained of color but exalted, insane with pride. He was talking quietly to the soldiers now, asking them what unit they were from. Someone translated the whole thing for me later. I realized for the first time how young they were. They all looked about sixteen. And then it happened.

The King, standing alone in front of the metal doors of the toilet stalls, drew himself very erect in his pink Saint-Tropez outfit.

"*Shoot your King if you dare!*" he cried. "*Kill your King if you dare!*"

It was a terrifying moment under the flickering fluorescent lights. There was no one in the line of fire but him. The officer hesitated. The faces of the soldiers were stunned, unbelieving. After agonizing seconds one of them dropped to one knee, then two more.

"*But we came to save the King!*" pleaded one of the soldiers.

The King threw out his hand toward them.

"*What are you waiting for to kiss his hand?*" he called. Ice. Steel.

And suddenly they were surging forward breathlessly to kneel and kiss his hand, while others shouted, "*El Malik! The King! We've found the King!*" I guess they didn't know he was the King. And they went charging wildly out into the corridor, crying *El Malik! El Malik!* They'd found the King, and the King went with them, and soon I heard the ripping sound of machine-gun bursts again. Some had come to kill him, and some had come to save him, you see. They had this little divergence on policy. I wouldn't have gone out there for love or money.

Gradually the room emptied out. I wasn't the only one hesitant to go strolling around the palace while the troops were settling their differences and I waited for quite a time with several others sitting on the marble floor amid the faint smell of antiseptic until I couldn't hear any more firing. The corridors when I emerged had a strange, let-down air, like the morning after New Year's Eve, a few soldiers wandering around aimlessly. I opened the door of the room in which I'd been questioned by Driss. He was lying sprawled on the floor on his stomach in a pool of blood. Dead. Out on the patio a thousand soldiers were milling about, willing to surrender but with no one to surrender to; they'd wiped out the palace guard. At their trial later the enlisted men among the insurgents were all found not guilty, misled by their officers. Soldiers and civilian doctors were giving first aid to the wounded now, mostly Moroccans in their Riviera glad rags, so honored at a royal invitation. The number of corpses was horrible, still being dragged together by the back gate. I looked for our people among the living but couldn't find anybody. No Omar, no Sandor, no actors or electricians. The camera and lights were gone already, the electric cables. The party food tents were a sorry mess, most of the fancy dishes spilled sickeningly over the ground, all tramped on. Passing one tent, I ducked in, started going through the top of a trash can and found my pistol immediately, slipped it in my pocket. Out in the parking lot, with everybody driving off, I looked for the car Sandor, Omar, and I had come out in, but it had left already. Sirens were sounding now as the ambulances began arriving from Marrakesh, and I went to where we'd parked our trucks and caught the last one, the grips still loading on the lights. With them was the same English stunt man who'd broken his ankle a few days ago out on the set, but he was gallivanting around with it in a cast. He seemed rather merry.

"Were you out there?" I asked him. "I didn't see you."

"Yeah, sure," he said.

"How'd you like the King's party?"

"Wouldn't have missed it for anything," he said, his blue eyes laughing. "I right enjoyed it."

It seemed like a peculiar thing for a man with a broken ankle to do, come all the way out, hang around to the very end after what had happened. And I hadn't seen him. I was certain I hadn't seen him. What had he been doing out there? He had ice water in his veins, that son of a bitch.

Back at the hotel that night, Sandor came into my room.

"What do you carry a gun for?" he asked with a funny look on his face.

"Me?" I said. "I don't carry a gun. Oh, the gun," I added quickly, figuring if he'd seen it with his own eyes why deny it? "Self-defense."

He looked at me.

8

THEY FLUTTERED ME. Imagine that. Not that my feelings were hurt. They fluttered CIA Director George Bush, why shouldn't they flutter me? I mean I could see it from their point of view. Here they'd been giving me all this money to lay on BULLMOOSE, and then suddenly BULLMOOSE behaves himself in a way that is let's say inconsistent with the way they'd thought he'd behave, although I'd warned them they were taking their chances with him. But it's only in the nature of prudence that they should wonder if I've really been laying all this money on Driss after all. You can see they'd have to wonder about that. Because they use fluttering not just to test your loyalty to God, to country, and to KUBARK. They're so in the habit of it they flutter you about expense accounts too while they're at it, because we can't exactly bring back signed receipts. So the fluttering technician straps on the pulse and blood-pressure thing and the respiration thing and the electrodes in my palms to record how much my palms are sweating and starts off with some bullshit questions, and then, *Was all the money given you by the station on operation* MOLLIFY *disbursed by you to the intended recipient?* And I say yes. And he says, *Did you by any chance retain even a small part of these monies for your own personal use?* And I say no. And he says, *Did you perhaps retain any of these monies temporarily for a perfectly justifiable reason with the intention of later restituting them to the station or to the intended recipient?* And I say no. All very slow. Then more bullshit questions and he looks at the polygraph, frowning, and says, *I'm having trouble with your answers to the question on disbursement of monies on operation* MOLLIFY. *What were you thinking about when I asked you those questions?* This is a little embarrassing because I know the technique is to tell you there's trouble so you'll panic and blab and confess the loot is stashed away in a numbered account in Switzerland, and the poor slobs are just trying to save taxpayers' money, but I am not only a very loyal-type guy regarding ODYOKE and KUBARK and KUDOVE and all that, it so happens I'm clean as a hound's tooth about money. And what is also a little embarrassing is the fact that, straight arrow though I may be, I happen to know personally that I could beat a fluttering even if I was crooked. Arrogance is all. As far as the polygraph knows it doesn't make any difference whether you're telling the truth or you're not telling the truth. I'm telling you you can beat any polygraph going as long as you Believe in Yourself. So we go through all the questions again, and still again, very slow, with lots of waits and pauses, and it takes hours. And I'm a little sorry for this guy, and weary, and just keep telling him I wasn't thinking about anything but that there money and how I disbursed it straight to the intended recipient and if the polygraph doesn't say I'm telling the truth then the machine's just goddamn busted, that's all. I wasn't sore at him. He was just trying to save taxpayers' money. They finally had to acknowledge me to be the straight arrow that I truly am. This was all up in Rabat.

There'd been a little boo-boo though. The only thing good was our deniability. Our deniability was terrific. Nobody would ever believe we'd have touched the whole thing with a barge pole, it was so implausible. BULLMOOSE hadn't been much of an asset, of course. There'd been some wishful thinking there. Not by me, I was just the cut-out and I'd passed along all my doubts, my profound and subtle analysis of character. Oh, yes, I had. It wasn't my fault they were visionary dreamers. There were operations officers back in Virginia who were going to be having deep thoughts about all this, second-guessing everybody as always. Thank God the coup had failed at least. All we needed was a bunch of Marxist colonels in power in Morocco, or a Kaddafi. It would have been Wheelus Field all over again. The BULLMOOSE thing was disappointing, I grant you. The theory and practice of this business was that if a guy took your money he grew to like it and depend on it and gradually conceived of this sincere affection for you, but that wasn't exactly the way it worked out this time. Although if the coup had been successful, who knew, BULLMOOSE might have been a secret asset in the new regime. It would have been better than nothing. And who knew which way these new guys would have gone, really. They might have split up. There might have been coup and countercoup. BULLMOOSE might have been a Moroccan Suharto. Anyway the coup had failed, hadn't it? You couldn't get disheartened just because you didn't get every detail just right.

"You're a chipper son of a bitch considering what's happened," said FitzWilliam. This was in the secure area at the Embassy, right in the *sanctum sanctorum*. Green metal office furniture all around. You'd have thought you were at the Immigration Service.

"Why not? I never promised you BULLMOOSE was loyal to the King. That was your idea. Anyway," I said, to cheer him up, "how do you know if the rebels had won they might not have set up a pro-Western constitutional democracy?"

"Just like all those other Arab constitutional democracies," FitzWilliam said mordantly, as if I was this *naïf*. Whereas he was the *naïf*. He was the one who had unreasonable expectations, that intelligence went off like clockwork.

"I don't see what you're getting so excited about," I said. "So what's the worst case? We wasted a little money on a bum asset. So what?"

"Listen, Nelson," FitzWilliam said, settling into a more comfortable tone. After all, he trusted me. He'd had me fluttered. "You were the last one we have any contact with who saw BULLMOOSE alive. How did he act at the palace during the coup? How did he seem to you?"

This was for the final operation report, I supposed. I'd thought about it a bit myself. It wasn't that easy to answer.

"Exalted," I said, trying to see it clear in my own mind. "As if he'd outsmarted us, of course. But there was something else, too. It was a little bit . . . It was a bit as if in the long run we'd be proud of him. It was odd."

"What does that mean?" said FitzWilliam, mystified, resettling his glasses on his nose. "Proud of him for what?"

"I have no idea," I said, shaking my head. "It was just a feeling he gave me."

"Well, if you have no idea, who does?" said FitzWilliam, irked. "You were his contact."

"What I don't know, I don't know," I said. "*Je ne lis pas dans les marcs du café.*" FitzWilliam hated me to speak foreign languages. "Anyway it's over now. We got off pretty light, I think. I have no regrets."

"*You* have no regrets!" FitzWilliam almost went through the roof, eyeglasses and all. "The goddamn nerve! Do you realize the whole moral position of your country could be compromised by a stunt like that! Not to mention KUBARK!"

Feeling the heat, I guess he was.

"What do you mean, 'stunt'? We didn't stage the coup d'état. We just had an asset who wasn't straight with us. The luck of the draw."

"The luck of the draw," FitzWilliam repeated, despondent amid his notebooks and filing cabinets. I saw now that he was a sensitive person, introspective and unhappy beneath his stylish exterior.

"Don't give in to this post-Vietnam demoralization, Fitz," I offered cheerfully. "So we lose a couple. Be resilient! Look at the Russians. They lost Egypt. Did they cry? Did they tear their hair? Did they wail, and swear never again would they ever, and say how horrid, and go to pieces? The hell they did. They kept coming."

FitzWilliam looked at me stunned, a little horrified.

"You're a trigger-happy maniac, Nelson," he said, aghast. "Do you realize the mood the country's in? Do you realize we have a new President? Do you realize the kind of scrutiny KUBARK is getting?"

This was ludicrous. First this gutless bastard sitting behind a desk pushes me up on the firing line, then he lectures me that we take too many risks. Anyway we didn't make up this game. What kind of public scrutiny was the KGB getting?

"I don't give a damn what kind of mood the country's in," I said flatly.

"Do tell, Nelson." He was supercilious again. "And what kind of thing do you give a damn about?"

I looked straight at him.

"I want us to win, Fitz. I intend us to win."

"Win?" said Fitz, the intellectual strategic thinker. "I'm afraid you'll have to define your terms."

"*I will not define my terms!*" I shouted at him. "You know what I mean as well as I do!"

We just stared at each other, FitzWilliam stiff and alarmed, me angry as hell. Actually I think I impressed him. I could see it in his look, a mixture of wariness and awe. All demoralized, he was. Gave him a little backbone, I did.

So there I stood revealed as a crazed super-patriot, with red, white, and blue blood in my veins, Old Glory tattooed on my heart. Did I really believe what I'd said to him? Well, you have to keep in mind that I spent most of my life engaged in deception and chicanery and just plain lying, so when I had a chance to speak sincerely it welled up at extra-strength, in distilled super-concentrate. And I thought he'd been making pretty heavy weather over one lousy bum asset, and this chickening-out defeatism got me riled up. Did I really believe what I said? *Win! Win! Win! Win!* It was funny. Actually I had a feeling I kind of believed it.

So KUBARK was okay, but it was my own deniability that was a little bit blown, if you want to know. Not that the operational environment was tough in Morocco, but here Sandor had suspicions, and Mouna had charged me right out with something I'd rather not mention in mixed company, and I don't know, I didn't seem too secure to me any-more, or to FitzWilliam either. It was time to go out of the fossil-stone business for a while and be an inactive asset. Always ready to answer the Nation's call of course. Ready to rally to the cause of freedom and democracy. But dormant now. He also serves who only screws around writing movies about Mohammed. I mean I kept the actual fossil business, which I had a guy run for me while I was in Marrakesh, but you know. Latent asset. Potential asset. As for Halil, that one hadn't come to much either, had it? Which was sad, because I'd felt Halil was perhaps even a true friend. But Halil was an accident really. It could have happened to any-body out there. No hard feelings, Halil? Actually our movie people had gotten off pretty light too, considering that more than a hundred people died out there that day. We'd only had a boom man shot in the leg, a script boy hit by a grenade fragment, and a makeup man trampled on when a stampede hit one of the food tents, breaking one of his ribs. He went around saying he'd been crushed under the weight of the collapsing caviar.

Meanwhile that crazy Kaddafi was beaming revolutionary broadcasts into Morocco for days after the coup failed. *Arise, Arab brothers! Revolt! Death to tyrants!* It must have been the first time we'd had any money on the same horse as the Libyans even by mistake. And the Moroccans were rounding up Libyans, including our Libyan. Not to mention the Moroccans they were rounding up. Half the general staff had been in on the coup, it turned out, and the commanders of most of the military districts, the commander of the palace guard, the King's brother-in-law. You really won-dered how they'd muffed it. The security police grilled the surviving coup leaders for forty-eight hours and I was a little bit nervous, say what you will, but nobody came after us. Joy. A happy ending. When the interrogation was over they took twenty-odd generals and colonels out to the mili-tary camp outside Rabat and shot them. Not such a happy ending for them, but you can't have everything. We watched it on television. They were chanting the *chahada*, real scary, as other officers ripped off their epaulettes and all insignia. Then they were tied to the stakes, their faces with that frightening, blank look, still chanting. No blindfolds. Before the command to fire, some of them cried, *Long live the King!* The screen went black for an instant as the shots rang out and when the camera came on again they were hanging there, sagging, tied to the posts, their bodies sprayed with blood, ripped to pieces. It was a little barbarous I thought actually.

We were all sitting in front of the television set at Douad's, the Moroccan production manager's home in the Medina, eating sticky cakes and mint tea while we watched the execution. Giggling women brought in big brass trays of gooey goodies, and later when we were done they brought brass pitchers of orange water and bowls for us to rinse our hands. It sounds as if we were unfeeling brutes, we should have been fasting or mourning or something, but there it was, we were having mint tea and sticky cakes. The show was prime-time Arab stuff, something like watching a real rough sporting event I suppose except you didn't bet on who would win. I mean it was terrible, really terrible, but the King must have thought it would do people good otherwise he wouldn't have put it on television, would he? Weren't we making an Arab movie? Shouldn't we immerse ourselves in Arab life, Arab folkways, watch public executions for Arab folklore? They'd certainly immersed us in their coup d'état.

Mouna wasn't drinking any tea. She was a little tense. I hadn't been seeing so much of Mouna since we had our little whatever it was; in fact I saw as little of her as I could manage. But things weren't really much worse than they'd been before to tell the truth. She used to hate me. Then she had this yen for me for a few hours. Then she went back to hating me again. It had its comforting side, like I knew where I stood with her. And it showed that sex was pretty shaky grounds on which to build a relationship. I mused on how little of a bond it created to be familiar with a woman's genitals. I mean like you can take a washing machine apart and study its plumbing, where the liquids squirt in and out. Do you love the washing machine? Old Mouna had inspected my plumbing and she positively loathed me. She was tense today.

"It's Ahmed who's the traitor, a traitor to Arab socialism," she said bitterly, meaning the King. She was on the side of the coup plotters of course, which was her radical Arabic chic and a little inconsistent for someone so greasy with the King's sister you might think.

Since Omar needed the King's support for his movie he couldn't really agree with this. Also Omar's true politics were somewhere to the right of Tamerlane. I was staying out of it.

"Oh, Ahmed isn't so bad," said Omar. "He's doing his best."

Mouna turned to him, breathing hard, her eyes narrowed.

"You talk like this when Arab blood has flowed?" she cried, her voice rising shrilly.

I had a sincere desire to get out of there. Why didn't they fight about Arab stuff in private? Our hosts had fled the room and were peeking in at us discreetly through a beaded curtain.

"But it was flowing anyway, wasn't it?" pleaded Omar. "You weren't out there at the golf course. There were a lot of dead people. Okay, okay," he said, conciliating. "Ahmed's a shitheel. Ahmed's a shitheel."

But Mouna didn't like this either.

"You expose the dissensions of the Arab people before foreigners?" she shrieked, almost shaking with rage.

I got it. She and Omar were Arab brother and sister; they shouldn't wash their family linen in public. If they'd only kept their mouths shut Sandor and I would have thought Arabs were always completely lovey-dovey, you see. We thought the to-do at the golf course and this execution were just good-natured fooling around. There was stirring behind the bead curtain. Sandor and I got up to go.

"No, no, stay," said Omar, frightened. "Stay! Don't leave me!"

"Sandor can stay," said Mouna coldly.

Which wasn't logical. Mouna should hate Sandor more

because he was a scheming Zionist Jew while I was this straight American gentile type, naïve, good-hearted, just an overgrown kid really. But she hated me much more than she hated Sandor, especially since she'd inspected my plumbing. It was interesting.

"Burt stays too!" said Omar desperately.

I looked back on my way to the door and he was gazing after me so beseechingly, like an abandoned dog, that I went back and sat down again. So then Mouna stormed out, going off in one of the production cars waiting out in the alley. And Sandor slipped away with her, the rat. And who was left holding Omar's hand in the Medina but me.

"She's rough," he confided, a little shaken. "It's getting very rough."

But life went on. *Mohammed* went on. The King forbade all social meetings among officers of the rank of captain and above and was so busy ferreting out plotters and potential plotters that a religious movie the Saudis might not like didn't seem so important to him anymore, and we took advantage of the respite to rush on with our picture so as to get at least the Mecca scenes in the can before the King was seized with another fit of Islamic puritanism. For Omar, a coup d'état, even one in which he could have gotten killed, came a poor second to the movie. As it did with me, too, of course. For Omar it was a case of money plus his devotion to mankind and religious ideals. For me it was more like just money, a far more emotional subject, really, which at times gave me the cold sweats, something my love of humanity never did. We still had to figure ahead to the day we might get closed down again. Where could we go? To no country that needed Saudi oil, obviously. So it would have to be a country that had its own oil — but also camels, which left out Venezuela, Ecuador, and Indonesia, not to mention Norway. Kuwait? Qatar? Dubai? Abu Dhabi? Not much cinema infrastructure there. In Algeria they'd made *The Battle of Algiers* and Z but you had these damn socialists. It wasn't so much the reworking of the scenario, but idealists were tricky people to handle, big prima donnas, hair-

99

splitting and shifting their ground all the time, you'd be arguing Frantz Fanon with them over breakfast. And the more we thought about it the more we thought that Libya was a pretty stand-up country, good straightforward fanatics, took no guff from anybody because of oil, that was for sure. Let bygones be bygones about Wheelus Field. Yes, sir, Libya, the big "L". That is, if you could stand Libya, compared to which Marrakesh was Paris apparently. I asked an American at the hotel who'd been there how we'd find it, and he said, "You want my advice? Don't go." Which was certainly succinct. Tastes differ though. And the nicest thing, as the word got out that we were shopping around for a new country to move to if we got closed down again, was that these various watchdog supervisors we had around began currying our favor, yes, sir, *currying*. And when our Libyan got out of jail, as he eventually did, it was a big day, we curried him and he curried us. We gave a Moslem champagne party for him in the hotel's conference room after we screened the dailies, and he climbed up on the little stage at the end and made a nice speech beginning *Arab Brothers*, which was no worse than "Fellow Americans" I suppose, but was a little spooky with Libya still beaming in these bloodthirsty regicidal radio broadcasts. He was a big, good-looking guy with black, curly hair, beautiful white teeth. He was information vice-minister or assistant minister or junior minister or something back in Libya and his name was Mohammed, like forty percent of the males in Arab countries. It led to confusion with both the picture we were making and its invisible hero but we had to live with it. In Spain we'd had a bullfighter named Jesus Córdoba that we tried to get into the movies once and the producer said, *We can't bring him to Hollywood with a name like that! They'd crucify him!* But "Mohammed" was okay. It was like Peter and Paul.

"How was it in jail," I asked Mohammed afterwards out on the set in one of the hot, dusty, mud huts we used as production offices. We were picking up the next day's call sheets.

"Very all right," he said tolerantly. "They ask me an interrogation or two. I don't give a hoot. Hey, Burt. How about we finish movie in Libya, no problem? Tripoli, Benghazi . . . Benghazi my home town. They lay out a beautiful carpet for us there."

This stumped me but was richly tantalizing, calling up images of magic carpets from the Arabian Nights, Cleopatra being unrolled from a carpet in front of Julius Caesar.

"Crimson carpet," Mohammed added. "Maroon carpet."

"They'll give us red carpet treatment? I'm all for it," I said. "How are the belly dancers?"

"I'm seriously, Burt," he said, as if all tomfoolery aside now. "We should make continuation of movie in Libya. Kaddafi would like very much."

"Would he really?" I asked, because the word that had gotten out on Kaddafi was that he was a little on the strict side himself religiously speaking.

"Oh, Burt!" said Mohammed as if I was wounding him personally. "Kaddafi . . ." He drew a deep breath and gestured as if he was calling on me to behold the glory of Allah's work, the sun, the moon, the majestic procession of the seasons.

"Burt," he said, "Kaddafi is a true man. His word is his bondage. If Kaddafi do something you don't like, you can say to him, *Kaddafi, I don't like.* You can say this. He listens. I know Kaddafi personally. When I don't like somewhere, I say, *Kaddafi —*"

"I'm all for it," I said, although I didn't quite see myself buttonholing Kaddafi to give him my likes and dislikes. "I'm all for sincerity. I'm all for speaking up to the boss."

"Here, Burt," said Mohammed. "Would you care to drink a cigarette?"

He offered me a cigarette. That's what they did in Libya, they drank cigarettes.

"No, thanks," I said, but sat down beside him on the little couch. Everyone else had gone for the day, driven back to town.

"Hey, Burt, listen," said Mohammed, dragging on his

cigarette, then waving his hands through the air unhappily as if the world was a complicated place but at the same time it shouldn't be. When two men of good faith such as he and I met we should be able to sit in manly simplicity and speak from the heart, sipping our sweet Arab tea and drinking our cigarettes.

"The problem is, Burt," he said, his voice gentle but regretful, "people from Christianity countries don't understand Libya. They don't understand how progressive-looking is Islam. But if we make big grosser in Libya, and they read in *Variety*, they will *see* Libya is modern country. People of Christianity just does not *understand* Islam," he said sadly. "Forgive me, Burt, but you know I don't want to criticize Europe and America peoples, you know this. But West people has extremely prejudicial thoughts on Islam, believe me, I know. It is my own sad experience in London. These Chelsea peoples laugh at Islam, which notwithstanding is very high religion. I give you polygamy."

"Right," I said. "There is polygamy."

Mohammed clenched his fist and punched the air as if to say, "But that's just it!"

"Polygamy is *extremely* ununderstood in Christianity countries," he said earnestly. "Look, Burt, suppose you have wife."

"Okay," I said. "I've got a wife."

"Suppose she gets sick."

"Okay. I've got a wife and she gets sick."

"Aaah," said Mohammed, spreading his hands eloquently. "Then who takes care of children?"

"Wait a minute, you didn't say anything about children. Don't worry, forget it. Okay, I've got a sick wife and children."

"Now I ask you fairly," said Mohammed, indicating he didn't want to force me in the least. "Which is better? You leave poor wife sick, children untended for, you unhappy, wife unhappy, children unhappy, everybody unhappy? Or you get new wife. *She* take care of old wife. *She* take care of children. *She* become fast companion of old wife. Old wife happy, new wife happy, children happy, you happy. Now I ask you, Burt, which? Fairly. Which?"

"But both Kaddafi's wives are in perfectly good health," I said.

Mohammed stared at me, stunned at the underhandedness of the question. You have this magnificent syllogism laid out, and this snake finds a flaw that threatens the entire beautiful structure, confusion enters, dark doubts yawn. Could this be a friend?

"I wouldn't want you repeat this anywhere, Burt," Mohammed finally said in embarrassment. "But I hear in Tripoli say Kaddafi's first wife nag him because he travel so much."

I didn't see where to take it from there. I was stymied. Did the first wife nag Kaddafi less now that she had a fast companion?

"Anyway you've got a point in case of sickness," I said. "If both girls are willing after all."

"Isn't it better than sending wife out into coldness of world?" asked Mohammed, taking heart again. "Isn't Islam kindlier?"

Here he was clearly under the impression that divorce in the West was like in the Koran, where you said three times to the woman, "I divorce you," and you were divorced. *I divorce you, I divorce you, I divorce you.* I was wondering whether to introduce him to the concept of Alimony as it was understood in the West when he started off again, improving Islam's image.

"Why should we take public health, social welfare, social security from West when we have this already in Koran: to give alms?" he said. "Why should imitate income tax from West when we have already this in Koran in seventh century?"

"The tithe, two point five percent, why, indeed?" I said.

"Why should we imitate after West women when Islam is kindlier to women? Islam woman is happier?"

"Happier? Really happier?" I said. "How can you tell? Don't any of them fight the system?"

"In Libya," Mohammed said gravely, "we have girls who are misbehaving girls, who go with different men. But when people says a girl is such a girl, this girl don't easily find husband, never finds husband. And I," he paused primly. "I agree with this. I think this is right."

"When a girl plays around you think she doesn't deserve a husband anymore."

"Plays," Mohammed repeated equivocally as if this might be debatable. If she only played at it arbitration might be called for.

"I mean if she's not a virgin she doesn't deserve a husband."

"Aah," he said, and then, deeply felt, "Ah, no. A girl's virginness is most precious possession she can offer husband." He extended his hands, cupped, as if he was offering something not only tangible but perhaps liquid. "I will never marry girl who is not virgin."

"But you're married already," I said. "Oh, I see. Even the third and fourth wives, they have to be virgins too."

Mohammed looked a little uncomfortable as if I'd sprung another trap on him. But God knows I wasn't trying to spring traps. If anything I was trying to help the poor booby out, smarten him up so he could get a reasonable set of answers ready in case he got to be foreign minister, which the way things were going might be tomorrow. Hadn't anybody ever asked him a tough question before in his entire life? Had he come straight from a Bedouin tent to the Marrakesh Hilton? What happened to Chelsea? He was sitting, dejected now, lonely and misunderstood.

"Don't feel bad, Mohammed," I said. "I'm sure Libya is a terrific place."

"Ngah," he said moodily. "People doesn't understand Libya. When Kaddafi says we cut off hand of thiefs, it so badly *done*."

Thieves' hands again. Mohammed raised his arms in exasperation, as if the whole PR operation had been muffed, a disaster. If only he had been the real Information Minister it could have been handled so much more deftly, there would have been no revulsion gap at all.

"They don't *explain*," he appealed to me. "First, before we cut off hand we ask thief *reason*. We ask him *why*. He can *explain*. Perhaps he doesn't thief anyhow? People in abroad countries doesn't understand thief has chance to explain!"

"We have that too," I said. "Trial by jury."

"And we ask him is he sorry," Mohammed pursued. "We ask him is he promise not to thief again. And it only if he *not* sorry, and he persist in thiefing, then we tell him we very much regret, very regretful, but for his own good, alas, we must cut off his hand. But abroad people doesn't understand this!"

He gestured in despair at that lousy Libyan PR department. You must admit fuller explanations like this would dissipate rapidly any apprehensions you might have about the appropriateness of hand amputation for theft. Thus are loathing gaps created simply for lack of good PR work. Mohammed sat dejectedly in his chair.

"There, there, Mohammed," I said.

His face brightened slightly.

"Tell me, Burt," he said, things looking up again. "What *you* think of Libya?"

Urgh. Couldn't we get off the subject of Libya? Did I have to say what I thought? I knew he was a big man in the Information Ministry and I wanted to wise him up, but couldn't I show my friendship some other way? The worst thing was that his face was all lit up now as if he knew that a man like me could only admire such a miracle as the reborn Libya. Its purity must reach out to me, pristine and shining across the desert sands. Mohammed's face was already softening with pleasure at the compliments that were coming. My brain clutched desperately at euphemisms. I wanted to be kind but I couldn't let him run around loose in this state. I had to give him at least a clue.

"Well," I said. "I have a feeling it might be a little bit stern as countries go."

You could see he'd missed the key word.

"Stern," I said. "Severe. Austere."

His face had fallen at the first non-eulogistic word.

"Severe?" he said. "*Libya?*"

He spewed public health for a quarter of an hour. It washed over me. Maybe there was a good point or two in there someplace. I don't know. Maybe with all that oil they took your appendix out for free. He was such a booby your mind wandered. "Religion-based," I said at some point and waves of gray, boring protest came from him. At "archaic" he almost hit the roof. It was true amazement. "But Islam is ever new!" he pleaded emotionally. "Always fresh! *Everything is in Islam!*"

Well, he couldn't expect me to accept that, could he? What kind of a lovesick lunatic had I gotten myself locked up with? I wanted to get out of there. I didn't want him to start crying for God's sake.

"Good old Mohammed," I said. "Would you mind if I called you Mo? I'm sure Libya is a really great place. I only ask the chance to see it for myself. And if the Moroccans throw us out, why not? I ask you. *Vive la Libye! N'est-ce pas? Vive le pétrole!*"

Mohammed took my hand.

"Westerners are cruel," he said.

I got a clammy feeling.

"Not really," I said, slipping my hand away again. "Mo."

He sat slouched on the couch beside me, a great hulk of a despondent baby.

"You make mock of poor Arab," he said pitifully.

So there I was, this merciless city slicker with my cruel ways taking unfair advantage of this zillionaire hayseed Bedouin information minister. But it was the "poor" that got me. *Poor* Arab? *Poor?*

"No, no, Mohammed, I assure you," I said, giving up on the "Mo." Try as I would "Mo" didn't seem natural. "I'm not making mock of you."

"Burt," he said, looking at me with his great calf eyes. "You are my friend?"

"Of course I'm your friend, Mohammed," I affirmed stoutly.

This was followed by an acutely embarrassing silence, at the end of which Mohammed moved forward to embrace me, and I braced myself. I confess I was still a little priggish about being kissed by men but knew you had to put up with it around Arabs. After all I'd been kissed on the mouth by Omar Sharif I told myself. How many guys do you know who can say that? It hadn't been so bad. It was dry. So I kind of steeled myself, and Mohammed's head grew closer and I felt warm lips on my mouth and he put his arms around me and wait a *minute!* It wasn't like Omar Sharif at all! This character meant business!

I pushed him away firmly. But gently though because of the points I had in the movie. I mean we might really be moving this picture to Libya. I owned a piece of this movie.

"Yes, yes, I am your true friend," I said, keeping the hanky-panky subverbal. But he got the message, took it not too badly, just a little bit of egg on his face.

"Good," he said doggishly. "Burt. We true friends."

Naughty, naughty. You naughty bugger you. See where this female-purity cult got you? Buggery in the desert is what I call it. T. E. Lawrence. The mystic silence of the sandy wastes. Above, the cold moon. Below, the warm rear end of a manly brother in arms. I'm telling you, friend, this guy wasn't kidding around. He had things in mind that were against the law of man and Allah. Man, anyway. Believe me.

The next morning I got a phone call from a friend of Harold Shapley from Long Beach, just calling to say hello, and we chatted about this or that, the usual polite stuff. There's a limit to the things you can say in a conversation like that, particularly if you've never met anyone from Long Beach named Harold Shapley, and I flew up to Rabat that weekend and FitzWilliam put it to me.

"*Cultivate* her? Jesus!" I said. "She hates me! You just told me I was through with all that!"

"We hear she's got connections in Beirut with the right Palestinians," said FitzWilliam. "That's where it's at."

"But she wouldn't trust me for one minute. You think we're going to use her to *infiltrate*?"

The whole thing struck me as repellently hazardous anyway, for me, because even if I kept my cards close to my chest Mouna would be bound to suspect me of exactly what I'd convinced myself she *didn't* suspect me of, my safety after that depending on her benign desire to keep me alive, a situation so fraught with risk that to enter it willingly you'd have had to be loco. Unless I could persuade myself that what Mouna wanted was peace and understanding among nations, with all men brothers, and something in it for one brother provided there was something in it for the other brother, like us putting the screws to Israel, for example. FitzWilliam reminded me of the *alte Kriegspiel*, and how if Mouna went along with us we'd fix it so if she played tricks her ass would be in the wringer too. Being in harness with Mouna would be a whole new relationship though, with me inevitably exposed a bit as the access agent always is, which was just one of those things, except that *Kriegspiel* or no *Kriegspiel* teaming up with Mouna to advance international peace would seem to call for a rather reckless person. It would be like aerial acrobatics without a net. I supposed there were people who worked without a net.

Well, FitzWilliam was a new man since I'd seen him last, I had to give him that. Last time I'd been in Rabat he was a whimpering piece of blubber, so demoralized I had to give him halftime pep talks. Now he was showing sterner stuff again, eager once more to send me forth into the jaws of death or whatever. His valor when it came to throwing me into perilous situations was once again, as I always knew it would prove to be, exemplary. He had the real stuff, old Fitz. Oh, yes.

9

THEY'RE ALL FAGGOTS. I'm not going to argue about it. Fuck you. Scratch an Arab and you find a part-time faggot. Scratch an Arabist and you find a full-time faggot. It just shows how little people know about things. How would you expect to know if your idea of an Arab country is Humphrey Bogart in *Casablanca*? If you were plugged into the fag underground you'd know about it, don't worry. Ask Guy Lockley.

I was staring out the plane window thinking about stuff. Mohammed the Libyan. Sex stuff. Mouna. They must have piss-poor contacts with the Palestinians if they were down to me cultivating Mouna, which I thought was a terrible idea anyway, pathetic, embarrassing, doomed to deep unrewardingness even if it didn't get me killed. The whole idea filled me with melancholy. The Don Juan squad, such low-level activity, truly the lowest form of government service. Did she really have connections with the right Palestinians back in Beirut? FitzWilliam didn't go into any detail about that. This KUBARK stuff was always just bits and pieces, very frustrating. They never gave you the whole puzzle. You never knew what the fuck you were doing. It was always just unintelligible minutiae, never anything interesting or exciting, because you never got the whole picture. You never got that full, rolling, epic sweep like in a movie, where everything fits together, everything is a whole, where God himself seems to be telling you what it all means, and if you can't understand you've still got the music, which certainly seems to know what's up. Which brought me back to that rolling epic *Mohammed Superstar*. The last coherent word I'd had from Omar was that I was supposed to stand by, prepared to rewrite the scenario in any direction to accommodate the sensibilities of whatever country we were going to move to if they closed us down. Would he really want us to go to Libya? The idea seemed decidedly unattractive to me today. There were people I might not want to see in Libya, for example. Anyway who knew what Kaddafi would think of my script. He was so unpredictable; there was no way of knowing in advance. It wasn't like Algeria. Kaddafi had just made a speech calling on the Egyptian people to rise and overthrow the traitor Sadat, and in the same speech appealed to Sadat to head a union of all the Arab countries — a little inconsistent, you might think. A real screwball. We'd really be putting our head in the lion's mouth if we went there. Yet our choice of countries was limited. Oil and camels. Camels and oil. Norway would be so terrific if it only had camels.

I looked down at the ocean waves far below. We were at about 30,000 feet and they looked frozen, long, silvery-white, motionless lines etched on the surface of a cobalt glacier. I remember when I was a kid at Santa Monica I used to think the waves sprang up only when they saw land coming. I thought it had something to do with the collision of ocean and land, that out in the middle of the sea there were no waves. But here we were right over the middle of the Mediterranean and there were real waves down there. You probably think I should be flying over deserts, great parched wastes, geological detritus, stuff like that, and that I should be on my way from Rabat to Marrakesh. But it so happened that I was on my way to Rome because I had this errand.

He was the only other person in first class. I recognized him right away from the pictures. Because of Mohammed I'd started to think of Libyans as great, hulking devils, but this one was quite normal size, a bit under average, vaguely studious-looking under his horn-rimmed eyeglasses. He was studying papers which he slipped in and out of his briefcase and looked a hint like Pier Paolo Pasolini, the Italian movie director, but was another Libyan, which was an interesting coincidence really. I took my time. I had plenty of time. The jets hummed on.

"Mind if I visit with you for a while?" I said, standing there in the corridor. "Break up the trip a little?"

He looked startled, but what could he say? He couldn't say no. I sat down.

"You've got work," I said. "I'm interrupting you."

"No, no," he said, shuffling all his papers carefully into his briefcase and snapping it shut, keeping it on his knees. He was civil. He smiled. He was a good sport. We had the cabin to ourselves.

"Yes, sir, Cleveland seems a long way away," I said. "I've got this travel agency in Cleveland. But don't tell anybody." I laughed. "I really hate to travel. The airlines like me to see some of these places so I can recommend them, and I jet around a little here and there during the off season, but frankly I hate it. Hate to leave the old carpet slippers. You promise you won't tell anybody now." I laughed again.

"Very much so," he said.

What the hell kind of answer was that: very much so.

"Have you ever been to America?" I asked.

"No."

He smiled equivocally. Maybe he didn't want to go to America. He wasn't much of a conversationalist. I checked out the cabin again. There were no stewards or stewardesses in sight.

"Let me show you some pictures of my wife and kids in Cleveland," I said, and handed him a nine-by-twelve manila envelope.

He seemed a bit perplexed, perhaps at the idea of someone carrying around nine-by-twelve photographs of his wife and kids.

"Go ahead look at them," I said. "I'm an amateur photographer. They're very good."

A stewardess came walking through the cabin and I extended my hand to stop him from opening the envelope. When she was gone I withdrew my hand. Still puzzled, he unwound the little string and slid out the sheaf of pictures, looked at two, made a wheezing sound, blenched, slid the pictures back in. He'd only looked at two pictures, which was too bad, because they were very good prints: him eating pussy, him eating cock, him buggering and being buggered, which was worse. They'd got him in with two girls and a boy and there was a lot of action of a kind he doubtless would not want Muammur Kaddafi to see. He was very pale now, the skin with a greenish yellow tinge, the sweat pouring down his face. He was staring out the window. I felt sorry for him. I kind of liked the guy.

"You don't have to worry," I said. "They're safe with us. We'll keep them from falling into unfriendly hands."

"What do you want?" he blurted out, still staring out the window. As if he didn't believe me.

"Nothing. Nothing at all," I said. "They came into our hands completely by accident. You might not believe that but it's absolutely true. You should be more careful, you know. We're your friends but there are people around who'd make nasty use of pictures like that."

"What do you want?" he said.

Absolutely nothing at all, we were his friends, I told him again and ended my friendly little visit and went back to my seat. Somebody else would pick him up in Rome. It was just in and out for me, an unknown face, someone he'd never see again. They'd nailed him in Rabat, which is a very favorable operational environment for us when we're going after a Libyan, which makes local Moroccans who give us a hand feel almost like super-patriots because of the meddling those Libyans do in other people's affairs. From Palestinians to the IRA. With their new oil money they were really extremely meddlesome.

The next day I was back in Marrakesh in my sweatbox at the Hilton, when a knock sounded on the open door and in walked Mohammed, eager and smiling, in his best green sport shirt. I don't mean I was receiving a visitation from the Prophet, who as far as I know didn't own any sport shirts. It was Mohammed Maziq, our movie Libyan — as opposed to other kinds of Libyans — the Information Ministry character Tripoli had sent to safeguard its investment in *Mohammed Superstar*. It was too bad we didn't have out an entrapment operation on him. He'd have been the easiest man to entrap since the *Duc de Guise*. But Information Ministry people were clowns. They weren't even worth entrapping. Mohammed was standing there proudly carrying a book. If he thought I was so fetching, why wasn't he bringing me flowers? What was this book?

"For you, Burt," he said warmly. "I give to you."

When I saw it was a book on Libyan history I had a feeling as if I'd eaten too much squash pie. I had a decisive feeling I didn't want to think about Libya anymore for a while, but here was Libya again.

"Thank you, Mohammed," I said.

"Read and understand, Burt," said Mohammed.

My heart was like weighed down with lead. Was he going to check up on me and make sure I read every page?

"Understand what?" I said.

"Libya!" he bleated.

There he went again. Love me, love my Libya. But I didn't love him either! What was this? "Read and Understand." Between *Read and understand* and *Divide and conquer* give me *Divide and conquer* every time.

"Drink deeply, Burt," said Mohammed, benign.

I couldn't stand it anymore. He made my mind go all numb. Wasn't he even embarrassed at being slapped down making a pass, the crazy bugger? Didn't he have any shame? He sat down on a chair.

"Burt, we go out on set?" he said. "We supervise shooting? Supervise shots?"

Anything but talk about Libya. Off we went. We walked out through the lobby and I found my Peugeot and we hit the dusty road to Mecca, passed Checkpoint Ali, and arrived on the set just after they'd broken for lunch. It was clear

Mohammed really saw us shooting the rest of the film in Libya now and figured he'd better get real knowledgeable if he was ever going to get to be Prime Minister or whatever it was he had his heart set on. After all he was already twenty-eight. As we came up to the executive-rank table in our desert chow hall Sandor and Omar were talking in loud voices.

"*And the Angel said to Muhammed, READ!*" Omar said excitedly.

"No! No! No!" answered Sandor, just as excited. "*And the Angel said to Mohammed: WRITE!*"

It was the old argument. Was Mohammed an illiterate or wasn't he? *Sura* ninety-six. Frankly I didn't care one way or the other. If the Arabs wanted the founder of their religion to be able to read and write it was okay with me, but Sandor and Omar had been arguing about it for months. We'd been through it time and again but it was all new to Mohammed Maziq the Libyan, who'd been spending most of his time in the bar of the Mamounia communing with the shade of Winston Churchill up to this point. Mouna was at the table too, her face set in a glare. Old Mouna. Mohammed and I took seats beside the three of them on the wooden benches. It was a real U.S. Air Force chow hall.

"What?" asked Mohammed, disconcerted, no doubt alarmed at references to his namesake being bandied back and forth so disrespectfully. You could tell right away he was going to put a crimp in the conversation. Sandor ignored him.

"Listen, you!" Sandor shouted at Omar. "You know like I do Mohammed was an epileptic! First you take away from me this. Now you want he reads and writes when it says right in the Koran, when the Angel says to Mohammed *Read*, he can't read! We'll be a laughingstock!"

He was having one of his fits of integrity. Mohammed Maziq's face was a study in something.

"What is this epileptic?" he asked warily.

"A disease," I said. "You fall down and foam at the mouth."

"Foam?"

"Brargh," I said. "Gargle, gargle, gargle. Brarrgh."

Being told there was no Santa Claus was nothing compared to this. It was more like the Pope having syphilis. The Pope and Santa Claus *both* having syphilis. Mohammed Maziq's face was incredulous, horrified, fearful. You have to remember he was a Moslem.

"Muhammed *sick?*" he said, his jaw slack.

"You stay out of this," said Omar and went on arguing with Sandor.

Sometimes Omar lost his head too. Here this character had at his command all the hydrocarbons of Arabia, maybe the only means of saving the movie, and Omar was insulting him.

"They're kidding," I said. "It's a joke."

But it didn't look like a joke. Sandor was holding his great grizzled head in his hands now and groaning, "I'm a nice Jewish boy from Budapest! Why is this happening to me? What am I doing here?"

"Come, Muhammed," said Mouna, her face bright. "Let's get something to eat." You had to go through the chow line. It was like the Air Force.

"Yuh, Mohammed," I said. "Let's eat." I tugged him by the arm. He resisted.

"Let's get something to eat, Muhammed, dear," Mouna repeated, but Mohammed wouldn't budge, swatting us away like flies. We weren't going to deflect him from taking part in this serious conversation with the grownups.

"You get," he said to Mouna disdainfully.

I was about to sit down again to serve as a buffer between this golden meal ticket and my crazy partners, but then thought, after all, what would be, would be. Mouna and I went through the chow line together. It was the first time I'd been alone with her since the last time I was alone with her. I wondered if she really knew important Palestinians. I sneaked a couple of glances at her and she seemed to be communing with herself, which was maybe just as well. This was miserable. I was going to make a fool of myself. I took some fried chicken, smoked ham, salad, honeydew melon, watermelon, and fresh figs. I was drowning my troubles in fruit. Mouna had already eaten and was modestly picking out a plate for Mohammed, which was unusual as she didn't often do things for people. She usually got people to do things for her. I noticed she skipped the ham. As I was drawing a cup of coffee for myself, I saw she was staring at me, her expression softer than it had been at the table.

"Well," I said. "Old Mouna. How are things?"

She just kept staring.

"Burt," she said at last. "I know you won't let anything in our personal relationship interfere with your higher duty to the production."

She had delusions of grandeur, that girl. And which of us had thrown the whole thing up over dinner in a hysterical fit? Humiliating poor Omar? Who'd called our good friend the King of Morocco a traitor to Arab socialism? I might have my diplomatic weak points but I didn't call anybody a traitor. Mind you, I was willing to forget.

"I ask for your respect," said Mouna. "If you have any feeling left for me at all."

I screwed up my courage.

"Mouna," I said. "I'll always have a soft spot for you. You know how I feel about you."

Implausible on the surface, you'll say, but it seemed natural enough once I'd said it. She blushed with a pinkness I'd never suspected her of. Imagine that. Just a little bit of kindness and all that hostility laid to rest. I was on the point of carrying the verbal reconciliation to a further stage when she turned and headed back to the table. As we approached, both Sandor and Omar were gazing at Mohammed Maziq with stunned looks on their faces.

"*Why electricity so wonderful? Why?*" Mohammed proclaimed confidently. "*In Arab countries before electricity we have candles. Why electricity more superior than candles? The Prophet have merely candles. In Koran is no electricity.*"

Both Omar and Sandor were speechless. I never found out how Mohammed got from the Prophet's epilepsy to the parity of electricity and candles. It was the *Islam has everything* approach.

"You must have some honeydew melon, Muhammed dear," said Mouna solicitously and swung her legs over the bench to go get it for him.

What did he care about honeydew melon. He was preaching the gospel according to Saint Muammar. And why Mohammed "dear"? Wasn't that going too far? Was the "dear" really necessary? They were talking about camels now.

"But we're going to need hundreds," said Omar. "We've got the two big battle scenes to do. Can you get hundreds of camels up to this place where you want us to shoot?"

"Why you need hundreds?" said Mohammed with assurance. "I get you a dozen camels. Do it with mirrors."

If Omar and Sandor had been stunned at the parity of candles and electricity, they were pole-axed now.

"What?" Omar blinked.

"Mirrors," said Mohammed with the pride of expertise. "Do it with mirrors."

There was a moment of silence.

"You mean," said Sandor, seeking confirmation, "you think that on *The Longest Day* they just had ten GIs and the rest was mirrors."

"Sure," said Mohammed, unshaken. "Why not?"

"Where do you put the mirrors?"

Omar started to interrupt but Sandor raised his arm as if to fend him off.

"No, no. This sounds like an interesting technique," he said. "I'd like to learn it. Where do the mirrors go?"

"In the camera," said Mohammed, a bit worried now.

"Where in the camera? What do you think it is, a kaleidoscope?"

I had a horrifying vision of what this ten-million-dollar movie would look like if we tried to multiply twelve camels into a thousand by means of some process shot, let alone mirrors, what the joins would look like, the discontinuous backgrounds, the panels of identically refracted camels like a fun fair. But Mohammed clearly thought he had penetrated into the heart of the secret mystery of the movies. It was done with mirrors.

"Technicians," he said with new buoyancy. "Technicians do it."

"How about some tea, Muhammed, dear," said Mouna. "Some nice mint tea. Sandor, get Muhammed some tea."

Sandor turned to her as if she was insane.

"I'll get it myself," said Mouna, rising.

She went to a hole in the rattan screening which separated us from the Moslem half of the chow hall. Through the hole you could call to the man who was dispensing mint tea on the other side. Why didn't Mohammed go eat with his coreligionaries on the other side of the rattan screening? There were probably a lot of guys who thought movies were done with mirrors over there. Mouna came back with a glass of the mint tea, a whole mint bush crammed in the glass. Mohammed took it without even looking at her.

Out on the set they were shooting another one of *the Moslems are coming* scenes. Actually it was the Meccan caravan that was coming and, unbeknownst to it, was about to be mousetrapped and cut to pieces by us devout Moslems for the greater glory of Allah at the famous mousetrapping at the Badr Wells in March, 624 A.D., in case the date has slipped your mind. And we go off with their treasure and camels and their survivors that we hold for ransom. One if by land, and two if by sea, and I by the Badr Wells shall be. Then we take the much-needed treasure, and Mohammed tells us we can kill all the captives nobody is willing to pay anything for, which seems fair enough really, after we've given them time to raise the money and all, and it's a very important date in Moslem history. Omar and I sat on this little hill, watching the horses and riders charge by under Sandor's direction. That crazy English stunt man was riding with a broken leg.

"Sandor! Why you waiting?" called Mohammed Maziq,

sitting further down the slope with Mouna. "Why you don't shoot?"

"The sun," yelled Sandor, pointing straight up. "The Meccans' faces are in shadow. Another few minutes and we get front lighting."

Mohammed nodded sagely. He was learning the business. He was going to be the Libyan Irving Thalberg. But waiting was tedious for him. After a time I heard his voice drift upwards, "Why electricity so wonderful? Why electricity superior than candles?"

I was figuring out his method. This was his way of mastering technology. You showed it who was boss. You didn't let it get a swelled head. He was proselytizing Mouna now. I'd have loved to hear how she answered that one. After about a quarter of an hour in the sun, they both rose.

"I'll take Muhammed back," Mouna called up to Omar, sitting beside me.

"Fine," Omar said, and Mouna and Mohammed trudged off toward her car, Mohammed following obediently, leaving me feeling rather aimless, not to say confused. What had happened? Here I had her blushing, and she's gone off with Mohammed.

"Where does that leave me?" I asked Omar. "I only came out here to bring him."

"I guess you can go then," Omar said. "Mouna'll take care of him. He's in good hands."

When I said goodbye to Omar half an hour later he said, "Tell Mouna not to forget to call Kuwait."

Back at the hotel I looked for her in the production office, the lobby, the upstairs bar, the downstairs bar, the swimming pool. I tried the suite she shared with Omar on the house phone. No answer. Thinking Mohammed might be able to tell me where she'd gone I tried his room too. No answer there either. I'd done my best. When Omar came back at the end of the day I was in my room reading a day-old newspaper which had just arrived at the hotel newsstand.

"She won't let me in!" he said, careening in, wild-eyed.

119

"Where?"

"In the room! The room! She's slid the bolt! I banged on the door! She won't even answer!"

"Why would she do that?"

Omar had a dead look.

"Maybe she's not there," I offered. "Maybe she's out someplace."

"Then who slid the bolt?" he asked excitedly. "The chambermaid? Who's in there?"

"You want to get the manager? They can get the bolt open from outside if they really need to."

"No," Omar said nervously, glancing around, startled.

"Sit down," I said. "Have a drink."

He got something out of the refrigerator, fumbled with ice cubes.

"Locking me out," he fumed. "She's gone too far."

"Let's go have dinner," I said, not knowing what else to propose.

Omar washed up and we went to the hotel dining room, him still wearing the polo shirt and Bermuda shorts he'd been working in all day. His mind wandered during the meal. He ate his food without tasting it, chain-smoked. "What's she doing up there?" he burst out several times. I had no explanations I cared to offer.

After dinner he tried the suite on the phone, but no one answered.

"Let's go up," he said anxiously. "Maybe she's unbolted the door."

As we came down the corridor leading to his suite we saw the door open and one of the room-service bus boys emerge, shutting the door again behind him.

"*What were you doing in there?!*" cried Omar, charging up to him.

The green-uniformed bus boy was flustered by the attack. He didn't have English and I translated into French. He'd been serving dinner.

"Who's in there?" Omar demanded angrily. When he saw

the boy hesitate he reached into his pocket and gave him a few dirhams.

Monsieur and *Madame* were in there, said the boy. This perfectly conventional couple, *Monsieur* and *Madame*. Omar let him go. From the handle of the doorknob was now hanging a card which said DO NOT DISTURB in English, French, and Arabic. Omar leapt at the door and began pounding.

"Come out! Come out!" he yelled. "I know you're in there!"

There was no sound from within. Omar tried the key. The door was bolted again. We stood there like idiots for a minute or so and I led Omar away, him mumbling dazedly, "She locked me out of my own room." Downstairs in my place with all windows and doors open in the hope of a breeze, he slumped dejectedly on the couch.

"Who do you think it is?" he said. "Who's in there with her? What do you think they're doing?"

"Eating," I said.

"I guess it's Muhammed Maziq," said Omar miserably. "The Libyan. What do you think of him?"

What did I think of Mohammed Maziq. What did I think of Mohammed Maziq and Mouna together, for that matter. Well, the situation was not without its ironies. It was even rich in irony.

"Maybe they're just talking," I offered cheerfully.

Omar looked at me.

"Maybe it's all perfectly innocent," I insisted. "How do you know? Maybe she's just spiteful. Is she sore at you about something?"

Omar shook his head, then asked wistfully, "Do you think she's doing it for the good of the picture?"

I didn't want to answer that one. It was what reporters call a *have you stopped beating your wife* question. The illuminated swimming pool outside cast ripples of light across the far wall of the room.

"She certainly has the good of the picture at heart," I said.

Omar stared absently out the window.

"Hey, let's take a walk," I said. I thought it would do him good.

So we strolled down Avenue Mohammed V under the trees. The scent of orange blossoms mingled with the odor of *keftas* broiling over charcoal in the nearby Medina, carried to us on the night air. The change had lightened Omar's mood. He had gone from wretched to wistful all by himself. Now he was reflective, detached.

"What should I do with her?" he asked thoughtfully. "When a man and a woman are as close as we've been, you can't end the relationship just like that. It's heartless. One incurs obligations."

"She doesn't seem to feel very obligated to you," I noted. "Anyway, what do you mean, what should you do with her? What choices are you offering me?"

"How can I get things back to the way they were?" he said, forlorn again. "It was so great at the beginning."

What could you say to him? As we neared the Medina the sound of Arab music and of high-pitched voices reached us. Flutes whined. Hands clapped in unison.

"There's no way back, Ome," I said. "Ditch her."

It didn't go in.

"For your own good, get rid of her," I said. "Get her out of here. She's nothing but trouble."

Omar frowned in distaste, as if he didn't like the Arab music, wailing now.

"Listen, Ome," I said. "I'm your friend. She's a bad person. How long can it go on anyway? You've got a wife and kids in Bel Air, remember?"

I was walking inboard, beside the buildings, and as I turned toward Omar and the street, with a vision of Bel Air and his Mormon quite clear in my mind, I saw out of the corner of my eye a motorcycle coming up Avenue Mohammed V at about twenty miles an hour with two Berbers aboard in turbans, faces wrapped to the eyes in their blue desert scarves. As the motorcycle drew near it slowed, both wrapped faces turning toward us as the man riding behind drew an automatic from beneath his blue robe.

I pitched forward onto the sidewalk in the shelter of a parked Citroën DS and shouted at Omar, *"Get down! Get down!"* and then just crouched there, my heart thumping, waiting for gunfire as I heard the motorcycle sputter, pick up speed again, and roar hoarsely down the avenue. There were no shots.

When the sound of the motor faded away I peeked cautiously over the hood of the Citroën. The motorcycle was gone. I turned to Omar. He was standing in the middle of the sidewalk, mystified, concerned.

"Burt," he said. "Did anyone ever tell you you were a little strange?"

"Omar," I said. "I want to know. Was the man on the back seat of that motorcycle carrying anything in his right hand?"

"A transistor radio," replied Omar, spreading his arms in bafflement.

"Uh!" I let out, leaning against the fender of the car with my head down between my knees, taking deep breaths.

"Burt, you're taking this desecration of the Prophet claim much too seriously," said Omar. "A Muslim would never resort to violence over a thing like that." His voice was sad. "With all that you've learned about Islam, you still don't realize that what Islam brings to the world is a message of peace?"

I couldn't take in what he said after that. As we resumed our walk I felt as if my head were filled with a huge bubble of giddy helium, as if the plane ahead of me in formation had crashed on landing, but not me. It certainly wasn't survivor guilt. I have never had survivor guilt. But I've had survivor euphoria a lot.

When I could finally hear what Omar was saying again, he was chattering along, his natural optimism rediscovered.

"Mouna didn't put through the call to Kuwait today," he said. "She never remembers. You want to come with me to Kuwait?"

"What's in Kuwait?"

"Money."

Here I'd been worrying a lot about money lately, but the sound of the word "money" this time made me very serene. It was good to know that there was money out there somewhere, at least. At least we weren't chasing after something imaginary, ineffable, always beyond the reach of mortal man. I slept very well that night, in fact. A little bit of imaginary danger. Hopes of great wealth. I'd been loyal to a friend. I'd shouted to him to "Get down!" and had tried to pry him out of the clutches of a vicious woman. It wasn't my fault if he didn't do what I said.

10

I HAD TO WAIT for the fires of Mouna's passion to burn
themselves out now. Which was really boring. You've never
known true boredom unless you've waited for the fires of
someone's passion to burn themselves out. This kind of
thing was demeaning. It really was. And it paid peanuts,
for Christsake. I just did it because I was patriotic. The
whole business sucked. There weren't even any bits and
pieces anymore. There were definitely no bits, and decidedly
no pieces. I just sat around, holding Omar's hand, telling
him what a turd Mohammed was — because the rival is the
heavy in a situation like that. The beloved is forgiven. *Come
back! Come back!* We held hands. And that ambidextrous
Mohammed! *Corriente alternativo, corriente directo.* You
can say that again. I had serious reason for knowing that
that circumcised son of a bitch was ambidextrous as hell,
didn't I? And now it turned out he loved Mouna more than
me. I was like crushed. But time went by. "If we didn't need
the Libyan money I'd kick his ass out of here in nothing
flat," said Omar, but lightly now. The tide was turning.

Panic. It was going to come around to me again next. I
could feel it. The long-awaited opportunity was about to
strike. It put me into a state of deep anxiety because of the
danger I would be running here of getting killed, not to
mention the effect Mouna had on my erections. My mind
had skipped over that problem. Perhaps we could get to be
friends again without there being any sex. Why couldn't I

cultivate her asexually? We could just be pals, go shopping together in the *souks*. I saw her one day in the corridor at the Hilton. I knew the thing with Mohammed was over just by the look of her. Maybe she was a oncer, I thought hopefully. Maybe when she'd had sex with somebody once and broke it off she never went back. We could be platonic friends, talk about native jewelry, native handicraft, Third World liberation movements. Fourth World. Fifth World. I'd go as high as she liked.

"How's the view from the second floor, Mouna?" I said.

She came to a full halt in the corridor and stood there as if we were going to have a talk. She'd been walking past me with barely a nod for a week, and now, suddenly, we were going to converse, talk about the old days. She said nothing but her face was open. I can't explain it.

"I just mean because your room is on the second floor and mine is on the ground floor," I said.

She didn't speak at all but just kept looking at me with this open look, smiling faintly. The sheer plainness of the look was odd. It had no pretension, no artifice; there was no twisting up inside to give the ball some kind of English. It was a look with no frills. It was as if you could see way inside to the person living in there. She was just looking at me, you understand. She was wearing one of her braless white jerseys. There were tiny, shiny drops of moisture on her skin from the heat. Her black hair was wispy.

"Come on in, Mouna," I said. "Along the corridor here to my place. Come have a drink."

"All right." She laughed. It was like a whole new person.

It was all very very relaxed. She was very relaxed. This new person was very relaxed. She sat there drinking gin and tonic, that well-known Arab highball.

"What do you think about the chuck wagon, Mouna?" I said.

Somebody had blown up our chuck wagon out on the set during the night. Big drama. A plastique bomb had blown the thing to smithereens. The land lay thick with *couscous* for miles around.

"Yes," she said.

Not exactly a full answer. She was free, open, and psychologically available, but she didn't happen to be concentrating on what I was saying.

"Somebody out there doesn't like us," I said.

She laughed and there was a manic touch of the old Mouna, a hint of hysteria in the black eyes. Sometimes the way she laughed made me uneasy. But she subsided and it went away and she went back to looking at me with this faint smile. It really made you examine your notion of the relationship between men and women when all a woman had to do was stop talking and look straight at you in a sustained, unconcealed way with no distractions or dilatory diversions and immediately you thought of sex. What's more I had the feeling that Mouna was thinking about sex. All my brashness came back in a rush. I stood up and walked over to her chair and stood there. Where did you sit? On the arm of her chair? On the floor? On her lap? I touched her damp face with my hand and suddenly saw her seize my hand and kiss it, which unnerved me. It was really very embarrassing and so unlike her, but she was still at it, humbly and gratefully kissing my hand as if I were the Pope. It wasn't even sexual. I had to stop her.

"No, no, Mouna," I said.

I couldn't decide whether to bend over or try to draw her to her feet, and tried lifting her by the armpits but she wouldn't lift, and finally, I had to kneel beside the chair. It seemed for an instant she'd rather kiss my hand than me, but she adjusted and it was all warm and wet in there, slippery tongue slithering around amid hard teeth.

We had to hurry before the magic spell was broken. I stood up. Locked the door. It was the usual drill, I suppose. Ha, ha, it's easy to say that now. We took off our clothes quickly, jumped onto the bed. I was in mad haste to get inside her before something happened to break the mood. I was in a nervous state. I spat all over her entranceway there to slippery her up; I didn't have time to play foreplay. And in another second I was in there, rocking away.

I couldn't believe it. I was so relieved. There I was inside her. And that was her all around me. And we were heaving and pitching and rolling and yawing in the time-honored maritime tradition. I'd felt there was a whole new current running this time and it was all different, but still in the back of my mind was that nightmare scenario from the other time and I'd been hyper-nervous but this was a new Mouna. It gave me a new perspective on her. She seemed less threatening when you had this kind of a handle on her. This inside handle. I had a funny feeling that I could rub all her organs from the inside this time, her pancreas, liver, spleen, gall bladder, as if I could reach them all, although I suppose I really wasn't getting any further than the vagina.

"Oh, I just love sex," she murmured with her eyes closed.

She had good muscles in her solar plexus. Looking down, I could see them contracting and relaxing, tangible evidence of her desire for me as she came forward each time to swallow me up. I could see the stomach muscles tensing under the soft belly part as if she were doing sit-ups or something, arduous physical effort under other circumstances but all for me now, concrete proof of my attractiveness.

"Oh, it's wonderful making love," she said, still moving now but peacefully, as if we were watching a sunset.

We were rowing a boat in the sunset. The rhythmic muscular movements. The aquatic feeling. The lapping of the waves. "Push in further," she said. Rowing. Rowing.

Afterwards it had all faded away and the sun gone down and we were beached, watching the afterglow. It's funny how the details are gone. I remember every horrifying, anguished particular of the time I'd washed out with her but details of the triumph are gone. You remember the failures, but I suppose one happy screw is like another. As Tolstoy said. There was mostly her cute solar plexus, the muscles under the soft part knotting up and then relaxing. And I remember her being quite hairy, proving this theory I picked up in Yugoslavia that hairy girls are more strongly sexed. We lay there peacefully in the afterglow, her resting her damp head on my damp shoulder.

"Are all Americans circumcised?" she said.

"No. Lots of them aren't."

"Why are so many?"

"Hygiene," I said. "Health. If it's healthy, we'll buy it."

It seemed to make her pensive.

"Why, because Omar's circumcised?" I asked. "Isn't Omar circumcised?"

Which seemed quaint. Here I knew him so well and I didn't even know if he was circumcised or not.

"Oh, *Omar's* circumcised," she said. "He's a Muslim."

It made me wonder if Omar was circumcised as a Moslem or circumcised as an American, and if Mouna had ever slept with anyone who was *not* circumcised. Maybe she'd been looking forward to it. It seemed like too personal a question to ask though and I wanted to get off the subject. I was tired of the subject.

"What's this scar on your stomach?" she said.

"Appendicitis."

"But an appendicitis scar should be here. What's it doing way over there?"

"I was little," I said, exasperated. "It's been moving over that way for years."

She really was an impossible woman. She made you feel you had to apologize for having a scar in the wrong place.

"Okay, okay," she said. "What's in a scar. You want to see something?"

She suddenly wheeled herself around and playfully rotated her pelvis up toward me, her face red and half embarrassed, laughing, spreading her legs wide offering full visibility as if she was going to demonstrate that she could squirt Jergens Lotion out of her vagina. She had no shame whatever that woman. She was absolutely shameless. I saw I'd broken through her reserve. If she told me she could squirt Jergens Lotion out of her vagina though, the romance was over.

"Look," she said.

Well, what is there to say?

There was a vague closing and opening movement. I guess she must have had muscles there. I'd never seen it before in a vagina and, who knows, I might never see it again. She was laughing, red faced.

So she was a more complicated girl than I'd thought. She was a mad Palestinian fanatic, anti-U.S., anti-Israel of course, anti-capitalist, quite humorless about all that. She had an aggressive, overbearing personality, capable of virulent hostility, with a strong strain of malicious hysteria. Very hard to get along with, by and large. Very vengeful. On the other hand, inside was this fun-loving girl who could do tricks with her vagina. She had this sustained, comparatively long-term relationship with Omar, which I wasn't certain I understood except by virtue of masochism on his part. She had relationships with other men, the latest of which were with Mohammed Maziq and me, which not only made you think it wasn't just her sex drive but that first, there were other goals, and, second, why him, and, third, why me? The Libyan was more understandable; but me she should have hated through and through. She had these great Palestinian contacts theoretically, a whole Palestinian Mafia, they told me, which had provided my ulterior motivation. But although I'd started this gambit under the impression it was my idea, this was rapidly supplanted by the impression it was her idea, and in the normal course of events you would wonder what was in it for her, like was I being sandbagged. She was a very attractive, dark, fanatic-type Palestinian girl. She had a good figure, a bright, lively, slightly hysterical intelligence. She'd had a sudden affair with this Libyan and now me. She wanted something, all right, but what? Was she leading me into a trap? She was copiously endowed with hair around her sexual parts, if that gave any clue to her character. This was what I thought of in my mind as the Yugoslav School. Not only was her vulva itself handsomely hairy, the hair filling all the space conventionally available, to the fold of the leg, but fuzz extended down the inside of the thighs for an inch or two, on all of which area I lavished great attention, which seemed quite well appreciated, not so much sexually I had the feeling but as a mark of esteem. In fact I finally decided that she wasn't especially interested in sex at all.

I was standing in my best beige tropical-worsted suit and a red-and-white striped tie on the curb halfway down a side street in Beirut. The sun was blinding. A blue Renault-12 slowed and came to a halt at the curb. A man in tinted eyeglasses leaned across the front seat and lowered the window.

"Hinkel?" he said.

"Right," I answered and opened the door and got in.

"Close the window, it's climatized," he said, and slammed into gear and sped down the street, taking a corner on squeaking wheels, then some more side streets, heading out of town, skirting the roadblocks. Then straight out.

He was in his late twenties, tanned, well built, well dressed, wearing a blue suit and tie, but I didn't have confidence in his driving. Mouna had probably told him everything about me, but false names were the rule. He was to be Ahmed, not very original. He tore along the highway as if the best sharpshooters of the Phalange were on our tail, setting occasional chickens flapping as we passed peasant villages on the road. He didn't speak, keeping both his hands high on the wheel. Suddenly he turned off to the left on a side road, went half a mile, stopped. No cars came after us. Ahmed turned the car around and drove back on the highway, heading back toward Beirut, turned off on another side road and stopped again. I didn't follow this at all; perhaps he knew what he was doing. Finally he sat back and turned to me with a smile gentler than I'd expected. The tinted glasses were pale and I could see his eyes clearly. They were emotional, liquid.

"And what are you doing in Lebanon?" he asked.

His English was very good, somewhere between British and American, but the manner was pervasively Arab somehow.

"You mean to what do you owe the pleasure of this visit?" I said.

"Well, yes," he laughed with a slightly embarrassed courtesy. "The pleasure of this visit."

"Well, I'm in business of a sort," I said. "We have branches throughout all the Arab countries."

"But you have very good connections with the American government too, Mouna said. Our mutual friend."

"Yes," I said. "I have some connections."

"And you know about us?"

Behind the glasses the eyes fastened on me hungrily, yearning to be close. I felt as if he'd moved physically closer. They like to touch you. It reassures them.

"Only what Mouna tells me," I said.

"Aah," he answered and in elaborate language and gesture laid it all out.

It wasn't completely implausible. This was a minority current within the PLO, Yasir Arafat's outfit, the umbrella organization. They disapproved of terrorism and felt that Palestine should be ready to take its place among the community of nations. It all sounded very nice. We'd certainly be interested in hearing what these fellows had to say, and they obviously couldn't communicate with us through diplomatic channels. I could fix something up. We could set up some kind of cut-out, access agent, telephone drill, dead-drop system. We'd also be quite interested in hearing what Yasir Arafat had to say in private, on a fairly regular basis. We were panting for stuff like that. They could give us the pros and the cons of arguments. Who won. We had various electronic devices that would simplify his task, but that was another threshold, farther down the line. He was an ardent Palestinian, this fellow.

"I feel it's only fair that you should let us pick up your expenses on this sort of thing," I said. "We wouldn't want you running into debt."

There was a faint withdrawal behind the tinted glasses. There was psychic distance.

"What expenses would I have?" he said distrustfully.

"Whatever comes up. I don't know. Travel. Incidentals."

"With signed receipts?"

He raised his chin sharply, making a *tsk* sound. Arab for no.

He'd heard stories. He didn't want us to burn him. You could understand his point of view. I laughed.

"We haven't done that for years," I reassured him joshingly. "We'll take your word for it."

He wasn't laughing. I'd hurt his feelings somehow. I also had the impression he was hiding something, but this was a common impression with Arabs. He had a wounded look.

"I don't want money to have anything to do with this," he said in a hurt tone. "We want to be your friends. Are you our friends?"

"Of course," I said, grasping his hand in a manly grip and looking him straight in his tinted glasses but feeling nervous. I was leery of the word "friend" with Arabs. They were deep, passionate, devoted friends while it lasted, but you did one little thing wrong and all that intense, burning feeling curdled and went sour and they wanted to kill you. I'd had Arab friends already, and they spent all their time brooding and tormenting themselves that you were going to betray them, and at the least little thing they turned murderous. I wasn't so hot on acquiring Arab friends. I'd rather give them money.

"When the time comes we will want your support," Ahmed said emotionally. He was still holding my hand. I was staring into his glasses as warmly as I could. They say we have cold eyes. Our eyes slide away coldly.

"What kind of support?" I said, knowing perfectly well he didn't mean a vote in the United Nations. He gave me a mental image of something on the scale of an aircraft carrier, or anyway hardware. I could close my eyes and definitely see hardware.

133

Ahmed didn't answer.

"When the time comes we'll see if you are our true friend," he said, wounded again. "We'll see how true is your friendship."

They were touchy devils, always getting their feelings hurt about something, always jealous, always expecting treason. You say I am your friend but am I your *favorite* friend? Mustapha tells you he is your friend but he schemes against you behind your back; only *I* am your true friend. You spent ten more minutes with Abdullah than you spent with me. You'd give me an aircraft carrier if you *really* loved me. But they could kill. They love the sight of blood.

Well, some of it made sense but some of it didn't make sense. Why were they coming to us? If you were a moderate Palestinian everybody knew you went to the Saudis or the Gulf Emirates, who were as conservative as anybody could want and whose subsidies were keeping the PLO even as moderate as it was. Were their channels blocked? Did they think we were the best way to reach the Saudis? Try it upside down. Suppose these guys were not beyond the moderate fringe of the PLO but beyond the wild-eyed, nut fringe. Then why didn't they go to the Libyans, who were bankrolling fire-eating rebel movements from Belfast to Dhoffar? A hazy recollection of Mouna and Mohammed Maziq floated across my mind. Maybe they had gone to the Libyans. What had happened? Well, we would see what we would see. I was wired. The boys at the station could play it all back, check around, plumb this enigma. It seemed worth going along with for a while. It might yield some good raw stuff. They could flutter him eventually if it came to that, check him out that way. Or would that offend his notion of true friendship? When you fluttered a guy there was this innuendo that maybe you didn't trust him. Maybe fluttering was incompatible with Arab friendship. I had the feeling we were leaving no Palestinian unturned though. I set up a communication system with Ahmed and he drove us back to Beirut, dropping me off as we approached the outskirts.

Then there were a few odds and ends. They got a lot of work out of me. They'd brought me to Beirut and I was this new face that nobody in Beirut had ever seen before. Now you saw me, now you didn't. In and out. They had some bric-a-brac they figured they could use me on. There was this security man at the Syrian mission whose wife had been sick for years and he needed money. In fact she was dying of multiple myeloma which is an expensive disease to die of, and I was kind of sorry for the guy. His family back in Damascus didn't have the money it used to have, apparently. I know this sounds a little heartless but you had to be practical: those were the guys you went for. Even the most leonine courage could be crushed by relentless adversity, so you put yourself in phase with relentless adversity. That was the business. That was the way it was done. They didn't tell me how they knew about the Syrian's sick wife and money worries. They only gave you what you needed to know. The problem with this Syrian was access. He went to the casino once in a while, penny ante stuff, to forget his troubles I suppose, poor guy, but casinos were tricky. There was no privacy. He took walks along the Corniche sometimes in the evening, which was a funny thing for a security man, but people were funny. He was a romantic, lonely security man maybe. He liked to gaze out at the sea.

His car slowed to a halt and parked on the landward side of the Corniche in the dark. We were following him too close and had to go past him and stopped about a hundred yards further on, figuring he would come walking by. It was a psychological law. People strolled in the direction they'd been driving usually. In a couple of minutes we saw him walk past on the seaward side, and I let him go by and then got out, started walking at the same speed behind him. He walked and walked. It was a beautiful night, warm and fragrant with a mild breeze coming in from the sea, with only sporadic gunfire. Oh, yuh, they were having this Civil War. But the militias hadn't shot up this district much yet, not to mention the Israelis, who came along later.

Lanterns were shining down along the seafront, festoons and garlands of light. Very pretty. Very lyrical. He stopped at a round observation post from which tourists would admire the view, when there used to be tourists. Two or three other people were there too, but the Syrian stood apart.

"It's a beautiful city you have here," I said to him. "Every time I come I admire it. They bring us here every three months on R and R from Riyadh."

I had to engage him in conversation. I didn't want him to just turn his back and walk away.

"I'm a doctor down in Riyadh," I went on. "When you live in Riyadh you really appreciate a place like Beirut. God, Riyadh. No show business. No movies. If they didn't give us R and R we couldn't stand it. Rest and Recreation."

He was looking at me curiously as if he didn't know how to take me.

"It costs them a fortune," I said. "What with the R and R every three months, and home leave, and transportation, and housing in Riyadh which is very expensive, and the other allowances, you know how much I cost them a year?"

"You are American?" he said with a small smile. He was dark, with black, wavy hair. Somehow his features seemed cramped.

"Uh, huh," I said. Then, "Yes," to make sure he got it.

There was no hostility. Sometimes the ones who were supposed to hate you the most turned out not to hate you at all. We're still very popular despite what anybody tells you. He didn't seem to have followed my story about money but I went on anyway.

"I cost them one hundred and twenty thousand dollars a year," I said. "Isn't that incredible? I'm not worth it!"

I laughed. He smiled.

"My salary is only a small part of that, but can you imagine? It's all the to-ing and fro-ing and the R and R and the house in Riyadh. But that's what they're willing to pay to get a good doctor to go to Saudi Arabia."

"Sow-dia," he said, pronouncing it in Arabic. "You American, you like Riyadh? How is Riyadh?"

"Never been to Riyadh?" I said. "My God, you haven't lived. Well, I'll tell you. You get the impression that the whole country from one end to the other is run by the CIA."

There was a slight stiffening in his face. His face was there but he was elsewhere.

"A liberal Lebanese like you might not like it," I said.

There was another stiffening of his face. He was even further away. He knew he was no Lebanese but he wasn't going to tell me. The romantic sightseers were out of earshot. I changed my tone.

"I know who you are," I said. "Play ball with us and we'll make it worth your while. Your money problems will be over."

He seemed to recoil an inch or two in the night. Perhaps it was my imagination. He muttered something under his breath in Arabic, the expression on his face frozen.

"*You cocksucker!*" he said.

It wasn't taking.

Very good English. Very idiomatic. I didn't take it personally. He just stood there, glowering in the dark. I didn't turn my back on him. Oh, no, I didn't. If he was armed, I was armed. In Beirut they shoot a man for sneezing. You never turned your back.

"Think it over," I said.

He made an angry arc around me and walked swiftly back down the Corniche toward the car.

Well, the way we were fixed, it was a cold-turkey approach or nothing. Nothing ventured, nothing gained. And a Syrian, it wasn't as if you might be offending a dear friend and true supporter. We should have Arabs do that sort of thing for us, but what local Arab would have done it? His life wouldn't have been worth a plugged nickel. The great thing about me was that if it didn't work, tra la la, off I flew and no one ever saw me again. It all left me feeling rather elated. To be called a cocksucker in the line of duty and feel unoffended, pure in heart. It was really quite bracing.

On my last day I saw Mouna in the lobby of the Saint George Hotel. She'd come on a different plane, on a different airline, and had been staying with her mother and father. I hadn't seen her in Beirut at all. She was very well dressed, in a chic khaki safari suit with military detailing. That kind of well dressed.

"The Phalange is setting up more roadblocks," she said, her eyes burning with rage.

I'd noticed this myself and told her so, and she appeared less tense.

"He says if he ever sees you again he'll kill you," she said evenly.

"Who?"

She wasn't supposed to know anything about that. It had nothing to do with her at all. But Beirut was this tiny place. No wonder they'd brought me in.

"Use your imagination," said Mouna.

It seemed to me she should have been slightly angry, as if I was this thug, as if I had bad manners, but you never knew with Arabs. It all depended on how they were related to the other person. *Shame cometh to a man when one of his neighbors, relatives, or a blood relation in any degree is humiliated.* Ibn Khaldun. It was all ifs and buts and bloodlines. It was only a partial ethic. There was a lot of waffling, too. They always had an out if they wanted one. *Thou shalt not kill without due cause.* The Koran. How was that for a waffle? But I wasn't worried about the Syrian. I didn't believe it. It sounded like Arab rhetoric to me. If he wanted to kill me he could have tried right there on the Corniche. Mouna was another matter. There I had to believe that *she* believed that I was useful to the Cause. As the man said who jumped out of the fortieth-story window as he passed the tenth floor, "So far so good."

At the station, the man beckoned me into his office.

"He says he'll kill you if he ever sees you again."

His mouth tightened. It might have been a smile. It wasn't FitzWilliam anymore of course, back in dear old Rabat. This one was a distinctly non-U type for a change, small, hard-eyed, with acne and a faint Southern accent.

"Where did you get that?" I asked him.

"We picked it up," he said.

"Listening in on people's conversations?"

"He said it to another Syrian. I'll tell you that much. So stay out of his way and get the hell back to Morocco."

I still thought it was a lot of hot air, big talk to impress his buddies. If he'd wanted to kill me why hadn't he tried up on the Corniche? Unless he was waiting for a clean shot at my back. There was that. I should have been disguised, I supposed. A dark wig and a pair of rimless specs would have done it. Unmeticulous tradecraft. Now I'd have to stay out of Beirut for a while. Not to mention Damascus.

To each his own airline. Mouna and I returned to Marrakesh via different routes, she arriving two days after me. She'd been visiting her parents, you see. I'd gone to get my teeth fixed. I did rewrites on a couple of scenes for *Mohammed Superstar*, which was still staggering along. Mouna introduced me to quite a few new people. I was expanding my contacts with the native population. It turned out there was a Palestinian diaspora, even in Morocco. Mouna had this whole life that I hadn't known about. She was a gold mine for contacts. Of course I was placing myself in the hands of old Mouna, who just might do me in some day, but she was our link to these Palestinians. It all reminded me of Ben Barka of Moroccan memory. I mean Ben Barka was on the French payroll all along, but until he bought the farm he went on revolutionizing, and Third-Worldizing, and Tricontinentalizing, as free and unconstrained as a revolutionary person could be — except deflecting some of those Third-World passions away from France, right? *Chose promise, chose due.* That was the point of it all. So now we were maybe going to use Mouna's friends to deflect something from somebody, just like Mehdi Ben Barka. Who if he hadn't nourished childlike dreams of cinema glory via my *rara avis* of a friend Georges Franju might be alive and well today, still deflecting.

So you see what sex, so often relegated to a humble position, could lead to if properly implemented. History was made at night. Actually we did it in the afternoon when

Omar was on the set. History was made in the afternoon. In point of fact this was all pretty low-level stuff, but interesting, piquant. I was meeting all these piquant Arabs through Mouna. All these Arabs of all varieties seemed to like me. I was very likeable. I had an attractive candor about me. I invariably felt sincere. In the low-budget movie of life I even had a persona worked out for myself. I was a loveable rogue. That was looking at it from Mouna's point of view. Actually from my point of view I wasn't a rogue at all if you want to know. I was as honorable a man as circumstances would allow. Of course circumstances these days were pretty complicated.

11

IT WAS DEEP, BLACK, viscous sleep, and there was hop-scotch down there, and penny candy, and childhood Monopoly games. And this cold, hard thing was pressing against my temple and somebody was talking in some funny language but I could understand everything, and I didn't like this man. *What day is it?* I thought in growing desperation. If I could only figure out what day it was I could straighten everything out.

"If you make a move we'll kill you," the voice said quietly. "Don't move, don't make a sound."

I was wide awake. There were two of them in the dim light. They'd come in through the window from the swimming pool. It was the barrel of a pistol he was holding against my head.

"*Doucement*, easy does it," he said in French in a low voice. "Relax. Okay. Slowly now. No fast moves or we'll blow your head off."

He removed his pistol from my head but he was shining his little super lumijet flashlight in my face. I was still anxious about what day it was. If I could only work out what day it was I'd have a hold on it.

"Okay. Slow and easy. You can sit up. Keep your hands in sight. Just sit there on the edge of the bed."

I sat up slowly.

"You sure you got the right guy?"

"You're Nelson, aren't you?"

"No," I said.

"Who are you then?"

"Farrell." It was the first name came into my head.

"Bullshit."

"No kidding. Randy Farrell."

"What are you doing here? In Marrakesh." His voice was low but clear.

"I'm a salesman. I work for a company that makes medical supplies."

"You don't look like a man who sells medical supplies. Keep your hands on your knees."

The other man was shuffling the papers on my desk with his own super lumijet.

"There's a hotel bill here that says Nelson," he said.

The first man gave a low laugh.

"And there's a mimeographed book here with 'Nelson' on it."

There was enough light for me to see that they were Arabs of some sort, but you couldn't have told from the accent. They were dressed in Western clothes. No light was coming in from the swimming pool. It was the middle of the night.

"Now you just sit there on the edge of the bed for a minute or two, and I'll tell you what we're going to do. If you step out of line or make any sudden moves I'll put a bullet in your brain like nothing. Makes no difference to me one way or the other."

"You've made your point," I said.

He leaned forward slightly.

"Now here's what we're going to do. You're going to put on your clothes. Then we're going to go walking out of here through the window there. We're going to go single file, my friend here leading. You follow him. I follow you. We skirt the pool. We probably won't see anybody, but if we do you don't say anything, just keep walking. If he speaks to you and says, 'Hey, Nelson, where are you going?' you say you're out for a walk with your friends and keep walking. If all this goes off without a hitch, you live. If the slightest thing of any sort goes wrong, I blow your goddamn brains out. Now is that a fair bargain?"

"Who are you?" I said.

"Curious bastard," he laughed. "What do you care? You don't need to know yet. Don't worry, we're not doing this for money. It's for the good of Morocco. We're patriots. Does that make you feel better?"

"Worse," I said.

"Get your clothes on."

I put my things on slowly by the light of their super lumijets. My .38 was in a drawer under some underwear but I didn't go anywhere near it. I didn't consider going near it.

"Can I comb my hair?" I said.

"No."

"Okay. But I'll look conspicuous if we meet anybody."

"Where's the comb?"

"On the shelf over the washbowl."

"Get it," he said to his friend, who handed it to me.

"Comb your hair here," the first one said. "You don't need a mirror."

I combed my hair.

"Did you understand everything I said to you before?" he asked.

"Say it again just in case."

"Are you trying to be funny?"

"Not me. Never. I just don't want to get killed."

He went through the whole thing again. It seemed reasonable. I had no questions. I really concentrated because if something went wrong I had a feeling this guy would shoot me. It was a very definite feeling.

"Should I take a toothbrush?" I said.

"What do you need a toothbrush for?" he came back, starting to smolder.

"Just an idea."

"Stand up."

He said something to the other one in Arabic.

"Move away from the bed. Raise your hands."

The other one stepped behind me and felt me down very thoroughly to make sure I hadn't concealed a weapon somewhere. In America they had you lean your hands against a wall to keep you off balance but these guys hadn't heard of that. This way if I'd managed to pocket my .38 in the darkness I might theoretically have spun around now, pulling the guy behind me around as a shield, but those things were dicey. If it hadn't worked I'd have been dead. Oh yes I would.

More Arabic.

"Okay, let's go," said the first one. "Follow my friend. Remember now. No tricks or I'll blow your brains out."

Off we went like three Indians, out the full-length window, onto the grass, springy underfoot, no one in sight. Overhead the stars were dazzling, no moon, the air cooler with the smell of gardenias. A very romantic night. Come to romantic Marrakesh. All lights were out in the refreshment house by the swimming pool, the chairs up-ended on top of the tables. A blue light was coming from the water of the pool itself. Someone had left the underwater lights on. The man in front of me walked steadily, with a rolling stride. Past the pool, it was darker and his navy-blue sport shirt was harder to see but I could make the rest of him out easily enough. He angled across the last few yards of lawn. No fences. No watchmen. No dogs. A terrific, old-world, low-security hotel. When we came to the road the leader turned right, the pavement hard under our feet now. The car was a dark-gray Peugeot 404, the same model as my own. The lead man climbed in behind the wheel.

"In," said the one behind me.

As I climbed in the back I could sense the pistol of the man in the driver's seat pointing at me. The other man got in the back with me.

"Now you just relax. Don't move," he said and tied a blindfold around my eyes. I heard him ripping off pieces of adhesive tape and then he taped the blindfold to my cheeks and forehead.

"Stick your hands out in front of you," he said.

The driver snapped what felt like regulation police hand-cuffs around my wrists.

"Scrunch yourself down on the floor there so nobody sees you."

I did it. It was cramped.

"Remember, I'm right here looking down at you and if you try anything I can pump six bullets into you in seconds. And don't speak unless you're spoken to. Let's go."

The car started, drove straight for a couple of minutes, turned, and turned again. Lying in a cramped foetus position on the floorboards, I felt all spun around and had no hope of figuring out what direction we were driving in, but was strangely tranquil. My fate was in the hands of the dealer now; there was nothing I could do about it. It was as if the whole thing was a load off my mind. I thought of my ex-wife in Switzerland, glad she would get the insurance money if it came to that. Fair was fair. I got into these sordid relations with women. I attracted the wrong kind of woman. It wasn't my fault. I had no important unfinished business. I didn't owe anybody any money. My accounts were neat and in order. And now these guys were in charge of me.

The Moroccans didn't speak. The windows were open and the night air was doubtless sweeping through the car up there but not much of it reached me down on the floor, where I could feel the engine vibrations coming through the floorboards. Were we passing other cars? We drove on, cramps coming and going in my legs. My hands started to go numb and I flexed them very discreetly. I was so squashed down I couldn't even take a full breath but had no intention of complaining. Still no sound from the two Moroccans. They said I didn't need to know "yet," which meant they had plans for me, I had a future of sorts. We must be way out in the country now, but heading where? Toward the Atlas Mountains? Into the desert? Were we climbing? Why didn't the Moroccans talk? They were lousy company. I liked it a lot better when they talked, told me to do things, we did stuff, action. I hated this inaction. It was a dreary trip. I've had better trips. We slowed. The driver shifted gears and we went off the highway onto a dirt road, and he shifted up again. *Rum! Dum! Dum! Bam! Bam! Bam!* Bumps in the road. *Talan ch-ch, talan ch-ch,* they say in Spanish for the sound of a railroad car riding smoothly. This was no *talan ch-ch. Bam! Bam! Bam! Clunk! Clunk!* We slowed and stopped. Doors opened. My companions jounced out.

"Out. Move it."

He was speaking in full voice. We must be out in the middle of nowhere. I climbed up onto the seat, stiff, filled with cramps, my right leg numb.

"Get going. The door's open."

"Wait a minute," I said. "I'm all dizzy."

I sat for a few seconds on the seat and then, still blindfolded and my hands manacled, cautiously felt my way out of the car. The air was cool and it was a very quiet, still night and no light was coming through the blindfold. In the distance I could hear faint sounds of animals. Goats? Horses? Cows? Did they have cows in Morocco?

"Would you mind loosening the handcuffs a little," I said. "Or I might get gangrene."

"Later. Put your hand on my friend's shoulder and walk."

It was pebbly and uneven underfoot. After twenty yards or so he stopped. I heard keys in a lock, a door swinging open, and my guide moved ahead. A hand pushed me from the back and I followed. There was a strong smell of hay, straw. The floor felt like hard dirt. Another door creaked open, another push, and I followed my guide. We were kicking our way through straw now. Were they going to bed me down with the cows?

"Lie down."

"Right here?"

"There."

I sat down on the floor, then stretched out. The straw wasn't too bad. Lumpy.

"Would you loosen my handcuffs a little now please?"

Someone released my right handcuff with a key, then

146

rattled it shut again. It sounded like the winding of a noisy watch.

"Hey, it's as tight as it was before. No kidding, I'll get gangrene."

He did it again and left it one click looser, then for the left hand.

"Listen to me," he said. "You're going to lie here and not move around much. Don't try to remove your blindfold. If you need anything ask for it in a low voice, but no useless talking. If you hear anyone moving around or any cars don't make the slightest sound. You know us well enough to know we don't like tricks. If you want to get through this thing alive you won't try anything funny. Do you understand what I've told you?"

"Yes," I said. "But could I ask you something? I don't want to pry but could you tell me what this is all about?"

He snickered.

"I mean, isn't there some mistake?" I asked. "What good am I to Morocco?"

"You heard what I said," he answered. "Anything you want, you ask my friend here softly. Any monkey business and we'll kill you. You'll be hearing from me. *Salut.*"

I heard the door swing open and shut. In a few minutes the car outside started and drove off. The silence seemed unnatural. No human noises, no birds. Only a thin hum of insects and an occasional distant animal bleat. I couldn't even hear my guard breathing. A low light came through the blindfold. I was still trying to figure out what I had been doing recently. I remembered there'd been a big commotion when the chuck wagon was blown up. But that was weeks ago. These couldn't be the same people, could they? Would Moslem religious maniacs kidnap someone to prevent a movie on the Prophet? Why didn't they kidnap Omar, who was responsible for it all and was a Moslem sort of, a traitor to his religion maybe when you thought about it.

Then an evil thought blossomed in my mind that I had felt budding for hours. *Did they know about me and* KUDOVE?

I didn't want to think about it. I just wanted to lie there and not think about it. *Mouna*. Her image came to me balefully like a noxious emanation from a swamp. She'd tipped them off. She'd fingered me. I'd always thought that to be done in by a woman would be a dashing way to go, but I'd been wrong. It was a miserable way to go, filled with nasty self-recrimination, demeaning, shaming, and left me feeling that if by some chance I got out of this thing alive I'd have to avoid wild women at all costs in the future, thereby destroying at one blow half the fun of life, which was miserable too, even assuming I had a future. So I'd been done in by a woman, one of the great, historic pitfalls. It was humiliating, but had happened to others before me. That strange feeling of fatalism and tranquillity came creeping back, as if nothing I could do mattered now anyway. Perhaps the whole thing had been preordained. Perhaps it was the Lord's will. It was out of my hands.

I slept. When I woke up I could see daylight through my blindfold and hear my guard moving about. I sat up and heard him leave the room and come back a little later and stand beside me. I could feel him. *Drink*, he said. I reached out my hands blindly, felt a warm bowl, took it, drank. It was sweet tea. "May I go to the bathroom please?" I asked, beginning my first day of life as an Arab. There was no water for washing, my guard said ahead of time. Water for tea but not for washing. So I did it the Arab way. You ate with the right hand, and did all your dirty business with the left hand, and hoped never the twain would meet. Just try it with handcuffs. When nature called, not to say yodeled, the guard would lead me out, into what I could tell was the great outdoors because of the smell and sounds and warmer air and higher light level through the blindfold, and I would do left-hand stuff as best I could. When for what I took to be lunch I was handed a bowl of plain *couscous*, which I held between my knees, I dipped into it with the fingers of my right hand, right-hand stuff. No cutlery naturally. The only trouble was that when you're manacled, whither the right hand goeth the left hand hath this tendency to go also. "Could you take off my handcuffs just while I eat please?" I asked. No answer. So I kept my hands as far away from each other as a handcuffed man can do and prayed to Allah I wouldn't get dysentery. It was the Arab way. No conversation from my guard at all.

Sounds: Insects, a kind of cricket samba. Birds now, chattering and cawing wanly. Domesticated animals way in the distance, bleating, neighing, mooing, whichever. My guard, breathing, moving around now and then. As sounds go, they weren't enough to keep a full-grown man interested very long. My heart leaped up when I heard what sounded like the turning of the page of a magazine or book. Was the guard reading something? How a man's horizons would expand if he could only read something. Could I ask him what it was? No. I did some sit-ups instead, then rolled over in the straw and tried push-ups and discovered that a man in handcuffs can't do them. You can't even get all the way down, let alone up. Your own elbows get in the way somehow, jabbing you in the middle of the stomach. I wondered if I could get up and do some deep-knee bends, jog in place. "Can I stand up and do some exercises please?" I asked. No answer. Smells, I would count the smells. Straw, hay, whatever it was. Anything else? If I pulled my shirt away from my chest I could smell my own underarm deodorant. A lot of good that did me. The hours passed. More right-hand stuff. More left-hand stuff. I could see through the blindfold that the light was failing, then it was night. The guard snapped on what seemed to be an electric bulb and the humming of the crickets got louder.

With darkness Mouna came into my mind again. She was responsible for all this, God damn it, which was both galling and unjust, and you could trust her to get me into the deepest trouble of my life to date. I mean when you came right down to it my relations with KUDOVE were essentially harmless and I was an extremely lightweight person; anybody could see that but her. I was loyal to my country. What was the matter with that? I liked a little innocent fun. It seemed to me I was a basically patriotic, fun-loving-type person who never corrupted anybody who wasn't dying to be corrupted to begin with, and it didn't seem fair to me that I should be lying handcuffed and blindfolded in a hut in the middle of Morocco because of the ideological bigotry of some malevolent maniac of an Arab female. I did some more sit-ups, then listened to the crickets. More hours passed. I began alternating now between acute anxiety and then sudden sleepiness. My tranquillity was gone. I wondered if this went on long enough if I would eventually go nuts.

. A car. First a dim thrumming noise, gradually growing louder, then a jouncing of springs, the motor roaring as a clumsy driver threw in the clutch while keeping his foot on the gas pedal, then *slam!* People piling out. Clear voices in Arabic. I could see it in my mind's eye, three or four young Moroccans stretching their legs, the car doors slamming shut again. Then I heard them making their way into the house.

12

ME AS AN ARAB LADY. Me in Arab drag. Me dressed up like
Golda Meir when they smuggled her across the border for
secret talks with Hussein. Fucking ridiculous, you think,
but the way they dressed their women, with veils, and all
the bedsheets, the whole bit, it wasn't that ridiculous, except
bulky. In size, I'm telling you, I was one bruiser of an Arab
lady. First they slapped more adhesive tape around my
blindfold. Then they took off my handcuffs. Then they said
take off your clothes, and I took off my clothes, stripped
down to my shorts. Then they handed me something and
said, *Put this on. Over the head.* And I reached out, blind,
and took hold of it, and with their help got it on. Then they
handed me something else and I put it on. And more stuff
and I put it on. And I could tell from the feel that these
weren't Western clothes, naturally, and thought they were
getting me up more or less like Rudolph Valentino until
they had me sit down on the floor and pinned a kind of
headdress on me, and veil, and stood me up again and
covered me with the all-over, all-weather tarpaulin, the
ultimate bedsheet, when I thought, hey wait a minute. Then
they handcuffed me, hands in front again, hidden slyly beneath the last garment. I was a handcuffed Arab lady. I was
a handcuffed Arab lady with eye trouble.

"This is the dangerous part, Nelson," one of them said.
"Watch yourself. Open your mouth and you're a dead man."

"Or woman as the case may be," I said.

151

I felt as if a mule kicked me in the stomach. For several panicky seconds I couldn't breathe, then, gasping, thought I was going to throw up. After a time the retching heaves stopped. I was lying on the floor.

"You think we're kidding around, don't you?" someone said. "You think this is some sort of joke."

"No, I don't," I said hollowly. "I do not."

And kept my mouth shut.

They had to tidy me up again and then off we went in the night, me jammed down on the floorboards of a car again, but more comfortable this time, a smoother ride. Other people's feet rested casually on my back, very relaxed. We drove and drove on paved roads. Swung left. Swung right. No one spoke. I was very hot on the floor with all my bed wrappings and was afraid the sweat pouring down my face would dislodge the adhesive holding the blindfold in place. It might slip and I'd get a peek at where we were, making my captors decide the calculated risk had gone too high, maybe better throw me away and start afresh with somebody new who wouldn't sweat off adhesive tape. The car turned sharply to the right, then turned again and I sensed we were coming into a city. We made many more turns, probably to throw me off, then the car came to a slow halt. Everyone got out but me. The car springs were motionless again, the doors open. No one said a word. What was I supposed to do? Should I just keep lying there?

A hand tapped me on the shoulder. I'd been given no instructions but took this as the signal to rise and I slowly climbed to a sitting position on the back seat. Someone got in the back beside me. Hands arranged my bedsheets, then tugged my arm. Outside I knew instantly I was in a city from the basic sound, like the faint throbbing of a distant generator. Somewhere far off delivery trucks whined, radios tinkled. *Walk naturally*, a voice said in a hoarse whisper as a firm hand gripped my arm, and I walked ahead blindly, steadily, relieved that my blindfold was still in place. I could hear the footsteps of the others around me. Don't ask me what we looked like. Just a bunch of guys bringing old grandma home in the middle of the night, I guess. Except for me being a little big it might have all looked perfectly plausible for all I know. The street beneath our feet was paved. After a few minutes' walk, part of it on a slight upgrade, I was yanked to one side, pushed. We were inside a building. The door shut. There was a faint chemical smell. My handcuffs and outer garments were removed. Then began a complicated series of peregrinations. I was spun around, led up a ladder onto creaky boards, told we were going to have to crawl through a tunnel on our stomachs, crawled, stood up again, was spun around again, led down a ladder, turned around, down a staircase, crawled on hands and knees for a long ways over damp tiling, stood up, bent down. *Watch out. Climb under this.* I felt it as I edged under. Wood. Then more turning around, climbing up and down ladders. And, you know, after all this, I had the feeling we hadn't gone twenty feet, we were pretty much where we'd been all along. The last stop was, *Down on your hands and knees. Crawl in there.* I felt chicken wire. Where were they putting me, in a dog kennel? They threw something in after me and said, "There are your clothes. You can take off the blindfold." I heard a padlock snap, a door shut, footsteps walking away.

Removing the blindfold was a blessing, but did not bring sight as the darkness was total. After staring into the blackness for several minutes it seemed to me I was seeing a dim haze, but could make out no shapes or objects. To my front, groping, I felt chicken wire several feet wide, to the left a plaster or terra-cotta wall, to the right the same, in back the same. The floor was a kind of rough tiling. In the back was a lumpy straw mattress. It was hot and I peeled off all the Arab lady's bed linen and stretched out on the mattress soaking wet with perspiration, which began to evaporate now, giving an agreeable impression of coolness. Well, it was a new life. Cool. No blindfold. No handcuffs. My stomach muscles hurt some from having been punched earlier, but still I lay there a happy man.

I dozed and came awake again all tense. I couldn't tell

if it was day or night but knew right away where I was. It seemed to me I'd known that all along while I was asleep. I was all anxious again. First my heart beat like a trip-hammer as if something dangerous was going to happen any second. Then suddenly time stretched out and it was indescribably wearisome and boring, an everlasting, nag-ging, unbearable emptiness. In the silence and darkness there was nothing to mark time by. I had no time sense. A minute was like a year. Then from a speck in the depths of the undulating dankness of my mind came a sweaty fear named KUBARK. If they knew about me and KUBARK my future was very dark. It didn't bear thinking about. But then I veered and became quite jolly. I don't know why. If it hadn't been for KUBARK I think I might have been deeply content.

"Turn your face to the wall!" a voice commanded. An electric light was on.

I rolled over obediently and heard the sound of many feet tramping into the room.

"Turn back now. Crawl through the hole. Sit just in front."

I rolled back again. I was in a middle-sized white room the end of which had been sectioned off with chicken wire as a lockup. The only way to get out was by crawling through a little grill door by the floor like a goddamn dog. They opened the door, which was padlocked. I crawled through and sat on the floor outside. Four Arabs in full Bedouin regalia were sitting along the far wall on stools, their faces wrapped up to the eyes as if against the blowing sands of the desert. It was Sigmund Romberg's *Desert Song*.

"What's so funny?" one of them said.

"Nothing."

"What are you laughing about then?" he said with an angry edge. He called me by the intimate in French, *tu*.

"I'm sorry," I said, crossing my legs in front of me and leaning back against the chicken wire, which sagged. "No reason. *Ne t'offense pas*. Don't get sore."

"Why do you call me *tu*?" he asked coldly.

"But you call me *tu*."

"But I speak in the name of the Moroccan people," he said grimly, and one of the other ones stepped forward and smashed me across the face with his open hand. My head reeled and my ears rang. They were right. There was nothing funny about this at all.

"Name," one of them said. He had a *sténo-bloc* and a Bic ballpoint pen. None of them had the faintest accent in French and were consequently no more Bedouins than I was. Arabs though.

"Nelson."

"First name?"

"Burt."

Born? Hollywood. That's where the hospital was. How far was Hollywood from Los Angeles? It was part of Los Angeles. This earned me wary eyes. What class had I been raised in? Working. Why not? My father worked. Father born? Illinois. Profession? Musician. The Los Angeles Philharmonic? No, he'd been musical director for Bob Hope. Who was Bob Hope? A public-spirited comedian. Had he been born in Illinois? No, he'd been born in England, now that they mentioned it. Did I feel guilt at having seized California from Mexico? No. I knew we'd taken it from Mexico but didn't think about it much, which was no doubt callous of me. University? I missed a couple of beats on this one, but figured I might as well tell them what they could find out easily enough for themselves. No, I hadn't gone to a university. I'd graduated from the U.S. Air Force Academy. I saw their eyes sharpen at this and their whole attitude alter. It was interesting how much you could see through Bedouin face wrappings. After a certain amount of exchanging of glances among my four inquisitors, one of them asked if I didn't feel I had betrayed my class, at which my ability to translate America into Marxist-Moroccan terms broke down. What was the class of Bob Hope's musical director? I couldn't think my way through it.

They'd taken this Air Force business very ill, and I wasn't overly fond of where this sort of subject could lead us either. How had I gotten from the Air Force to the movie business, they asked. Well, ever since I'd been a little boy in Methodist Sunday School, I said, it had been my ambition to do my bit to make movies which would give people spiritual uplift, bring spiritual happiness into their lives. It was embarrassing to talk about myself in such icky terms but this was no time for irony. Irony was no man's friend. What was needed was a positive attitude. And it was true, what was more. It was kind of true. There were true elements in it. But then why the Air Force? Well, I could understand their being puzzled. But what I'd really wanted was a life of public service, and defending my country in the Air Force was serving the public. But I realized now that I'd probably made a lot of mistakes, which was why I was trying to make up for them by writing this pro-Moslem movie so that all men could live in peace and brotherhood. Unless they felt that a movie about the Prophet was sacrilege, in which case just say so and I'd be happy to hear their point of view. I'd give them a fair hearing. I'd give them more than a fair hearing. I'd admit my mistakes. If they'd just tell me what the mistakes were I'd admit them.

They looked at me steely-eyed now in silence.

"Why do you tell us all these lies, Nelson?" the leader said.

"Lies?" I said. "What lies?"

"What are you really doing here in Morocco?"

"Making a picture. Writing this Mohammed picture."

"And what else?"

"Well, I've also got this little fossil stone business."

"And anything else?"

I answered after a natural interval.

"No," I said. "Nothing else."

Two or three of them laughed.

"Nelson," the leader said. "You were at the golf course massacre, weren't you?"

"Yes."

"Why weren't you killed?"

"Well, everybody wasn't killed. I wasn't the only survivor."

"You can think of no reason why you might have been spared when hundreds died?"

"No," I said.

They were silent, just looking at me.

"Luck?" I said.

They paused ominously.

"Nelson," the leader said, his voice angry. "The West has robbed the Arabs of their greatness."

I had a funny tight feeling in my chest. I didn't see what I could say to answer this. It wasn't the kind of remark you could find an answer to that they would necessarily like. What if they'd lost their greatness on their own without us having robbed it, or they'd never had it to begin with? I had to be very careful.

"You have destroyed the Arab's honor by sullying his women," said the leader icily. "You take away the Arab's honor. This debt must be paid."

I saw him coming so early this time it seemed to be in slow motion. The end man rising, striding forward, his hand swooping in an underhand swing because I was sitting on the floor and *zock!* on my ear and cheekbone, my head spinning.

"*Vermin!*" he said and spat on me.

Women, women, I thought as my ears rang. What's this got to do with women?

13

WOMEN. I LAY THERE in the dark feeling really afraid. *Ird.*
Hushûma. Honor. Shame. They killed for things like that.
My mind went back to two Arab villages in Jordan when
we were making *Lawrence of Arabia*, Kufr al Ma and Deir
Abu Said. Three boys from Deir Abu Said were picked up
by police riding in a taxi with a girl their own age from a
very good family of Kufr al Ma. Her father was the ex-
Mayor and the family was related to the regional Pasha, an
ex-Jordanian Senator. It didn't seem too serious at first.
The Kufr al Ma tribe felt their *ird* had been besmirched by
this boy-crazy teenager, but its elders began negotiations
with the Deir Abu Said elders over a financial compensa-
tion for the injured tribe. Arabs think money is very honorable, even more honorable than I do, and the payment of a
price proves the offenders acknowledge their misdeed and
restores the injured parties' *ird*. The two sets of elders were
also negotiating over "sanctuary," an arrangement under
which a third tribe would safeguard the property of the
three boys' families when they were banished from the
area, as was also necessary to restore the injured tribe's *ird*.
Even the boys' distant relatives who didn't get banished
would have to secure sanctuary to protect their property
from raiding on the part of the girl's kinsmen, who were
considered morally justified in stealing and plundering as
much as they could from the boys' tribe to compensate for

all the harm that had been done to them. No one thought about any harm done to the girl. Only the men counted. Meanwhile, when word of the negotiations reached the Pasha, the girl's relative, the ex-Senator, he became indignant, feeling that a money-and-banishment arrangement in return for amnesty was not enough, and he called in all the leading dignitaries of the region and demanded that they refuse amnesty to save HIS *ird* now. It was getting bigger and bigger. They refused amnesty. Then the ex-Mayor and the ex-Senator took the girl for a medical examination, where it appeared, as feared, that she was not a virgin. And bright and early the next morning, the day of the great Moslem "Festival of Sacrifice," the girl's father took his penitent teenage daughter to the boys' home town of Deir Abu Said, right to the house of the boys' guardian. And there, standing on the guardian's doorstep, in the clear, dry desert air, he drew his beautiful Arab dagger, which glinted in the early sun, and stabbed his teenage daughter to death. Killed her. Blood all over. Her begging in terror and screeching and gurgling blood. Then dead. Now you think this man murdered his little daughter. But the Arabs explained it to me. Actually he did this noble thing, saving the tribe's *ird* and effacing the *hushûma* felt by all the girl's kinsmen because she wasn't a virgin. It was the *boys'* tribe which had really murdered her, as the father proved by going through the mechanics of the thing on the boys' tribe's doorstep. The news of the father's virtuous action reached his home town just as the men were leaving the mosque after the Festival prayers and they marched in a body to the police station to cheer him as a hero. He was released without punishment. The boys' families all had to leave the area as well as dozens of other families of their tribe, because of the part they'd played in murdering the girl by being related to the boys, you see. Only very distant relations of the boys were allowed to remain on condition they paid a bribe known as the "sleeping camel." For all the trouble he'd caused his family one of the boys was murdered by his father. Either

that or he was murdered in connection with another im-
broglio that had nothing to do with this at all. And so the
sun sets on romantic Arabia.

That's the kind of story you remembered when a bunch
of Arabs accused you of sexual misbehavior with an Arab
woman and you were lying in the dark in a chicken wire
cage wondering what they were going to do with you. Fears
for their honor when their women were involved incited
these people to really gruesome behavior. It happened all
the time. In Cairo a young man in his twenties had just
murdered his widowed mother for keeping company with a
new man. It shamed his father's memory, he said. No punishment.

A great national hero in Egypt is a soldier who heard his
sister had become a prostitute, tracked her down, and killed
her. He's alive and happy today, celebrated in song and
legend, kind of an Egyptian Audie Murphy. *When a man's
tree grows into another man's garden he must cut it off.*
Women were these trees that grew into other people's gardens. You tried to hold this down in advance of course by
cutting off part of the woman, which is to say her clitoris
and all that. Great nauseating subject. Great ungenteel subject. Great undiscussed subject. Great unreported subject
by Westerners because it's so disgusting they can't bear to
think about it. Practiced from Morocco to Oman but dwelt
on only by me as I lay in my sweaty black cage of chicken
wire and wondered what these murderous bastards were
going to do to me. I'd seen what it looked like, man; it made
you want to throw up. I'd asked Mohammed Maziq about it.
He and another Libyan giggled. "Peasants," he said. Peasants
did it. It was a very low-class thing to do. But I'd heard it
was done even by the Arab bourgeoisie. Was it done by any
families he knew? He didn't answer, his eyes evasive.

Women. I was really very afraid. I didn't know if it was
day or night. I couldn't sleep. *Ird. Hushûma.* I'd sullied
Arab women, they said. But who had I sullied but Mouna?
It struck me now as a searing injustice that they should
consider Mouna an Arab, because I realized now that I

160

thought about it that Mouna was about as Arab as Vanessa Redgrave. It was absurd. She was a Christian. She had a Western upbringing. She shared Western sexual morality, even more so. There was nothing Arab about her at all, except she happened to speak Arabic, and she looked a little Arabic. How could they count her as an Arab? They were counting her though. I was kind of shaking. What were they going to do to me? It was all illogical even from the Arab point of view, I thought desperately. If they were going to do it by the book the Arab way it all had to be by bloodlines. First, word had to get back about his daughter's misbehaving to Mouna's father, a banker back in Beirut, at the Intra Bank, I think. He didn't give a damn. I swear to you as God is my witness that he didn't give a damn. And if he did give a damn this is what he'd have to do. He'd have to get on the plane and come to Marrakesh. Then he'd have to grab Mouna and drag her along the corridor at the Hilton and kill her in front of Omar's door, because he'd sullied her most, hadn't he? With his Mormon wife back in Bel Air? Then he could stab Mouna again if he wanted to in front of Mohammed Maziq's door, because he'd sullied her too, and some other Arabs had sullied her, Omar said. Why pick on me because I was a Methodist? I was hot and sweating and my mind was in a seething rage, and I was desperate and shaking with fear that they were going to castrate me, and I was furious because it was so unjust. They weren't even doing it right. The point was that someone of Mouna's blood should kill *Mouna* to wipe out the dishonor to their blood. They were supposed to kill Mouna! Okay, let them do it even in front of my door at the Hilton. Let them shame me. I'd willingly leave town in disgrace. I'd pay them a sleeping camel. And these guys weren't even related to her! They were doing it all wrong! I lay there all sweaty and sleepless in the dark, and was terrified and enraged and felt there was no justice. So far they'd only slapped me, which was comparatively almost a pleasure; they could do that as long as they liked. But I was very, very afraid of these savage Arabs who cut things off people, including

161

tongues. I'd heard that too. Maybe so I wouldn't be able to boast how I'd sullied Mouna. And I was lying there in such fear about Mouna and getting things cut off that I completely forgot to worry about KUBARK. Maybe they didn't know anything about KUBARK. Maybe I was just up on this sex rap. The thought brought no solace.

The light went on. A Bedouin with his face wrapped up came in and sat on the stool, very casually, and pointed a submachine gun at me through the chicken wire and released the safety catch. I could hear my heart thumping.

"Clint Eastwood," he said.

I said nothing. It didn't seem to call for an answer.

"Clint Eastwood," he said again.

What was I supposed to say? What was he talking about? Was I Clint Eastwood? Was he Clint Eastwood? Was Clint Eastwood a mutual friend?

"You Clint Eastwood," he said. He didn't speak French like the other ones.

"No," I explained to him. I was not Clint Eastwood. Nor did I know Clint Eastwood. And would he please put his safety back on? I was behind all this chicken wire and even if I were to sweep it all away with a mighty paw like King Kong for example he'd still have plenty of time to release his safety. In the meantime just a fraction of an ounce of careless pressure on the trigger and I'd be splattered all over the wall.

"Clint Eastwood," he said.

"The safety catch," I pleaded quietly. This time I gave him urgent sounds and gestures. All that stout chicken wire (pointing). The trigger (pointing at that). What if he dozed off (dozed)? Just the tiniest little bit of pressure on the trigger (trigger) and paff! paff! paff! I'd be filled with holes (holes). In agony (agony). Dead (dead).

Silence.

"The safety catch," I said. "That little gizmo there."

"Guh. Guh," he said. Something glottal. And then appeared to unbend as if to say, *Oh the safety. Is that all. Why didn't you say so? Sure, why not?* He put the safety catch back on and seemed to be smiling under his desert mask.

"Clint Eastwood," he said.

Clint Eastwood again. He couldn't seriously think I was Clint Eastwood, could he? Could it be that I reminded him of Clint Eastwood? And then it came to me that I was merely supposed to express recognition, establish a link. We both knew who Clint Eastwood was, didn't we? He was an American like me, wasn't he? My guard had only wanted to satisfy himself that I *knew* of Clint Eastwood. But of course I did! *Bien entendu!*

"Right, absolutely!" I said. "Clint Eastwood! Big Hollywood star! Spaghetti Westerns. Italy. In Hollywood now. Clint Eastwood. Absolutely. My wife was a big fan of Clint Eastwood's. Do I ever know of Clint Eastwood."

My guard seemed reassured.

"Olly Wood," he said.

"Right," I said. "Big star of Olly Wood. Clint Eastwood. I know of him very much. I know of him quite a lot. Very definitely. Clint Eastwood."

The guard was satisfied now and sat peacefully, but still keeping his weapon trained in my direction, interfering with my thinking. It was hard to concentrate when someone was tracking every little movement you made with an automatic weapon, even with the safety catch on. It made you self-conscious. After about an hour he left and turned off the light. It was an odd system. With the light on I required an armed guard with a submachine gun, but with it off the wire cage was enough.

Blackness again. It was hard to think in the dark. Perhaps I needed exercise. Now that I'd seen what my cell looked like in the light it felt psychologically much easier moving around and I did some sit-ups and push-ups and stoop-falls, then jogged in place. But it felt very strange doing exercises in total darkness, as if it was all internal, as if there was nothing out there. Most peculiar of all was the jogging. Although I tried hard to stay in one place I kept drifting around as I jogged, bumping into the walls or the

163

wire. To me it seemed as if I was absolutely staying in one place and then out of the night these walls would come and hit me. I was very hot now, pouring sweat, and sat cross-legged on the floor. They hadn't fed me yet.

I heard footsteps crossing the room outside and the light came on. A man in a KKK-type face mask unlocked my dog kennel door and I crawled out. He gave me a stool and I sat on it. A second one came in wearing a similar mask, the masks looking as if they'd been made out of sugar sacks, with eye and mouth holes snipped out with scissors. The eye holes hung down lower than their actual eyes, giving them a hound dog look, but I was certain these were two of the four who had questioned me before. The second one was holding something behind his back.

"Stick out your arm," he said. "Clench your fist."

"Why?"

"We want to relax you."

"But I'm already relaxed."

"This will relax you more."

He had a hypodermic needle, disinfectant, cotton swab, the full kit. I was terrified and threw a tantrum. I was allergic to sodium pentathol, scopolamine, all that stuff! I screamed at them. I had a weak heart! I would die! They looked lackadaisical, as if when a man's time had come, it had come. Just put in a very small dose! I begged them. Just give me a quarter of a dose! I carried on so the first man finally took a revolver out of his belt and put it right at the side of my head. "The needle or a bullet," he said. It calmed me down.

I clenched my fist. The other one fumbled for a vein, at last got it in. I looked the other way; I think he didn't give me the full shot. For a few seconds nothing happened.

"Get off the stool, lie down, and start counting," he said.

The floor felt very soft, as if I was on a foam-rubber mattress. I got to eight and my head began to swim, and I dozed off. It was like taking a nap at the beach. You could hear the ocean. When I woke up all four of them were sitting on their stools staring at me. Four hound dogs. I had a worm's-eye view of them this time from the floor, which was very comfortable.

"Hiya, fellas," I said. "What's up?"

They seemed amused at this, although I didn't see why.

"How's things in the kidnapping business?" I said.

It was a little like being drunk, but more like good kif. I'd had this stuff before when I broke a collarbone doing judo in the Air Force.

"You don't ask the questions, Nelson. We ask the questions," said the leader.

"Okay," I said.

They paused.

"Let her rip," I said.

They looked at each other as if they were going to have to put up with this.

"Give us the names of all the people who are working on this motion picture of yours," the leader said.

"Aw, come on," I said. "You don't need me for that. Call the publicist. You can find that out from anybody."

I was pervaded by a sense of *bonhomie*. I felt pretty good.

"What's the name of the King of Morocco?" the leader said.

"The King of *Morocco*," I said. "What kind of a question is that? Don't you know the name of the King of Morocco?"

"Just answer the question, Nelson."

I thought. It wasn't as easy a question as it seemed. Actually I knew perfectly well who the King of Morocco was but it would take me a little while to find him. I'd kind of misplaced him.

"You know I'm Nelson," I said to while away the time. "But who are you, *amigo*? What do I call you? Señor No Name?"

"Why do you speak Spanish?" asked the leader.

"I was raised by this crazy Mexican," I said, which seemed rather entertaining as I said it. "English is my mother tongue and Spanish is my maid tongue."

"And French?"

"Oh, I don't know. Why shouldn't I? Who is he anyway?"

I didn't have this stitched together right and my questioners were looking at each other. But I thought the conversation was rather enjoyable myself. It had *bonhomie*.

"What do you think of the King of Morocco?" the leader asked.

"He's an asshole," I said. "I guess. Isn't he?"

"We're asking what you think," said the leader, the questioners looking at each other again.

"He had a lot of guts that day at the golf course, believe you me."

"And what do you think of the golf course *coup*?"

My mind stopped. There was a numb area. Way off someplace there was something to watch out for.

"He really can give a party," I heard myself saying.

"What party are you talking about?" the leader said.

"No."

"No what?"

My mind was like wet dough. I couldn't think of anything. This wasn't such a great conversation after all.

"Missed," I said.

"Missed what?"

"The *party!*" I shouted at them.

They laughed and there was *bonhomie* again.

"Ha, ha," I said. "The King's an asshole. You can quote me."

They asked me more stuff. When did commercial airliners come and go? How many kilometers was it to Rabat? They were trying me for coherence and consistency under a truth drug, I think. Good luck to them. My mind wandered. I thought I'd take another little nap. I was on the beach at Venice, California, trying to make a phone call at a public phone box, but something was wrong, they wouldn't give me the number. And this girl with a whopping Southern accent comes up and says, "Ah'll do it," and says to the operator, "But he already *put* in the money. All raht. Here's mah brother now." And she hands me the phone. And then

166

these jokers from *The Sheik of Araby* are back telling me I'm an enemy of the Moroccan people.

"Why?" I said.

They explained it to me. They had reasons. I don't remember. It was all woozy. Amid a swirl of other items there was a membership card to the Club Méditerranée they'd found in my wallet and something about the Club Méditerranée having a quota system; it was anti-Moroccan. Who owned the Club Méditerranée, they asked me. I didn't even know. Some Jew? Edmond de Rothschild? It was all making me sleepy. I was heading back to Venice, California. Where did that girl come from? Who was she anyway?

"We are going to get a million dollars' ransom for you," someone said.

My eyes opened.

"Who?"

"For you. We're holding you for a million dollars' ransom."

They were all staring at me. It was very quiet.

"You're not serious."

"Yes, we are," the leader said solemnly.

I could hear my pulse pounding in my ears.

"Who's going to pay that kind of money for me?"

"Your masters in Hollywood," he said. Just like that.

"Hollywood!" I gasped. "There's not a penny of Hollywood money in this movie!"

I could hear Arab music somewhere outside.

"It's all Arab money!" I cried. "I always told you your intelligence was rotten!"

They sat there stolidly.

"If that's the case," the leader said, "then the Saudis will pay."

"But it's not Saudi money either! It's Libyan money!"

"Do not resort to lies, Nelson," one of them warned.

"But it's not a lie," I said, exhausted. "Ask anybody."

There was an amount of exchanging of glances among my interrogators.

"The Moroccan government might pay," said the leader.

"Why should the Moroccans pay?" I moaned. "They

wouldn't give a used jelly bean for me. You should have grabbed Omar at least. A million dollars. Do you realize? Are you out of your mind? Rabat?"

They didn't know anything, I thought mournfully as I lay there on the floor. It was hopeless.

"Did you ever work in Hollywood?" the leader asked.

"Once," I said disconsolately.

"For what company?"

"Fox. Look," I implored them. "Nobody is going to pay a million dollars for me. I'm not worth it. You've got the wrong person, I swear to you. A million dollars? This is a big mistake. It really is. Now you gave me truth serum, would I tell you a lie? Let me go and all is forgiven! It so happens I'm a true friend of the Moroccan people."

"*La Fox* will pay," said the leader.

"*La FOX!*"

This was the stuff of tragedy.

14

THEY CAME. They went. I crawled out. I crawled back. They
gave me cold *couscous* to eat. I shat in a wastepaper basket,
washed myself with my left hand, ate with my right hand.
They left the light on. I did push-ups. I ran in place. They
gave me Régis Debray to read, an electric razor. They
brought me an underground doctor in a face mask, who took
my blood pressure, listened to my heart with a stethoscope,
tapped my knee with a rubber hammer, told me I was in
terrific shape. What the fuck did he know. I was dying
from nervous anxiety and he tells me I'm in terrific shape.
My blood count was okay too, he said, so they had underground laboratories. Did anybody out there even know I
was gone? Were they looking for me? Were there police
sweeps? Roadblocks? Every so often the lights would flicker
out and a guard with his super lumijet would stand and
aim a pistol at me through the wire and say, "If they come
in, you get it," then the lights would go on again. The drill
was not something I enjoyed that much and I wasn't so
anxious to have them find me actually.

The Politburo came and talked to me for about an hour
every day, because it would have been cruel and unusual
punishment to leave me with only Régis Debray. I told
them time and again that it was all a big mistake, hell would
freeze over before anyone was going to pay a red cent to
ransom me, my market value was nil, but they persisted in
thinking they had hold of something real valuable. I was

worthless, I told them. No, no, they said. Worthless. Valuable. Worthless. Valuable. They finally brought me a tape recorder, my dreams of glory come true, at last I would address the world. *Dear friends and well-wishers*, I said. *I am alive and in good health. These revolutionaries are giving me plenty of couscous and are really quite a nice bunch. Although they say they will really kill me if you don't come across with some money. This is me okay. I am a little anxious, but what can you expect?* I don't know what I said. Presumably it was so people could recognize my voice, if they cared. "Why don't you give me some more of that sodium pentathol?" I asked them. "That was groovy stuff." But no more of that for me; they had to watch their supply. Time dragged on. I was going crazy. Actually it wasn't so bad. Now that it looked as if they weren't the kind of Arabs that cut off things that grew into other people's gardens I felt a lot better. This was the new Arab, a type I hadn't seen much of but was glad to see emerge. It was an untested mutant but I was all for it. Probably straight from Saint-Germain-des-Prés. No torture, humane treatment, just a slap now and then. It showed you what a French education could do, and also the benevolent potential of socialism as a creed, and was kind of an interesting experience in a way, I supposed, though not without anxieties, like would they kill me.

When I'd finished Régis Debray they gave me a copy in French of Marighela's Brazilian "Mini-Manual of the Urban Guerrilla." *Kidnapping figures known for their artistic, sporting, or other activities who have not expressed their political views may possibly provide a form of propaganda favorable to revolutionaries, but should be done only in very special circumstances and in such a way as to ensure that people will view it sympathetically. But kidnapping American personalities who live in Brazil or who have come to visit here is a most important form of protest against the penetration of U.S. imperialism into our country.* Glug. There it was. My arrest warrant. Like you had to be careful with kidnappings, but if they were *gringos* go right ahead. I read the Mini-Manual three times from cover to cover. It felt spooky to see things from their point of view. I was drawn into it for whole moments, as if I was this guerrilla who thought it was a most important form of protest to kidnap Americans. But then I became this American again who wanted to get the hell out.

I almost immediately was able to tell my captors apart even behind their masks or face wrappings, from the way they moved, from their general shape, from their voices. The individual particularities of their masks became as personal as faces. The odd snippings of a scissors seemed to reveal character. One's mouth hole was bigger than the others. One's eye holes were cut asymmetrically and gave him a loony look. The leader, at least the one who talked the most, was a stocky man with a noticeable eye blink. In my mind I called him Blinky. In fact it gave me comfort somehow to give them all names. One, thinner than the others, was String Bean, although not very tall. The drooping eye holes gave them all a hound dog look, but one even more so than the others, and him I called Bird Dog. The one with the large, rectangular mouth was Big Mouth. The nonspeaking guards were harder to personalize, although Clint Eastwood would of course forever remain Clint Eastwood. I could never figure out if the two who'd grabbed me the first night were in the group. I still had a sharp impression of the abduction scene, and my abductors' presence, and could see their hard, dark, intent faces in the glow of the flashlight, but the scene seemed too different, too far away, nothing like this life in a dog kennel. I'd have to see them again in a similar setting. That had been a thrilling, romantic ride that night though. It had been dangerous but we were going places. I had pleasant memories of it.

The interrogations were a mess, the same material over and over again. They kept after me about my connection with the Golf Course Coup but never came up with a theory. How could they figure it out; I could barely figure it out. They kept hinting they knew I was a special person, which was always disquieting, but they never exposed a clear theory on that either, and no help were they going to get from me. No, no. And there was the ransom. I told them to ask the Libyans for the money, but it was funny how they backed away from that. They asked me who else had money in the picture and I told them Abu Dhabi. Why didn't they go ask the Abu Dhabians, I told them, a good, reactionary, feudal regime, honored member of the United Arab Emirates? They didn't buy that either. Even *partners* of the Libyans were privileged. I was a Royal Moroccan tool, they told me, a tool of King Ahmed. Absolutely not, I said. I was a Libyan tool. Moroccan. Libyan. Moroccan. Libyan. They told me I was amoral, had no conscience, was a frivolous man. They explained to me that frivolity was a psychological defense, that I had a typical colonialist attitude, that I didn't respect Arab culture. They told me I had used Mouna Saadi and cast her aside as soon as my lust was satisfied. I almost suffocated. Real up-to-date intelligence. I'd shagged her two days before they grabbed me. And what kind of Arab morality was that? It sounded more like Fannie Hurst to me. But I didn't argue. Better to be the man who cast Mouna Saadi aside as soon as his lust was satisfied than other things I could think of. How was old Mouna, I wondered to myself. Did she love me in August as she did in July? What was going on in the great world outside?

Sometimes my captors and I had long debates with lots of ideological give and take about colonialism and capitalism as if they were brainwashing me, which I didn't mind. Let them wash my brain a little. But then they'd spoil everything by slamming me one. Everything was relative. If you thought they were getting ready to cut something off you then a few *baffes* seemed like a bagatelle, but when you were deep in an ideological debate with free interplay of ideas and they belted you it made you sore. It spoiled the intellectual pleasure of conversation. Capitalism was the exploitation of man by man, they told me. Whereas, I said, socialism was the opposite. For a little thing like that they slammed me. What kind of an equal conversation was that? And I didn't like slamming just on general principles. One slam led to another slam. And where would it end? My mind would drift back now and then to Mouna, with her high ideals, a light unto the nations, who reminded me in a funny way of a French girl I knew who had such high ideals she'd managed to sleep with two crowned heads (Middle East), two conservative prime ministers (Europe), two revolutionary leaders (Africa), and Che Guevara. All in her efforts to spread the light. Sometimes they were down to asking me how we grew oranges in California. Morocco grows oranges.

They were inconsistent as hell about the ransom. The night they'd grabbed me, one of my captors had said they weren't interested in money. Then these guys told me they wanted a million dollars. Then one day a new one comes in and says they're not interested in money again. Why didn't they shape up! Make up their minds! I was guilty of collaboration with a corrupt tyrannical despotism by even being in Morocco, this one said. A man of conscience would have refused even to come as a sign of moral disapproval, and I would have to take what was coming to me. Which had its own logic, but what was coming to me? Polarization, that's what was coming to me. Polarization? Was I going to be polarized? How did you do that? "No, *crétin*," he said. "Morocco is going to be polarized." By what? By this spark. He was very serious. *Iskra*. It had a very gritty taste to it. It made me depressed. I didn't want him to tell me about the spark. He thought, they thought, that this, I didn't even want to hear about it.

Had it occurred to them that they might be overrating me a little, I asked them. First they thought I was so loved and cherished that people were going to lay out a zillion dollars just to get me back. Now they thought I was so widely despised that capturing me was going to make them national heroes, or divide the country up, the Nelsonites and the anti-Nelsonites, as if I was the Dreyfus Case or somebody. Mobs were going to surge through the streets. *Free Nelson! Down with Nelson! Up with Nelson!* "These things take time to ripen," String Bean said in a hard voice. So I was supposed to languish in this people's prison in Marrakesh waiting for objective historical circumstances to ripen in Morocco. First the delicate blossoms would appear. Then, slowly, the fruit would grow heavy on the branch. And finally, when the scent of wisteria was in the air, the full round fruit would fall: socialism, human brotherhood, from each according to his capacity, to each according to his need. They sat there, all five of them now, looking at me. Of this humble clay were they going to fashion a revolutionary fruit. Me.

Books. I devoured books. Avant-garde socialist stuff, they brought me: Che Guevara's journals, *The Protocols of the Elders of Zion*, which I'd been hearing about all my life but had never read, printed right in Cairo. The *Protocols* are one hell of a book, let me tell you, hard to read really, very deep, but when it got a grip on you, you couldn't put it down. There's this secret world government of Jews, are you with me? And these Jews are causing depressions, and inflations, and assassinations, and national debt. They're behind every political party without exception (in the West I guess), using liberalism as a blind just to bamboozle people. And they're undermining morality too, and promoting atheism. In fact just about everything bad you've ever heard of is caused by Jews: monopolies, the armaments race, wars, alcoholism, prostitution, secret police, blackmailing . . . Jews invented plutocracy, the rule of gold. They invented the visual media to turn Gentiles into unthinking submissive beasts. They're placing their agents as governesses and tutors in Gentile homes to corrupt the young. They had subway systems dug so if anybody gives them any trouble they can blow up all the big cities, after which they can inoculate remaining resisters with frightful diseases. I'm telling you the *Protocols* really turned my head around about Jews. I knew it was taught in Egyptian schools and had been strongly recommended by Adolf Hitler and Nasser, not to mention Idi Amin, but when I read it, wow, it was dynamite. In the last sections it's real scary, foretelling the future, which is kind of like Orwell's *1984*, but with Jews out in the open now, and everybody Jewish. It really sent chills up and down your spine.

My captors were just the tiniest bit embarrassed about it, I had the feeling. It would serve as an antidote to what we got in America, they told me. It explained the Israeli lobby. "The Israeli lobby," I said. "It explains fallen arches." Don't be smart, Nelson, they said sternly. A famous Jew once boasted publicly that three hundred Jews, who all knew each other, controlled the destiny of world capitalism. Look how many American Cabinet members were Jews. These guys were a little batty on the subject of Jews. They were internationalist and socialist and humane, and then they came to Jews and to Israel and they changed from the New Arab into the Old Arab. But the *Protocols* were really something, and since they didn't give me anything else for a while I reread it. God, in the West we couldn't get away with stuff like that anymore. Maybe I was pitching this Mohammed movie too high for Arab taste. Maybe they'd think it was highbrow. Deep down in my heart of hearts I secretly envied the wacky Russian who'd concocted the *Protocols*. Here I wrote nourishing stories about peace and friendship and how thou shouldst fear no evil even though thou walkest through the valley of the shadow of death, and wholesome accounts of Communist plots, and was well paid for it, but aesthetes sneered. And this crazed Russian probably on starvation wages puts together this pathetic fake out of a fifty-year-old French satire on Napoleon III, dressing it up with slavophile ravings, and it circles the world a hundred times, the most influential book since *Origin of Species*, and now even when it had passed out of style in the West it still held a large part of the world in thrall: just because the Czarina happened to have it on her when the Bolsheviks gunned her down in the basement in Ekaterinenberg. Such shabby stuff, no uplift in it at all. Maybe I should be more crazed.

Say what you will, confinement gets a man down. Here I was in this Arab underground prison, destined perhaps to pass away without ever having won any hearts or any minds at all for all I knew, with church attendance dropping, and this semi-literate Russian had earned immortality. I wasn't paranoid enough, that was the trouble with me. I should learn from the *Protocols*, drink deep. Then they gave me another book fresh off the Cairo presses by some guy named Dr. Abdullah al-Tall about the Jewish custom of bleeding Gentile children to death because they need their blood to mix with this unleavened bread at Passover. They place the Gentile kid in a barrel fitted out with lots of hollow needles which pierce the kid's body and drain off his blood, and have the additional advantage of being excruciatingly painful which the Jews feel purifies the blood for Passover. The Jews have lots of interesting customs like that, says Dr. Abdullah al-Tall, who I guess should know since he's a doctor. Adolf Eichmann was a "martyr who fell in the holy war," he says. Drink deep. Drink deep. But it was hard to drink deep of stuff like that. It didn't go down easy. There were times I felt that between me and my captors there was this gulf. Me and Dr. Abdullah al-Tall were engaged in a desperate struggle for the hearts and minds of the Arab people. I was taking the high road, trying to bring out their better selves with my truly superior Mohammed movie, while he was going the low, easy, crowd-pleasing route with his barrels of hollow needles. And who would win? Somber thought. Dr. Abdullah al-Tall maybe.

"Nelson, prepare yourself," Blinky said one time with excitement in his voice. "We're going to bring a major international journalist to interview you."

"Hot dog. Who?"

"Never mind. You'll find out in due time. We want the outside world to know how well we're treating you."

"You're not treating me so hot," I said. "Where's my peanut butter?"

"Be serious, Nelson. We're not murderers, and the best way for you to get out of this is to just tell this journalist the truth."

"Aren't you afraid he'll give you away?"

176

"He'll be blindfolded. Don't worry. We know how to cover our traces."

Days passed. No journalist.

"Nelson! Attention! Sit by the grill!"

The door opened and a girl with a sugar sack over her head was led in. She wore an ankle-length skirt made up of ninety-two pieces of blue denim at various stages of bleached-outness. Her well-manicured hands grasped anxiously the shoulders of one of the Moroccans who preceded her; she seemed unsteady of foot. The Moroccans sat her down on a chair right in front of me and lifted the sugar bag off her head. Underneath was a blindfold and they removed that too. She was very pretty, about twenty-five, with brown stylishly cut hair, and in addition to the skirt wore a blue chiffon blouse and Indian wrist bangles. Around her neck hung a gold grandpa pocket watch, and from her shoulder a Sony TC-120 tape recorder. The Moroccan honchos sat back along the wall on stools, clearly intending to monitor the interview. I was sitting at about the level of this girl's knee and felt like a monkey in a cage. She looked flustered.

"Oh, I didn't know," she said in English. "I was expecting someone with shorter hair."

"I've been here a while," I offered, wondering how the Moroccans were going to be able to follow the conversation in English. Perhaps they were there to make sure I didn't bite her fingers if she stuck them through the wire.

"It looks as if it was pretty long to begin with," the girl giggled.

I didn't see why we should be talking about my hair.

"You are Birdie Nelson," she said, bending forward, seeking confirmation.

"No," I said. "I'm Burt Nelson."

"But you are the one who's the prisoner of the National Liberation Council?"

"I suppose so," I said. "Who are they?"

"They're the ones who took you prisoner. These people here."

"Well, if I'm their prisoner, and you say they're that, I guess they're who they say they are. Who are you?"

She blushed slightly and smiled.

"I don't feel I should say."

I looked up at her, of necessity, and waited.

"I'm embarrassed," she said, flushed now, the heat beginning to get to her. "I didn't think they were really going to take me to see you, so I don't have my questions structured."

"That's all right. I'll ask you questions. What's going on out there?"

"Should I start my tape recorder?" she asked. "I only have one cassette."

"Why don't you leave it off for the time being," I said. "When we come to something good we can put it on then."

She smiled bashfully.

"Are you a journalist?" I said. "If you don't mind my asking?"

There was a flutter of hesitation.

"I'm just beginning," she said in a sweet voice, pushing her knees to one side and trying to lower herself to get closer to my level.

"May I ask where this story of yours is going to appear?"

"That all depends."

She took a deep breath.

"I feel it's only fair to tell you that I am a convert to Islam," she said, "and that one of my principal reasons for conversion was the position of women in their society, which I feel is more future-oriented."

"You're kidding."

"From a societal point of view," she added thoughtfully.

"How long have you been living in Arab countries?"

"I've arrived rather recently," she said evasively, perspiration beginning to show on her face. "But Arab men I know very well have given me a great deal of information."

"What Arab country are they from?"

"I don't think I should say."

"Does it begin with an 'L,' otherwise to hell with it."

There was a flicker of something before she repeated in

her syrupy way that she couldn't say. I asked her about the world outside and she couldn't say that either. I looked at the Moroccans. They seemed neutral. Did they have English? What were they making of this?

"Well, let's get on with it," I said. "What do you want to ask me?"

"Oh," she said, disconcerted. "Yes." She fished in her brass-decorated Moroccan leather handbag for a note pad and ballpoint. "Should I start the tape recorder?"

"What have we got to lose?"

She set it turning with a distrustful pushing of buttons.

"Uh, where were you born?" she said, and went on like that, but by the time we got me up to the fourth grade she was suddenly warmed up and proceeding under her own power.

"Tell me," she said, her eyes glistening. "Deep down, didn't you secretly want to be taken prisoner by the National Liberation Council?"

"No."

"Without consciously being aware of the desire," she said, "don't you think that something within you desired it? Because you were so careless? The secretly wished accident is a very well known phenomenon, you know."

"No."

"I don't say you planned it," she added hurriedly. "I don't mean you openly said to yourself, 'I wish that the National Liberation Council would take me prisoner.' But somewhere inside, don't you think something in you desired it without the desire being structured? Something in your unconscious? Some unconscious desire to pay for American sins?"

I couldn't believe this girl. "No," I said again.

"Because it's not enough that we should pay them more money for their oil," she crooned. "We have to pay for all the bad things America has done in the world. Someone must atone. Don't you think you had some such unconscious wish? Which is why you're where you are?"

"What in God's name's the matter with you?" I snapped. "Why don't you at least ask me questions instead of giving

179

me your opinions? I do not want to atone. I want to get the hell out of here. You can atone if you like."

Water off a duck's back. She looked at me with commiserating eyes.

"I am atoning," she said sadly.

"Well, good for you. Then change places with me and you can atone some more."

She shook her head pityingly.

"This is an outrage!" I protested. "Here I am rotting in this lousy People's Prison, and instead of a journalist they send me the likes of this."

"I can understand that you're upset," she said. "I know that imprisonment causes resentments. The problem is to avoid boredom and despair. So you structure your time, don't you? What do you do, play cards?"

"No."

"What do you do?"

"I knit."

"Do you really?"

"No."

"What *do* you do?"

"Push-ups." This woman was driving me crazy. "I can do a hundred push-ups."

"Is that a lot?"

"Of course it's a lot. Haven't you ever tried to do push-ups?"

"Is that enough to keep your mind active? Do you read?"

"I would love to read but the lending library here is kind of thin. Marighela's *Mini-Manual of the Urban Guerrilla*. Guevara's *Guerrilla Warfare*. Dr. Abdullah al-Tall's *The Danger of World Jewry to Islam*."

"Perhaps I should have brought you something," she said, troubled.

"Well, it's too late now."

"I have some excellent revolutionary literature. Or the Bible perhaps? Are you into Christianity?"

"Am I into Christianity," I said.

And it went on. I begged her to tell me what was happening outside. Were there any new wars? Revolutions? Was anybody looking for me? Were they writing about me in the *Los Angeles Times*? But that was against her instructions. She asked me if I believed in the principles of the American Declaration of Independence, that a government drew its power from the consent of the governed, and that the people had the right to overthrow any government they no longer felt represented them. I told her it was a hell of a place to have a free discussion on political philosophy, me in the slam with machine guns pointing at me, her on a tourist's visit to a People's Prison. Then I figured I might as well humor her and said what the hell, if it was in the Declaration of Independence it was good enough for me. Whether or not the Moroccan government had the consent of the governed I didn't know though, being a foreigner. Let them fight it out maybe. May the best Arab win.

"So I can write that you realize there's nothing personal about your being captured by the National Revolutionary Council," she said. "But that you see they're dedicated idealists, and you were captured because of collective guilt, and you realize that your execution would be an act of social justice. In a way."

"What execution?"

My throat was dry. I didn't take in anything after "execution."

"Oh." Her mouth worked nervously. "Perhaps I spoke out of turn."

"Spoke what."

My heartbeat was thumping in my ears. Several attempts at smiles flickered and died on her face.

"Oh, nothing." She fidgeted with the grandpa watch hanging around her neck. "I don't think I'm at liberty to say. I have certain obligations to representatives of the N.R.C."

I tried to keep my voice calm so the Moroccans sitting along the wall wouldn't think I was threatening her.

"Listen, you little creep," I said. "When you get out of here you're going to go straight to the Marrakesh Hilton and find a Libyan named Mohammed Maziq."

"The American Embassy's been notified already," she said, her eyes enlarged. "I'm at liberty to tell you that."

"Forget about the American Embassy. Unless I miss my guess your friends here are operating on Libyan money. But I don't think they've got it through their heads yet that Kaddafi isn't going to like their mucking around with the author of a movie that's got big Libyan backing. Now you can save the Revolution. You can save the financing of the Revolution. You go to the Hilton and find MOHAMMED MAZIQ and tell him what they're going to do to me! He's a Libyan government Minister!"

"I'm sorry," she said, blinking her eyes. "I'd like to help. "But the Libyans have all been expelled from Morocco. There aren't any Libyans here anymore."

It was like a seagull flapping along over a beach, zooming and falling, and wheeling around and gliding down the length of the beach again, then turning and heading out to sea. And then he was gone.

15

IT WAS NIGHT. I think it was night. I woke pouring all over with sweat. The room wasn't quite pitch black. From the direction of the doorway came the dimmest pearly fog. The guards were out there somewhere.

Chicken wire. Nailed with a thousand bent-over nails to two wooden uprights bolted to the walls at either end, unmoveable. Not nailed to the tile floor though. Held down only by a third wooden upright in the middle, this one bolted to nothing, just jammed in place between floor and ceiling. The V.C. on night reconnaissance patrol could creep only a foot an hour and slowly turn those Claymore mines around on you while you were looking right at them. Noiselessly. *Inshallah*.

Slowly I moved toward the middle upright and grasped its base with both hands. It wouldn't budge. But the top seemed to have a tiny bit of play, jammed not quite tight against the ceiling, and I took the base again in both hands and gently, gently pulled. Nothing. No movement. Bracing myself, I carefully increased pressure as I pulled again, prepared for the post to give way abruptly, set to block it so it wouldn't slip noisily. Pulling, increasing pressure gradually, my foot in front of the post now to block it if it suddenly came free, I was bathed in sweat, my back muscles straining because of my odd position on the floor. Slowly I pulled again, harder, straining in the dead silence, blocking with my foot, straining, straining, sweat running into my eyes, my mind a hot blur, one last iota of strength. Click. I'd loosened it. I felt faint and stopped to rest. I knew I could move it now. The next time it was the tiniest bit easier, cautiously increasing pressure, desperately straining and then *gleek*, a small squeak as I moved it a quarter of an inch. I tried to raise the post as I pulled, after that, diminishing its downward thrust against the floor. Again I stopped to rest, wiping my wet hands on my trousers. Four or five more displacements and I heard the first faint twang from the chicken wire. Moving this slowly and noiselessly how long was it going to take me? I thought in a panic. Pray for the night to last, darkness. If a guard came by on his rounds, I'd have to try to pass it off as a joke, I supposed. He'd see the humor of it, I was sure. If not *zzap*, too bad. They were going to kill me anyway.

In an hour the chicken wire was really starting to sag and I took the support post in both arms, raising it the tiniest amount. Agonizingly, a millimeter per second, sweat running from every pore, I eased its base toward the center of the cell, the top of the post rotating outwards, producing a tourniquet effect on the soft chicken wire, slowly distending. From what I could make out in the darkness a gap of perhaps two feet had opened between the top of the wire and the ceiling, but climbing up over the wire mesh would be impossible without making a huge amount of noise and, laboriously, millimeter by millimeter again, I edged the base of the post back toward the upright position and began raising the now slack bottom of the wire mesh so I could crawl underneath. Any sharp twang of metal and all would be over and I worked at the speed of a snail, wriggling along on my back now, holding the bottom of the wire up with my hands. Almost to my surprise I made virtually no sound but the slowness was agony, muscle tensed against muscle to displace the border of the wire mesh only a microscopic bit at a time. To move my body an inch was like carrying a hundred-pound sack of cement a mile. When I could no longer support the wire with my hands I rested it on my legs and continued scraping along on my back. It seemed an eternity before I was clear of the wire and stopped, lying on my back on the tile floor, exhausted. But press on, I must press on, and I turned over on my stomach and began crawling toward the door of the room. A finger, then another finger, then the hand a quarter of an inch. Then, spreading my body weight over as large an area as possible, legs, arms, inching my chest a fraction forward, then my pelvis, like a snake. I crept my way to the open door and got my first look at the room beyond. Very dim. I scanned carefully, using the night-vision technique from the military, never staring straight because of the night-blind spot at the center of the retina, but peering thirty degrees off.

It was an empty room of indeterminate size, a barely perceptible luminescence coming from the far corner of the ceiling. As I crept forward I heard a faint, rasping, throat noise and my blood ran cold. Someone was breathing quietly in the darkness. Where was he? Was he sleeping? I realized the dim luminescence was coming from a type of ceiling window the French call a *vasistas* and began writhing toward it, even more cautious now that someone was in the same room. The breathing gradually grew louder, alarmingly clear, until approaching the spot under the *vasistas* and raising myself with excruciating care I could dimly make out the scene and the sleeping body. A ladder leading to the roof. Glass *vasistas* at the top. At the foot of the ladder a shadowy form, sleeping on its side, maskless. Where was his weapon? I hovered over him in the blackness and couldn't locate it. I could make out torso, arms, legs, a dim face. He seemed fully dressed in Western shirt and trousers, lying on a rumpled mattress. In order to climb the ladder I'd have to step over his body. It was possible to do this in silence, and maybe even to climb the ladder in silence, but to force the *vasistas* open at the top would surely wake him. *Where was the gun? Where was the gun? Where was the gun?* My stomach turned over as I realized that the stakes had gone to the limit now and I thought for a second of creeping back quietly to my cell, but I'd gone too far. There could be only two ways out of this night, no fast talk, no jokes. Either I got away or I died.

Where was the gun? It had to be somewhere around his waist or in a pocket. But what if he cried out? It had to be faster than that. It had to be very fast. On all fours I crawled over until I was directly beside his head and slowly raised myself. As I reached a full standing position the body on the mattress began to stretch and ease itself and half roll over while I froze in fear, not breathing. Was he still asleep? Were his eyes open?

"*Ashkayn . . .*" he said groggily.

I kicked him in the head as hard as I could, aiming for the temple. It made a sound like chopping into a watermelon and I fell on him and grabbed his throat, under the jaw, feeling not for the windpipe but the arteries that brought blood to the brain, pressing with my thumbs. He'd made a first convulsive spasm but was offering no resistance now, lying still, motionless. I kept pressing with no notion of time, trying to count, ten, twenty, losing track. A few seconds should bring unconsciousness and thirty death if I had my thumbs right. I released the pressure. All was stillness. He wasn't breathing. I pressed again with my thumbs, time seeming to stop, counting to thirty, forty, fifty, repelled by the body's inertness. But then patted the repellent thing down. His pistol was in a trouser pocket and I took it and slipped it into my belt. Quietly I felt around on the mattress. No other weapon, only a paperback book and a towel. A cloth? What was it? I pushed the end of it inside the waist of my trousers, thinking I would wrap it around my hand to break the glass at the top of the ladder, and cautiously began to climb, consumed with a horror that someone would walk into the room and snap on the lights and *zap*, that would be the end. In a dim phosphorescence at the ladder's top I examined the glass *vasistas*. It had only the ordinary pin-in-hole fastening and all I had to do was carefully unhook it and slowly raise the glass, pushing it back with a tiny squeaking sound until it blocked and hung on its locked hinges.

Out on the flat roof, the night was filled with a faint silvery light and there were dull nocturnal noises. I was in the middle of the Medina. Around were dim roofs, some higher, some lower, with low walls dividing one house from another. But where were the alleys? I'd hoped the Koutoubia minaret might be lit to give me a sense of direction but no buildings could be seen against the dark sky. About a quarter of a mile away was a glow of reflected lights. Was it a square? A night café? I was in desperate haste to get away from the corpse at the foot of the ladder but walked toward the glow at a slow-motion, silent pace. At the edge of the roof was another roof, lower, beyond that a much higher house with a blank wall. I'd be trapped. I reversed my steps and moving in the opposite direction came to a five-foot wall and clambered up and over. The new roof I was on surrounded an area of darkness that I realized was a court. Dropping down into that would just put me inside somebody's house. And whose house? I skirted the court, still quietly because people were sleeping down there, and climbed over another wall, about four feet this time, and then another one a few yards farther on, and rested behind it for a moment. I was going away from the lights but every additional roof that separated me from the ladder I'd climbed brought a giddy headiness. Freedom.

A *vasistas* creaked in the night behind me and I heard the dull thumping of two or three people erupting onto a roof and hushed voices in Arabic. I stayed low behind the wall and felt in my pocket for the revolver and took it out and cocked it, feeling I had a brief advantage over them since they'd just come out into the night from brightly lit rooms and wouldn't be able to see for several minutes. *You just come after me in the dark, you sons of bitches*, I thought. *You just come after me.* I listened, hardly breathing, for the sound of footsteps coming in my direction. *Whump. Thud.* The sound of someone climbing a wall. Then: *Pad.*

Pad. Pad. Pad. I turned and squatted behind my wall, peering back over the top, but could see nothing. He was still on a lower roof. I extended my pistol waiting for him to appear over the next wall, but discovered in clammy sweat that there was not enough light for me to see my gun sights. I crouched lower, with my gun arm resting on the protective wall, aiming by feel at the spot on the next roof where I expected him to come climbing up. And there he was, a little over to the left, a gray shape, standing now about fifteen yards away, his right arm at waist level as if carrying a pistol.

"*Mash yootutch*," he called back in a low tone to the others, and then came on, step after step, gingerly, blind as a bat. I didn't move a muscle. Another few seconds and he arrived at my wall and placed both hands on its top, gave a jump, twisted, and sat backwards on the wall preparatory to swinging his legs over. At the same time he jumped I rose, took two steps, and fired once into the back of his head.

I heard a muted sound and for an instant thought my pistol hadn't fired, but he slumped sideways onto the wall. My heart racing, I found his right hand and extricated his pistol from his fingers.

"Hammad!" someone called softly. "*Wasstih?*"

The night was as still as before but I walked away briskly, as if I might now be Hammad. The next wall I vaulted, walked on, hoping desperately I would come to a street.

"Hammad!" someone called.

I was above a dimly lit alley, two stories down, with a street light in the distance. Would it lead to a dead end? If they bottled me up in a lighted alley they could cut me down in seconds. Behind me on the roofs their eyes were gradually getting accustomed to the darkness and they'd soon be coming after me. I let myself down over the outside wall, hanging by my hands, then fingers, dropped fifteen feet onto cobblestones, leapt up and, terrified of being in the light, sprinted off to the left. The alley seemed to end in a great double wooden door in the shape of a Moorish arch, then I saw it turned sharply to the right, then left again, and I dashed on. It widened now, still eerily empty, pink-earth walls and street lights and closed doors and not a living creature. I could hear no sound of pursuit but kept running, zigzagging as the street zigzagged, coming to occasional small open places, fountains, benches, all deserted. The street seemed to be following the general shape of a crescent, and I began to be afraid I was running back to where I came from, but saw a square coming up. Trees. Three parked cars. Benches outside a closed café. Deserted. I paused for a second, my chest heaving, and heard the put-put-put of a motorbike. Soon a Moroccan in a khaki uniform appeared riding a black Solex. To avoid any misunderstanding I made sure both pistols were stuffed deep into my pockets. He was almost past me now, heading away.

"Officer!" I called after him.

He kept on put-putting, not even turning his head.

"Au secours! Monsieur l'agent! On m'assassine!" I cried.

He still kept on, not even looking back, and I ran after him, outraged. I didn't care whether it looked that way or not — people were trying to kill me! What was he waiting for, me to be dead first? Soon I came to a larger square, opening out to streets automobiles could drive on, and there was a parked taxi with a driver at the wheel. I ran to it and tried to open the back door. It was locked, the window closed. The driver raised his chin bleakly as if to say, "What's up?"

"Take me to the police station!" I said, turning to look behind me to see if anyone was coming.

"I'm not going that way," said the driver and rolled up his window.

I pulled out a pistol and fired a round into the window by the rear seat. It turned all white and started to fall to pieces like rock candy. I pointed the pistol at the driver.

"The next one's for you, buddy. Open the back door."

The driver's face turned gray and he reached behind him and unlocked the door and I climbed in, sitting on the lumps of broken glass, my pistol still in hand.

189

"What police station?" the driver said.

"How do I know what police station?" I said irritably. "Any police station. The big police station."

As we got underway and hundreds of yards began to separate me from my former captors I began to feel all faint and weak and drowsy, as if I was going to fall asleep, and I just sat there on the back seat, inert, not caring whether I got cut by the glass or not, my right hand with the pistol lying lifeless beside me on the seat. I didn't even know where we were driving. We were outside the Medina now. Greenery. Marrakesh's Beverly Hills. I assumed he was circling the Medina by the outer road, but I began to have second thoughts about driving into a police station in a commandeered taxi with a pistol at the head of the driver. What if he gave them a quick spiel in Arabic and they shot down this mad gunman before I had a chance to give my side of the story. I didn't want any misunderstandings. I was this famous kidnapee, but who was to say they'd recognize me? And what was I doing shooting up taxicabs and driving in armed to the teeth? I didn't want to have to give a five-second explanation in a foreign language after which, if they weren't satisfied, they shot you.

"Take me to the Hilton," I said. "I changed my mind."

The driver slowed the car and made a U-turn. The sky was beginning to get light.

"Don't worry, I won't hurt you," I said. "I just escaped from some revolutionaries."

The driver said nothing.

Coming into the drive at the Hilton I still had my pistol in hand, but didn't want to go walking out of the cab toward the hotel and have my driver do something whimsical like reach into his glove compartment and put a bullet through my back. I just didn't.

"Get out of the car!" I ordered.

When I was out on the pavement I marched him in front of me into the lobby, still covering him with my pistol, which seemed a bit strange even to me, as if I was holding him as a hostage, but I couldn't figure out what else to do. I'd drawn a weapon on him and shot up his car and it didn't seem to me I could count on his good will anymore. Two night clerks behind the desk looked shocked. No one else was in the lobby.

"I'm the man who was kidnapped," I said calmly. "I'm covering this man here because we've had a little difference of opinion. Call the police."

No one moved.

"I'm Mr. Nelson," I said. "I'm a guest at the hotel. Don't you recognize me?"

I didn't recognize them, I thought. Why should they recognize me?

"These revolutionaries came and grabbed me," I said. "I'm lucky to be alive."

Seeing I was getting nowhere I said, "Give me that phone."

"I want my money," said the taxi driver.

"You sit right down there, you fuckhead! And don't move or I'll blow your goddamn brains out! Don't worry, you'll get the cab fare."

"And how about the window?" he growled, but sat down.

The phone rang for quite a while. Sandor sounded very sleepy.

"Sandor," I said. "It's me, Burt."

"*Burt!*" he cried. "*Where are you? How are you?*"

"I'm okay," I said. "I'm right down here in the lobby. I'm coming up to your room. Here, tell these guys I'm on the up and up."

"*Did they let you go?*" asked Sandor.

"Yuh, they let me go," I said. "I was eating too much of their *couscous.*" I handed the telephone to one of the clerks.

"Nobody follows me, you understand?" I said to the clerks and the taxi driver, his face surly, sitting now on a lobby couch.

I covered them both with my pistol and slowly backed across the lobby, turned the corner and walked swiftly to the elevator. Pressing the button, I still kept the empty corridor covered with my pistol. Even on Sandor's floor I couldn't bring myself to lower it and walked down the corridor, weapon at the ready. A chambermaid came around the corner with a tray.

"Don't be afraid," I said. "I'm not a burglar. I'm just coming to see a friend."

"Burt!" said Sandor, looking as if he had tears in his eyes. He wanted to hug me, the crazy Hungarian.

I backed my way into the room and bolted the door.

"You know how to shoot?" I asked him and handed him my pistol, which still had four rounds left. I reached into my left pocket and dragged out my second one, seeing it in the light now for the first time. It was a Smith and Wesson. I broke it open. Fully loaded.

"You cover the balcony," I said. "I'll cover the door."

"Take it easy, Burt, for Christsake," he said. "Take it easy. You're safe here."

"Oh, yeah? I was lying in a bed just like this and those two motherfuckers came right in the window. Anybody I don't like comes in that door I'm blowing his fucking head off."

"They're calling the cops," said Sandor. "Take it easy. How are you? Are you okay?"

He sat down on the chair across from me in his pajama bottoms, the hair on his chest gray.

"I'm terrific," I said. "I never felt better in my life."

"You're shaking like a leaf, Burt."

"I am not," I said. "I'm just out of breath."

"Maybe lie down a little, get a little rest," he said. "Rest up."

I lay back but wouldn't give him my second pistol, not on your life.

"You keep watch," I said.

"Maybe I give you a tranquilizer," said Sandor.

"I don't want a tranquilizer! Keep your eyes peeled, god damn it!"

I lay there with my eyes closed and felt really terrific. It came in waves, exultation, then a hollow, empty feeling, then funny surges of nausea and I thought I was going to throw up, then, that ebbing, nothing, just a dull gray nothingness, then in a minute or so I was feeling terrific again.

I saw it was broad daylight out. But the sun rose early in the summer. It seemed sad it would be such a long time until breakfast.

16

"BURTON! I AM SO HAPPY! I am so extremely overjoyed!"

And he really did hug me. But no kissums. No, no. It was that big lunk of a Libyan, Mohammed Maziq.

"We had so anxiety!" he boomed. "We so involved with your safety! We strain every ounce!"

"Hey, what are you doing here?" I said. "I thought they ran all the Libyans out of town."

"Hah, hah!" he laughed jovially and winked. "We are Arab brothers."

I didn't get it. "Now wait a minute," I said. "I don't want to go into details but I thought that your guys and these Moroccan guys had this little falling out. You'd all been expelled, they told me."

"Some came," Mohammed said philosophically. "Some went."

He made this fatalistic Arab gesture with the open hand, palm outwards, which I never figured out completely but I think meant kismet, it was in the hands of Allah, or maybe give up hope all ye who enter here. Anytime an Arab couldn't explain anything this was it. Allah's will. Kismet.

It was the next morning. Sandor was sitting on a straight-backed chair looking slightly enigmatic.

"We are so passionately overjoyed for you, Burton," said Mohammed. "We delight to have you again among us."

"And I delight to be among you, too, old buddy pal. And

why are you calling me 'Burton'? You never called me Burton."

First I was Birdie, now I was Burton.

"I always think Burt is a diminuation of Burton," said Mohammed, puzzled.

"Well, it's logical, I'll give you that," I said. "But here I had such hopes for you and you were looking for me under a false name."

Mohammed made me a funny sign, then turned on the hotel-room radio quite loud, like to throw off bugs for example. He leaned his head close to mine and whispered conspiratorially.

"Hish. Burt. There is no reason of which to be ascared. You will be released."

I looked at him, baffled. Drawing intelligence out of this guy was like swimming in salt water taffy. I edged the radio even louder and spoke softly into his ear.

"What do you mean, I'll be released? I'm already released. I released myself."

We looked at each other again. No communication. He crooked his finger at me.

"Burt!" he whispered. "We have influence! We are friendly with these geezers! *You will have been released!*"

I would have been released. I just sat there. Stunned. Sick to my stomach. The radio was playing what sounded like an Arabic version of "When Irish Eyes Are Smiling." I tried to sing it in my mind, *when Arabic eyes are smiling*, but it wouldn't fit. Mohammed's face was all eager, eyes alight. He thought he was giving me good news. I wasn't reacting the way he expected though and his smile faded slowly, giving way to a look of concern.

"You mean it was all for nothing," I brought out. "They were going to let me go. I almost got myself killed for nothing."

He looked puzzled.

"Who was that goddamn dumb girl? On her last visit to the condemned man."

"A misunderstanding!" Mohammed whispered after a pause. "I explain them you are friend! You are friend of Arabs!"

"You mean you explained to your friends," I said dully. "You explained to them I'm an all-right guy, better they should have grabbed Elizabeth Taylor."

"Yes, yes, yes!" whispered Mohammed. "I explain everything. Elsbeth Taylor. You are in absolute safety."

Well, there was no point being sore at him. He'd really tried to help and it probably would have worked if I'd only given it enough time. It wasn't his fault.

"That's nice," I said weakly. "Thank you, Mohammed."

He turned to Sandor, who looked reflective. Sandor felt Mohammed's eyes on him but avoided them, I noticed.

"But how's the picture going?" I asked. I hadn't given it much thought lately. "How's the movie? Where is everybody?"

I'd just woken up but I thought at least Omar would be coming.

"They're in Libya," said Sandor with a trace of uneasiness. "I was going to tell you. They closed us down while you were away. The sets, the studio, everybody's in Libya. Kaddafi, he's taking us in thanks to Mohammed here. We're going to shoot the big battle scenes in the Libyan desert. Kaddafi can go 'up yours' to the Saudis."

Sandor made the "up yours" sign, that part of American culture he had taken most deeply to his heart. Mohammed beamed. It wasn't every chief of state who could say up yours to the Saudis. Oil shall make you free. They were all in Libya.

"The Moroccan checks are rebounding," said Mohammed with strong disapproval. "These are not high-class people."

"*Ai-yi-yi*, are the checks bouncing," said Sandor. "Once the Moroccans are out, then they don't pay nothing. Their own people they don't pay. Lawyers we've had. This movie, I'm telling you, Burt, it's going to make legal history from Casablanca to Baghdad already. Now we're in the Libyan national budget."

So there I was like Rip Van Winkle. I go off to play a little ninepins with these Moroccan dwarfs and I come back and my pals are gone and I hardly know anybody and everyone's gone to the promised land in Libya. Where it was a whole new ball game, I guess, and the future wasn't bright but was black and oleaginous, which was better. This was a petro-movie we were making. I told you. You've heard of petro-dollars. This was a petro-movie.

The first thing the Moroccan cops wanted was to find these dastardly terrorists who had so abused me and might commit other mischief and we set off early in the morning with something the size of a mobile brigade. As soon as they'd gotten word I'd escaped and learned from the taxi driver where he picked me up, they'd cordoned off a whole section of the Medina, and if anybody needed to go to work or do an errand or make *pipi* on the other side of a police roadblock it was too bad, they had to wait until I had my nap. Heavily armed police and armored cars were everywhere. Starting from the square where I'd shot my way into the taxi, and passing first through a bristling roadblock, I tried to retrace my steps of the night before, with the police following me patiently and deferentially. I was their retriever dog.

Everything looked very different though. In the black, still night in the deserted streets I'd thought every wall and turning would be engraved in my memory forever, but now the sun was blinding, the streets bubbling with people, men in skullcaps, women in veils, children, most of them staring at us. Buildings whose front walls had struck me as blank had only been shuttered, I realized, and now little shops and workmen were everywhere, making shoes, repairing clocks, peddling vegetables, the streets filled with pushcarts. The jumbled houses were so hard to recognize that all I could go on was the geometry of my escape route in my head, the lefts and the rights and the half-rights and leftward curvings, and I worked my way back up the main thoroughfare and its tributaries. The hardest part was identifying the house where I'd dropped off the roof. I pictured the eerie night scene in my mind. Was the dark, deserted alley this babbling runway? Had this wall street lamp provided the faint light I was afraid I might get shot by? It was unlit and insipid now in the dazzling sun. I reversed myself and walked back and found the Moorish-shaped wooden door and then returned to where the police were waiting. This was it all right. A ladder was brought and sirens wailed as police cut off the block. Troopers with automatic weapons climbed the ladder first.

As soon as I got to the roof it all fit together and was easy, no more distractions. It had been black and now it was pink-earth and baking in the sun, but the geometry was all there, if much smaller. It had seemed to me I was going miles over the roofs and here it was just a few yards, almost pathetic. The wall where I'd shot a man in the back of the head was neutral, noncommital. But when I reached the glass *vasistas* I'd climbed out of, it was like coming upon some ill-remembered but frightening memory from infancy, a rattlesnake sleeping in the sun that might still bite me.

"That's it," I told the police. "Down in there."

The assault force took up positions on all the surrounding roofs and entered the adjoining houses and set up machine guns in the alleys. When the whole outfit was in place, an officer with a bullhorn droned in echoing Arabic warnings to come out. Silence. No one emerged, neither from the *vasistas* nor, judging from the walkie-talkie reports, from the front door. More crackly buzzing warnings to no effect. Finally a lieutenant broke the glass *vasistas* with an iron bar and fired in a series of tear-gas shells. Still nothing, and police wearing gas masks and carrying submachine guns swarmed down the ladder. The whole building was empty, a deserted warehouse, no bodies living or dead. My captors had probably cleared out within minutes of my escape taking their casualties with them.

I didn't go into the place until days later myself when the tear gas was gone, although you could still smell it. Here was the room granddaddy crept across on his belly and killed the first Indian. And here was granddaddy's cell, and granddaddy's chicken wire. I was a free man again but I still didn't like that place. It made everything seem small and squalid and oppressive. It was as if I couldn't breathe while I was in there again and I was glad to leave.

I told the police everything I could remember, descriptions, about the American girl, little slips made by my captors. Maybe they'd been about to release me, but did they do it? No. I didn't have that from an unimpeachable source anyhow. I could impeach him any day. Then FitzWilliam and my friends in the fossil stone business were interested in what had happened, naturally, and they debriefed me. I mean I put it into a different perspective for them. They had their own perspective. They'd taken it all very well, I must say, me being a hostage in a sweltering People's Hell-hole with these bakehead Moroccan Tupamaros maybe getting ready to put a bullet through my brain. FitzWilliam and the boys in the shop hadn't so much as turned a hair, had borne up under the strain admirably. Real valor, they had. *Mucho cojones*. The public pressure on them was staggeringly nonexistent, of course. Burt Nelson? How did you say his name was spelled? They'd never laid eyes on me. They told the Moroccan government that too, don't worry. Oh, they disowned you. You were on your own. What did you expect? Free our intelligence operative? If something went wrong you went out without the Purple Heart, *amigo*. Resign yourself.

The Moroccan police gave me a security man now in case my revolutionaries might have a grudge against me for something or other and this Moroccan bodyguarded me, and I wasn't sorry to have him really. I was kind of jumpy. I had black thoughts. Death in the sunlight didn't seem so bad; why was death in darkness so scary? Morocco made me nervous now. I don't know. I had the feeling someone might have hard feelings against me, might take a pot shot at me just out of meanness. A sore loser. Somebody like that.

Well, I was the hero of the hour. I was this jumpy hero. They flew me up to Rabat and I met our ambassador Mister Rentschler, who wasn't so bad if you liked ambassadors.

And the Moroccan Interior Minister, their top cop, the notorious Mohammed Abboukir, who had done in Ben Barka personally, I heard it said. And they even gave a little reception for me at the palace and I met the King, whom I'd met before in a men's room but he probably didn't remember. And here he was again good as new, all smiles, in a business suit even as you or I. My first king. The first king I'd met socially. *Monsieur Nelson! Monsieur Nelson!* They all thought I was the cat's ass, the King and everybody. I got to stay in a hospital for three days, where they gave me tests. They thought I was crazy, I think. They thought I'd broken under the strain. Except when I was at the hospital I wore these huge shades all the time, and no pictures and no press conferences, hell no, because of people who might have known me under other names, for example, or that Syrian just the other week who said he'd kill me if he ever saw me again. Like him. Because I don't want to be indiscreet but I was not the most lily-white-innocent American abductee that had ever been abducted. I was not your ideal case. So it was no interviews because I'd been under such nervous stress, and I had to wear dark glasses because of the damage done to my eyes during my long periods in darkness, and for God's sake no pictures for fear of reprisals against my family or I don't know what. Morocco has the kind of press where, out of ten stories on the front page of a morning newspaper, six are about the King working tirelessly for the good of the country, minimum five pictures. Him supervising things, Him signing decrees, Him receiving dignitaries. With that kind of press you didn't have to worry so much. The Interior Minister, Abboukir, took quite a shine to me. It was the opportunity I'd had to kill someone with my bare fingers, I guess. "Monsieur Nelson, your embassy was most concerned for your welfare. You have good friends." This with a broad smile on his coppery face, his eyes slightly slanting. I checked him out at the shop and got this feeling he was on our payroll. I sensed it. The Interior Minister. How was that for a penetration?

It was fun being at the palace, all the servants in fancy costumes, the place ablaze with air conditioning. A Moroccan army major came up to me near the end, a rather imposing figure, but with these hot Arab eyes.

"What will you think of us Moroccans?" he asked, very flowery.

I told him not to give it a thought, and had the feeling he wanted to tell me something. We were off in a corner.

"What do you do for a living?" I said, although he had his army uniform on. I was the last of the kidders.

He gave a small smile and looked somehow stiffer.

"I commanded a battalion in the Moroccan brigade on the Golan Heights," he said, meaning in the October War against Israel in 1973.

"Uh, huh," I said, smiling. It was a decent battle credit. They'd done all right.

"And you know what was waiting for us when we got home?" he asked after glancing about, a quick play of the eyes. "Immediate transfer to other units. Not even leave to visit our families."

"Well, the King invited you to the big party," I said.

"No promotion," he said, sticking to his point.

"None of you?"

"None."

His eyes fastened on me intently as if he'd said it all. I surely grasped the configuration. He smiled bitterly. But I didn't speak.

"*Le dix-huit brumaire,*" he said. "*Le retour d'Egypte.*" This was a reference to General Bonaparte's return from Egypt as a conquering hero. He promptly overthrew the regime. Well, yes, it was something you had to watch out for.

Why was he telling me this? I was just the celebrity of the hour. But if he talked to any of our known spooks the other Moroccans would have noticed, I supposed. I had the feeling I was expected to pass this on. What made him think that I — An interesting case.

"We must play tennis together some day," I said.

"No," he answered embarrassed. "Not tennis." Looking at me with these crazy Arab eyes that said, *Do you love only me?*

"We'll get together somehow," I persisted.

"Perhaps," he said.

I got his coordinates and red-flagged him for the boys in the shop. They could figure out a way of contacting him, maybe via some local. It was always worthwhile keeping in touch with the disgruntled ones. The gruntled ones we had already. Not that we wanted to subvert the King. Far from it. What we wanted was to protect the King from himself in a way; we could do it better than he could. And this major plainly wanted to talk to us, didn't he? Surely we should listen, keep an open mind? Right there in the palace right under the King's nose, how daring of him. I had a feeling something might be cooking again. I red-flagged him.

I was still jumpy though. I looked behind me a lot.

17

"SANDOR, WHAT ARE YOU still hanging around in Marrakesh for?" I asked him. "Why aren't you in Libya?"

Because the King's love for me was not such as to rescind the expulsion of our movie. I was back in Marrakesh. Real life. Thank God it was cooler.

Sandor made a noise like "taahh!"

"But who's directing the picture?" I said. "Who's picking the locations?"

"Our fearless leader!" exclaimed Sandor, now gay, exuberant.

"Omar?" I said with some surprise because Omar didn't have a clue on how to direct a movie. The mind reeled. The flesh shrank.

"Listen," said Sandor. "In Libya Kaddafi's running this crazy-man Moslem country, am I right? Here in Morocco a Jew is okay. A little Jew here, a little Jew there. A little to, a little fro. They need you for something? It's a deal. They're not fanatics. But in Libya? A Jew direct a picture about the *Prophet*? Omar tells Kaddafi he's the director, now he runs around making believe to direct."

"But what's going to happen?"

"What happens is that in a couple days I go and save the picture. From the burning caldron I pluck. Omar still pretends to direct but I whisper in his ear."

"But why aren't you there now?"

Sandor sighed.

"Listen, I been there already, last week. And we have one of our Moroccan actors with us. And then he flies back to Casablanca to see his old mother for Ramadan or something. And he's a hometown boy so the papers want to interview, and everybody's curious about this new country Libya, yesterday this nothing, these hicks, now so rich. So naturally he tells the papers Libya is the shithole of the universe, and the Libyans see this and they're so mad, like hornets, they can eat barbed wire. *Never that mamzer in this country sets foot again!* Except he's in the picture already. He doesn't die until the big battle. So now I got to take him somewhere to some kiddie's sandbox and shoot him dying, so you should think there's this big battle going on in the background. One camel I'll take and make him run around in circles."

Real life. Marrakesh had a flourishing branch of the *Club Méditerranée*, which Sandor had taken to using as his home away from home since our production company left town. It was a singles bar in the sun, his Fountain of Youth. The average age of the young French vacationers must have been about twenty-five, with bevies of young women in bikinis splashing around the swimming pool, calling people they didn't know *tu*. The French call people *tu* when they're children in school but once they're grown up you have to be married to them, or related to them, or they have to be bohemian or have loose morals or something like that for you to make *tu*, otherwise it's *vous* — except for the *Club Méditerranée*, where in the interests of sociability and financial gain the creators had institutionalized regression to childhood. Sandor loved it. A hundred and ten years old and with young women in bikinis around he was still a spring chicken. *Gnädiges Fräulein! Gnädiges Fräulein!* He kissed their hand; I don't know why. He was like an aged archduke frolicking with his milkmaids around the May Pole, except that he called them *Gnädiges Fräulein* and they called him *tu*. All these poolside Aphrodites knew he was connected with a big movie so they gathered around him flirtatiously despite his gray hairs. "I am in love with a beautiful redhead from Bordeaux!" he told me, pointing out a high-spirited girl with freckles, punching a beach ball as she grew pinker by the hour. "She torments me something horrible," he moaned. "You read *Death in Venice*? I write *Plotz in Marrakesh*."

There was this big American girl always lying around the swimming pool too. Blonde, very pretty, bland face, big knockers. Every time I walked by the pool she'd stare at me with a wishful, yearning look that made me think that she, too, had heard about the movies, a look compounded of the magic of it all, plus self-interest, unreasonable aspirations.

"Got enough suntan oil there?" I said.

"Oh, yes," she replied, giddy.

It was a kind of staring you couldn't even call staring. It was too soft. She just kept gazing at me like a ninny. When I moved, her face followed.

"Getting a good tan, I see."

"Not on the face," she cried anxiously, as if afraid I might make her get a tan on the face.

Her name was Janie Holt. She was twenty-three. She came from Wilmette, Illinois, and had gone to New Trier High School, like Charlton Heston, Ann-Margret, Bruce Dern, and Rock Hudson before her. She was a photographer's model and I'd never seen one yet that didn't pine to be a movie star. She was a Virgo. That's how the conversation went. She was based in Paris but had "fallen in love" with Marrakesh when she'd come down to shoot a nylon-stocking commercial on a camel. She was all by herself this time and was having erotic dreams.

"Erotic dreams?" I said.

"Yes," she giggled.

"What happens in these erotic dreams?"

"I'm all alone in the middle of the desert and a beautiful Arab boy rapes me."

"A nice looking girl like you has dreams like that?" I said, thinking it was the most derivative dream I'd heard in quite a while. "What is Wilmette coming to?"

"Oh, you movie men," she said.

"I'm a slow starter," she whispered to me that night, her eyes like a baby's up close, and indeed it took quite a bit of work to start her up, and even then she was very placid, billowing softly along, and suddenly knitting her brow as if she was concentrating very hard on a math problem and *ooh! ooh!* And then looking upon the world with dew-filled eyes. "Like two savages!" she whispered in my ear, her words roaring against my eardrum. She was an Arcadian, this girl. She suffered from the persistent misconception that backward cultures were more virile. I took inventory. There was a lot of girl there. She was soft all over, and big, and it was paraphernalia that had provided healthful entertainment and needed diversion for at least one exalted personage, wearied by the cares and burdens of high condition: the Shah of Iran. He was still the top of the line in that market. He'd flown her out to Teheran first class, and a royal limousine had been at the airport to take her to the palace.

"He was waiting for me in his dressing gown," she whispered. "We danced the tango."

"Does he dance a good tango?" I asked.

"Oh, yes!" She was enthusiastic.

So there. Shake the hand that felt the pussy that was felt by the Shah of Iran. I too had my place in history. And I was always curious about money. I wormed it out of her. Want to know the authentic going rate? Two million old francs, which is to say twenty thousand new francs, or $5,000 plus some loose emeralds, for one hour's deep tango. You've heard of the Hesitation Waltz? This was the Penetration Tango. The emeralds were the tip.

"And he had me back a second time a month later," she whispered delightedly, hugging herself.

That made $10,000 and twice as many loose emeralds. It was a good living.

"I'm just the type the Shah likes," she said, starry-eyed. "Tall. Blonde. Blue eyes. Big things." She meant breasts.

Her room at the *Club Méditerranée* was like Ali Baba's cave, native rugs and hand-worked leather cushions strewn about. A low ceiling took the shape of a Moorish dome. From outside came the sound of bubbling oriental fountains, for the club was in the form of a toy Medina, with toy patios open to the sky. Janie's room was lit by cylindrical brass lamps with holes punched in them, as by a nail, which shed a curious, dappled light on those voluminous breasts of hers. Actually, with its authentic lamps and rugs, the room was the finest example of Beverly Hills Moorish I had ever seen outside of Beverly Hills. Surrounding all of this, you understand, was this great, crummy, authentic Moorish city named Marrakesh, but when even genuine Moors wanted to create an earthly paradise, an oasis of delight amidst the desert sands, they built it in Beverly Hills Moorish, proving the vigor of our national culture. O Rodeo Drive! O Dream of Happiness! O Leopard Woman! Because I had accepted from Jackie Bisset the theory that girls of baroque proportions looked much more naked than girls with slighter builds, and it was true that when Janie Holt walked around the room unclothed she looked naked indeed, but the odd light gave her this leopard-woman look. She looked like a neg print from an African fantasy movie. "Do you like them?" she asked hopefully as she knelt over me on the bed, which made the breasts loom out alarmingly. Well, yes, I liked them, but was getting sick and tired of Ali Baba, and the other Arabian Nights, and would have really liked to scrutinize these prize-winning breasts under more nativist, patriotic forms of lighting, like Beverly Hills Tudor, for example, or Beverly Hills Cape Cod. For sheer bulk and weight I had to give it to her; they were really something, which I said, which made her girlish with pleasure. But I don't know. In my heart of hearts I was reserving judgment. The air conditioning was glacial and I caught a cold.

So her name was Janie Holt. She was from Wilmette. She was this Virgo. She had truly huge bozooms. She was a placid fuck. She wanted to get into the movies. She'd been had twice by the Shah of Iran. And she was beginning to make me nervous.

It was a cosmic malaise maybe. But also, she'd been awfully easy. It had to cross your mind. We did it to them; why shouldn't they do it to us? I mean was it love for the movies or had somebody planted her on me? It so happened I had the one invincible defense against entrapment: Total Blatancy. They couldn't shame me. I was unshameable. But of course they might not know they couldn't shame me. They might think I still had some shreds of latent shame. In which case they could think they had a zinger. The spook business made you paranoid. Here I was safe as a human being could be, with my bodyguard outside the door, me securely ensconced in the bed of this strongly built girl, a second line of defense almost. But you always had to keep going over things in your mind, seeing if you could read scenes from different angles, looking for the worst. It poisoned your life sometimes, permeating it with a noxious effluvium of apprehension and suspicion and counter-suspicion. You couldn't relax. You couldn't enjoy easy nooky. It robbed life of its goddamn savor.

I introduced Janie to Sandor the next day. *Gnädiges Fräulein*. He kissed her hand too. It was his Old World style; she brought him back to his youth in Budapest. When her attention was distracted he made noises like an out-board motorboat, proving he was the product of two cultures, the Old World and the New. "Come out to the set!" he invited her. "Come watch me I shoot the world's biggest battle scene ever takes place in a kiddie's sandbox!" Janie went out there with him, thrilled. She rode the camel. She sent postcards back to Wilmette. And I still thought she might be a plant.

"Tell me, Sandor," I said. "What's Libya like? Is it really that bad?"

We were sitting in the hotel lobby. Sandor leaned forward and took his gray head in his hands.

"Arabic lettering everywhere," I said to help him out. "No

Latin alphabet. I'm getting my passport in Arabic. No booze
I guess. Booze is illegal."

Sandor groaned.

"Booze is illegal, booze is illegal," he repeated disdainfully. "*Iced coffee is illegal!* You think I kid you! Wait till
you get there!"

He made it sound a little forbidding.

"How's Mouna?" I said to change the subject to something light and fluffy.

"Say, Mouna pulls me aside last week and she says to
me with tears in her eyes: *I love this man but I despise his
profession.* I say to her: *So suffer.*"

"Which man?"

"Our fearless leader," said Sandor as if who else?

"Well, because there was Mohammed there. And other
guys it seems to me for all I know."

"No, no, I don't agree with you!" Sandor admonished me
heatedly. "You're sexist *trafe*, you are. A fella cheats a
little on his wife, he can still love her, can't you? So why
not Mouna? Why can't she *shtoop* a little on the side and
still love Omar? I'm telling you these girls are right. She's
a good *zaftig* girl. A little hot in the pants, so what's bad?"

He was so eloquent he quite carried me away.

"Hey, Fouad," I said to my security man.

He was sitting a few seats over in the lobby, looking
around beady-eyed to see if anybody was getting ready to
shoot me. He didn't like me sitting in the lobby or being
anyplace outdoors except when moving fast in a car. Best
of all he liked me in an upstairs room with him outside
the door, and when you came walking down the corridor
he tracked you with his eyes, his hand near his holster. If
there was a sudden explosion or a car backfired he shot you
I guess. I wasn't supposed to talk to him in public either.
A nameless assassin shouldn't realize Fouad and I had any
connection. While the nameless assassin was getting a line
on me, Fouad would be getting a line on the nameless
assassin. And then *zzblap!* Fouad would get him.

"Hey, Fouad, what's the drill when I go to Libya?" I

asked. "You come out in the car with me. And you go through customs with me. And you come to the foot of the embarcation ladder with me. And then it's *salut*?"

"That's it," said Fouad, looking away as if he didn't know me, his narrow face aloof.

"I mean you don't ride on the plane with me even if it's *Royal Air Maroc.*"

"I don't think so," he said as if he was giving me the time. "I'll ask."

Which was a long answer for him. He wasn't very talkative. Whenever I spoke to him the expression on his face said, "Who is this bum? I never saw him before in my life."

"I got the tickets already," I told Sandor, who had finished his actor's death scene. "We change in Rabat. Maybe I should send Omar a telex saying we'll be getting in the day after tomorrow."

"Three days it takes to telephone," groused Sandor. "An urgent cable? Twenty-four hours."

"I better get it off then," I said, and drafted the telex and took it to the desk clerk with instructions to move it as soon as possible.

We were sitting in the gardens half an hour later, Sandor telling me we should change the title of the film to *The Magnificent Mohammed,* when a bellboy in a caftan started making the rounds of the lobby calling, "*Monsieur Nelson au téléphone. Monsieur Nelson au téléphone.*" A call for Mr. Nelson. They signaled me to a house phone down a short corridor.

"I have a message for a Mr. Nelson," said a male American voice when I picked up the receiver.

"This is Nelson. Shoot," I said.

"Is this Mr. Nelson?"

"Yes, it is."

"I've a message for you, sir."

He did the "sir" short as in the military.

"Let her fly," I said.

There was a pause.

"Fire away."

The line was silent.

"This is Nelson. You can give me the message," I said.

"I'll read you the message," said the voice. "Are you ready?"

"I'm as ready as I'll ever be."

"Here's the message: ACCOMMODATIONS TRIPOLI DIFFI-CULT WEDNESDAY. COULD YOU DELAY ARRIVAL TWO DAYS. REGRETS. Signed: DONALDSON."

"Old Donaldson," I said. "Who's this?"

"The message is signed 'Donaldson,'" said the voice.

"Donaldson's an old friend of mine," I said. "Who are you?"

"Cut the comedy, Nelson," said my correspondent and hung up.

I sat down in the lobby again and thought about this or that for a while, then went to the travel desk and changed the reservations to two days later.

"Why Friday?" asked Sandor. "What was the matter with Wednesday?"

"I have this legal stuff to clear up because of my kid-napping," I said. "It'll take a couple of days more than I thought."

"Maybe I should go ahead by myself," Sandor suggested. "Maybe Omar is on pins and needles for me to arrive."

"Sandor," I said. "Wait a couple of days for me. What's a couple of days?"

"Maybe duty calls," he said.

I looked at him, and he looked back for a second and then blurted out, "I blame it on you. If Omar blows him-self up on one of the land mines Rommel left from the *Afrika Korps*, I blame it on you."

Janie needed to go back to Paris and we had one of those tearless partings. I wouldn't say I was screwing her to a fare-thee-well. I was screwing her and I was saying fare thee well to her. She asked me if we might do a movie before long where we could use a girl like her, and I said maybe, I'd try, who knows, with her links with Islamic culture. Because what intrigued me most about Janie was

the Shah. Experts were always going on about the "sensuality" of Islam, at least in the afterlife, as opposed to Christianity, where the afterlife is strictly non-sex. And here Janie had been on the receiving end of real Islamic sensuality, although it looked as if the Shah didn't want to wait for the dark-eyed *houris* of paradise. He wanted blue-eyed *houris* in the here and now.

"You know, I've been in Moslem countries all this time," I told Janie. "And doing all this Mohammed research. And I still haven't been able to figure out if in Islam women go to heaven. The subject didn't happen to come up while you were with the Shah?"

I knew perfectly well the subject didn't come up while she was with the Shah, but I mean we were lying there skin to skin, pelt to pelt, genital to genital, to each his own. We'd mixed juices. It created a certain intimacy. She'd experienced Islamic sensuality.

"Because it says in the Koran," I explained, "that on the day of judgment good male Moslems go to the Gardens of Delight. *They shall recline on jeweled couches face to face, amidst gushing waters and abundant fruits. And theirs shall be the dark-eyed houris, chaste as hidden pearls. For Allah created the houris and made them virgins, loving companions for those of the right hand. Sura 56.*

"It sounds like a celestial cat house," I said. "Where do good Moslem women go? For that matter why don't the *houris* have earlier lives like other people? And, last, how do the *houris* stay virgins? I can't get anyone to answer me. Unless they have throw-away, biodegradable *houris*. Use them just once, there's always a fresh supply. The Shah must know about things like that. He didn't say, for example, *Until we meet again in that great Las Vegas show in the sky*? Something like that? You know, the life to come?"

"He's a Sagittarius," she said.

It would be hard to work Islamic sensuality into the Mohammed script anyway, I supposed, given Libya. Maybe in some other script.

Janie rolled over and, cupping her hand around my ear, whispered loudly, "Do you want me to wear anything?"

I drew a blank. We were both lying there stripped, me with my cold. Wear what? When?

"You know," she whispered, her eyes dancing. "Garters?"

"No, that's okay," I said. "Just plain naked is all right."

But she got up anyway and put on a garter belt and black stockings, although I thought nowadays girls wore only tights, and stood contemplating herself in the full-length mirror, beaver very prominent. I supposed that was the true function of garter belt and stockings now, to make a beaver more dramatic.

"Oh, that really is pornographic," Janie said indulgently, as if she rather fancied herself in this get-up.

Well, she didn't have to put on black stockings for me. I didn't ask her. And the Shah? Was he a garter-belt-and-black-stockings man? I asked Janie. It was true. The thought of the two of them tangoing around the palace with the Shah in his dressing gown and Janie in the outfit she was wearing now was picturesque, to say the least. It all left me with even deeper thoughts about the irresistible ascendancy of Western culture. *Yanqui no! Garter belts sí!* And what the hell kind of a girl was this Janie Holt? Raffish. Shady maybe even. Glug. I still had these suspicions about Janie. Once a spook, always a paranoid. You had to be realistic. Why not? Why shouldn't they? That was the way it was done, wasn't it? It was that damn Morocco. I had to get out of there. Too many people knew me; I was almost a public figure. My nerves were still a little shot from the kidnapping. Those two men I killed made me nervous. And a feeling I had that something might be cooking in the Moroccan military made me nervous. And even easy nooky made me nervous. I had to get out of Morocco.

Sandor and I were diddling around with the script in his room the morning our plane would have been putting down in Rabat if we'd flown the day we'd originally planned on, when suddenly there was martial music on the radio, *drrrum-ta-ta.* And it seemed this Moroccan Air Force F-5 fighter flight had just tried to shoot down a plane the King was on as it, too, was putting down at Rabat, shooting it full of holes all right but the King, who literally must have had a rabbit's foot up his ass, got away, landed, safe. And we had the usual routine, you know, martial law, and tanks in the street, and, earlier, antiaircraft guns firing at these rebellious pilots, who were strafing the shit out of the airfield. And in truth it would have been a very impractical day to fly into or out of Rabat airport, with a lot of dead. And Sandor was looking at me very funny, but not saying anything. And I said, "What good luck it was we weren't flying through Rabat just now, eh, Sandor?" And he kept looking at me funny.

But say what you will I was puzzled. And then twelve hours later we heard on the radio that the Interior Minister, head of the whole security system, my old buddy pal Mohammed Abboukir — we were like *that* — had just been executed by firing squad. You get it? Don't you get it? Our guys got wind of the thing, otherwise I wouldn't have been warned, and they naturally told the Interior Minister, figuring of course he'd tell the King. But Abboukir wasn't as loyal a friend of the King's as one might have thought. No, he wasn't. In fact he was in cahoots with those diabolical pilots who were up there in the sky in their F-5's waiting to blast the King to pieces. And what do you know our warning never got through! All those good intentions on our part come to such naught! *Así es, mi viejo.* Murky, huh? These things were filled with murk.

And I went outside the door of Sandor's hotel room and there was my security man out there, seemingly vigilant. But this security man was put there by order of the now defunct Interior Minister, I reflected. And this Interior Minister was plotting all that time against the King. What I'm trying to get at is, if an Interior Minister was plotting to chop down his own King, how much could he really care about protecting Burt Nelson? I mean deep down. A fellow just didn't feel secure in a situation like that.

18

LIBYA! LAND OF FREEDOM! Kaddafi ran a taut ship. He ran
a taut desert. Nobody was going to take any pot shots at me
in Libya, no, sir. It was such a relaxing feeling. A good,
stable regime. No *coups d'état* since King Idris. No angry
dissidents, underground malcontents, Monteneros, Tupamaros, *Brigate Rosse*, protesters, riffraff like that. Law and
order. Koranic law and order. Deep sleep at night. Deep
dreams of peace and pristine unpermissive societies where
they don't permit you to do frigging anything but the peace
is beautiful, man, wow.

Tripoli had a great waterfront, palm trees and curving
esplanade just like La Croisette or the Promenade des
Anglais, dating from when Libya was an Italian colony.
When you looked close the streets were filled with sand
and dead cats and antique garbage and Coke bottles and
used condoms. Street sweeping hadn't been invented yet.
So the secret was don't look close. A great boom was underway; there was no doubt about that. A dozen ships or more
were always standing off to seaward waiting to get into the
harbor to unload. Construction sites were everywhere, scaf-
folding, cement mixers. As soon as the buildings were finished they seemed to start falling apart, which meant more
scaffoldings and more cement mixers, I suppose, work for
everybody, activity in perpetuity. Every hustler and indus-
trial con artist in the world had hit the Libyans for some
project or other. Someone had built them a glass factory

and when the keys were being handed over at the end said, "It's too bad the sand you have here isn't right for glass." And somebody else built them a brick factory and said at the end, "It's too bad the clay you have here isn't right for bricks." And somebody else built them a tuna-fish canning plant, when the Libyans not only don't have any tuna fleet, they don't have any fishing fleet of any description. And ministers got sore at you when you were hesitant about the wisdom of this empty tuna canning factory, explaining to you that it was going to act as an incentive to Libyans to get out there and *catch tuna fish*. It was Monopoly money for them. There was a severe labor shortage even in unskilled trades, which made you wonder why the U.N. had to support idle Palestinian refugees in camps when this nearby province of the great Arab nation was panting for labor to build its tuna fish plants which it was paying for with Monopoly money. And every morning at breakfast time the dining room of the hotel would be jammed with dynamic international businessman types, Americans and Germans and Swedes and Italians and French, all there to sell something to the Libyans. Maybe one European secretary you'd see as one of these dynamic businessmen dictated a dynamic letter. That's what you got in the way of women in Tripoli. Because compared to Libyan women the women in Marrakesh had been bawdy licentious hussies. They'd been veiled but you saw two eyes. In Libya you got one eye. The bedsheets the women wore over their heads they pulled down over one side of the face, then back over the mouth of course, and if they didn't have a hand free to hold the sheet right up close they held it in their teeth, all wet. One eye. Male hookers in the hotel though. Oh, yes. Midnight Sheiks. All you wanted of that.

The American oil company people lived outside town in a golden ghetto with this intoxicating Xanadu called the company commissary, actually like a small local supermarket on the outskirts of Fresno. And their kids went to a school whose athletic equipment was marked somewhat generically "OIL COMPANY SCHOOL." Not "Exxon" or "Mobil" or "Occidental" but "Oil Company School," in case the Libyans were to decide to nationalize it further or maybe change its name every six days. You could never be too neutral. Oil Company School. I knew there wasn't going to be any hootch. The country was dry as a bone. At the hotel they served fizzy blue and green soft drinks. The U.S. oil guys made their own Sneaky Pete, a rotgut they called "flash." Kaddafi had promised to let in real Christian booze for the movie company but somehow this hadn't come about yet, and in the meantime if you made friends with the oil people there was flash. Outside the U.S. ghetto of course nothing was readable in the whole country, all squiggles and swipes and curlicues. I could pronounce a little Arabic, but I stared at my name in Arabic printing in my passport for an hour without mustering any real confidence I would recognize it if I ever saw it again. The writing was all flourishes and embellishments, with the critical wiggles of it almost microscopic, it seemed to me. Despite what a person might think even their Arabic numerals weren't like our Arabic numerals. Two was like a backward seven, and four was like a backward three, and eight was an upside-down "V," and zero was a dot, and it turned out our Arabic numerals came from India. We should call them Indian numerals. I couldn't read a word of the damn stuff. It was hopeless. Mohammed Maziq said he'd been to London and there hadn't been any signs in the Arabic alphabet for him; why should Libyans put up signs in the Western alphabet for us? It was logical if cheerless. Near the airport outside Tripoli some good-hearted American had Scotch-taped to an Arabic road sign a weather-beaten piece of cardboard bearing the forlorn, unsteadily hand-printed message "AIR-PORT," like an appeal for help. *Save me. No one can find me out here.* Signed. *Airport.*

The morning Sandor and I got in from Morocco we had them show us the footage Omar had been shooting on his own. He was off at the moment scouting locations in the desert.

"Well, we'll see what our fearless leader has been up to,"

said Sandor as we sat on folding chairs in an improvised screening room at the hotel.

When it was over he sat stunned. The sequences had been stiff, stilted, the actors ill at ease. They were slightly incredible. Sandor struck himself on the forehead with the palm of his hand and gazed about desolately.

"The first thing I tell him," he said. "Always. The first rule of the director. *One.* You got to reread the scene when these guys last met up. To see what's cooking between them at least, what kind *tsimmes* they're making. *Two.* You got to read the scene when they *next* meet up, to see what you go into, what kind *tsimmes* they make next time."

He gave a look of despair.

"These guys hasn't met in fifteen years! They hate each other! They're from different branches of Mohammed's followers! No sooner he dies, they fight! They're going to kill each other to death!" Sandor mourned a moment in silence then wailed, "What am I doing here! I'm a nice Jewish boy from Budapest! I tell him, he doesn't listen! *Run, here comes Sandor.* He should learn how to direct a movie only."

"Be diplomatic with him," I said. "Don't hurt his feelings. His heart's in the right place."

"Where's that?" said Sandor despondently.

"Show me the dailies from when I was in the clink," I said.

These had been shot under Sandor's direction and looked very professional. Hundreds of people on camera. Good movement. Good angles. But Sandor didn't even like his own dailies now.

"They look like animals," he said, revolted. "Fighting and clawing to touch their holy stone. If I let him he turns this into the greatest anti-Moslem propaganda movie the world has ever seen. Like Tannenberg! The Russians march straight into the swamp! Feldmarschall von Hindenburg, the hero of Tannenberg! The man who stands there while the Russians march into the swamp."

Outside in the lobby we ran into Guy Lockley, our star. I didn't mention him before because I'm anti-star, although

Lockley wasn't too bad. Big Brit Shakespearean actor but human, you know, the human touch. The move to Libya had put him past his stop date and he was now getting twenty thousand human dollars a week on overtime.

"Well, I must say, you'll do anything to get attention," he said astringently. It was the first time he'd seen me since I was taken captive by those creeps.

"Hiya, champ," I replied.

"Giving trouble to all those divine policemen," said Lockley. "Making everyone a nervous wreck. News bulletins. You'd think you were Greta Garbo or somebody. Topsy escaping from Simon Legree. You all right?" he asked in a change of tone, eyeing me.

"Sure."

"I should hope so," he said, tartly again. "The nerve."

"Do you know which direction Omar went in?"

"My dear, I do not," answered Lockley disgustedly. "He's out there communing with the God of his ancestors in the desert, I assume."

He waved his hand vaguely. Everywhere in Libya is desert.

"I think he's gone to El Alamein," someone contributed.

"How could he go to El Alamein?" humphed Sandor. "El Alamein is in Egypt! I know where he is."

We took a driver from the production office and Sandor, the driver, and I set out in a Land Rover to find Omar.

It might not have been El Alamein but great stretches of desert had never been cleared of the German mines Rommel left during the war and we needed to keep a careful eye on military maps with red zebra hatching indicating the uncleared minefields. *Danger.* Under a scorching sun, with the dust caking on our lips, we finally spotted Omar's Land Rover halted at the foot of a sand dune. Omar and the British production manager were standing outside their car, Omar staring up at this great mound of sand. He was in an exalted state. As we drove up, he turned, the light of enthusiasm in his eyes.

"Burt! How are ya, m'boy?"

It was the first time he, too, had seen me since I'd been in captivity, and he was my bosom buddy, and we'd been through thick and thin together, and I'd escaped with my life since he'd seen me last, and we were very close. As I opened my mouth to tell him how I was, he said, "How do you like this for a location!"

I closed my mouth again.

"Pretty good," I replied after a second.

"The majesty of it!" Omar breathed. "The silence. At such a spot you can see the infant Islam, this tiny sect, but destined to fire the spirits of men for centuries, engaged in its first struggles. The hand of God reaching out to Man. This Islam destined to grow and grow and spread and spread."

"From the rock-bound coast of Morocco to the sunny shores of Indonesia," I said.

"Indonesia," said Omar. "And here you get it at its inception. This tiny little new religion, so rich with its promise of peace. Look at that sky! Almost white. The color of tranquillity."

"This is going to be a battle scene, Ome," I said.

"Naturally. How do you like it, Sandor?"

"Well," Sandor said. And you could tell he didn't like it. "Omar, here you got an hour's shooting a day at best."

Omar looked bewildered under his beige golfing hat.

"The light." Sandor gestured resignedly. "We're facing here due east. In the morning the sun's behind the sand dune, it comes up, all rear lighting. At noon an hour you get maybe, then all afternoon with the sun going down it's like everybody's staring straight into a projector, no side lighting."

"So what do we do?"

"I look for a place over south. Then we get side lighting in the morning, side lighting in the afternoon."

Omar wasn't stubborn. It seemed to him that it was almost his own idea.

"Oh, I've met Kaddafi, Burt! What a man," he burst out. He was even more enthusiastic now.

"There's a leader who knows what he wants," Omar cried. "You can talk to him, Burt. You can really talk to him. I told him our various professional movie problems, and he understood immediately, picked it all up instantly. Very quick. And Burt! We showed him the footage from Morocco! He loved it! He definitely loved it! He sat there in his shirt sleeves, imagine that, a chief of state, very natural, very relaxed, definitely loving it. And you know what he says to me? You remember how worried we were about offending devout Muslim sensitivities, and those crazy Saudis, and not showing Muhammed, not even his shadow, you never even hear his voice on the soundtrack? Well, I show him the footage and he says, *Where's Muhammed*? And I explain to him that we don't want to offend devout Muslim sensitivities by actually showing the Prophet. And he says (Omar shrugged), *What's the problem? You get a good actor.*"

"We're not going to have to reshoot all that Mecca stuff," I said, terrified. "I'm not going to have to rewrite the script with dialogue for Mohammed now, I hope. I drove myself crazy writing this script leaving Mohammed out. If I put him in it's a whole new script."

"No, no," Omar reassured me. "He said we *could* get an actor if we wanted to, as far as he's concerned. It shows how tolerant he is. And he's supposed to be a religious fanatic, does his prayers five times a day. It's what I've been telling you all this time about Islam. It's very tolerant!"

"I'm glad," I said. "I mean that's what we say in the film so I'm glad it's straight stuff."

"And he speaks beautiful Arabic," said Omar. "With the purity of the true Bedouin."

"You never met a Bedouin in your life," I said.

"Oh, Burt, come on! I can understand him much better than those Moroccans! They made such terrible noises. They always sounded as if they were strangling. You have to have generations of pure Bedouin behind you to sound like Kaddafi."

"What are you talking about? His mother's Jewish," I said.

"What?" said Omar.

"What am I letting out, a state secret? Ask him, the next time you see him. I'm not kidding. He's half-Jewish. Dust off your Jewish Mother jokes."

"Here, I've got to talk to Burt on the way back," said Omar, grabbing me by the arm. "Dennis, you ride back with Sandor to keep him company."

We climbed into his Land Rover and Omar shut the door with a worried look, as if making sure the desert wouldn't overhear our conversation. The driver had almost no English. The two Land Rovers got underway, heading back to Tripoli, sand raining against the mudguards.

"How can she ask me to give up the movies?" Omar asked intently, fidgeting with his hat, wiping the sweat off his forehead with his sleeve. During the talk about Kaddafi and the birth of Islam he hadn't fidgeted at all.

"The movies are my life!" he declared. "She wants me to work for the Palestinian cause. George Habash, the PFLP. Not Arafat because he's subsidized by Saudia Arabia, not pure enough, not Marxist enough, only Habash and Black September. She wants me to give up all this, my whole movie career, my whole reason for living, everything, and place myself, my money, artistic talent, business acumen, everything, solely at the service of the Palestinian people."

"Mouna," I said.

Omar was silent, staring out at the desert as we drove. If I'd said "Helen" he might have corrected me but as it was he didn't find comment necessary.

"I'm no Palestinian," he said. "She's the Palestinian. I'm no Marxist. I'm no serving monk. She says to me, *You must choose me or this filthy profession.* Very piss-elegant. I think she's bananas. I think she's going bananas. I don't think she's got all her marbles anymore. Very elevated she gets. I must choose, she says."

He crushed his hat between his knees, staring at the desert.

"I told her it was over," Omar said severely. "I told her it was finished. I told her last night."

"Well, that's that," I said. "That's taken care of."

"In the morning she was just as bad. She wakes up in the morning and her first thought there in bed is of her Palestinians. Have you ever heard of such a woman? I told her it was over. I told her again in the morning."

"You mean you slept with her," I said.

Omar smiled weakly.

"I guess I shouldn't have," he said.

"You mean you said, *We're through*. And then you had yourself a little poontang. And then you said, *I hope you understand we're through*."

"She gets demanding at times like that," Omar explained apologetically. "When she gets excited like that she rapes me. I guess I shouldn't have done it. It weakens my position."

"It does weaken your position," I said.

So there you were. Where were the hostages of yesteryear? One day you were this famous ex-hostage and everybody invited you out, you met the King, the Interior Minister (now defunct), the U.S. Ambassador, headwaiters gave you the best seats in restaurants. And the next thing you knew there were new hostages, more bloodcurdling acts of terrorism, and you were a back number. *Remember me? I'm the guy whose left little finger was amputated by the Eritrean Resistance Movement in Asmara in the summer of 1974, remember?* Nobody remembered. Nobody asked me about the new attempted *coup d'état* in Morocco either. A whole flight of F-5 pilots tries to shoot down the King of Morocco; this movie company has just been filming there; and not a single person in the company asks me about it. They were trivial people, these movie people. They had no interest in world events. You know what they were interested in? One of our English actors had picked up this beautiful Moroccan boy in Marrakesh, and he'd brought him along with him to Libya, this mad passion, but the Englishman flew to Rome one weekend to talk business about some upcoming movie and left the beautiful boy behind in Tripoli. And while his protector was off in Rome this beautiful boy was co-opted by Guy Lockley, you might say, which was logical because Guy Lockley was a bigger star and made more money and what do you expect, so he co-opted him. And now there was High Drama in the air because the other Englishman and Guy hadn't met since this co-optation, and everybody on the production had grabbed his scenario and was racing through noting which scenes had been shot and which scenes hadn't, figuring out when Guy and the other Brit would do their next scene together. A battle scene! Gadzooks! Perchance they wouldst do unto each other dastardly deeds! I tried to bate my breath but it was harder than you might think.

Really out of a desire for serious conversation I went by the shop, and it was a sad sight. I mean we were really the underdogs in Libya; you could feel it. The Libyans were running so many operations with this Monopoly money of theirs that the boys were going out of their minds trying to keep track of them. The Libyans were shipping arms, and bankrolling, and intervening, and finagling, from Belfast to Ouagadougou, much more than us. Oh, Lord, yes. The CAS budget they had from all that oil! I mean we were pikers by comparison. They were running all those big hijacking and hostage operations; it was notorious. These Libyans were the most frenetic interventionists of any interveners anywhere, bar none, and it was very hard to buy anybody in Libya because everything was so expensive. Hotels were expensive and automobiles were expensive and people were expensive. Just the ordinary bread and butter KUTUBE stuff cost a fortune, and KUCAGE, forget it. Libya was a very pricey place. The boys were working like mad counting stacks of Libyan money, which was printed up absolutely crazy, with the words reading backward from right to left like most Arabic, but then, brace yourself, the digits reading from left to right. That is you were reading along comfortably in one direction about the Islamic Republic of Libya and you came to some figures and, *zip*, you had to change direction, then, *zip*, back in the first direction again for more words. Zigzag. What was all the Libyan money for? I don't know; they didn't tell me that. To lay around on some Libyans, I guess. Or to take it out via diplomatic pouch and lay it around abroad to make it look like Libya was behind something. You made a false-flag recruitment, say. Let the guy think he was doing it for Libya. Or you wanted to get somebody sore at the Libyans, so you spread Libyan money around to make it look as if the Libyans did some repulsive thing that they maybe even didn't. It had to be plausible of course. Like take the Kurds. That was really a sophisticated operation. Unless the Libyans paid off people abroad in oil dollars. In which case this was for laying on Libyans.

"Count it," he said. This was another of those FitzWilliam types. Amherst maybe this time. Wesleyan.

"What do you mean count it?" I said. "I can't read Arabic."

"I'll give you five minutes to learn to read figures in Arabic," he answered scornfully. "What are you, stupid? They're on every milestone."

Actually it wasn't so hard. But only the digits. Pink money. Blue money. Purple money. Life-Saver colors.

"And you count it out right in front of him when you give it to him," he instructed me.

"What if he gives me an argument?"

"You can say yes and no, can't you?"

"I don't know in Libyan."

"*Aywah* and *la*-glottal stop. If he argues say no."

"Why don't you send someone who speaks Arabic anyway?"

"We're short-handed," said the man, not very loveable. Not a man you could love for himself.

A shack by moonlight. This Arab walks into the glare of my headlights, showing his hands, then climbs into the front seat beside me, holding a flashlight while I count the money. He counts it again himself then sticks it in his jacket, mumbling something in Arabic. "*Elahfoo,*" I say. He makes no acknowledgment. It might have been the wrong dialect. Crazy stuff. Crazy stuff. You never knew what you were doing with that KUDOVE. Bits and pieces. Dribs and drabs. You could be paying off your own grandmother. It was dreary. It was menial. It was boring. It was dumb. They never told you enough to make it fun.

I saw Omar when I got back late that night sitting in the rooftop lounge of the hotel by himself, staring out over the rubble of Tripoli toward the Mediterranean. He'd disappeared at dinner time and there'd been a rumor that Kaddafi had called for him to consult about the movie, but it occurred to me that he might just be ducking Mouna. Now he was probably afraid to go back to his suite. A peppermint highball was in front of him on the table, ignored. I tasted it when I came up. It was a pure peppermint highball. Omar hardly looked at me.

"Get another room," I said. "There are empty rooms."

He didn't answer but just kept staring out dispiritedly over the harbor, very beautiful in the moonlight.

"He says it's sacrilegious," said Omar somberly, still not looking at me.

"Kaddafi."

Omar nodded mutely.

"How can he say it's sacrilegious?" I asked. "You told me he said he loved it. He wanted us to get an actor to play Mohammed."

"So he's had second thoughts," said Omar in ill temper. "He's changed his mind. He's mercurial."

"Why?"

"He wants to unify with Egypt again," Omar snapped. "Syria, the Sudan, Tunisia, Saudi Arabia. One Arab nation. How do I know why? Maybe he wants to buy Paramount from Gulf and Western."

"But we just got here. Why didn't he think of this before?"

"How the fucking hell do I know why he didn't think of this before!" exploded Omar. "Because he's a crazy lunatic fuckhead, that's why! Because he's unstable! Because he doesn't keep his word! Because it's not in the Koran! Because if God had meant man to make movies he'd have given him a built-in Arriflex!"

He was breathing hard.

"Where do we go from here, Ome?" I asked dismally. "Who's going to take us in?"

Omar slumped back on the cushions of the lounge chair in a state of collapse, a look of utmost desolation on his face. He didn't answer.

"What's the budget now?" I said quietly.

"Fifteen million," said Omar without looking at me.

It made most KUCAGE operations seem modest.

"The move from Morocco to here brought it from ten million to fifteen million," I said.

He nodded.

"If the Libyans welsh on their agreements the way the Moroccans did we're through. Is that it? We go under." It was getting really grim.

"It's not the money," said Omar, giving his head a barely discernible shake. "It's finding a place."

I tried to cheer him up. I had a lot at stake myself. My dreams of financial greatness were tied to this nutty movie, and I'd realized all along I was lucky to have someone like Omar who really believed in it. His lunacy, which blinded him to some of life's realities, was a precious commodity when it came to an enterprise based so heavily on hope. I gave him one of my best pep talks ever. *Fight, Ome! Fight!* All we needed was a country that wasn't too fanatic about its religion and had oil so it could withstand Saudi pressure. "Camels," murmured Omar lifelessly, and in a moment, "infrastructure." That eliminated Qatar, Bahrain, Dubai, Abu Dhabi, and all of those. "We're running out of countries!" moaned Omar. "An Arab country with oil that's patriotic about its religion but isn't too fanatic, has some infrastructure, communications facilities, camels, isn't too fundamentalist about the Koran, isn't too socialist or pro-Russian, is reliable and can keep its word . . . How many countries are there left! There aren't any like that!"

227

"Iraq," I said.

Omar sat stock still for a moment and then shuddered.

"Iraq is the worst," he said. "The last time I was in Iraq they threw me into a toilet."

"Why?"

"How do I know why?" he bristled. "I come into the airport at Baghdad. All my papers are in perfect order, visa, passport. I can talk Arabic to them like a dream. *Bark! Bark! Bark!* They throw me into a toilet stall and lock the door and keep me there for three hours and then throw me onto the next plane out. Public executions. Ugh. *Errrgh!* They execute people in public to keep their spirits up, morale high. Has an edifying effect on the onlooker."

He sat as if revolted, then almost seemed to panic.

"We'll get killed," he said. "They're fighting Kurds. They'll think we're Kurds."

"The Iranians are supplying the insurgents in Iraq," I said, ticking them off. "But the Iraqis are supplying the insurgents in Oman. Also the South Yemenis. While the Iranians are supporting the *government* in Oman. Also — "

"It's all so complicated," cried Omar. "And I went into the movies because I wanted decent values. I wanted to live the life of art. The Saudis are merciless! They're persecuting us!"

"Well, we're up against a strong religious taboo there," I said. "Thou shalt not worship graven images."

"Who's asking them to worship them?" Omar said, exasperated. "I just want them to have them around."

"Thou shalt not have them around either. You know that."

"Then why are there pictures in the Saudi Arabian tourist office?" he raged. "Of Mecca!"

"But not of the Prophet," I said. "No screwing around with the Prophet."

"Why?" bellowed Omar, people in the lounge turning around to look at us. "He's not supernatural! You told me so yourself! Only the Koran is a miracle! Why can't there be pictures of the Prophet like there are pictures of Saint

228

Peter and Saint Paul and Saint Matthew and Saint Mark and Saint Luke and Saint John and Abraham and Isaac and Joseph in Egypt?"

"Not to mention the Virgin Mary," I said. It struck me he'd reeled off a lot of saints' names for someone raised in the Moslem religion. "Because they've got a taboo against pictures," I said. "Particularly religious pictures. Are you just learning this for the first time? Go argue with the King of Saudi Arabia. He wants to pray in Jerusalem and wants to walk there on foot and he doesn't want any Israelis around defiling the road. It's got to be holy Arab ground the whole way."

Omar sat as if stunned, but not by anything said by me.

"Whereas Jerusalem being us Christians' number-one holy city and not our number-three holy city," I said to brighten things up, "I think a Christian U.S. president ought to be able to walk there on foot without any Jews or Moslems around. I think the Mount of Olives should be undefiled by un-Christian foot."

Omar suddenly got all choked up with emotion.

"A masterpiece, a masterpiece we have here," he said with tears in his eyes. "And it might never see the light. A film rich with a message of peace for humankind."

It wasn't often you heard Omar use the word "humankind." The tears left his eyes and he stared out over the moonlit roofs and the sands and the harbor with a visionary look, a man who saw a better world, shining with hope, where men laid up treasure upon earth but recycled it for the benefit of humankind, and the lion lay down with the lamb.

Whereas out there over the harbor what I saw was a world of limited objectives, one of which was me being rich. It was less inspiring, I grant you. It didn't inspire the multitudes. It didn't have that exalted, millenarian appeal, or promise salvation, no lions and lambs. So Omar would take the high road, and I'd take the low road. And I didn't give a damn who got to Scotland first just so we got there.

229

19

"FOR THINE IS the oil and the fullness thereof," I said to him the next morning but he didn't think it was funny. I thought it was kind of funny.

"Look at the lilies of the field," I said. "They promote not; neither do they hustle."

"Fuck you," said Omar.

I was just trying to cheer him up. I guess he wasn't a Christian. We were in the sitting room of his suite after breakfast, trying to think our way out of this.

"Quit horsing around," snapped Omar. "Give me an Arab hero they've heard of in Topeka."

I didn't follow him. If *Mohammed Superstar* was a boff, we were going to take more petro-money and make more petro-movies and we'd be on the prowl for more petro-heroes. But *Mohammed* wasn't a boff. For the moment it was dead on its feet. Omar caught my puzzled look.

"We take the footage we've got," he explained with optimism flowing in him again. "And we just hang some other Arab story on it, that's all. Then we've got no problems with religious taboo and all that jazz. How about Saladin?"

Well you had to admire his bounce-back quality. *De l'audace, de l'audace.*

"And the Mecca scenes?" I said.

We'd shot big scenes with Mohammed driving the idolaters from the Kaaba, like Christ driving the moneylenders from the Temple except it was Mohammed driving the idolaters. It was hard to see how you could work in Saladin.

"Junk it!" Omar declared. "Cut our losses! Move forward! The *one if by land* and *the British are coming* sequence we can still use. It's all-purpose stuff. You just write us another Arab historical story that fits the action. Remember *Speed is of the Essence?* When all those drug-addict movies started to die Paramount just took the footage, knocked out the drug nonsense, and made a beautiful little love story out of it?"

"It still bombed," I said.

"What's the matter with Saladin?" said Omar. "A famous Arab. Everybody's heard of him. I say Saladin."

"Wait a minute, Ome, take it easy. Saladin's the twelfth, thirteenth century, something like that, the Crusades. We'd have to have medieval armor, Richard the Lion Hearted. And wasn't Saladin a Kurd?"

"He was not!"

"I think he was though."

"Okay, smart guy," said Omar, getting indignant. "You're the one who knows so much about history. You're trying to tell me that the Arabs are such a spiritually impoverished race they don't have any great men? Any legendary heroes?"

"But Topeka, Ome. You said Topeka."

"I'm sure there must be some." Omar scowled. "We've just got to get ourselves together."

I offered him Almanzor, the one who took Granada. I offered him Gibraltar. "Gibraltar?!" he objected. "Gibraltar's a *rock*." First there was the guy, then there was the rock, I said. He was the Arab who conquered Spain. We could start with the rock and work back to the guy. It was better than Almanzor where you didn't even have a rock. Nobody had heard of him, period. This seemed to open whole new avenues to Omar. He grew more chipper.

"How about doing the Old Testament in Arab dress?" he asked. "Like *Green Pastures?* The Bible the way these crazy Arab darkies see it. It's a cute idea actually. Yasir Arafat plays De Lawd."

In the middle of this last remark by Omar I'd heard the door open and out of the corner of my eye had seen Mouna come into the room. We hadn't met since I'd arrived in Libya and what with the tension between her and Omar I'd been wondering what she was like these days, how we'd get on. We'd been pretty friendly those last weeks in Morocco.

"Be serious, Omar, for Christsake," I said.

I looked at Mouna directly. She was standing in the middle of the room now, white with rage, her eyes wide and fixed, staring at Omar. A lot of white around the eye.

"Hiya, Mouna," I said. "Long time no see."

"You unprincipled swine!" she spat out, quivering with fury, still glaring at Omar. She hadn't given me a glance.

Well, that surprised me, you know? Such hostility. It was so excessive. And all for Omar. Nothing for me. No welcome home? No affectionate greeting for an old teammate and comrade in arms? Omar was sitting with his head fearfully hunched down between his shoulders, looking as if he was considering running out of the room.

"Come on, Mouna," I said. "He was just kidding. He doesn't really think Arabs are darkies. Give us a break. We're trying to figure out a way to save the picture."

Her eyes swung wildly around to me.

"*You keep your mouth shut!*" she screamed.

"Mouna . . ." said Omar apprehensively, and then jammed. Nothing would come out.

"Say, Mouna. What is this?" I said. I was a man of peace. "We're working! He was just joking! Fight with him some other time."

She ignored me and slowly began to circle Omar physically as if she was moving in for the kill, as if she was going to dart in another moment and try to strangle him. Her hands were like claws. I don't know what she was going to do to him.

"Hey, Mouna, take it easy," I said. "For that matter, Mouna, would you mind leaving us alone please? We're trying to save the picture, damn it. We've got a lot on our mind. In fact we're desperate. If we don't think of something the whole picture's going to go up the pipe."

"You filthy hypocrite!" she snarled at me, turning right back to Omar.

Actually I didn't object to the word "hypocrite." It was just one of those words, like "fascist."

"Mouna," I said. "We've got work to do. Would you mind getting out of here?"

She was circling Omar again. His eyes were darting about. I think she was really going to try to choke him.

"Mouna!" I shouted. "Get out of here! Take your principles and fuck off! Who do you think you are anyway?"

She let out an interesting noise, I guess it was a squeal, and suddenly turned on her heel and stamped out of the room. She was a true believer though, I guess. She was sincere. She wasn't one of these people, *Down with the consumer society but this has nothing to do with my three-picture deal with Warner Brothers.* No, no. She had integrity.

"There you go antagonizing her," said Omar reproachfully.

"Antagonize her! What was she doing to you? Is that the thanks I get for coming to your defense? What were you going to let her do, chew you up into little pieces? Get tough with her, for the love of Mike! She walks all over you!"

"But Arafat's a god to her," said Omar in a hushed, cautious voice. "You can't take Arafat's name in vain when she's around. How would you like it if she spoke disrespectfully about Thomas Jefferson or somebody like that?"

"That really would shake me up," I said. "So what are you telling that to me for? Tell it to yourself. I never kid around with her about Yasir Arafat. No, sir. Never. You're the one. You're the one who brought his name up.

"Anyhow I thought you were going to give her the boot," I added as an afterthought. "What happened to that? What's she doing still butting in here as if she owns the place?"

Omar nervously rubbed his hands together.

"She's very high strung," he said anxiously.

"I think she's a menace, having her around," I said, glad to have her out of the room. "I think you should get rid of her. I think you've got nutty taste in women."

There was a knock at the door. It was Mohammed, our Libyan. There were a lot of Libyans in the act now but he was our original Libyan, the muck-a-muck from the Information Ministry. He was wearing a dark green polo shirt, the Prophet's color.

"Omar!" he cried. "Burton!"

There was great shaking of hands and hugging. He was just in from Morocco, where he'd stayed to wind things up. But now we were wound up in Libya. What good could he do us now? Also he'd had an affair with Mouna too. We all had a richly interwoven relationship.

"What are you doing around here when we're licking our wounds, you bum?" I asked him. "Your boss just closed us down. He's kicked us out. We're through."

"No, no!" boomed Mohammed, his face all smiles, beautiful teeth. "We have not losed everything! We can widdle Kaddafi!"

"Widdle?" I said. "You mean diddle. We can diddle Kaddafi?"

It was a nice thought.

"No, no!" cried Mohammed. "Widdle! Widdle!"

Omar shot something at him in Arabic, got an answer, and sank into an armchair, unnerved. "Wheedle," he said weakly. "We can wheedle Kaddafi. We can get around him."

"Yes!" said Mohammed. "We can go around him! He has true heart, is true Arab generosity. He understands your trouble you are in. I speak to him! I widdle him!"

"God damn it, for Christsake, Mohammed!" I said. "Widdle you! Have you spoken to him yet or haven't you? I hope that's your lucky shirt you got on."

"Ah," said Mohammed, raising a finger with a twinkle in his eye as if to say patience, patience.

234

He had a plan.

Things had been happening in the outside world that these movie people knew nothing about, you see. For Omar there was only this movie. Of course I was a person of much broader interests. A few days earlier a Libyan Airways 727 with a pilot who'd been flying the Tripoli-Cairo shuttle for months overshot Cairo by a couple of hundred kilometers, which was a hundred and twenty-five miles. And it overshot the Suez Canal by a hundred kilometers too, despite all those Egyptian antiaircraft tracking stations, why didn't they warn it? And since all this was happening before Sadat went to Jerusalem, and Israel gave the Sinai back to Egypt, this meant the 727 had crossed over into territory controlled by the Israeli military, very edgy people about that sort of thing. So the pilot of the 727 was tooling along with landing gear up and passenger blinds down fifty miles inside Israeli-held Sinai when Israeli F-4's scrambled and vectored out and challenged him, but he ignored them. He thought they were Egyptian Migs. I was a pilot myself and if you thought F-4's were Migs, forget it. Not to mention their wing markings. So the Israelis, thinking the 727 might be loaded with explosives, flew simulated attack runs and fired warning bursts. And the pilot still ignored them. Quixotically, he still thought they were Migs. *Vete a saber.* You figure it out. So then, kiddies, the Israelis shot the 727 down in the Sinai Desert, a hundred civilian passengers dead, and the world was in an uproar. The Arab world was in an uproar. People were upset. The Arabs were calling on Kaddafi to avenge them. *Avenge us, O Kaddafi!* They wanted him to shoot down El Al planes over the Mediterranean with his Mirages. But what wasn't known to the general Arab public, and I just happened to come by as a piece of incidental information, was that Kaddafi's Mirages needed ground-control equipment to navigate and that beyond a hundred-mile-or-so radius they didn't know where the hell they were.

So Kaddafi had these problems on his mind, you see. How to avenge yourself beyond a hundred-mile operating radius. Which no doubt contributed to his erratic behavior toward us. Here we were egocentrically thinking only of our movie while poor Kaddafi had these real problems on his mind. But if the shooting down of this Libyan plane that couldn't tell Migs from F-4's had brought misfortune upon us by causing Kaddafi radius problems, it was also going to lead to our salvation. This was Mohammed's plan: The Israelis were sending the dead bodies from the plane back to Benghazi and a mass burial would be held there and Kaddafi was going to attend. So we would go along too, you see, very conspicuously, filming and documenting, and documenting and filming, to show we were in sympathy and were Friends of the Arabs, which was very important. And all this would cause Kaddafi's light to shine upon us again when he got over being upset by the crisis. When Mohammed said "friends of the Arabs" I caught a glint in Omar's eye that meant as plain as day, *Now don't screw this up, Nelson*, which I resented. Why should I screw it up? What did he think I was, some kind of wild man? Just because I didn't lie down in front of Mouna like a doormat? I wasn't crazy. I was a friend of the Arabs. I was a friend of the Arabs.

I was real curious to see Mouna again though in private. There were levels and levels inside that Mouna. She had a separate room from Omar now. There was a long pause after I knocked and I felt somehow that she was in but wasn't going to come to the door. When suddenly it opened and she was standing there, hollow-eyed, in her bare feet, a couple of inches shorter than I was used to her being. I had expected her to react at seeing me but she took me in with no surprise, her eyes smoldering, haggard. Her look bespoke passion, bitterness, hatred maybe. True hatred? For an instant she did absolutely nothing and on an intuition I stepped inside and closed the door behind me, turned again and found her leaning against the wall with her eyes shut. I stooped and kissed her and she began to shiver.

"You just want to abuse me," she said, her voice hoarse, eyes still shut. "To demand and denigrate. I who have asked

236

you for nothing. Who have given you selfless love, asking only to hold you in my arms, feeling your warmth as my own."

I didn't recognize us from her description. I don't know, it just wasn't the impression I'd had of our relationship up to now. The style was peculiar. It made me a little uneasy.

We went inside and sat on the edge of the bed and I was wondering whether to apologize to her about Yasir Arafat when immediately her hand went to my fly. She got it out and began rubbing it up and down with a quick, agitated motion as if she was polishing brightwork, but with a remote, resentful look on her face as if brooding on some remembered injury. When I tried to move off a bit she kind of growled, making a low threatening noise in her throat, hanging onto me, still polishing it as if it was silverware. Closing her eyes, she bent forward and engulfed it in her mouth, still making these growly noises, but I had only the back of her dark head to look at now, bobbing up and down, which was kind of lonely. It was a little impersonal, nothing to look at, no one to talk to. I was a little scared of her. Whether she loved you or hated you, she was always so angry. Soon we were stripped and lying on the bed doing the usual drill, Mouna rumbling ominously, her unseeing eyes half closed. Angry nooky. Wrathful nooky. It was interesting in a way. When she came her eyeballs rolled up so you could see only the whites. This was all in broad Libyan daylight. The next time around her eyes were almost closed, just a thin line of white visible between the lids.

"I want to hold it," she announced aggressively.

Her all over. You'd never catch her asking gently could she hold it? Or would I mind if she held it please? She grabbed it as if it were a broom handle. This gave me the notion she wanted the general action to continue, but she rebuffed further caresses on my part.

"I despise Omar," she said fiercely, handling my joint watchfully. "He's contemptible."

Well, now maybe this was funny of me, but there was only a very limited number of subjects I wanted to talk about while a woman was handling my joint and one of them was not Omar. He was just not sexy to think about.

"He doesn't have a scrap of idealism in him," she seethed, her hand active. "Not a shred. He'd never sacrifice anything for anybody."

I still said nothing. I just wanted the subject to go away. Mouna now glared at the corner of the room, still stroking.

"That's why I've given everything to you," she said vengefully. "You're everything he's not. That's why I belong to you so utterly."

This made me uneasy again. Actually I'd have settled for a lot less than utterly. The responsibility was too great. Mouna closed her eyes and drew closer and once more I thought she wanted some action, but she firmly rebuffed it.

"No, let's just lie here like this," she said. "It's so restful, so beautiful." She went on stroking slowly. "Just lie there, my darling, while your beloved ministers to your every wish."

Provided I wished what she wished.

"I just love holding it," she breathed fervently. "It belongs to me, I know it." Which was overstatement surely. I mean what the hell. It belonged to me.

Mouna's hand stopped moving and she wasn't doing anything with me anymore, but she wouldn't let it go either. We both lay there motionless and she held it tight in her right hand, her eyes shut. But there was nothing she'd let me hold. It would have spoiled her restfulness. Soon she appeared to be slipping backward into a half-sleep, still holding on to me. Her dry lips parted and I heard parched sounds but couldn't understand them. Was it English? Arabic? What was she doing, reciting mantras? Then her eyes opened a sliver again with just a thin line of white showing, her lips moving, making these parched sounds. It was spooky. She was getting very spooky.

In another day she had a poster of George Habash up on her wall. Try having some woman treat your joint like a cocktail shaker with that looking down at you. Talk about lonely. Omar didn't fire her. Mouna stayed on working for this brink-of-disaster movie of ours, but she and Omar led separate lives now, the Palestinian diaspora coming out of the woodwork again. It turned out Tripoli was filled with Palestinians, doing the jobs the Libyans were too backward to do since they'd never had a British Mandate. You had to remember we were sitting right on top of the world's greatest spawning ground of covert action operations of all types, a major Libyan growth industry. Mouna's Palestinian friends were all panting to meet me, no doubt eager to build bridges and wean us from our unhealthy attachment to Israel. And the boys at the shop were still panting to meet Palestinians, part of their eternal quest for the eternal moderate, which sometimes made the Holy Grail seem a positive cinch. Everybody wanted something from somebody else naturally. That was the way it was. The operations in Morocco had had names like MONSOON, MONGREL, MOTORBOAT, MOTOWN. Here in Libya they were called LIPSTICK, LILLIPUT, LITTORAL, LITANY. I never walked into the shop but they had something ridiculous they wanted to saddle me with. I was going to Benghazi? It just so happened that they had this Mercedes-Benz on this complicated registration deal. Somebody had sold it, and somebody had bought it, and this agent in Benghazi needed it. And since I was going to Benghazi.

A postcard came from Janie Holt, who'd been to Iran again.

Dear Burt,
Maurice and I are having the yummiest time in Teheran.
I know you'll like each other.
Love,
Janie

Which was very nice, but who was Maurice? That Janie scattered enigmas at every turn. Was Maurice the new boy friend? If so, why should we meet? And if "Maurice" was code for Mohammed Shah Pahlevi, why should I meet him either? What was I supposed to do, play the maracas while they danced the nudists' cha-cha-cha? That silly Janie had such access to power, such closeness, such true proximity; she felt the real charisma of the charisma. But what could you get out of her? It was such a waste.

Mouna saw the postcard and bristled at the sight. I don't need to tell you about the burning hatred Mouna felt toward Iranians, who were friendly toward Israel then. But Mouna had lots of burning hatreds, fellow Arabs weren't spared either. Mouna and her friends hated Iraqis, for example. Now would you have known that? It was because of the infamous *stab in the back,* she told me, her face white. In Black September, 1970, the PLO thought the Iraqis should intervene to save it from the ferocious Jordanians, but the Iraqis didn't do a darn thing. It was the famous non-stab Iraqi stab in the back. Not to be confused with Black *June*, when the *Syrians* invaded *Lebanon* against the PLO, which was more of a stabbing-type stab in the back, until the Syrians switched sides. You had to keep all this stuff straight. And Mouna was hating Omar quite a lot these days too. *How can you bear a man who lives for such sordid commercial motives*? she asked me, her lips curling in contempt. The night before the rest of us went to Benghazi for the big funeral, Mouna suddenly flew off to Beirut in the hopes of meeting Leila Khaled, no less, the famous hijacker lady. *I want to devote my life to my people*, Mouna told me before she left, her eyes burning menacingly. *You may never see me again*.

Then we went to Benghazi.

20

O, BUNCH GRASS, including alfalfa grass! O tropical desert
shrub! O plantless rock desert! O plantless sand desert! O
temperate green xerophytes even here and there! There
were thousands and thousands of miles of the stuff. It was
big. It was horrible. Libya's big. Never in my life will I cross
that bugger again in an automobile. What an idea that was.
Mohammed, Omar, and me, we whiled away the carefree,
desiccated hours telling tales of brave deeds of yore. "We
beat America in first war against States," said Mohammed
in a mood of urbane satisfaction, happily drinking a cigarette. "We sink two American ships, *Philadelphia* and *Intrepid.* You shall see. I think we beat America again." Now
you will not necessarily recognize this as an account of our
war against the Barbary Pirates, most of which did indeed
take place in this very hellhole we were driving in, Tripoli,
no one having heard of Libya yet. It was in the Marine
Hymn, from the halls of Montezuma to the shores of Libya.
In the American version, needless to say, we won. Mohammed really filled you with such disdain for these tacky new
nations clutching at the most ludicrous crumbs to give themselves a sense of importance, brainwashing their poor subjects into quite absurd delusions of greatness, considering
that we'd blown the thieving little fuckers clean out of the
water, in our history books. Well, you couldn't expect any
help from Omar, so as we drove across this Death Valley
East I set out the facts of the case for Mohammed's benefit.

First of all the *Philadelphia* hadn't sunk at all. We voluntarily ran it upon an uncharted reef off Tripoli harbor, and it surrendered and the pirates took three hundred brave U.S. tars prisoner and held them for ransom, a technique still popular in the area, as you will have noticed. And the pirates didn't sink the *Intrepid* either. It so happens we sank the *Intrepid*. I mean we filled it to the gunwales with gunpowder, and a crew of thirteen men sailed it into the harbor at night to wreak havoc. And just as it should have been nearing the docks there was this great blast and it kind of blew up with all hands, no survivors. It wreaked itself havoc. The pirates get no credit for it whatsoever. I explained this, too, to Mohammed. The greatest U.S. exploit of the war was us creeping back onto our own *Philadelphia* and setting it on fire. These slimy pirates captured it when it ran aground but it didn't do them any good. Then Eaton and O'Bannon and the Bey of Tripoli's smarter brother and a motley invading force of six hundred Arabs and other delinquents they'd picked up in Egypt marched across the desert in the opposite direction from the way we were driving, but never got past Derna, never did get to Tripoli. The fact of the matter was the war ended in a standoff. The Tripoli pirates gave us back our brave tars and we gave them sixty thousand dollars, which must have been worth millions then.

But if you really want to know the truth, like say you were going to make a movie about it, without altering a single fact you could go either way with it depending on who put up the money. If Hollywood came up with the financing you could play it like *55 Days at Peking*, which we also made in Spain. You emphasized the audacity of the enterprise to begin with, the bravery of our brave tars, particularly that night going in on the *Intrepid*, poignant last moments, and the fearlessness of the boarding party that burned the captured *Philadelphia*, in the background these shifty Tripolitanian jackals always breaking their word, and how the pirates gave us back our tars. That way it was an American victory. As in our history books, in fact. If the Libyans put up the money you emphasized the audacity and bravery of

242

these early Libyan-nationalist tars, particularly their bold capture of the grounded *Philadelphia,* coming out in such little boats, a plucky little country not letting itself be pushed around by this oversize bully, and ending with world public opinion forcing sixty thousand dollars out of the U.S. in war reparations. This way it was a Libyan victory, as in the Libyan history books. It was all in what side you showed the action from, who you made good looking and who you made homely, who acted nice and who acted like a jerk. You could also work in how the treacherous American jackals left their mercenaries in the lurch, taking their Marines and their puppet Hamet back on their ships and sailing out to sea, abandoning their native troops on the beach. There was that. As the Americans put to sea, their Arab ex-auxiliaries were attempting to escape the Bay of Tripoli's sanguinary vengeance by fleeing on foot across the desert, disappearing at this point from the pages of even Libyan history and quite likely dying of thirst. Used in the epilogue, the dying of thirst in the desert would provide a powerful dramatic lesson to any Third Worlders so gullible as to trust these Americans with their fine talk about freedom and democracy and bearing any burden and supporting any friend. The epilogue part of the story Mohammed didn't know anything about and I kept it to myself. Let's put it this way. If Mohammed was willing to settle for a draw on who won our war with the Barbary Pirates and didn't know about the dying of thirst part, why should I hand it to him on a silver platter? This was all while we were driving down along the coast of High Barbary where it had all taken place, otherwise known as Libya. Ten parching hours from Tripoli to Benghazi.

The camera and generator and other equipment came by road too in a truck, and this whole elaborate campaign was because we were sucks, trying to worm our way back into the good graces of the new master of the Barbary Coast and world cinema, Moamer Kaddafi.

Benghazi. I told you about Tripoli already; you can imagine Benghazi. The Israelis had finally sent back the bodies of the passengers killed in the shooting down of the 727 and the mass funeral ceremony was going to be held in a big empty lot, with all the coffins lined up in rows on the sandy ground in the 110-degree heat. Thousands and thousands of desert people had thronged into the city by camel and on foot, traveling all night to get there, and were now assembled, a muttering, illiterate mass, waiting for the ceremony to begin. We were all set up with full camera and sound crews, but had left Sandor behind in Tripoli in case things should take an anti-Jewish turn the way things sometimes do.

"This is wonderful, this is just great!" cried Omar, bubblingly unaffected by the heat, directing his cameraman to get in the multitudes, the coffins, the mourners. We were all on a fifteen-foot steel-tubing platform with a plunging view of the coffins and the spot where Kaddafi was supposed to appear. Mohammed Maziq was with us and we were very conspicuous perched there above the crowd, where Kaddafi couldn't help but see us.

"Do we have film in the camera?" I asked Omar, who got offended.

"Don't you see he's got a magazine clipped in?" he said tartly.

"I thought maybe the magazine was empty."

I didn't know just how sincere we had to be.

"I'm going to give the footage to NBC London as soon as the ceremony's over," declared Omar reprovingly. "I'm going to fly it there at my own expense."

"Who are all those guys," I asked Mohammed, nodding at a cluster of distinguished old gentlemen in flowing white robes at the front of the coffins, near a brigade of officials in Western dress.

"Imams," said Mohammed. "Holy people."

The hordes of Bedouins and Benghazi locals pressed against us, and from atop our platform it was as if we were floating on a sea of white-clothed Libyans, stirring and tossing and rippling. As I looked out over the eddying sea suddenly a great shout went up, with the veil-less Berber desert women shrieking their piercing war whoop. Turning back toward the front where the officials were I saw Kaddafi in his khaki uniform, bare-headed, intent. There was a tremendous uproar, with people screaming and raising their fists. Our camera was rolling, panning out over the crowd and then back to Kaddafi. "What are they shouting?" I asked Mohammed.

"*Avenge us, O Kaddafi, Avenge us.*"

"Against Israel," I said to show I was following.

Mohammed gave a small movement as if he didn't necessarily endorse the sentiment but acknowledging that that did seem to be the implication.

All at once a teenage boy broke through the cordon of police and security men and bounded out among the coffins like a jackrabbit, climbing on top of one coffin and yelling something with an enraged, rabid look on his face, shaking his fist, then dashing toward Kaddafi until he was submerged by the muscle power of a dozen guards. I asked Mohammed what he'd been shouting.

"Hail, Kaddafi," answered Mohammed without missing a beat.

"But it didn't look as if he was saying, *Hail, Kaddafi.*"

I turned to Omar. The shouting was in some kind of dialect, but he'd understood it. His face was very glum. We were still rolling.

"He said, *You have betrayed us, Kaddafi. The Egyptians have betrayed us. Shame. Shame.*"

"Egyptians?"

I was puzzled because you've got to remember this was all before Egypt broke with the other Arabs and got friendly with Israel and Sadat was still an Arab Brother, not an Arab Fink. In fact he'd done pretty well in the Yom Kippur War and far from being a traitor was really something of a hero, a genuine Arab hero. This was in the large view.

Now suddenly hundreds of youths were breaking through the police cordon from every direction, dashing over the coffins, shouting. It was pandemonium. The crowd surged forward, and backward, and people were running every which way and screaming, and our platform began swaying, and men were grabbing the steel tube structure and shaking it.

"My God, the camera!" cried Omar. "We're not covered by insurance! Save the camera!"

Which was very professional of him but from my point of view if it came to a choice between saving the camera and being torn to pieces by the mob, to hell with the camera. It looked as if the platform was really going to collapse so I carefully climbed down on the side away from the people who were shaking us and sat on a coffin with everybody charging about like mad and watched Mohammed plead with the demonstrators to leave the platform standing, wondering dully what the basis of his appeal might be. Freedom of the press? No great nation without untrammeled communications media? Omar climbed down now too and sat on the coffin beside me, saying nothing, speechless, staring vacantly. It was like being in the middle of a human fireworks display, with a great roaring, everybody running in a different direction. Over the public address system I'd heard Kaddafi trying to continue the ceremony for a few minutes, but then he got alarmed and packed up and went.

After a while the riot seemed to run out of steam. Miraculously, the platform was still standing, if wobbly, the camera intact. We were all alive. Higher powers decided that the ceremony should go on, and even without Kaddafi the pallbearers came forward now to carry the coffins to the cemetery. Filming this thing as a means of ingratiating ourselves with Kaddafi had become somewhat moot by this time, not to say preposterous, so we left the camera and crew behind us and Mohammed, Omar, and I — me in a *kefiya* borrowed from one of the drivers — trudged after the unruly mob as the hot wind rose, blowing the burning desert sand in our faces.

"Say, Mohammed," I brought out as we marched along behind the crowd, which was still erupting in cries and angry shouts. "What do these people have against the Egyptians? Aren't they brother Arabs?"

Mohammed made the Arab gesture for it being in the hands of Allah. Only Allah knew. Take it up with Allah.

We tramped for what seemed like hours behind the coffins in the hot wind and sand, with the crowd rumbling balefully. At the city outskirts in sight of the cemetery all hell broke loose again, men charging about like maniacs, pallbearers dropping their coffins, coffins breaking open, everybody screaming in Arabic.

"Egypt betrayed us. Vengeance," Omar translated joylessly after we'd withdrawn to the edge of the crowd.

"What? Who?" I said.

"Maybe we go," said Mohammed, deciding that no further good will could accrue to any friends of the Arabs watching this spectacle.

"Wait a minute! Why Egypt?" I asked, exasperated. "What did Egypt do? It's Israel they're supposed to hate!"

But suddenly everybody was running back toward the center of town, the whole insane mob, shouting curses about Egypt, Sadat, the Egyptian army, vengeance, betrayal, Egypt had betrayed them, Sadat had betrayed them. They tore through the streets.

"They run after Egyptians," explained Mohammed.

"Well, that's logical," I said.

It was hopeless. Everybody charging about. It was a real riot, I guess. We left the cemetery and coffins and made our way back to our hotel, Omar so withdrawn as to be almost catatonic, stumbling along, one foot in front of the other. Idly the three of us watched the rioters from the hotel steps. "They're looting the Egyptian Consulate!" someone cried excitedly. The former palace of King Idris. Then they sacked the offices of Egyptair and an Egyptian export-import company. The crowd was attacking Egyptians on sight, the word came. "How does a Libyan recognize an Egyptian?" I asked, just as a gang of white-robed madmen started throwing rocks and bricks at us in front of the hotel. We nipped into the lobby where we could still see the rioters from behind a big plate-glass window. Glass didn't seem to me to be the best imaginable shelter from people throwing rocks but

Mohammed said, "No! Symbol! They throw symbols." "They look like rocks to me," I said, but he looked imperturbable and manly. "Only little rocks," he said, and I didn't see why I should be more chicken than a Libyan, so we stayed there.

"But tell me, Mohammed," I said. "Would you mind explaining to me? It seems elementary, I know, but why Egypt? What does Egypt have to do with it?"

"These Benghazi people," he said, dissociating himself. "I Tripoli. Maybe foolish people."

"Foolish or not foolish, they've got to have something against the Egyptians, don't they?" I insisted. "Real or imagined?"

Omar was no help at all, staring inertly out at the mob. Mohammed laughed self-consciously.

"You don't get me in trouble, Burt," he said sheepishly, "but Egyptian have higher life. Higher standard of life, more education. He come to Libya, get better jobs from Libyans maybe. These simple people."

At this point I felt it would be rudely undiplomatic to remind anyone that it was the Israelis who had shot down the Libyan plane, as if I'd be stirring up trouble, inciting Libyans to race hatred against Israel over an unfortunate border incident when they seemed to be perfectly happy hating people of their own choosing, come across in the ordinary course of events.

A crack. A thunderclap. A crinkling, tinkling, melodious falling and deafening crash and it was as if God's ice machine had broken down and we were standing up to our ankles in shattered glass and people were screaming, and I hightailed it out of there and up the service staircase with Omar at my heels, to hell with the elevator, and we barricaded ourselves in Omar's room. There are crazy ways to die but I was goddamned if I was going to be lynched because a mob thought I was an Egyptian.

Safe in the icy, air-conditioned room I wiped the freezing sweat off my face and it turned out to be blood. A flying splinter of glass had cut open my cheek. A couple of inches higher, I realized, and I might have lost an eye, and this unnerved me for a bit as I put Omar's aftershave lotion on the cut, which hurt like a bastard.

The life had gone completely out of Omar again, drained out of his eyes and his whole body as he sat slumped by the window. Our operation for earning Kaddafi's good will and inducing him to rescind his shut-off on our Mohammed movie was a total shambles at this stage, and even our most ardent supporter would have to admit that the idea of finishing the film in Libya was dead for good this time. Omar had both his heart and his pocketbook totally committed to making his soul-movie about the Prophet and was taking it hard, even harder than I was. Soon the camels and the sand dunes of Libya would know us not. And who was to say what other Arab-oil-camel country would come forward to shelter us from the harsh winds of bankruptcy. I was even beginning to wonder, and I had morbid doubt about it for the first time that day in Benghazi, if *Mohammed Superstar* was ever going to get finished anywhere. Omar was right. We were bearers of a message of peace and brotherhood to the world. But did the world want to hear what we had to tell it?

"Five Academy Awards we could have won," said Omar, his voice sepulchral, from beyond the grave. "Best film. Best male lead. Best direction. Best original screenplay. Best music."

"Don't be discouraged, Ome," I said. "We'll find some place. Or we'll turn it into the story of El Gibraltar, remember?"

I stared out the closed window at the white figures still swirling and eddying below. It didn't look as if they were going to set the hotel on fire like Sheppherd's Hotel in Cairo, and no one had followed us to our room to lynch us. We were perfectly safe. It was just a street mob. But suddenly through the glass I heard the whining snap and ping of small-arms fire and felt exposed behind that big glass window as if someone was going to open straight up at us any second with automatic weapons. How could you know?

"Would you mind if we sat in the bathroom, Ome?" I said, because solid walls were better.

Although no one was firing anymore. They'd stopped firing.

I was prepared to take some good-natured ribbing on the point but Omar came along like a zombie and sat down on the lid of the toilet seat without even asking why. I sat on the edge of the bathtub.

"Do you think we'd have a chance with Iraq?" Omar asked somberly.

"I don't know. You're the guy they threw in the toilet."

"I'd let bygones be bygones," said Omar.

"It's okay with me if it's okay with you," I said. "But it might be from the frying pan into the fire. I mean, Iraq."

Omar just sat, slowly taking heart. He was a congenital optimist.

"Maybe Iraq isn't so bad," he said hopefully. "They're no worse than anybody else really maybe."

I didn't say anything.

"What's so bad about Iraq?" he asked cheerily. "Give me details."

I reminded him of the Kassem *coup*, and how after machine-gunning the royal family the Iraqis had hitched Regent Abd al-Ilah to the back of a truck and dragged him through the streets of Baghdad, with people in the crowd screaming in delight and dashing up and cutting off pieces of Adb al-Ilah for souvenirs, first his sexual organs, then both his arms and legs, crying *Allah is great*, just like in our movie. The *coup* leaders laid the corpses out in the center of the city and everybody joyously stamped on them and ran automobiles back and forth over them for hours. Then Abd al-Ilah's body without the arms and legs was hung from a balcony and the crowd went wild and stabbed it with pointed sticks, and people climbed up and whittled off slivers to celebrate.

"Maybe he wasn't popular," said Omar.

Kassem cut off Abd al-Ilah's head and sent it to General de Gaulle, who curiously enough didn't accept it, I recalled.

"I don't think Abd al-Ilah was very popular," said Omar. "Anyway who are we to criticize? You know, after what we did to the Hollywood Ten? Each country has its own life style. If you were an Arab, Iraq wouldn't seem so bad. Look at Saudi Arabia."

I looked at Saudi Arabia. In Saudi Arabia they chop off people's heads in the central square in Riyadh on Friday afternoon, and flog people for drunkenness Mondays and Thursdays, and the blood spatters gaily over the crowd assembled for family entertainment, and the little tots laugh. When you ask the Saudi Attorney-General about it he says, "But it's a free show for the whole town!" Public flogging, the poor man's television. It was not for us to disturb these hallowed folkways. Iraq, indeed. Why not Iraq?

The goddamn car. Burned to a crisp. You'd have thought it had been made of sugar, all black and melted and geflooey. Windows exploded, hood buckled, the insides still smoking. The rioters had burned quite a few. I met the guy late that night down by the port. He was the strangest looking deep-cover man I'd ever seen, luxuriant, flowing black hair and beard, face like a Coptic grave painting, a rich, melodious, very loud voice, a louder laugh. He was a Kuwaiti, and saw the funny side of the present situation about the car. He had a strong sense of fun. "Iraq?" he boomed, and told me a complicated story about Iraq and a scorpion asking a frog to let him ride on his back across the Euphrates. The frog says, *Are you mad? A scorpion's sting can kill you.* But the scorpion answers, *I can't sting you though, don't you see? Because then I'd drown.* So the frog takes the scorpion on his back and frog-swims out onto the Euphrates, but halfway across the scorpion's habits get the better of him and he stings the frog anyway. As the frog dies from the scorpion's poison he turns around and asks him, *Why? Oh, why?* And as the scorpion goes down drowning he answers, *Because it's Iraq!* He had a strong sense of fun about the car.

The story had its pot-and-the-kettle side considering what we'd seen that day in Benghazi. So long as I'd been in Morocco I'd thought the great terrible place was Libya. But I no sooner got to Libya, which largely lived up to expectations, than it started looking as if there was an even terribler place up ahead. It was like, *If you think Libya's something, wait till you see Iraq.* And that's where we were going.

When we got back to Tripoli the next night, I checked in at the hotel desk, went up to my room, took a shower, and was walking down the corridor on my way out again when I caught sight of an Arab in a blue suit waiting in front of the bank of elevators and I kept on walking. Past the elevators without breaking my stride as if I'd never had any intention of taking an elevator. Who me? I had some perfectly routine business down at the other end of the corridor. I kept my face blank, eyes averted. He didn't turn to look as I passed. The only trouble as I walked along with unaltered step was where to go. As I reached the end of the corridor there was only the little room where the chambermaids made toast and coffee for the morning breakfasts and I stepped inside and stood against the wall behind the door. Footsteps approached outside and I drew my .38 and cocked it. They came to a halt just outside the door.

"Burt," I heard. The voice was tentative.

I said nothing.

"Burt, are you in there?"

It was Sandor.

I eased the hammer down and slipped the pistol back into my armpit holster and peeked out the door cautiously.

"Come in," I said.

Sandor walked into the room dazedly. I shut the door after him and stood back against the wall again. The door had no lock.

"Burt," he said, as if talking to a potential madman. "What are you doing in the broom closet?"

"It's not a broom closet," I said. "It's the floor kitchen."

Sandor gazed about at the hot plates and coffee pots. It wasn't much of an explanation, but what was I supposed to tell him? That there was a Syrian standing at the elevators who'd said he'd kill me the next time he saw me? When I'd caught sight of him I didn't even think "Syrian."

I didn't know whether he was a Syrian, Libyan, Moroccan, Algerian, Lebanese, Saudi, Kuwaiti, or what. It was getting hard as hell to remember who was who and what you'd said to which. But there was something instantly ominous about his features. He meant trouble. That I remembered. He might still be out there.

"There's a nice view from this side of the building," I said, waving my hand in the direction of the window, because it was a floor kitchen with a window.

"Sit down," I said.

There were stools. Sandor sat down warily as if humoring a dangerous maniac. I was still standing against the wall. *What was that Syrian doing in Libya?* And me without diplomatic cover. Libya was starting to make me nervous. I had to get out of Libya. Sandor and I admired the view from the floor kitchen for a while. It was on the landward side.

"Hey, Burt, you feeling okay?" asked Sandor.

"Sure."

"You really like it in this place?" he asked, mystified but considerate, me still with my back to the wall.

"Sure," I said crisply.

So what if I liked it in the floor kitchen? Was he so normal?

21

We didn't go to Iraq. You'd have to be out of your mind to go to Iraq. What we did was we went to Cairo, proceeding by indirection on a cushion-shot strategy. I liked Cairo anyway. I liked the faded grandeur, Cairo this shabby lion, but still with some of the old pizzazz. The Egyptians were lovely to us, even putting us on television in kind of a *Meet the Mullahs* program, meet us, these big personalities. Egypt was easy-going compared to some Moslem countries but there were people around who thought this movie of ours was a theological outrage so we met them head on in the mass media, and *bammo*, we really wiped them out. First of all we presented our actors, because in a battle between show business and religious faith show business is really sexy. Then we presented Omar as an Arab who'd made good in Hollywood, which was hard for the Cairenes to resist. Then without showing me on camera we talked about me as this Methodist who despite his deep commitment to Christianity found so much that was admirable and exemplary in Islam that he'd made it his mission to help Omar spread the light of truth. We couldn't present Mouna unfortunately because she had chosen to make her mark in life as a guerrilla or hijacker-person or something like that. And we didn't present Sandor because you never knew. Egypt of course didn't have a drop of life-giving oil and it was all just a prestige play to impress the Arab boondocks. That was our game. Cultural diffusion from metropolis to hinterland. You smiled at a girl in Cairo and the Gulf States came down with the clap. So we got all this prestige, stars of stage, screen, and Egyptian television, and on a winning wicket set out on a tour of the Persian Gulf, which we humored the Arabs by calling the Arabian Gulf, and which in any case produced forty percent of the oil on the world market and was the place we just had to go. So we did our sheik-to-sheik tour of this here Gulf, as our own sheik-to-sheik salesmen, although wanting to buy as much as sell really, looking for a place where we could finish our film in peace. All we needed were camels, sand dunes, oil for independence, not too much religious bigotry, politics not too left-wing, a bit of infrastructure; you know the list. We really didn't have to worry about their politics being too leftist because when you ventured into the Persian Gulf you were getting into real Koran-belt territory with social views resembling those of Vlad the Impaler, where despite decades of anti-Israel policies from the Kremlin these sheiks still believed there was a Moscow-Jerusalem alliance against the Arabs. I mean these were bizarre people.

Blip. Blip. Blip. Blip. One after the other. We had a big hunk of Abu Dhabi money already and even they wouldn't have us. We took on the right kickback consultants. We promised jobs as assistant director to sheiks' nephews. We promised dinners with Jeanne Moreau. We promised dinners with Ursula Andress. We promised dinners with Raquel Welch, the absolutely top girl in this category of girl; she'd do that for us, wouldn't she? But it was *zip. Nada.*

And you should have seen those sheikdoms. All around, sun-baked rock, sand, desert, not a blade of grass for hundreds of miles. The day before yesterday their tiny capitals had been sun-parched villages of dried mud, but oil had made the desert bloom. It had not been very good at making it bloom anything horticultural, but it had made it bloom a lot of concrete, and steel reinforcing rods, and even skyscrapers with mirror walls tinted the color of smoke. Wherever you went there were dozens of construction sites with the skeletons rising of skyscrapers to come, for Allah had ordained that on these waterless wastes should rise a series of mini-Manhattans. Fine, wide boulevards ran a few hundred yards. Doha had a six-lane highway which served mostly for the display of rusting automobiles, strewn by the roadside. Dubai had a tidal creek, which made it the Venice of the Gulf. Through the streets of all these places sand was constantly shifting and flowing and blowing, a relentless reminder of the desert so close. In my mind I pictured thousands of ill-paid menials stationed at the gates of these miniature rising Manhattans, eternally but hopelessly trying to beat back the invading sand. When the oil gave out these would be the world's first skyscraper ghost towns. The poor labored valiantly to keep alive a few eucalyptus and acacia trees along the new boulevards, watering and tending without rest. The rich labored valiantly to brush the dust from the grooves of their hi-fi records of Om Kalsoum. Everywhere were men in long white nightshirts, women in black leather masks that left the face marked for life, oven-like heat, dust, dust, dust. The nights, needless to say, were magic. On a night off, if you wanted excitement, you went down to the main street lined with glass skyscrapers and hung around hoping a donkey would come by. And if you were in the mood for real action you could go to the airport, where every once in a while a plane took off for some other place on the Gulf, and you were in spiritual contact with the great world beyond. Leaning on the guardrail by the tarmac, you could dream romantic dreams about distant, glamorous places like Pittsburgh, or Detroit, or Buffalo, N.Y.

This time I'd gone to the airport in the afternoon to pick up Omar, who'd been up the coast on our perpetual mission. He was big enough so he didn't need to be met, of course, but what else was there to do? The airport looked as if it had been inaugurated that morning and was just open for business, outside all tinted glass, inside white marble. Men in business suits strode about purposefully in the arctic air conditioning. A few huddles of ragheads conferred solemnly. Near me someone must have done something nice for somebody because two men in *dishdâshas* were doing that Arab triple thing with the right hand as if they were saying, "I am yours, heart, mouth, and head." Or perhaps it was, "neck, nose, and head." The real ragheads did that. I was sitting to the side in an upholstered plastic chair when I saw through the glass a limousine pull up outside and an Arab lady get out, dressed in long black robe and black veil, the full regalia. She came trotting in briskly through the glass doors with a bevy of humble domestic types scurrying around her carrying luggage, suitcases, trunks, overnight bags, weekend bags, duffel bags, tote bags, all very expensive and European. This was a lot of excitement for the Persian Gulf. I noticed she was wearing smart, black, high-heeled sandals. She walked girlishly into the center of the hall, glanced over, paused, then started in my direction, but walking very differently, stealthily, carrying her weight forward, as if sneaking up on a chicken. When she got to about ten feet of me she stopped, drew in her breath, and blurted out in English, "It's you!"

I rose. I don't know why. She cried, "Burt, darling!" and threw her arms around me and kissed me right through the black veil. It was like kissing a handkerchief. It was the kiss which ended all desire. She seemed aware of this herself and unhooked the veil somehow and hissed, "It's me!" then hooked the veil right back up again. I'd had a lightning glimpse of this pretty American face, twenty-five years old perhaps, cute nose, no lipstick, then the veil again and just the eyes, well made up, heavily rimmed in kohl, the whites very bright.

"He's been just dreadful to me!" she said urgently in a low voice. "You don't know what I've been through. And I could have done so much for Arab women. Persecuting me! Not even letting me make the poor things aware of their oppressed state. Absolute total refusal to see! Trying to turn back the clock of history. Have you ever seen oppression? I mean absolute, stark, brutal oppression?"

There was a tiny pause in which she caught her breath. "Excuse me," I said. "Who are you?"

She blinked. Then, in a tone of reproach, "Nancy Hinton."

Well, I had a name. Now if I only knew who Nancy Hinton was, I'd be all set. I stood there. She stood there.

"The one from Marrakesh," she said. "When you were in the People's Prison. I was the one that visited you from the Boston *Woman's Paper*."

"Would you mind taking that thing off your face so I can get a look at you please?" I asked.

She glanced over her shoulder furtively and then drew the veil aside, leaving her face exposed for perhaps fifteen seconds, the face startled but alert, eager to please. There she was. It was her all right. This knocked the wind out of me completely, and I backed up a step and sat down, stunned, didn't even look at her. My head was buzzing. In a moment she was sitting beside me on the upholstered plastic bench, very solicitous, gently taking my hand, but with the veil on again.

"Why don't you take that rag off your face," I said irately. "They're going to think you're an Arab woman, holding hands, kissing strange men in public. You're going to get stoned."

She blinked again.

"With rocks," I said. "They throw rocks at you until you're dead."

"Oh, dear," she said, and gingerly removed the veil, glancing about.

"Take off the whole head thing," I said. "Slide it off. It's a mess anyway."

She slipped off the headscarf and gave her head a shake to fluff out her hair. When this was done I felt I was talking to a person at least. She returned to an attitude of solicitude. She was certainly pretty. Weak intellect though.

"You seem disturbed," she said with concern. "Is there anything I can do?"

"Listen, lady," I said.

"Nancy."

"Listen, lady. Do you know I almost got whacked out in Marrakesh? Do you know that you were the one that came and announced my death sentence?"

"But you were the class enemy," she said imploringly. "You were the capitalist-imperialist-warmongering Imperial Penis!"

"Holy shit," I said numbly.

"You were the cancer of history. You were preventing the improvement of human nature. You had to be removed so that mankind could advance."

I couldn't believe it. I just looked at her.

"Lady," I said. "Whatever I was then, I am now. Why are you holding my hand? Why the goo-goo eyes? What are you wearing that goddamn black window curtain for? You're on the side of history? Terrific. Good luck. But old Burt Nelson was holding up the line of march, so he was going to have to get wasted, which you thought was perfectly okay. But how do you think *I* felt about that! What makes you think I'm your friend?"

Her face went from surprise, to compassion, to self-pity, to plaintiveness. Taking my hand in both of hers now, she said beseechingly, "I've been through a lot too, you know."

I don't say I'd have done it but an image was passing through my mind of strangling her, when suddenly I looked up and Omar's plane had landed and the passengers had all gone through the passport-stamping and Omar was standing right there looking, well, quizzical.

"Uh, Ome," I said, a little disconcerted. "Oh, Omar Hammoud. This is, um, a person I used to know, tried to get me whacked out once."

"Nancy Hinton," she said, rising, smiling, shaking his hand. Social Register. I hadn't noticed before. I still hadn't gotten my balance back. Once upon a time I'd been a prisoner, a wretched thing, cooped up, filled with anger, and she'd been a free creature. She'd come in with heaven's air still in her lungs, with the glorious air of freedom around her. But now I was free again myself, no more chicken wire, no more handcuffs, and I trod the earth with unfettered step, and looked at Nancy Hinton and she was this little jerk. Omar was all smiles though. In his look of a moment before I'd been able to see that his trip had been fruitless, but Nancy Hinton had filled him with the joy of life again. "Some tomato," he said.

"He's an antique," I explained. "He still calls girls tomatoes. Well, Miss Hinton. Thus are we banished from our country's light. To walk the paths of endless night. If our paths cross again, I hope you're the one in prison, and not I."

All at once she gripped my hand. Scads of people were standing around by now. Omar was right there. All her porters were standing at a distance with her bags. Sandor was approaching. But she held my hand tightly and, giving me a look of an intensity of which I would have thought her face incapable, whispered, "Don't leave me!"

Now I get some strange looks from women. I get looks that have women's telephone numbers written in them. I get looks that say: I am free Wednesday afternoon from five to seven. But this look from Nancy Hinton had no qualifications. It was open, naked, unmistakable. It said: I am yours.

"Look, fellas," I said. "You go back to the hotel while I sit here for a while and talk with Nancy about old times."

As we sat there waiting for her plane she gave me some kind of hard luck story, woe and misfortune, the usual thing, but I was thinking all the time about a Mexican girl I picked up at the Palladium when I was a kid. We drove into the canyons north of Sunset, Benedict Canyon and Coldwater Canyon, all filled with fancy places now but there were a lot of empty hills then, and we got out and rolled around on the grass, Indian wrestling, her keeping her legs together, clamped like a vice. Suddenly, my spirits flagged. It seemed to me that God had placed a curse on men about sixteen, that they should waste the force of their youth wrestling with girls in the Santa Monica Mountains, with the girls fighting them every inch of the way, so, like Job, I surrendered to God's will and quit. The Santa Ana was blowing, that some call the Devil Wind, drives men mad, but I always liked it and I was lying there in the moonlight with the tall grass rippling in the warm dry breeze, serene, when this Mexican girl took my hand and in a small voice said,

"*Besame.*" Kiss me. But the trouble was that I was tired of kissing her. It had bad associations in my mind, me struggling, her fighting me furiously like the Mexican troops at Buena Vista. The little voice said, "*Besame,*" again, so I told her that, no, I didn't want to kiss her. I was all exhausted. Unless she promised me More, in which case I'd kiss her. As I watched her in the moonlight, her face hurt and resentful, I had this sense that I was not being very diplomatic and that there were secrets of the female heart that perhaps I didn't know yet, but I was stubborn. I felt that I was wasting the best years of my life wrestling fruitlessly with girls and it was wearing me out. Also, I was curious. This was the first time that a girl had asked to kiss me and I had said no, that I had denied myself to a woman. It was an absolutely original idea and I was wondering what it would feel like if I held out. If she had given me a notarized statement that great things were ahead, of course, then I'd have kissed her. But I never received the notarized statement and never even tried that hard to get it. So Juanita Sanchez and I lay there in the grass in the Santa Monica Mountains as the Santa Ana blew, her all humiliated, me savoring the strange taste of voluntary chastity. And I've never regretted anything so much in my whole life. I can't tell you how many times I've thought back to that girl. Perhaps I missed out on one of life's great experiences. Perhaps whole worlds would have opened before me. Where have you gone, Juanita Sanchez? Over the hills, I guess. Over the hills and far away.

"No!" said Nancy Hinton, returning from the reservations counter. "No, no, no! The plane doesn't take off from here. It leaves from up the coast. You want to come along with me in the car and keep me company? Oh, please! It's only a couple of hours. The chauffeur will drive you back."

She was standing there, all agitated, wearing her veil and headscarf again. I didn't remember her being this animated back at the People's Prison in Marrakesh. She had been rather halting of speech, if I remembered correctly, groping her way from one piece of jargon to the next. Now she was really quite lively, the jargon positively tripping off her tongue.

"This is my brother!" she said to her assemblage of medieval retainers, proudly extending her arm toward me at full length. They smiled and mumbled and bowed.

At the glass door of the airport building the chauffeur was waiting, and I was her brother here, too, except that he was wearing a European chauffeur's uniform and saluted me, British style, hand flat, palm forward. I felt odd not returning the salute, and then there was the vehicle. Well, I supposed you could call it a car. It was definitely smaller than a Nimitz-class aircraft carrier. It was a Silver Wraith, or Silver Spectre, or Silver Spirit, one of those Rolls Royce things. Never had luxury been so unappealing. As all her husband's fanatic-looking Islamic retainers loaded her gear into the trunk I stood there with my heart in my boots, wondering what Juanita Sanchez and the Santa Monica Mountains were getting me into. How could they possibly believe I was her brother? How did I happen to be there? Did she even have a brother? Her husband was going to be sending a posse after us! This was really asking for trouble.

But off we went, and were out of town almost immediately, into that heroic emptiness known as the desert. Well, I'd seen deserts, and I'd seen deserts, but this was the worst. Rock, not even sand, with for decoration the occasional rusty oil drum or car wreck. When the wind blew, eddies of empty Pepsi-Cola cans whirled in the dust. The road was dusty, straight, bleak, endless. Nary a village, nary a green, growing thing, nary a turn in the road, only every twenty-five miles or so another of the world's most desolate gas stations. You couldn't even see the Gulf, which was over to the east somewhere, who could tell? Was this the desert into which John the Baptist walked and heard the voice of the Lord? Maybe it was all the fault of the Rolls. Maybe if it hadn't been for the Rolls I could have walked alone into the holy emptiness of the desert and eaten locusts and wild honey in a camel's hair coat. First the moon would rise and fall. Then the sun would rise in its glory, but it too would fall. Then, again, the blackness of night, and I would hear the voice of the Lord. I don't know. Maybe there was something in the desert after all but you just couldn't get at it when you were riding in a Rolls.

Inside, the Rolls was huge. The smell of its soft red-leather upholstery filled the air. It had all-gold metalwork, a fitted white-lynx rug, fresh orchids in little vases fixed to the uprights. Set into the partition dividing us from the chauffeur was a refrigerator, stocked with caviar, Pepsi-Cola, Seven-Up. I drank some Seven-Up from a champagne glass. The air conditioning was humming, the stereo playing the score from Sergio Leone's *Duck, You Sucker*. Beside the refrigerator was a television set and I could have played a movie. I could have seen *Duck, You Sucker*, or *A Fistful of Dollars*, or *For a Few Dollars More*, or *Once Upon a Time in the West*. The windows of the Rolls were tinted a dark, smoky gray so that we could see out but nobody could see in, which was academic for the moment because there was nothing out there but rock and rusting wrecks. But what was important was the window between us and the chauffeur, which was opaque from his side, a mirror, so in the social sense Nancy Hinton and I were alone, alone in the desert.

She'd married this Arab, it seemed, the owner of this armored cruiser we were riding in and eleven others, all with different color upholstery, and then had come down here to live on the Persian Gulf, where she was trying to lift women from their oppressed state. There were difficulties, of course. She didn't speak Arabic. That was one. And her rich Gulfie husband, the Sheik's nephew, wasn't giving her much support. She was trying to write a book about Arab women, or a series of articles for the Boston *Woman's Paper*, and he even seized her notes, burned them up with bricks of dried camel dung in the servants' court. Now she was running away. Would I join her in the fight?

I hadn't really been paying close attention. My eyes as we drove had been on the desert horizon, which wasn't sharp. Between the beige desert and the pale-blue sky was this greenish, pearl, translucent zone, the colors cooler because of the tinted windows. It was like looking through giant sun goggles.

"What fight?" I said.

"To liberate Arab women." Her eyes sparkled. No veil.

"From what?"

"From Arab men."

This Nancy Hinton had a gift for removing all belief in the power of rational discourse.

"Wait a minute," I said. "Excuse me. But would you back up a little please? The last time we met, if I may say so, you were under the impression that in Islamic society women had attained true equality. You had it on good authority."

"But that's what they told me!" she said earnestly. "It's not my fault if it isn't true."

"Who told you?" I said. "Who's the 'they'?"

"My husband. And his friends."

"And where did they tell you this?"

"In Chicago."

"Well, I grant you, Chicago is really a terrific place to get off profundities on sexual equality in the Arab world."

Nancy looked puzzled.

"But you're chastened now, aren't you?" I said. "You're contrite. You'll never be gullible again. Will you."

Nancy's face became very sulky.

"You're trying to make it look as if this is my fault somehow," she said petulantly, throwing herself back against the red-leather cushions. "What am I supposed to do when people tell me something, just not believe them?"

"Well, that is one of the options open to you in this harsh world," I said. "What's more, I think you know that. I think a lot of times people tell you things you don't believe. The question is: why did you suspend your inborn skepticism on this curious occasion? And you swallowed it whole." It came back to me. "Didn't you convert? Aren't you a Moslem now?"

I looked into her eyes, which were murky, like the horizon, but more emotional. In their depths I could see confusion, bewilderment, pain, a sense of abandonment. In a few moments she timidly took my hand. Tears came to her eyes as she turned her head away and gazed into the desert.

"Don't leave me," she whispered.

There are fights you don't want to win, you know? I never saw a feminist go down so fast. Get up! I wanted to tell her. This was terrible. What was I going to have to do, marry her? She had a husband already! This was disreputable, not to mention dangerous. Why did she have to pick on me? I hardly knew her, for God's sake.

"You're right," she said tearfully. "You're right. You're right. It was wrong of me. I'll never believe anyone again."

"You don't have to go that far," I said placatingly. "You can believe someone every once in a while."

But this was too subtle a nuance for Nancy, and she lay her head on my shoulder, still holding my hand. Any moment now we were going to stop in a village and a mob of enraged Moslem fundamentalists were going to drag us out of the Rolls and tear us limb from limb, but Nancy was peaceful.

"You know where they have true sexual equality?" she said softly after a time.

I had absolutely no desire to play games and was silent.

"Go ahead, guess," she said.

"Angola."

"Oh," she asked, brightening. "Do they have sexual equality in Angola?"

"How the hell do I know," I said. "It would surprise me."

"Guess again," she said cheerfully.

"Ethiopia."

"No." She smiled.

"Albania."

"No." She was quite pleased now. She had a secret.

"Well, then, I give up. I have no idea. Where, oh where, do they have sexual equality?"

"Do you really want to know?"

I gave a groan, which she took as a sign of intellectual curiosity.

"North Korea," she said proudly.

I pitched forward, almost landing on the lynx rug, and then righted myself, holding my face in my hands, trying to shut the world out. I wanted the chauffeur to stop the Rolls in the desert and I would walk home. That was another turning point in my life right there. Maybe, I thought, some of life's great experiences were not worth having. Or maybe it just proved you couldn't go back, and that Juanita Sanchez was gone forever, gone with those purple flowers on the jacaranda trees up Mulholland Drive.

"Are you all right?" asked Nancy.

"Fucking North Korea," I said.

"I don't see why you're taking it that way." She didn't know whether to be offended or not. "It's a perfectly decent socialist society."

"Kim Il Sung," I said. "Gahhh!"

"I don't see why you're carrying on like this," said Nancy. "I just want a better world."

I think I passed out. I must have been hyper-ventilated. From there on I considered myself intellectually brutalized and not responsible for anything. She went all soft and clinging again and I rubbed her like you're supposed to. I used two fingers, three fingers, the flat of my hand. I went in circles. I went up and down. I went slow. I went fast. I was gentle. I was firm. I was regular. I was irregular. She was gasping, and panting, and choking, her mascara running down her face. But you've got to remember there were all these yards and yards of black curtain material, and it was only when I saw two long, astonishingly white legs shooting up out of all that yardage that I thought: *Who started this? How did this get started?* First I put her left foot into the armrest. She had on high-heeled black patent-leather sandals. Then I wondered if I could get the foot into the hand loop on the wall without the shoe. Then I thought I'd pull her down on the lynx rug, but we hit a rough stretch of road and it went *dub dub dub dub dub dub dub dub dub dub* and I didn't like it and hauled her back onto the leather seat again. And then, the nimble little devil, she threw both legs into the air as if she were going to do a backwards somersault and lodged her heels up on the roof someplace. I would have thought that would be a terrible position for her, bent almost in two like that, but she volunteered it. And on we went, and on the Rolls Royce drove at eighty miles an hour, and I was very distracted because through the windows I could see the desert all around us and I was really horrified and thought that now we truly *were* going to get torn limb from limb, but Nancy shuddered and moaned and there was just no stopping. *"Uh! Uh! Uh!"* she gasped, and it was a strange and bizarre experience because of the danger, I think. Never before had I committed adultery with a Moslem convert in the back of a Rolls Royce in the Persian Gulf.

I was dazed. Her skirts were down now. I drank some more Seven-Up from a champagne glass as the stereo boomed movie music, then sank back beside her on the seat, where she snuggled up to me affectionately. It created a link, I guess. I stared out at the desert, ever the same. I could see the back of the chauffeur's head but he couldn't see us. That was the theory. If it turned out to be a bad theory then we really might die out there. The Rolls rode beautifully. It was no Ford Fiesta. Nancy stirred.

"Have you ever read the Gnostic Gospels?" she asked.

"Is that what you do down here on the Persian Gulf?" I said. "Read the Gnostic Gospels?"

"Well, they found them down here," she objected.

"No, there," I said, pointing west. "Straight across the Arabian peninsula plus the Red Sea. In Egypt."

"Really?"

"Uh huh. There was this Egyptian, and he and his brothers were hacking off the limbs of this other Egyptian who'd murdered their father, and they ripped out his heart and ate it. Local custom. But then they got scared that this might create some ill will, so they took these papyrus books they'd

267

just found in a big earthenware jar on the Jabal and placed them in safe-keeping with a priest. And the priest showed them to Ali, and Ali showed them to Mahmood, and the next thing you know they were sold on the black market in Cairo, and that's how darkies were born."

"What *are* you talking about?" she said.

"Don't believe me? Check it out."

"But it's a whole new theology!" she cried excitedly, sitting forward so she could look at me. "They've got a whole new Trinity."

"The Father, the Son, and the Holy Mother."

"That's right! Because "spirit" in Greek is feminine. How did you know that?"

"I know all that stuff," I said, watching the side of the road as we passed a rusting truck. A big event in the desert.

"And God had a Mother."

"You mean Jesus had a Mother."

"No, God had a Mother, too!"

"Oh, yeh. The one who went around saying — every time God said, 'I am the Lord of Creation,' she'd say, 'Shut up!' "

"Well, yes, in a way. And Jesus's chief disciple was Mary Magdalene, but it made Peter jealous so they rewrote the whole thing, leaving Christianity the male supremacist institution it is today."

She flopped back against the seat, scowling at the light fixture in the roof. She'd been disillusioned by Islam, you see. But that didn't make everyday Christianity any better. She'd been shopping for something new in *The Woman's Guide to Religion.*

"Tell me," I said. "Have you actually read the Gospel According to Thomas, and the Gospel According to Philip, and the Apocryphon of John, all of that?"

"Not actually," said Nancy, a hint embarrassed, fidgeting with her robes. "A girl friend of mine from Chicago was visiting me a few months ago. She told me."

"Where are you from in Chicago?"

This was the second one. Janie Holt was from Chicago.

"Lake Forest."

268

"So this is the Lake Forest Gospel you're giving me here,"
I said. "This is the version of Christianity currently sub-
scribed to by the ladies of Lake Forest."

"Women."

"The women of Lake Forest."

"Well," Nancy said broodingly, crossing her arms over her
chest. "God is bisexual. You can't deny that."

"God is *not* bisexual!" I said, irked. "God is neuter! Which
isn't exactly big news since it's been the official doctrine of
the Church for two thousand years. Don't you know anything, you dummy! What are you, some goddamn Quaker?"

"I *am* a Quaker," she said. "I mean, I was a Quaker before
I was a Muslim."

"I knew it," I moaned. "The worst kind."

Nancy gave a little laugh and turned to me with a sweet-
sad look, shyly reached for my hand. And it was a slow
descent, from the Spirit to the Flesh, which she seemed to
like quite a bit, in between bouts of feminism, exophilia,
and *Fernweh*; that's what the Krauts called it. Nancy was
a practitioner of feverish, shuddery sex, which was very
ardent and intense but impersonal somehow. On the way
in she was sweet and fetching and we had a definite person-
to-person relationship, but as the fever mounted her focus
blurred, and the moment came when her eyes closed and
she broke contact and went into a quivering trance and, you
could tell, I could have been anybody. So I thought my own
thoughts about the Gnostic Gospels, some of which were
real strange, like the ones in which you had Jesus as an
oriental guru, a Jesus of enlightenment and spiritual understanding. Now I was accustomed to the Jesus of sin and
repentance. Sin, repent. Sin, repent. But this gnostic Jesus
came, not to save me from sin, but to guide me to spiritual
knowledge, and once I'd attained enlightenment Jesus
wasn't even my spiritual master anymore but I was right up
there with Him, which I confess I found profoundly repug-
nant. The way I liked it, Jesus was up there, and I was down
here, which was the way it should be. And the only condition under which I would have introduced this debased

oriental thinking into a Jesus movie would have been if we
had a guaranteed market for the picture in India and I were
blending Christianity in with Hinduism, but my heart
wouldn't be in it. *"Aaah!"* cried Nancy, shaking all over,
snapping her head from side to side. *"Aaah! Aaah! Aaah!"*
So there.

"Listen," she said later. "What's your favorite sentence?
The most powerful sentence you ever heard?"

We were still riding through the desert in the Rolls. It
was a way of life. I was getting used to it. We'd cut the
stereo.

"I don't have a favorite sentence. What is this? What's
your favorite sentence?"

"Guess," she said, snuggling up.

"How can I guess? With all the sentences there are in the
world, how could I possibly figure out your favorite?"

"I'll tell you then," she said.

"Okay."

"You want to hear it?"

"Sure I want to hear it. Shoot."

"Property is theft," she said demurely.

Well, what did I expect? North Korea. Lake Forest. An
apostate Quaker. Why not?

"Property is theft in Lake Forest," I mused.

"Oh, definitely," she said. "In Lake Forest most of all.
Now tell me yours."

"I told you. I don't have one."

"Oh, come *on,*" she pouted. "Make one up."

"O Orgasmic Woman! Hail!"

"Oh, really!" she said. "That's not a sentence."

"All right," I said. "Sit up."

She sat up, facing me on the back seat, a modern Islamic
woman with a Sassoon cut.

"Are you ready?"

She nodded her head vigorously, eyes bright.

"You're a little dummy. You know that."

"Don't change the subject," she said.

"All set?"

Again she nodded, eagerly, as we shot through the desert.

"*I am the Resurrection and the Life,*" I said.

She flinched, looking at me with something approaching horror, which was a little odd because until recently she had at least believed in Ulluh.

"That's not fair." She pointed her finger at me. "You don't believe in that." She drew in her breath. "No, you *do* believe in that."

She threw herself against the upholstery.

"My God," she gasped. "I've just fucked a religious maniac."

She writhed around to face me again.

"Do you believe in that? Do you believe in that or don't you?"

"Believe in what?"

"What you just said."

"I didn't say I believed in it. You just wanted a powerful sentence."

"You believe in it though!" Again her finger was pointing. "I can tell!" Her arm dropped. "My God, I knew no good would come of this."

Well, well, well, the old smoke ball. Whether I believed in it or not I'd figure out later but in the meantime it was a hell of a line. It made "Property is theft" look really miserable by comparison.

"*I am the alpha and the omega, the beginning and the end.*"

That was another good one, packed a real wallop. It scared the wits out of her as we bowled along in the Rolls. I gazed out into the barren desert and realized that the wilderness of Judaea had been like this.

"*He that cometh after me is mightier than I,*" I said. "*He shall baptize you with the Holy Ghost, and with fire.*"

She thought I'd gone crazy. But I wasn't crazy at all. She was the one who was crazy.

22

ON S'EST QUITTÉ SANS REGRET, as they say. She was glad to get rid of me, actually. I have this harsh side. When they want to whack out Burt Nelson I never again feel the same toward them somehow. I have this cold, uncaring feeling. She hadn't tied in with my Moroccan Tupamaros through her husband at all, I discovered, who talked Third World talk only when he was in Chicago, but through these radical women, who often acted as if they were in natural and total alliance with everyone who had a touch more melanin in their skin than we did. They were so resentful of the Capitalist-Imperialist Penis that they hadn't noticed that there were the Islamic-Fundamentalist Penis, the Tribal Autocratic Penis, and all these other penises including even the Marxist-Leninist Penis. So Nancy boarded a plane for London with a disappointment or two on her record, but with the sexual millennium still out there. Perhaps she was even gaining on it.

Her chauffeur drove me back, as promised. I was not stoned to death, *la preuve*. And two nights later I met another Western girl at the airport, when we were all moving out. I take no credit for being such a hit with women at airports on the Persian Gulf because I was just getting them on the rebound from Islam, as it were. In fact, to any male who had the time I would really recommend abandoning the singles bars on Third Avenue and giving the airports of the Persian Gulf a try. It might be seasonal. I wouldn't know about that. But the women are definitely there. When I saw this good-looking French blonde sitting by herself waiting for a plane out I had the definite feeling that she had not come this far to sell Avon cosmetics. There she sat in the coolest of Paris threads, wearing what she called a *salopette* but looked to me like authentic bib-type Arkansas overalls. Is this what a poor Arabian sheik got from the mail-order house when he ordered the latest model girl from Paris? The Arkansas dust bowl? The irony was too bitter. No wonder he drank. *Il picolait*, she said. But these girls had their problems, too, I realized as she explained them to me that night in Kuwait, where we stopped over. Life wasn't a bed of roses for them either. A whole month Chantal had spent in that joyless brick kiln, waited on hand and foot and dying of boredom. No television. Old movies on cassette. No Yves Saint Laurent. No Courrèges. No Kenzo. The sheik drank all the time. Impotent. I'm only telling you what she told me. I didn't ask for all these details. At last she was leaving in bitter frustration. And she who had dreamed of being the Farah Diba of Qatar or Sharjah or Ras al Khaimah.

It came out that the woman Chantal admired most in all the world was not Betty Ford, or Golda Meir, or even Isabelita Perón, the best nightclub dancer ever to become president of Argentina, although in jail now after a run of bad luck, but Farah Diba, the Shabanu of Iran, whose career she had been following in *France-Dimanche*, France's *National Enquirer*. Because, if the Shah was still in, she was still in too, of course. For the French, who had concerned themselves with Iran's dynastic problems ever since the great Saroya, Farah Diba was the living embodiment of the feminine ideal, it seemed, dedicating herself entirely to the life of art and the spirit, like Jackie Onassis. Chantal said the Shabanu had studied architecture at Paris's Ecole des Beaux-Arts, and she appeared to be something of an honorary Frenchwoman, representing the best in French dress, cuisine, culture, catering. She'd been the guiding spirit behind the Iranian monarchy's 2,500th birthday party, Chantal assured me, where they'd created 2,500-year-old traditional ceremonies, 2,500-year-old music composed by the latest modern composers, 2,500-year-old food provided by Paris's spiffy Potel and Chabot, an unprecedented example throughout of animating the dead raiments of the past with modern chic. It was Farah Diba who stood behind everything that was culture in Iran, said Chantal, who was a real fan of the Shabanu's and had hoped to emulate her on a smaller scale until all had ended in bitterness in that brick kiln with no television. Culture. Elegance. Moral values. Religion. Stylish clothes. Farah Diba stood for all that, and as Chantal climbed on top of me that night, beginning an earnest reciprocating engine motion, it came to me as if in a revelation: *Iran! Why don't we make "Mohammed Superstar" in Iran?* Why hadn't we thought of Iran before, I wondered, amazed. Just because it wasn't Arab? It had all the advantages, oil, devotion to Islam, all that, but without the religious bigotry so inimical to film culture! I had another one of these absent-minded erections during which I did some of my best and most creative thinking. It didn't make any difference that they were only Aryan! A Francophile film buff as empress and defender of the faith was exactly what we needed! One who had learned love of the cinema at the knee of the Cinémathèque's great Henri Langlois! The passion and depth of Islam. The tolerance and love of visual art of the West. At last, after all these months, the thing had the right feel to it. Somewhere out there I heard a plaintive voice calling, *Serre-moi les fesses,* and as Chantal churned tenaciously onward a strong tide of optimism and hope swept over me, a feeling of impending triumph. *Iran! Stand back! We were coming!* To think Chantal was only three heartbeats away from the lady she so admired. To the chiming of celestial spheres and a dull popping like toilet plungers it went like this: her, me, Janie Holt, the Shah, Farah Diba. How was that for Tinker to Evans to Chance? I was beginning to get the feeling the Shah and I were really related. I really felt close to him.

By the time we got to Teheran I'd worked out the master plan of a whole new scenario. I'd turned it into a triptych, like a *Moslem Space Odyssey*. Omar was in touch with all the right Iranians in the secretariat of the Shabanu, who was truly in charge of everything that was culture in Iran. She was the culture behind the throne. Chantal had been perfectly well informed. These were the people who wanted to get Tom Hoving of New York's Metropolitan Museum of Art to set up a whole art complex for them in Teheran so they were the right people. Straight off they wanted us to turn the movie into the story of Cyrus the Great of Persia, not Mohammed, which was kind of like impossible. The costumes wouldn't fit at all. But I was ready for them and zapped them with my counteroffer, my genius triptych.

We start with Cyrus, right, the whole story of the big first days of the Persian Empire, minus the Battle of Marathon, which they lost. Cyrus, Cambyses, Darius, Xerxes, they were all the same to me. They could have their pick. But everybody is *expecting* Mohammed. They are prophesying him, like the people are prophesying Christ in the Bible. In fact the Persians are even bigger prophesiers of Mohammed than the Arabs, and there were a lot of connections between Islam and Persia's Zoroastrianism. I looked into it. Anyway that's what the Iranians say. Zoroastrianism has lots of dualism, the good god Ahura-Mazda being the Supreme Creator, but he's up against the bad god Ahriman, the two of them eternally at war, the first responsible for everything that is good and pure and beautiful and the second responsible for darkness and evil. Ultimately Ahura-Mazda is going to win but man must play his part. Zoroaster's three commandments are: good thoughts, good words, good deeds. By living a life of righteousness, man strengthens the forces of Good and weakens the forces of Evil. In the afterworld he's called on to account for his sins, which he finds all inscribed on the record along with the favorable side, and his fate is decided as his soul passes over a bridge known as the "Accountant's Bridge," an interesting variant on the Saint-Peter-at-the-Gate routine. In the end Ahura-Mazda wins the final victory and the Kingdom of God is established on earth. Actually I thought Zoroastrianism was a first-rate religion and had to hold myself in and packed all of this — Cyrus, Cambyses, Darius, Xerxes, Ahura-Mazda, Ahriman, prophecies of Mohammed, and the Accountant's Bridge — into a ten-page treatment, a marvel of compression.

Then, Part II, we come to the Mohammed Superstar part, which we'd almost finished shooting already, except that now there's a Persian who's an important friend and close follower of Mohammed, to give the Iranian angle. Actually there's a stranger referred to somewhere in the Koran and I felt it was legitimate to make him a Persian. He could have been a Persian. It gives the Iranians someone to identify with in this part of the story. All of this we had pretty much in the can already. Then Part III would be the White Revolution, Shah Mohammed Pahlevi, the present-day Shah of Iran, or perhaps his father, or the two of them together, and how they are carrying out the final mission of Mohammed, the last word in Islam. It was hard to work up an instant treatment on this part so I left it very brief and general and figured I'd take my cue from the Iranians. The whole thing was a beautiful three-phase triptych on Islam through the ages. First the ancient Persians who prophesy, then Mohammed who does the heavy stuff with the help of a Persian friend, then the final fruition, the modern-day Persians: Iran. It was Islam seen from an Iranian angle. Of course we had to anticipate a certain coolness on the part of the Arabs, who had a tendency to view Islam as an all-Arab show. But you had to go where the money was. I grant you it had shifted a bit from where we started. We began with a Marrakesh One-Two and now we had a Teheran One-Two-Three. That was the shape it was in when it went up to the Shabanu, a relative of mine almost.

We waited around for days, enjoying the rich life of this exotic metropolis, the crowds on the Teheran streets, the markets, the banks, the exotic high-rises, the exotic automobile traffic, the exotic gasoline fumes, breathing in deep lungfuls of the health-giving carbon monoxide. Wouldn't it be funny if we ran into Janie Holt, in town to dance the tango with the Shah? There was no sign of her though. Sandor felt lucky because the Iranian flag is just like the Hungarian flag only upside down. Not to put too fine a point on it, I thought Iran was a shitty country. But it was a shitty country in a Western way, if you know what I mean. There was that familiar disgusting spirit of greed and frantic acquisitiveness, the rapacity, profiteering, the old repulsive lust for status. Actually it reminded me of us a hundred years ago, with Jay Gould and Jim Fisk and Boss Tweed and Chet Arthur and the robber barons and the Crédit Mobilier scandal with half the members of Congress on the take, Rugged Individualism, the old American Way. Needless to say the new Iranian plutocrats had the same feeling of community with the destitute Iranian peasantry that J. P. Morgan had with the destitute workers in American sweatshops. But Teheran had this huge new supremely corrupt middle class, which meant that the money was filtering down quite a lot, whereas in Saudi Arabia and the Gulf States, with as much oil but far fewer people, only the sheiks and royal families got rich. So Iran was a triumph of the old-fashioned American Way, if you looked at it right, and if you gave the Iranians a hundred years I was confident it would all come out okay. Except they didn't have a hundred years, *amigo*. There was that.

You know Omar was a very nervous-type cat, and pacing back and forth waiting for word to come down from On High that our treatment was accepted, he got the notion that we should butter up some Iranian Islamic authorities as a second line of support, to forestall fundamentalist opposition, just as he'd done in Egypt, his Al Azzar Strategy, which hadn't worked actually, but it wasn't the fault of the strategy, it was the Arabs who were crazy. Proceeding on the Arab model wasn't such a great idea in Iran though, I didn't think, despite the advantages it had given us in the Arab countries. Although between you and me anybody in his right mind could see that as an Arab Omar was pure

Beverly Hills, in the Arab countries he'd been an Arab brother, a coreligionary, a fellow Moslem. All doors were open, at least until they were shut. But none of this cut any ice in Iran. First of all the Shah himself, the Light of the Aryans, had a marked contempt for Arabs, calling the Libyans and Iraqis "crazy, bloodthirsty savages," and who could argue with him? So what good did it do to be an Arab in Iran? When Omar spoke Arabic it was the language of the Book, terrific; but Iranians spoke this Aryan language, Farsi. So you think, well, at least Omar was a Moslem. But Omar was a Sunni. These Iranians were Shiahs. They were two completely different kinds of animal. They hated each other. In the interests of our screenplay I figured I ought to delve into this Shiah business a bit because, it being Iran after all, I might have to work in some of the Shiah stuff, weave the Shiah stuff in with the Sunni stuff, making Islam whole again after all those centuries of bitter strife.

It wasn't going to be easy; I saw that right away. First of all the Shiahs were still in a rage because Ali, their man, Mohammed's son-in-law, got shafted out of the Caliphate by these mangy Omayyad Sunnis. They stabbed him to death, actually. This happened in the Seventh Century, you understand, a little dynastic squabble, but the Shiahs were still foaming at the mouth over it. *Ali! Ali!* It was as if I was still sore because Andrew Jackson beat John Quincy Adams in the election of 1828 and was going around screaming *Adams! Adams!* And this had been before Charlemagne, 1,300 years ago. So for the Sunnis, there were the Big Two: Allah and Mohammed. But for the Shiahs, it was the Big Three: Allah, Mohammed, and Ali. Although Ali's two sons, Hassan and Hussein, were also very popular and had also been done in by the Sunnis, and their tombs, at Najaf and Kerbela respectively right across the border in Iraq, were the holiest shrines of the Shiah sect, where you could see pilgrims crying and screaming and sobbing their hearts out for Hassan and Hussein as if they'd just been assassinated yesterday. And so maybe it was the Big Five: Allah, Mo-

hammed, Ali, Hassan, and Hussein. In fact when the Ayatollah Khomeini got himself exiled for opposing the Shah's
land reform and female emancipation in 1963 he'd holed
up on just the other side of the Iraqi frontier right there in
Najaf, which was where he still was, sending out anti-Shah
vibes of a mystical as well as a temporal nature. This was
before the Iraqis deported him and he had to send his
mystical vibes all the way from Neauphle-le-Château in
France. Because there was this whole mystical side to the
Shiahs too, which the Sunnis didn't have at all.

The Cycle of Prophecy having come to an end, you see,
Ali, just like that, began the mystical *Cycle of Imams*, of
whom there were twelve, not conveniently grouped together
like the Twelve Apostles, unfortunately, but strung out over
about three hundred years. Now here was where it got interesting. These Twelve Imams, about whom the Sunnis don't
know beans, were *semi-divine* personages, mediators between the human and the divine. So the Cycle of the Imams
began with Ali, the Fourth Caliph and First Imam, and ran
along pretty well, I guess, until the Twelfth Imam, Mohammed al Ghaim, in 940 A.D., when the *Great Occultation* took
place, with Mohammed al Ghaim suddenly disappearing,
becoming the "Hidden Imam" — to return at the end of
time! Now this is the spooky part. The Shiahs say that since
the Great Occultation everything that has happened in the
whole world is the secret history of the Hidden Imam, with
the Shiahs alone knowing the secrets of the imams and the
hidden meaning of the Koran. You and I could read the
Koran and we'd understand the words, you see, but we
wouldn't get the hidden meaning; only the Shiahs knew
that and they weren't talking. Of course you could argue
until hell froze over about just what this hidden meaning
was, and about who had a direct link-up with the Hidden
Imam. I was sure the Ayatollah Khomeini in exile over in
Iraq was certain he was in direct, two-way, electronic communication with the Hidden Imam all the time. But the
Shah was, too. The Shah had even *seen the Hidden Imam*,

he said. It was a subject which didn't leave much room for reasonable debate. And they didn't even swear Sunni oaths, you know. They had their own: *Ya Imam Hussein! Ya Imam Hassan!* All wrapped up in their imams and mysticism, they weren't a bit like the Sunnis. If you want to know the truth, I had the feeling that the Shiahs had worked out this whole mystical back-channel because they'd lost the Caliphate; that was all. It was so they could say to the Sunnis: You've got the Caliph? You've got the Koran? Okay. But we know the *secret* meaning of the Koran! We know the *secrets* of the world that your Caliph doesn't know anything about but that the Hidden Imam tells us. It was strictly dissident stuff, a loser's religion, until by some fluke it got itself declared the official religion of the state of Iran in 1502 A.D. So, I didn't want to alarm you earlier, but with the Shiahs it was really the Big Fourteen: Allah, Mohammed, and the Twelve Imams. But with the Twelfth Imam being assigned this Second Coming spot — the Messiah, no less — it made it look as if he really outranked Mohammed, who was only a prophet after all, which made it a little confusing. I mean it would be hard to work into a screenplay.

And the more deeply I delved into this Shiah business, and the more I saw of these real Iranian Shiahs, the more somber the whole thing got. Well, I'd been running with this Sunni crowd, you see. Now you know me as this notorious Islamic apologist — which is to say notorious Sunni apologist, because all the Moslems I'd ever met were Sunnis. Well, I hate to admit it but the Sunnis were a pretty sophisticated bunch compared to these Shiahs. Okay the Sunnis were a bunch of murdering bastards, but they had style; they had a certain *je ne sais quoi*; here and there you found dribs and drabs of modernism. But the Shiahs were the pits. Wandering through the squalor of the Old Town with an Iranian, I came upon a sign: ALL BELIEVERS ARE CALLED UPON TO TAKE PART IN THE FLAGELLATIONS IN COMMEMORATION OF THE MURDER OF IMAM HUSSEIN. THE PROCESSION WILL LEAVE THE HAJJ ABDUL AZIZ CARAVANSERAI NEAR THE GATE

OF THE CAVE. BRING YOUR OWN CHAINS. All around, starving urchins in rags. Because the Shiahs were great believers in "dying power," the mystic willingness to die, as the world was soon to learn. It was very depressing. I confess I'd started out with an initial favorable impression of Iran. I'd thought, they were Aryans, what the hell, must be worth a little something. And I'd been bowled over by the superb corruption of their new middle class, the way they spread the money around. I wasn't so sure now though. Corruption wasn't everything. Visions of Jay Gould and Boss Tweed and the Crédit Mobilier scandal were fading fast and it was sinking in on me that, Before Oil, Iran hadn't been more advanced than the Arab countries, it had been more backward. All ripples of modern thought had been stopped dead at the Sunni-Shiah frontier. And what was most depressing of all was that the whole thing made me deeply gloomy about the chances of our movie treatment up there with the Shabanu and the Shah of Shahs. We'd been very much heartened when we heard that the Shah was going to change the Iranian calendar from the Moslem system, which started from Mohammed's flight from Mecca to Medina and according to which we were in about 1354, to a new system of his own, which was going to begin figuring time from the foundation of the Persian Empire by Cyrus the Great, putting us in the year 2,500-plus. We'd taken this as a sign of an awareness of antiquity, history, ancient religions, the basis of the first segment of my terrific Islamo-Iranian triptych. But that was all stuff I got out of books. I was like those intelligence analysts back in Langley, getting everything out of reports without ever setting foot in the place. Then I come to Iran and it knocks me for a loop. What did these Iranians know about Ahura-Mazda? Zoroaster? All I was hearing was *Imam Hassan!* and *Imam Hussein!* Every holiday they were either shrieking with joy for the birth of one imam or wailing with despair at the death of another one. What happened to good old Mohammed? If the Will of the Iranian People were taken into account our movie was dead. Our only hope was that the Shah was so aloof from vulgar prejudice, with this monarchy mania of his, that he'd be delighted to see Islam as the meat in an Iranian-monarchy sandwich — Cyrus as bread, Mohammed as meat, and himself as bread again — and that he would remain firm in his commitment to a *politique de grandeur*. He was the Shah of Shahs, wasn't he?

Omar, of course, was still champing at the bit to go round up some Iranian holy men to get them on his side, and I had to sit him down on my knee and explain to him about the Sunnis and the Shiahs. You know, like the birds and the bees. You understand he knew there was such a thing as the Shiah sect, but it stopped there. Which was odd because the only place outside the Iran-Iraq area where there were really lots of Shiahs was Lebanon. But it was, imams? Ali? *Connais pas.* "You know you Sunnis murdered the Imam Ali and the Imam Hassan and the Imam Hussein?" I told Omar. "Deicide, baby. A tough rap. Hard to beat. And you have the good luck to be named after the Caliph Omar, who usurped Ali's throne personally and conquered Iran. They burn your effigy on High Holy Days. They curse mules in your name. *May God curse Omar!*" It shook him up. And frankly I couldn't think of a worse group of potential supporters for our flick than a gang of Iranian mullahs. They didn't like dancing, they didn't like music, they didn't like images graven on 35 mm film stock. They hated the Shah for taking land away from them in his land reform and for letting women vote and go around in bare faces without their black chadors. If the Shah was for it, they'd be against it. If a Beverly Hills Sunni was for it, they'd spit on it. It didn't look good. But Omar had the valor of invincible ignorance. In the Arab countries they'd treated him like somebody, and he'd begun to think he really was somebody. Anyway he had a lot of energy, too much energy, it was unhealthy. Fired up as he was, in a day or so he announced to me that he was going in for an audience with Ayatollah Badran Shirazi. To "get the feel," Omar said. To get the lay of the land. Not that he was hoping to come skating in from the other side and hit the Culture Ministry as a protégé of the mullahs, which would have gotten him thrown in jail directly. He just saw himself as the man who could bring together the warring social factions of this great nation, could bind up the wounds, bring peace and national union behind Allah and Mohammed, and even the Twelve Imams, what the hell, could bring about *l'Union Sacrée Nationale!* Something modest like that.

"Why don't you go along with him to see that mullah or ayatollah or whatever," the man said down at the shop. "It would be interesting to hear what those guys have to say for themselves."

Because I went down to the shop. It was IRRITATE. IRRIGATE. IRRADIATE. Same old stuff. This case officer was named Spivak, blond curly hair, rather genial and smiling for a man in this line of work. Actually I'd met him years before at a party in Paris and he'd said he was in the antique business, which must have been his deep cover at the time. He traveled a lot, he'd said; his name was Feldman then. He didn't know about me and I didn't know about him. Spooks that pass in the night, you see. He wasn't your ordinary dehydrated Camp Perry type though, as you might guess from his antique-business cover. Spivak had kind of an artistic temperament, warm and generous, kind-hearted. A lot like me, really. At least that's the way he was at parties. So here we met again.

"What do you mean, 'hear what they've got to say for themselves'?" I said. "They're not going to tell me anything they wouldn't tell a political officer from the embassy."

"Well," Spivak laughed, "the Shah doesn't like embassy people dealing with the opposition. He feels it would undermine his authority."

"Well, that's never stopped you before," I said. "Send one of your own people over. Send some deep cover man. Send someone who speaks Farsi. Send a cut-out."

"The SAVAK keeps close watch." Spivak smiled. "It's

pretty hard to make a move in Iran without them knowing about it."

It took me a second to soak this in.

"But we trained SAVAK," I said. "I thought they did what we wanted, more or less. Now we do what *they* want?"

Spivak surveyed his desk for a while then raised his eyes. They had a hard look. He was less warm than I remembered him.

"We're under orders not to have any contact with the political opposition," he said.

Then silence.

"But how about me?" I asked. "Wouldn't I be a contact?"

"No," said Spivak. "You'd be going on your own."

"What do you mean, going on my own? You're telling me to go."

"No," said Spivak. "If you think about it for a while, I think you'll realize you're going on your own."

Like he said, I thought about it.

"I just love the assignments you guys give me," I said. "Cold-turkey approaches. Fanatic hostiles. Guys who are going to kill me the next time they see me. Assignments that aren't even assignments, I'm out there all by my goddamn self."

"Nelson! Don't dramatize! This is a nothing! You go see some old man in black drapery. You visit a little. You get the feel. Maybe you'll get the feel of things."

So that made two who wanted to get the feel, these guys and Omar.

"I think this is an outrage," I said. "I don't see why I should have to go see some old mullahs like I'm walking on eggs. I think if you need these religious nuts to support the regime and the Shah's too stupid to realize it himself then you should do the straight, honest, democratic thing. You should pay them off. You should buy them."

Spivak was looking straight at me and I saw this quick flicker in the eye, this shadow. It lasted only a split second but I saw it.

Son of a bitch. I'd hit the nail on the head. That's exactly what they were doing. Or going to do. Or wanted to use me to do. Or they were arguing back and forth, some said yes and some said no, but the yes's were winning. I'd hit it! That was it! I'd seen it in his eyes! I knew it like it was gospel! I knew it like it was fucking Sacred Writ!

"Spivak, you devil," I said.

23

CYPRESS TREES LINED the long driveway. The air was heavy
with the scent of roses. Near the house were weeping
willows, flowering acacias, luxurious, well-tended shrub-
bery. A fountain splashed in a white marble pool in which
swam black and gold fish. In the distance loomed the bare,
angular shapes of the Alborz Mountains.

The house was Beverly Hills Persian, which was like
Beverly Hills Moorish, only Persian. Vulgar *nouveau riche*
imitation, you know, inspired by an antique model but
without true understanding of the ancient idiom. The
whole layout was really exactly like one of those seven-
million-dollar Beverly Hills estates north of Sunset, except
where was the retired Indiana business-machine tycoon to
whom this place should rightfully belong? Instead there
were all these strange Iranians. This wasn't where the
Ayatollah lived, of course. In Iran, you went to a friend
whose uncle was the chief-of-staff of a cabinet minister
whose niece's father-in-law had gone to school with the first
cousin of the Ayatollah's special assistant. That was the
way you did it in Iran.

Rose bushes. Fountains. White arcades. Skinny servants
in white coats. A grand entrance hall with Beverly Hills-
Persian rugs on the floor, heavy maroon velvet drapes by
the windows. Across the room was coming a suntanned
Armenian-looking gentleman with beautiful gray hair,
great, dark, liquid eyes under beautiful gray eyebrows,

gray suit, lavender shirt, pearl-gray tie. His hands were raised as if in praise of some deity.

"Welcome, agha. Welcome, agha. You do great honor to this modest abode, this mud hut. Please grace it with your footsteps. I am your slave. I am earth beneath your feet. Come, agha, come."

Omar mumbled, "Nice of you to ask us," which suddenly seemed very pallid, and our host led the two of us toward another expensively dressed, gray-haired gentleman, two carpets farther on, who turned his soft, large-eyed gaze upon us.

"His Excellency, the exalted Mr. Ferydoun Jambani," said our host, "one of the illustrious leaders of our Agriculture Ministry, without whose eminent guidance the ministry would not be able to function, and on whom even our Sublime Shah leans as on a strong tree in matters of agriculture. I have had the honor of claiming his Excellency's friendship for many blessed years."

His Excellency inclined his head, smiling.

"I am nothing," he said. "May your shadow never grow less."

Our host turned to Omar.

"The exalted Mr. Omar Hammoud," he said, "one of the enlightened, progressive leaders of the Hollywood cinema in America, in whose delightful shade I have learned much of the world of motion pictures, and who, despite his governance of one of the great film studios of Hollywood, is an Oriental even as we, whose father was a pillar of the eminent modern state of Lebanon, who gave much good counsel to Lebanon's president. Our noble guest is also a devout Muslim —" he interrupted himself, now addressing Omar. "My son knows by heart hundreds of the verses of the Book, agha, in your own language, sacred to us also."

Now it was my turn.

"The exalted Mr. Burt Nelson," said our host, "a scholar, a very learned man, a poet who has written many, many great books, very admired in his country and the world, and who is now engaged in a learned work of pious devotion

287

with Mr. Hammoud to demonstrate by means of the cinema the ecumenical unity of Christianity and Islam. Will you honor this humble gathering with the recitation later of some of your ecumenical poetry, agha?"

"I am unworthy —" I began.

"No, no. It is we who are unworthy, agha. We are your servants."

And he led us on, through many more introductions to dignified-looking people in expensive, stylish Western dress, with me in something of a daze, thinking numbly to myself: man, I'm never going to be able to use any of this dialogue. "This mud hut." "May your shadow never grow less." "May your head never ache." "*Shash. Shash. Shash*," they were all saying, too.

"Forgive me, agha," I asked, trying to get into the swing of it. "But I do not know your beautiful language. What is the meaning of this *shash* that so many of your exalted guests say?"

Our host smiled. "It means, 'I crush my eyeballs,'" he said benignly. "It is to show how much we are honored by your visit, how much we honor you."

"Thank you, agha," I said, my mind reeling again, thinking to myself: well, that's the top all right. Surely there is no greater honor than that.

There were about two dozen people at the party, about a third of them women, but the women seemed mostly engaged in supplementing the efforts of the flock of servants to keep the men attended to every minute. Some of the men were lounging on the carpet in one room playing what looked like poker. Others were in a second room, also lounging on carpets, playing some other card game. A third group in another room simply lounged with cushions behind their backs, heads, some lying with their heads on their neighbors' stomachs, a number of the men holding hands, tweaking each other's ears playfully. Through an oriental arcade into still another room, I could see tables heaped with a bewildering assortment of foods, fruits, delicacies. But our host was addressing himself to Omar again.

"Dear Mr. Hammoud," he said. "I know how cruel it must have been for you, an Oriental, in the cold formality of California, sitting stiffly upright in chairs, eating at hard, unyielding tables even among friends when your heart must have yearned to stretch out on our oriental carpets with a cushion at your back, eat of our oriental foods instead of Jell-O and Coca-Cola. Come, agha, come. This is your home. Stretch out." Now calling to the servants. "Food for the agha! The agha is hungry!"

There was a look of panic in Omar's eyes as they laid him out on a rich carpet, stuffing pillows and cushions under him. He couldn't have been hungry at all since we'd just eaten a full meal at the hotel, but in a few minutes the servants had stretched a sheet sprinkled with rosewater beside him and begun setting out silver and brass platters covered with cucumbers in yoghurt, stuffed grape leaves, steaming rabbit with crushed walnuts and pomegranate juice, saffron rice pilaff, great irregular pieces of bread looking like pale beige paper towels, apricots, quinces, grapes, silver bowls of shelled pistachio nuts, almonds, sherbet set in crushed ice, loukoum, halva, tiny crystal glasses in silver holders for thick syrupy coffee and black-cherry tea, a samovar, a bottle of arak, over it all the heavy scent of rosewater. It would have taken a week to eat all that stuff, and there must have been a chorus of six people around Omar crying, "Eat, agha, eat," with the lady of the house, contrite, "You must forgive us for these poor morsels, agha." Omar cast me a look of desperation. Well, it served him right for passing himself off as this Oriental. Let him pay the price.

"And you, agha," our host said to me. "Perhaps you would like to lie down beside your friend. I'm sure you must have many endearments to exchange. This is your home, agha. But perhaps you do not care for our Persian foods."

"Your kindness overwhelms me, agha," I said. "May it never grow less. But I thought I would circulate among your other exalted guests, to bask in the brilliance of their personages."

This sounded too sunny for hot weather and I decided to go for shade. "To shade myself in their leafy coolness," I said, but this didn't sound right either. I wasn't quite getting it.

"Agha does not like our Persian food," said our host.

"But indeed I do," I protested. "I simply can't resist Persian food." And to prove it I bent down and took a section of Omar's massive supply of loukoum, then scooped up a handful of pistachio nuts and threw them in my mouth too. Unfortunately this left me with a mouth full of gooey pistachio nuts, which shut me up for a while. I sat cross-legged beside Omar and slowly munched it all down. Some Iranian bigwig was lying beside Omar patting him on the head and urging him to take off his coat, his tie, his shoes, his socks. Soon I stole away and found the man I was looking for. This one, a banker, had a much firmer manner than the others.

"The Ayatollah is a stern man, agha," he said in another salon, with a splashing fountain outside the open window. "He grew up as a boy on my uncle's lands and he still has great respect for our family, but all this" — he gestured about the villa — "he disapproves of our Western ways. He was very angry when our sublime Shah took lands of the Mosque to distribute among the peasants, and when he gave women the right to vote. He feels women should still wear the chador, agha. He does not like this tennis. I am not certain you will like him."

"Do you think he likes motion pictures?" I asked.

My companion smiled wanly.

"No, agha. I would be very surprised if he liked motion pictures. He is against our sublime Shah's entire White Revolution. But he is a holy man, learned in the Law. He has spent his life in study." Then, afraid of overstating his case: "But he is a moderate man also, agha. He is not filled with bitterness like the Ayatollah Khomeini in Najaf, who fills the air with maledictions daily against our Shah, he whose mother was a dancer."

"The Shah's mother was a dancer?"

"No, agha," said my partner, shocked. "The Ayatollah Khomeini's mother was a dancer. And he also has pederastical tendencies and is an agent of our enemy Iraq. But you ask about the Ayatollah Shirazi and whether he would like motion pictures. No, agha, I would not think he would like motion pictures."

Another exalted guest approached and the ritual eulogies were gone through. This gentleman was from somewhere high in the administration too, apparently. The Shah couldn't make a move without him. I was gaining status as a poet every minute. This newcomer paid the usual tribute to our great ex-President Richard Nixon, still very popular among our friends in the Third World, who haven't figured out Watergate to this day. "Your Great Leader," he said. "Your Fallen Leader." The new man was a gentleman with views on the greater world and we were soon talking about the international scene.

"You should not concern yourself with the affairs of other countries, agha," he said kindly. "Vietnam was a woesome mistake, you should learn from this. In the New Hemisphere perhaps . . ." He made graceful motions with his hands indicating that perhaps the New Hemisphere was debatable. "But in the Old Hemisphere, no. You should not concern yourself with these matters, agha."

Still another distinguished-looking gentleman came drifting up. I was definitely the party's star turn. This one's theory was that our policy in world affairs was dictated by Betty Ford. It seemed to be another popular view, illustrating as it did Iranian ideas on female and male personality traits. Princess Ashraf was offered as a further example.

"We men are too emotional," the theorist said. "We cry and have delicate sentiments. It is the women who are strong, harsh. Betty Ford should not interfere with foreign countries, agha."

"You speak wise words, agha," I said. "Betty Ford should definitely not interfere with foreign countries. Nor should the United States. And I think we should not interfere with Iran either. As you know, agha, despite your great and fully deserved oil revenues, your country has a heavy budgetary deficit thanks to your sublime Shah's laudable and highly ambitious economic plan, and we are helping you to meet this budgetary deficit by means of large loans. But I think this is truly no concern of ours. I think your eminent country should be left to handle its own affairs without any outside interference from us, agha. And if the Russians come sweeping down out of the north, that, too, should be no concern of ours. It would be the will of God, agha, would it not? Kismet?"

This set off a chorus of protests.

"No, no, agha! We have offended you. If the Russians came, that would not be good at all! We are your friends! You must help us! We have offended you, agha. Let us talk of something else."

"Me?" I said. "Offended? Not me."

"Yes, yes, agha. We have offended you," said my first companion, the banker. "Let us talk of something else. I am your slave. May your head never ache."

But it did ache. What I wanted was to talk to some of these harsh women, but, dressed in Ungaro and Karl Lagerfeld dresses though they were, they were entirely occupied with plying the guests with loukoum and halva. I finally extricated Omar from the manly embrace of other members of the gentle sex, and the ride back to the hotel was refreshing as the bracing spirit of Lutheranism spread through my soul via the cushions of the Mercedes-Benz limo.

"Enjoy your oriental evening?" I asked Omar, who was slouched back lifeless, bug-eyed. "Your escape from Jell-O and Coca-Cola? The return to your ancestral oriental ways?"

I had to nudge him to get an answer.

"Wacko!" he said in horror. "This country's completely wacko!"

"Well, they put up I don't know how many million dollars to make James Michener's *Caravans* with Anthony Quinn, that MGM put in turnaround ten years ago," I said. "The Shah's brother-in-law produced it, in fact. Let's hope they've got sense enough to bankroll a movie about their own prophet."

"But they say such horrible things," replied Omar. "*Shash. I crush my eyeballs! It's disgusting!*"

"Well, the Arabs say, 'I kiss your feet.'"

"But they don't mean it!" protested Omar. "They're just being polite!"

"These people don't mean it either," I said. "That wasn't a mud hut. They're not our slaves. They don't think we're exalted. They might not even like us."

"But 'crush my eyeballs.' It's disgusting even if they don't mean it! Where do they get expressions like that?"

We were driving down a tree-lined boulevard. The warm air sweeping in through the open windows carried with it the smell of lemon trees and flowers.

"Their reality principle is weak," I said.

"What kind of bullshit is that?" said Omar, disgusted. "How's your reality principle?"

Off in the night, we could hear dimly the sound of oriental music. But it didn't orientalize me. No, sir.

"Strong," I said.

I'm not often out-gunned intellectually. Actually I am very smart. But look what it took to be an Iranian ayatollah. First to become even an ordinary *mullah* you had to know the Koran, of course, plus the *hadiths*, Mohammed's traditions which are something like Supreme Court decisions, plus the *fiqh*, otherwise known as the Law, which was worked out from the Koran and the *hadiths*, I guess. Then if you memorized the whole Koran you got to be a *Hafez*. And if you memorized 300,000 *hadiths* you got to be a *Hojjat*, or vicar. And if you still kept boning up maybe you could win a certificate of *ijtihad*, or interpretation, and you became a *Mujtahed* and were considered qualified to pass on all matters in heaven or upon earth, like say rent control or maybe interest rates. And from this very restricted group of *Mujtaheds* a number of *especially* learned men emerged as *Ayatollahs.* The depth of this liberal education left me humbled and in awe, particularly remembering that most of the memorizing was of precepts like: The blood of an animal whose blood spurts is impure, but the blood of a mosquito, whose blood does not spurt, is pure. The blood of a man is impure, but blood that flows between a man's teeth is pure if diluted with saliva. In fact, eleven things are impure: urine, excrement, sperm, bones, dogs, pigs, non-Moslems, blood, beer, wine, and the sweat of the excrement-eating camel. It was all good stuff to know if you wanted to immerse yourself in Iranian culture, filled with helpful, homey details. There are principles to be observed while drinking water, for example: sucking it up rather than gulping it down, drinking upright invoking the name of God, and recalling the martyrdom of Hazrat Aba Abdullah and his family while cursing their murderers. Among the eighteen principles to be observed during meals is resting on the back after eating and placing the right leg over the left. Urinating is regulated too, of course. It is forbidden to urinate while facing Mecca. On the other hand it is forbidden to urinate while facing directly away from Mecca. And if facing toward or directly away from Mecca, do not think for one second that you can escape this injunction by merely turning your member so as to urinate sideways. The whole body must be turned sideways. It is also forbidden to evacuate while facing the sun or the moon, unless your genitals are covered. During evacuation it is forbidden to eat, dally, or talk, unless praying to God. It is recommended to go into the place of evacuation with the left foot first, come out of it with the right foot first, keep your head covered while evacuating, at the same time carrying your weight on the left foot.

It was a genuine intellectual achievement to remember all this stuff, I thought admiringly, although in a small corner of my mind I still had some reservations as to how well this would qualify you to set wage-and-price guidelines. Because the ayatollahs had the answer to everything, you know. It goes without saying they had discovered that coeducational schools and unveiled women were obstacles to a wholesome life, in addition to being moral and material affronts to the nation and contrary to divine will. But they had also discovered that cursed Western medicine was a complete failure at handling typhus, typhoid, and other such diseases, which were only curable by old-fashioned Iranian remedies. And they'd discovered that running water remained drinkable even if containing excrement, provided you couldn't taste it. And they had Islamic economics, too, which I will spare you. But the most impressive thing about the whole system was how it placed at its center, not the individual, but the community, which was what the modern world so needed. As the Ayatollah Khomeini himself said in Najaf: "He who governs the Moslem community must always have its interests at heart. This is why Islam has put so many people to death, to safeguard the interests of the Moslem community." And these strictures weren't all rigid and unyielding either. Far from it. Take, "It is forbidden to urinate on the grave of a Believer, unless this is intended as an insult." You see? It wasn't unconditional. It allowed for the human factor.

A few days later we were sitting on the floor of a stark, almost unfurnished white room with our interpreter, waiting for our audience with the Ayatollah Shirazi, the moderate ayatollah. The atmosphere was more than austere. It was ascetic.

Omar was sitting there, expectant in his best duds. Giorgio Armani eggshell-color suit, blue paisley tie from Rodeo Drive.

"I want you to know," I said in a low voice, "that this is the craziest idea I ever heard of. Where do you think we are, in Cairo? The mullahs here are in the Middle Ages. You think the Ayatollah is going to back a movie of any description about the Prophet? They're against all movies!"

"But it's all been cleared," whispered Omar urgently, leaning forward. "It's all set up. He's going to go along with it. Anyway, didn't you tell me that this guy's mother was a dancer?"

"No, I told you the Ayatollah Khomeini's mother was a dancer. And I don't know that for a fact either. The man who told me that was bad-mouthing him. How would I know if his mother was a dancer?"

I looked at Omar and saw he wasn't getting it. Deeply imbued as he was with Middle Eastern culture, I could see he was thinking: Gee, imagine being the son of Ruby Keeler, wouldn't that be fun?

"Omar," I said. "In this part of the world dancers are prostitutes."

"What?" he said, startled, but before he could get his bearings again in swept the Ayatollah Shirazi in black robe, black turban, followed by three other mullahs and a man in Western dress. The Ayatollah was a man in his sixties, tall, gray-bearded, pale-skinned, unsmiling. Giving his robe a stately swirl, he sat cross-legged against the wall across from us, absent-mindedly, as if we were not in the room. We had risen but now sat also. The man in his retinue in civilian clothes, still standing, spoke to the Ayatollah in Farsi, gesturing to us. The Ayatollah gave us the faintest nod then looked away again, his face expressing no interest or curiosity. I had the feeling he didn't have the slightest idea who we were. Now our interpreter rose and addressed him on our behalf in Farsi. The Ayatollah gazed at the wall behind our heads, his turban higher on the forehead than seemed right. At last he spoke, quietly, his face still abstracted. Our interpreter translated:

"The Ayatollah understands that you are engaged in a book explaining the tenets of our Faith to the West. He commends you."

A book, eh? All cleared, eh? Let Omar talk his way out of this. I waited for more from our interpreter, but nothing was forthcoming. I glanced at Omar, who had the look of a rabbit caught in the coils of a boa constrictor, the eyes protruding.

"What would the Ayatollah like to see in this book?" asked Omar, as if restricted in his breathing.

Our interpreter spoke Farsi, the Ayatollah answered, and our translator translated again.

"The truth of our Faith is plain for all to see, but the West does not understand that Islam is all, Islam explains all, Islam is perfect. The West talks to us of freedom but does not understand freedom and corrupts our people. Freedom is following the will of God."

It was seamless, I thought. It was self-contained. It let no air in. Let Omar handle it.

"I am not unacquainted with Islam myself, Ayatollah, being a Muslim," said Omar, gathering courage, although I didn't see why. "But the West is obsessed with materialism. How can it best be made to see the truth of Islam?"

Working back and forth through the interpreter, the Ayatollah's answer came back:

"I do not condemn everything from the West. There is much I can accept. Until now you have kept the good things mostly for yourself, such as your wealth and economic progress. But we are not afraid of your science, of your technology, of your machines. We accept your atomic power plants, your aircraft, your telephones, your television, your air conditioners. We accept all that. But it is your evil thinking that we fear, and against which we must protect our people."

It seemed to me that it was the evil thinking that was producing the air conditioners, and that Omar and the Ayatollah were at cross-purposes anyway. Omar was asking what Islam had to give, but the Ayatollah was saying what Islam wanted to take. I thought Omar should pick up from air conditioners and from there proceed to motion-picture cameras, but he thought of himself as bearing a great moral message and instead picked up from evil.

"What kind of evil prevalent in the West should we most combat, Ayatollah?" asked Omar. "Materialism? Inhumanity? Godlessness?"

"What you do in America is your own affair for which you will answer before God" came back, suggesting a lack of zeal on the Ayatollah's part to lift us from the slough into which we'd sunk. "But our people must not be corrupted, must not be led to commit abominations."

"Like what?" said Omar, which sounded strangely naked, as if you owed an ayatollah more syntax. And indeed Omar had to rephrase this for the interpreter, "What kind of abominations must your young people not be led to commit?"

"You have exported many bad things to us," replied the Ayatollah, who wasn't buying Omar's fellow-oriental line at all. "We do not want our youth to be corrupted by alcohol, by music that deadens the senses, by uncovered women (his tone rising steadily, the voice grating). You have led young Iranian women to wear make-up, to go into the street exhibiting their necks, their hair, their figures. These women can be of no social, political, or professional use to their country because, by so uncovering themselves, they distract men and upset them. Your music thickens the mind and leads to pleasure and ecstasy, thus discouraging clear thought. All this poisons our youth, leading it from Islam! This is what the West has done! It must end!"

Omar had had a strategy, cockeyed though it was. Give the Ayatollah a shot, and then make a case for putting his position to the peoples of the world even more convincingly by means of the cinema. But he'd given the Ayatollah his shot and he'd come up with prohibition of music and alcohol, and covering up women. It might play in Qom but it wouldn't play in Quincy, Illinois. It wasn't a bit like my screenplay.

"Ayatollah, there is much truth in what you say," said Omar reverently, more mealy-mouthed than I had ever seen him, although I'd never seen him before with an Islamic divine. "Islam has superior spiritual values. In the West there is too much license, certainly. I, too, am a Muslim and —"

"If the flesh of your finger rots, do you not cut it off?" interjected the Ayatollah angrily.

There seemed to be a translation breakdown here. Either that or the Ayatollah wasn't listening on the Farsi end.

"Abomination! Abomination!" cried the Ayatollah, which confused things further.

"Yes," said Omar ambiguously, trying to get him back on the track.

Something alarming was happening to the Ayatollah now, his eyelids flickering, the eyeballs white. Either he was having an epileptic fit or he was talking to the Hidden Imam.

"We know that in some countries women are free to give themselves to men to gratify their lust!" he now thundered, back to earth again. "And these countries feel that death is too severe a punishment for an adulterous woman. But does not one cut off the rotting finger so that the poison does not spread to the hand? The arm? The whole body?"

Omar blenched.

"Yes," he said weakly.

"The rot must be cut out! You must write this in your book!" ordered the Ayatollah.

Omar was paralyzed. First, we were not doing a book but a movie. And what the Ayatollah had to say was so unappealing. He wasn't even paying lip service to humanitarianism. Was this the final message of Islam? Amputation? Omar was speechless, his eyes wandering desperately, and I thought I might as well speak up. What were they going to do, put me in mullah jail?

"Ayatollah," I said. "We had been planning to do a book, but what would you say to a motion picture embodying your ideas? It might have a lot of impact. We'd been thinking of telling the West about Islam's peacefulness and tolerance, but if you wanted us to show how the sight of women's necks distracts men's minds and disturbs the social order we could work that in too. We're flexible. Aren't we, Omar?"

While this was being translated I looked at Omar. He was in a state of shock, and I whispered to him, "What's the point of sounding him out on a book when we're going to make a movie? Speak up, man!"

The Ayatollah hadn't answered yet and was giving me a

look intended to turn me to stone. But I didn't turn into stone that easy. Omar was still in shock so I carried the ball again, apologizing for my ill-considered jest, the cinema as everyone knew being an abomination upon earth and an ally of the enemies of God. I humbly confessed that we did a lot of wicked things in America, dulled our senses with music, allowed women to show their necks, but we respected other people's religion and holy ways and if the Iranians wanted to decapitate women for adultery that was their business. Then I finally got him in position and zinged it to him: okay, Ayatollah, baby, which side are you on, God-hating Russia, or America the Beautiful, land of the free and home of the religious? KUBARK had to take a global view, after all. It was my global-view question. It was my Henry Kissinger question. I mean, it was the real stuff.

"Isn't this fun?" I whispered to Omar while this was being translated. "Forget about the movie, Ome, he's never going to go along."

Strangely, the Ayatollah was very serene, almost bored. America had invented the Communists, who did the bidding of America, he said. Capitalists, Communists, were all the same. Now I'd heard weird, but this was weird. I told him I wasn't concerned with little local Communists but the Soviet Union, the Biggies. Had we invented Lenin? Trotsky? The Ayatollah said he'd never heard of them. I couldn't believe it. "I am a man of God and not concerned with particulars!" he said angrily, after which the conversation was a shambles, with the Ayatollah barking, "In my long life I have always been right!" and me struggling valiantly to get the idea across that there were two kinds of whitey. There were these Communist whiteys up in Russia, hateful bastards with their police state, and very rough on religion including Islam, but maybe he'd like them for all I knew, it was up to him. On the other hand there were these other democratic whiteys in Western Europe and America, an easygoing, more likeable crowd really, but in any case different from the first whiteys up in Russia, considered by most people to be antagonistic even. I felt I owed it to

300

KUBARK to get him to see there was a distinction. It was a little elementary, but a necessary first step, wouldn't you say? It put him into a rage though.

"First you talk nonsense," he railed, "then you expect me to make sense out of your statements. Capitalists, Communists, democrats, whatever you call yourselves, all do the bidding of the Great Satan! All are enemies of Islam! We want this to be our country! And now I have spoken enough! I am tired! Go away! Go away!"

Well, it was as clear an answer as I was going to get, I figured. It was him against the united Capitalist-Communist Front. The conversation had no place to go after this and I sat in silence while the Ayatollah rose and, drawing his robes together disdainfully, swept out of the room.

"Mullah Murtazavi, may I speak to you for a moment in private please?" I said to a member of the Ayatollah's suite, and he looked at me, face expressionless, and led me into a side room where we both sat on the floor. He wore a white turban and was much younger, perhaps thirty. He stared at me with a kind of neutral gravity, neither friend nor foe. I took a package wrapped in cloth out of my attaché case and set it on the floor between us.

"This is for the upkeep of the mosques, and for the Koranic schools," I said clearly.

He nodded, inclining his head briefly in the Iranian way, and took the package within his robes, his face still expressionless. There was no thank you, no smile.

"You understand what this is for, Mullah," I said clearly.

He inclined his head again.

"You know who I am?"

Again he nodded, staring solemnly into my eyes.

Riding back to Teheran in the limo, Omar was gazing despondently out over the parched fields.

"Well, I'm sure glad the Ayatollah was one of the moderates," I said. "I'd sure hate to meet one of those extremists."

"Crazy son of a bitch," replied Omar.

"I don't see why you say that. He's no crazier than Peter

the Hermit." Seeing Omar didn't answer, I continued, "The priest who preached the First Crusade. Without which there would have been no Cecil B. DeMille."

Omar was staring joylessly out the window.

"Cheer up, Ome," I told him. "He couldn't have done us any good anyway. He was a very interesting fellow, actually, taught me a lot about Islam, and very consistent, I think. Because if you keep yourself firmly anchored in the Tenth Century, all these Communists, capitalists, socialists, John Birchers, must all seem pretty much alike. Why should the Ayatollah have to distinguish among these different kinds of modern riffraff? What business are they of his?"

There was still no response from Omar.

"He concentrates on important stuff," I said. "Like, 'It is forbidden to eat the flesh of a recently sodomized donkey.'"

Omar gave a start. "You made it up!" he cried.

"Nope."

"But how do you know what the donkey's been doing?" Omar said, his face alarmed and bewildered. "What do you do, ask him?"

But soon he had sunk back into his gloom, leaving me with my own thoughts, which were mostly about how subtle the world is. If they supported America we gave them money, to help them do what they already wanted to do really. But if they loathed America we gave them a little money anyway, depending on circumstances, to soothe their discontent, undermine their will, declaw them a little. As part of his austerity program the Shah was cutting off his funding of religious education and general subsidies to the Mosque, one of the most baroque blunders in Iranian history, but we were taking up the slack. Here the mullahs hated us, but we were helping them anyway. It was a very advanced concept.

In the bar at the Inter-Continental I met an American television correspondent named Jensen who told me that we should induce the Shah to liberalize his regime. The Shah should reach out, he said, encourage a loyal opposition. It sounded nice. The intellectuals, the leftists, the

Moslem clergy provided a vast, untapped source of liberal strength for the nation, he said. He sat there with his face from an Arrow shirt ad and told me that the Moslem clergy was a great liberal force. "Civil rights," he added enthusiastically. "If the Islamic clergy is brought into the political process here, Iran will have a new birth of civil liberties such as the world has rarely seen." There were people running around loose saying things like that in those days. And he was a correspondent of network television.

"Are you going to get up there on the box and say that?" I asked him.

"Oh, sure." He smiled.

"Tell me," I said. "Just out of curiosity. Have you met any members of the Islamic clergy?"

"Well, I just flew in," he replied amiably. "But we have staff here. We're well informed. We know what's going on."

"Do yourself a favor, Jensen," I said. "Go do an interview with one of the ayatollahs."

Soon one of Jensen's Iranian informants came to meet him in the bar, silky black hair, lustrous eyes. He spoke excellent English and was even a fellow Californian in a manner of speaking in that he'd graduated UCLA. I asked him what he'd majored in. "Theatre arts," he said blithely. So, I mean, how could Jensen give much weight to my opinion compared to that of a genuine Iranian graduate of UCLA's Theatre Arts Department?

It was a quiet time in Teheran. One of the Shah's sisters got into a contract squabble with her foreign business partner and, piqued, had him thrown into jail. So much for due process in Iran. Outside Teheran things were more spirited. In Qom, there were riots to commemorate the 1963 riots. In Isfahan, a bomb exploded at the Shah Abbas, the country's most famous tourist hotel. In Meshed, bombs went off at the U.S. Information Service and the British Council, not counting the traditional bulldozer bombings because the populace didn't like the Shah's vast, modern plans for renovating Meshed's Holy Shrine. And two U.S. Air Force colonels were assassinated, plus a SAVAK brigadier general.

So in the provinces there was turbulence, but the best Teheran had to offer was a scandal about top officials who organized the pilgrimage to Mecca taking bribes from pilgrims, something that went over rather badly with the thousands of religiously fervent poor idling on the streets of Teheran and who were bitter about not being able to go to Mecca anyway, the government-fixed price being $2,000 a head. Because there were lots of miserably poor people out there on the streets in Teheran that the new oil wealth was passing by completely. And again, in the Old City, I kept seeing these shabby-looking posters, which I could recognize now in their Farsi lettering: THE RETURN OF THE HIDDEN IMAM IS AT HAND. It wasn't the way a civil-rights movement usually heralded its advent and left me with an uneasy feeling. Maybe the Hidden Imam *was* coming.

I reported on the Ayatollah to Spivak down at the station. Spivak was cheerful, smiling, his blue eyes a-twinkle. I ran it through: the money, the hand-over, the Ayatollah.

"He didn't seem very grateful," I said. "Are you sure the money's getting to him? Are you sure he knows where it's coming from?"

Spivak raised the palms of his hands and smiled wearily as if to say: don't worry about it; we'll take care of that part of it.

"What do you make of him though?" Spivak asked. "The old Ayatollah?"

"Not much give," I said. "I hope you're not counting on him for any active good will. For any new birth of civil liberties or anything like that."

Spivak chuckled.

"But tell me, what do you make of the whole thing?" he asked expansively. "The whole Iranian situation."

"For Christsake, Spivak," I said. "You've got people here who've studied Farsi fifteen years. You've got assets all over the place. How do I know what's happening here?"

"Just your general impression," he urged me. "It's not everybody who gets to meet an ayatollah. We don't have many direct contacts on that side. I told you. Just your impression."

"Well," I said. "The mullahs are not devoted friends of our great God-fearing republic. Just a subjective view."

Spivak laughed. "And?"

"You got them neutralized? Terrific."

He laughed again. "And?"

"And what? What do you want me to tell you? You've got everybody from Richard Helms to sanctimonious ladies who lecture us about what swine we were in Vietnam agreeing that the Shah reigns secure on the Peacock Throne. What do I have for you, that I keep seeing wall posters that the Hidden Imam is coming?"

Spivak laughed outright.

"Are you asking us to pay attention to ill-printed pentecostal gibberish on ramshackle walls in the Old City? Christ is coming?"

"Well, I certainly wouldn't pay attention to anything that was ill-printed," I said.

He got a pompous look on his face.

"And maybe Christ is coming, Spivak," I said. "How would you know? This fucking place could blow sky high."

Although I suppose it wasn't his fault he wasn't raised to believe in Our Lord Jesus, missing, *For as the lightening cometh out of the east, and shineth even unto the west, so also shall be the coming of the Son of man.* It left its mark. It left its mark.

Walking back to the hotel I came to the definite conclusion that Christ wasn't coming though, at least not for a while. And that the Hidden Imam wasn't coming either, at least not as long as we continued our subsidy to the Mosque. But soon a Sunday-school teacher named James Earl Carter cut off secret KUBARK payments to Iran's Moslem clergy as an act of shining rectitude. And you know what happened then. A whirlwind did appear in the heavens, and, lo, the earth was shaken of a mighty wind. And a great beast rose up out of the sea, and all the world

305

worshipped the beast, saying, who is able to make war with him? And the sun became black, and the moon became as blood, and the kings of the earth did hide themselves in the dens and in the rocks of the mountains.

Yes, sir. All in St. John the Divine, which you'd think a Sunday-school teacher would have read. And when the great riots started he refused to sell the Iranians tear gas, because we could not support repression, you see. And as the end approached no one in Washington even bothered to read the published works of the Ayatollah Khomeini, nothing more or less than his *Mein Kampf*, because the Sunday-school crowd knew that men of the cloth were dedicated to love and peace and welcomed Khomeini as a "saint," because weren't they all for human rights together? And so we got the Great Beast. It was the kind of thing that gave morality a bad name and made us soldiers of the Lord bitter. *Behold, saith the Lord, I have made thee small among the heathen: thou art greatly despised; for the pride of thine heart hath deceived thee*. Obadiah. Bitter as gall was it in my mouth, and I did rend my garments and cover myself with sackcloth, and curse he who defended not Zion when the Assyrians swept over the field, bent on our destruction.

When I got back to the hotel, there was a letter waiting from the Ministry of Culture and Information turning down our movie project.

24

WHAT THE SHABANU would have liked was a *film d'auteur* in the Marguerite Duras style, *Persia Song* she thought it should be called. A budget of a quarter of a million dollars perhaps? A half-million? Never in my life had I encountered such contemptible penny pinching on the part of a crowned head greasy with oil riches when a major production in Hollywood budgeted half a million for a screenplay alone. I was disgusted. What a mistake it had been to come to Iran, leaving behind the Sunnis and our friends the Arabs, who thanks to Omar considered us all soul brothers. These Iranians were lousy, maggoty, money-grubbing Aryans. And such indifference to religion. They didn't give a damn about higher values. Just wait till they tried to cross the Accountant's Bridge.

Well, I went into the shop again. I can't tell you how boring it was. IRRIGATE. IRRITATE. Now that I had real problems of my own it all seemed so tiresome. I was downhearted. I'd been up so high, now I was down low. I was sick and tired of KUBARK. After all I'd done for them, let them do something for me now. But what could they do? Despite wild ideas people were getting these days a few thousand dollars was still a lot of money for most KUBARK operations and *Mohammed Superstar* was so high in the millions now I hated to think about it. You could have saved Angola for half the budget of this dumb movie. I could have asked KUBARK to pull some strings but they weren't going to squander a major effort on a crazy flick when they had tricky liaison operations to worry about. Was *Mohammed Superstar* in the U.S. national interest? They were selfish. They had something going with Kurds; I couldn't even figure it out. They were mad for Kurds all of a sudden. Kurds were this freedom-loving people fighting for independence or autonomy maybe up in their free mountain homeland in Iraq. Actually there were Kurds in Turkey and Iran too, and later they would be fighting for their free mountain homeland in Iran, but for the time being the boys were only het up over the ones in Iraq. *Kurds wha hae wi Wallace bled. Kurds wham Bruce has aften led.* That kind of thing. *Welcome to your gory bed. Or to victorie.* Quite stirring, really. It was a joint operation with the Iranians, from what I could gather, who were third cousins of the Kurds, more or less, who were also Aryans, I think, but basically it was one of those deals where the enemy of my enemy is my friend, sometimes known as *let's you and him fight.* I mean, the Iranians wanted the Kurds and Iraqis to fight because they hated the Iraqis. Like later the Iraqis wanted the Kurds and Iranians to fight because they hated the Iranians. Human nature, you see. I couldn't quite figure out how we'd gotten into it. Because the Iranians had asked us, I guess. They were definitely the enemies of our enemies, the Russians, who were out there somewhere. Personally I thought the Iranians were money-grubbing Aryan creeps, I didn't care whose enemies they were, and I couldn't wait to get back to our Semitic Arabs, who personally had always treated me perfectly okay, although on the face of it I must admit the Kurds looked pretty good. You had to have a lot of guts to stage an uprising against odds like that, pinning down sixty-five thousand Iraqi combat troops up in the mountains. Very brave I'll bet they were. Very noble. Of course I'd never met a Kurd. Maybe if I met one I wouldn't like him.

I was lying around the Teheran Inter-Continental, very dispirited, very despondent. This movie of ours was teetering on the brink of no more countries to go to, annihilation, and all KUBARK cared about at the moment was Kurds. Actually you could work out a perfectly reasonable Kurdish angle on *Mohammed Superstar* if you wanted to. I mean Saladin was a Kurd. But it was ridiculous. The budget for this damn film was more than KUBARK was giving the Kurds for Kalashnikovs to fight with! I'm not kidding. The Kurds were getting sixteen million. This little flick of ours had been over fifteen million in Libya, and now that we'd been kicked out of there, what were we? We must be over twenty million. With all the cost of moving and renegotiating contracts and everyone on overtime you could cry with black despair at the thought of it, it was so depressing. And to think that if this movie could only come in a winner I'd be able to retire and devote myself to good works. The Kurds were too small a market anyway. The Kurdish angle on Mohammed, what kind of a market did that open up for you? *Who were the Kurds? Who knew anything about Kurds? What friends did they have except us?* Even their fellow Aryans the Iranians were only helping them out of hatred for the Iraqis. The Kurdish market would pull in what, twenty thousand dollars in film rentals? They probably didn't even have movie houses up there in the mountains, fighting all the time. It was damn depressing. Well, we had drained the cup to the bitter dregs, and now we must eat the dregs.

Iraq. The very name struck a chill in my heart. Faisal murdered. Abd al-Ilah murdered. Kassem murdered. Aref murdered. But it was the only one left. We'd come to it through a process of elimination. It was the only country we hadn't tried where we could possibly finish the picture. It was our last chance. It was also the place where these Kurds were fighting, which was a curious commentary on something, and probably meant that the whole northern part of the country would be under martial law, but Omar was determined. What was our alternative? It didn't bear thinking about.

Omar came charging up to me in the bar, looking very excited. He'd given up smoking.

"She's coming!" he cried.

"Who's coming?"

He sat down on a bar stool in his natty eggshell-color suit, gripped my shoulder, gazed feelingly into my eyes and said, "Mouna."

"What do you mean she's coming? Is she an act of God? Don't you have anything to say about it? Coming from where? Coming to do what? How does she even know where we are?"

Omar looked puzzled.

"The telephone," he observed gently.

"You mean you asked her?" I said. "You called her on the phone? You invited her of your own free will?"

"I just called her for a little chat," he said soothingly. "To tell her we're going on to Baghdad."

He talked as if having her on our side would give us some tremendous advantage, bolster our courage, be a terrific asset to us in persuading Iraq to do this impossible thing.

"Omar," I said. "The last time I remember her with you she was trying to strangle you. She hates you, Ome, for God's sake. She hates you, me, the movie, religion, America. Don't let her back on the picture! I'm telling you! She's got all these crazy political ideas! She's not loyal to the picture!"

"No, no," said Omar fondly. "She was just excitable that day."

"Omar," I said, my voice low. "Are you crazy? That woman hates you. I'm telling you. What's the matter with you?"

I could see it wasn't going in and I gazed around the bar. Ye Olde English Pub. Come to Teheran to get drunk at Ye Olde English Pub. What could you do with him? He was hopeless with women. He fed the hand that bit him. He'd take anything from her. There was no limit. He was like another movie producer I'd worked for once. To cloak his identity I will call him by the fictitious name of Darryl Zanuck. That girl was so mean to old Darryl, although she

310

thought I was real cute. He took it all. He wasn't selfless though. Omar was more selfless.

Soon there she was, in the lobby of the Inter-Continental, in a new pink pants suit, big sunglasses. She'd failed in her career as a guerrillera but she'd gotten herself some new clothes. You never knew what end to grab her by, that Mouna. It wasn't so bad when you hadn't had much time to think about her, but when you'd been turning her over in your mind you got apprehensive. You kind of braced yourself before the plunge.

"Hello, Mouna," I said.

"Oh, hello, Burt," she said, opening her handbag. She had more important things on her mind apparently.

She seemed to know another man standing beside her at the reception desk. Not that they spoke.

"Who was he?" I asked when he'd left with a bellhop for his room.

"Who?" said Mouna.

"That guy who was standing right here."

"I wouldn't have the foggiest idea," said Mouna, turning around to look at the empty space where he'd been standing. "I think he was on the plane."

I couldn't see her eyes through the dark glasses.

"Well, you're coming back aboard for the last round, Mouna," I said.

"Yes," she said. "You might say that."

There was something evasive about her. It was hard to say what. I was slightly embarrassed. Actually I didn't care whether I ever went to bed with her again but I wanted her to commit herself. I was used to Mouna declaring her feelings very assertively, so even the mildest degree of reserve struck me as evasion and I felt I didn't know where I stood with her. She slept by herself that night. She didn't sleep with me.

I came upon her the next day standing in front of the hotel restaurant with two young men in business suits. They weren't talking. They were looking about in idle aimlessness. But they knew each other. You could tell. When people are by themselves there's psychic distance. The eyes are different. *Vamanos*, said one of the men to the other in a low voice and they walked off, two unremarkable figures, conservatively dressed, dark suits, one wearing eyeglasses. You couldn't have expected them to know I understood Spanish. What were they? I'd just heard the one word but it had sounded slurred and South American. Venezuela? Colombia? Something like that?

"Who were those two?" I asked Mouna.

"Which two?" she said, looking about in elaborate innocence.

She was lying.

She slept by herself that night too.

Omar was on the phone day and night to his bankers, his Arab brothers, sheiks who owned a piece of the action but didn't want us around offending the faithful by actually filming. He was pulling every string he could pull, getting leads to every influential Iraqi possible. He was going to Baghdad all right. He was hopeful. Once they'd seen his shining Hollywood Arab face they wouldn't be able to resist him. They were slaughtering Kurds up in the mountains and he thought he was going to talk them into letting us make a film about the human kindness and tolerance of Islam. The Kurds were Moslems too and a lot of good it did them. And you should have seen Omar with Mouna. Thick as thieves, as if the twain had never been separated, all gung-ho to win the big game in Iraq. And Sandor too. He was eating out of her hand too. They all had themselves talked into it. They were in a state of religious enthusiasm. Tolerance! Peace! Islam! Iraq! Damn it, *I wasn't going to go*. I'd just made up my mind. Let them go to Iraq by themselves. Couldn't they see the whole thing was over? Who would have thought it would end this way? Us still apparently rich. Still staying in the best hotels from Izmir to Kabul. Still spending other people's money like mad. But with bankruptcy staring us in the face, at least staring Omar in the face. And me, too, really. All my dreams of financial independence. And what about all those months of honest labor, trying to create understanding and tolerance. Well, it was back to Christianity, which was a better religion anyway if you want to know the truth. I went by the shop again. I was very wretched and cast down and even being a Christian didn't help. Or it didn't help enough.

"Baghdad?" said Spivak. "Iraq?"

Sure Baghdad, Iraq, I told him. What did he think I was talking about, Baghdad, Illinois?

"Go," he said. "Go along with them."

I waited, slightly puzzled. What could I do for him in Baghdad? Anyway I didn't want to go to Baghdad.

"There's a what-do-you-call-it you could give to someone for us," said Spivak. "A package."

His face had a closed-over look today. There was something missing from the expression.

"Why don't you send it by diplomatic pouch?"

"Awkward with the Belgians. They watch the Belgian Embassy like hawks. Do us a favor. We'll make it up to you. If this movie of yours flops you maybe could use a little helping hand. We could steer some interesting stuff your way, a guy with your connections?" Spivak smiled. "*Le showbiz?*"

They knew how to reinforce patriotism with self-interest. KUBARK and showbiz? I suppose you never knew. If Islam was this fucked-up hateful mess we knew it to be, and Christianity was on the wane, I suppose you had to be practical. I'd gotten my whole start in *belles-lettres* thanks to them. I suppose you had to think of things like that.

"You won't have any trouble getting it aboard the plane," said Spivak. "We'll see to that."

I went back to the hotel and told Omar, okay, deal me in for Iraq. You'd have thought they'd all been smoking loco weed. Omar, Mouna, and Sandor. Two Arabs and a Jew. Let them test their wily oriental minds on the Iraqi Minister of Industry.

The night before we were due to fly to Baghdad I went

313

by the shop to pick up the package. It was a nondescript tan suitcase.

"What's in it?" I said.

"That's all right," said Spivak.

His face didn't give away much today either. Where was the golden boy with that spontaneous artistic temperament? That cheery twinkle in his bright blue eyes? We were sitting in an ordinary-looking government office. Light green walls. The shades were drawn but luminous, the building very brightly lit from outside by spotlights to discourage second-story men.

"What do you mean 'that's all right'?" I said.

"It doesn't make any difference," he answered.

There was a pause.

"Hey, *hombre*," I said. "You think I'm going to carry stuff and not even know what it is?"

A little ripple of distaste went over Spivak's face as if he was going to have to step on a bug, but he snapped open the suitcase right there on the desk. I was beginning to figure as much, but I gasped. I was a little stunned.

"Hey, *amigo*. Do you realize what you're giving me here? Do you realize what you're asking me to carry?"

"You're one of our best people," he said.

Flattery didn't cost anything.

"You'll get it aboard," he went on. "There'll be no problem. We'll take care of that side of it."

"Wow. Boy, oh, boy."

Spivak laughed. "Remember to wear gloves," he said.

"I didn't say I'd do it yet. What's it for?"

"That I can't tell you," he replied with a cold sound in his voice. "I don't know myself."

"Well, I wish 'em luck. Holy smoke."

"Remember to wear gloves," he said.

"I didn't say I'd do it yet, I told you! I don't owe you guys anything. I'm still thinking it over."

Spivak let out his breath in a long *sssssss*, looking at his fingernails.

"Think," he said. "Think away."

314

I was wiping the fingerprints off the suitcase a couple of hours later back at the hotel. It was a slow, boring business. Your mind wandered. So much of this KUBARK business was boring, people didn't realize. It was so undramatic. No suspense. Everything handled by remote control. Other people took the risks. You never really knew what was going on. You never got the big picture. In my movies there was always epic sweep, feeling, significance. The KUBARK stuff was all unintelligible junk. In fact its boringness was why I had to escape into the wild, soaring realm of my imagination. It was ironic really because most screenwriters who worked on action movies were puny, pathetic little geezers who couldn't win an arm-wrestling match with Mia Farrow. Whereas I, so manly and combative of appearance and with my military background, carried within my bosom a sensitive poetic spirit, which was why in my movies there was always a soft lyrical undercurrent. They were probably too delicate and idealistic for most people nowadays; that was the whole trouble. I was a member of the Old School. If we'd been making a good straightforward film about hate instead of love and kindness we'd probably have had no trouble with it at all.

There was a knock on the door and I stood the suitcase in a corner.

"Mouna," I said.

Her face was unsmiling.

"I just wondered if you had any aspirin," she said, her eyes furtive.

"No," I said. "I'm sorry."

She acted as if she was going to go off, since I didn't have any aspirin.

"Come in though. Come in," I said, feeling a little hypocritical. I'd been wildly opposed to letting her come back on the picture, but I'd gotten used to her again now. I wouldn't want to say I really liked her, but for a malicious hysteric she wasn't too bad. You felt there was exhilarating passion smouldering in her. It was interesting, a relationship with Mouna. It had its thrill-seeking side. She had these black, burning eyes. She had big breasts. I hadn't been laid since the Persian Gulf. Mouna came walking in suspiciously, looking about as if she'd never been in a hotel room before.

"Sit down," I said. "You haven't told me about Beirut, devoting your life to your people."

She gave me a hard, resentful look. I shouldn't have said that maybe.

"I'm glad you and Omar have patched it up," I said, feeling that would be better.

Mouna gave a bitter laugh, making me think I shouldn't have said that either. Conversation seemed to founder. I couldn't think of anything to say to her. She didn't appear to want to leave but talk wouldn't come. I got her clothes off and hoisted her onto the bed with her showing no enthusiasm. We lay there naked side by side and she was remote. I had sex with her and she was still remote. She didn't enjoy it for one minute, I'll bet you anything. What did she do it for? And she still had no aspirin.

"How do you think this is all going to end?" she said, staring off moodily as we cooled off under the air conditioning. Suddenly it felt like wintry winds blowing down from the Hindu Kush. I pulled up the covers.

"All what?"

"All of this," she said. "*All* of this."

"We're going to have a happy ending," I said. "You together again with Omar. You go off into the sunset. The two of you. Why not? We all go off into the sunset."

"We must have our freedom," Mouna said somberly. "We must have our own land."

It gave me a chilly feeling. I can't explain it. It seemed too big. I'd been expecting something more personal. As we lay there naked in bed we talked about the great world out there since that was what she wanted, Mouna brooding, nursing her hostilities, a bad word for everybody. With Mouna even the enemies of her enemies weren't her friends. The Iranians were her enemies because they were supplying oil to Israel. And the Kurds were her enemies because they were pulling Iraqi troops off the Israeli front. But the Iraqis were her enemies too because they didn't support the PLO in its death struggle with the Jordanians, who were also her enemies. And the Saudis and Gulf sheiks were reactionary. It was as if Mouna was going down under the weight of all these enmities. They took their toll. She did some preoccupied banjo-strumming and I climbed on top of her again. She might have gotten something out of it for two or three minutes this time. Her eyes closed. She drew some sharp breaths. But then she went all inert.

"That's all right," said Mouna, folding her arms beneath her head. "You go ahead. You finish."

As if it was no fun for her anymore of course but she'd lie there and I could keep slogging away into her thing if I found any pleasure in it. It was honest of her, I suppose. It was like you took raw liver and you warmed it up to body temperature.

"You go right ahead," she said, staring off. "You keep going until you're done."

I should have taken it as a sign.

25

THE SUN WAS SETTING over romantic Iraq. With its sand
dunes and oil rigs, its happy, laughing people, its hope of
a better future. I leaned forward and peered out the plane
window. Way down there. You couldn't tell whether the
little buggers were laughing or not. There weren't any
sand dunes either, or any oil rigs yet. I can't tell you what
it looked like. A corrugated wasteland of reddish rock
stretching to the horizon. God's stone quarry. God's artillery
range. God's disposal ground for atomic waste. How could
anybody live down there? Iraq. Ancient Mesopotamia. Ur
of the Chaldees was down there someplace maybe, Abraham's home town, baking in the sun. I looked at a map.
Actually we were still over Iran.

Well, Iraq might be a horrible, barbarous, blood-lust-type
country but you couldn't have told it from thirty thousand
feet even if we were over it. And to tell the truth the Iraqi
Airways people had been absolutely darling to us as we got
aboard their plane in Teheran in First Class, because it
was First Class all the way as long as our Libyan and Abu
Dhabi money lasted, yes, sir. And he that traveleth First
Class shall neither hunger nor thirst. But it was the *viaje
de la ultima esperanza, amigo.* And if you want to know
what I really thought it was the voyage of no hope. I didn't
think we had a hope. *Iraq? Iraq with a "Q"? Baghdad?* It
was ridiculous. And Mouna. Mouna and Iraq, an unbeat-

able combination. She was the one who had been fouling things up all along, for God's sake. As a liberated Arab woman she was a constant provocation to the conservative Arabs who were deciding our fate. Throw her out! It was hopeless. People were so irrational. The whole thing was hopeless. The movie was through. We were through. We were bankrupts on the loose. I had this ending feeling. It was on me strong. Yes, my little *muchachos*, our little story was ending. *Mohammed Superstar*, this terrific movie I've been telling you about, this message of peace and good will to a strife-torn world, was never going to be made, it looked like now. It was sad, but that was the way it was. I could feel it. The sun was setting on romantic Iraq.

Mouna and Omar were sitting side by side to the right of the aisle, Omar pensively sipping a martini. Eat, drink martinis, and be merry, for tomorrow we may be making documentaries on ecology. Sandor and I were just behind. Mouna was rather withdrawn today, Omar flapping about as we got aboard, acting oddly protective. They'd worked things out somehow. Don't ask me on what basis. It was a funny relationship. But Sandor liked her too, really. What was so wonderful about this woman that everybody could see but me? It seemed to me she was an anti-social hysteric, subject to psychic storms and tempests, but familiarity had bred contempt, I suppose. Or more exactly, familiarity had bred nooky, and nooky had bred contempt. Nooky had bred a skeptical attitude. Nooky had kept me from putting her on a pedestal. But Omar had his nooky with her and he put her on a pedestal anyway. It was the difference between me and Omar. With Omar nooky led to idealization. With me it led to realism. Actually Mouna was her usual imperious self, just a little withdrawn. She got her way in everything. Allah forbid she should fake an orgasm. She was wearing a beige pants suit, big shades, her new style.

"Voom!" said Sandor, beside me. "Vroom! rrRRRR! Woof! Woof! Ah-hooo! Ah-hooo! Boing-boing! Ring-a-ding-a-ding! Oh-oo-oh-oo-oh-oo-oh-oo! (police car)."

It was an anthology of sex cries. He liked one of the

319

stewardesses. Pushing Methuselah and he still lit up like a pinball machine when he saw a girl he liked. When she was past us he made a weighing motion in front of his chest as if he was hefting two great pumpkins.

"How do they grab you?" he whispered.

"They grab me, they grab me," I said.

What were you going to say about breasts? Breasts were breasts. She was a little overweight actually for my taste. They were all a little overweight. They made you think of all those centuries of near-famine. With a background like that when you got a little extra flesh on the bones, a little extra fullness, what roundness, what joy, what beauty. To me it looked like fat. The stewardesses were dressed in pink skirts, pink caps, figure-fitting white blouses. They had these placid faces, big, dark eyes. The one Sandor liked had the most sharply delineated breast line. They were all overweight.

"Hey, listen," whispered Sandor. "You know what would be nice? They dressed the stewardesses like belly dancers! What a business they'd do! *Dah-dee dah-dee dah dah, dah-dee dah-dee dah dah.*"

He sang whining, belly-dancer music, making movements with his hips suggesting Little Egypt on a bad night.

"I like a nice *pupik*," he said judiciously. "Belly button. There's nothing like a nice *pupik*."

Him and his *pupiks*. Despite his obvious liabilities this character was being brought along to Baghdad as the man who'd shot the chariot race in *The Song of Jesus*, known in the trade as "Mandel's Messiah," but he was under a strict ban of silence on Jewish jokes, Hungarian jokes. No airing of his solutions for the Middle East or who should have sovereignty over Jerusalem. Just religious piety from him as from all of us, and as far as I was concerned that excluded *pupiks*. Iraq was the place that kept its few remaining Jews in a state of virtual imprisonment like hostages. I'd told him. He knew anyway.

"Hedy Lamarr had a nice *pupik*," Sandor said.

He glanced down at the armrest.

"The rash is all gone from your hands," he observed with surprise.

I'd been wearing gloves when we came aboard because of a rash on my hands.

"Hey, Burt, how come these girls can dress up all modern, Playtex bra, everything, but the girls down on the ground, they still got to wear veils?"

"I don't know," I said. "To keep passengers happy. In Iraq the international air passenger is king."

"Listen, just between you and me it's a little *meshuga* anyway. You get these almost full-grown girls, real titties on them, they go walking around with skirts up to their *tochis* and no veil. Suddenly somebody comes along, *You're fifteen years old now, you're a woman.* And they wrap them up in fifty yards of bed sheets, they're not safe for a man to look at anymore."

"Puberty rite," I said.

"Hey, Burt." He whispered behind his hand. "Is that when they cut off the clitoris and all the business? These stewardesses, they got a clitoris, yes or no?"

It was a grizzly thought. I hadn't thought about it since I'd been a prisoner of those Moroccan Tupamaros. It didn't seem polite to look straight at a girl and wonder if she had a clitoris.

"I wouldn't know. Ask our Arab expert, Mouna."

"I'll ask Mouna," said Sandor. "Hey, Mouna," he called forward in a hoarse *sotto voce*.

"No, no, I was just kidding!" I caught him but already Omar's face had appeared, inquisitive, peering around the side of his chair. Mouna didn't turn.

"Nothing," I cut Sandor off. "He just wanted to know if Mouna had the last script changes."

Mouna rose and walked back down the aisle carrying a copy of *La Revue du Liban*. Omar turned as far around toward us as he could, his face concerned.

"She's a little tense today," he said, his voice hushed. "I think it's because of Iraq."

"Why Iraq?" asked Sandor.

"1970," Omar said, looking about cautiously. "You remember, when the Jordanians shot up the fedayeen in Amman. Mouna says the Iraqis had a whole brigade stationed right there in Jordan, and the Palestinians were counting on them to come to their rescue and smash the Jordanians, but they just sat there, didn't attack the Jordanians, didn't do anything. The Palestinians say it was a stab in the back."

The Iraqi stab in the back again. "You remember the Iraqi stab in the back, don't you, Sandor?" I said. "The famous stabless stab in the back?"

"She's tense today because of these Iraqis," said Omar, rolling his eyes to indicate the Iraqi plane crew.

"Why wasn't she tense in Teheran?" I asked. "She hates them too. Why should the Iraqis make her tenser than the Iranians?"

"Factionalism," said Omar with slow-motion emphasis as if he was astonished at me. "The closer they are, the more they hate each other."

"I think you're the one that makes her tense," I said. "Fawning on her all the time."

"No." Omar smiled contentedly. "We've got it all worked out. She's agreed to stay on if I devote myself to the Palestinian cause after hours. She's under quite a bit of strain, you know. It's no bowl of cherries living with a man in this business. Worries all the time, uncertainties."

This had gone farther than I thought. It also seemed to imply he thought he was in a business. Only I seemed to know we were bankrupt.

"And me with Chloe back in Bel Air," reflected Omar. "That doesn't make it any easier for a girl."

"Now that you mention it, how *about* old Chloe back in Bel Air?" I said. "How are you going to sort that one out?"

"It might not be possible to solve without pain for someone," Omar said with the stoic attitude of somebody who didn't expect any of the pain to be his own. "Surgery might be necessary."

"Who's going to get the surgery? I thought you were through with Mouna."

"How does this no-fault divorce work?" answered Omar. "No matter what I do, it's not my fault? Chloe drove me to it?"

He saw Mouna coming back up the aisle with some new magazines and broke off abruptly like a schoolboy when the teacher comes back into the room, hastily snapping around front again.

So that's the kind of stuff we talked about as we flew over Iraq: which Arab countries cut off women's clitorises and no-fault divorce in California. Not entirely unrelated subjects, I suppose, all part of the great romantic merry-go-round of love. Actually I was still curious about this clitoris thing, which was gruesome but pretty important after all if it was your clitoris. I knew the practice was very widespread, but, country by country, who did you ask? Of course we had Mouna who definitely still had hers, but somehow I had the feeling she might take the question as implying a certain criticism of Arab culture. And they said there were no more taboo subjects. Go ask an Arab sheik if his wives had their clitorises cut off when you're trying to make a movie about Mohammed. Go ahead. What's more I didn't see any possibilities for clitorectomy as a petro-problem-movie either. I didn't think Arab society was ready for it yet, no, I didn't. Although it would sure give a fresh twist to the old boy-meets-girl flick. We could defend orthodoxy if they wanted, what the hell. Boy meets girl with clitoris: nothing but trouble, demands. Boy meets girl *without* clitoris: peace and order, domestic bliss. It would sure be a fresh twist on the old boy-meets-girl formula.

I checked my watch. It was ten minutes after the hour and I got up to be in position on time, walked back through First Class, some Arabs, European businessmen staring out the window. Then Economy, three-quarters empty, Arabs and Europeans, reading, dozing. At the water cooler, the jets louder, I took a paper cup, filled it, drank it slowly, leaning against the bulkhead. A hostess was asleep with a blanket over her legs on the last seat of the compartment, another one busy in the galley behind. At thirteen minutes after the hour a young Arab in a blue suit walked carefully back down the aisle to get a paper cup of water also. He avoided my eyes. He had a narrow, intent face, a thin black mustache, soulful brown eyes. Finished with his water, he leaned against the opposite bulkhead, putting him on a slight diagonal from me. I discreetly checked my watch and he discreetly checked his watch, and at exactly quarter after I said, "Stretching your legs?"

"Yes," he said, almost as if saddened, his eyes dog-like. "I am stretching my legs."

I waited.

"It is cooped up always to be in the same cockpit," he said with more animation.

"What's your favorite sport?" I asked.

"Water polo," he said briskly.

"And your favorite spectator sport?"

"Spectator? Ice hockey," he said, tightening his lips.

"Okay," I said.

I moved casually and with my foot tapped the suitcase where I'd left it on the floor at the end of an empty row near the back. I bent as if gazing out the window, glancing back at the water-polo player. He'd seen. Back in First Class I was very relaxed. "I've got a present for you," I said to Sandor, and gave him my paper cup. Two men from the front of the compartment rose and walked back along the aisle.

The stewardess brought us our snack, real china dishware, real cloth napkins.

"No pork east of Athens," Sandor said secretively, but as if announcing, "No land beyond the Volga," or perhaps, "Remember the Maine."

"No *trayf*," he said.

"What's that?"

"Food Jews aren't supposed to eat in Hungary."

"And in America?"

"Anything goes in America," he said, carefree. "Everybody eats everything."

He really spent half his time thinking about Jews though, that Sandor. It was Jews this, Jews that. He was a professional Jew, I guess. A quarter of an hour later we were talking about the war and he said, "You know what they used to say in Berlin in the Nazi time?"

"What?"

"It's all the fault of the Jews and the bicyclists."

"Bicyclists?"

"Sure. On the walls in the U-Bahn they wrote it. The Jews and the bicyclists. To show what nonsense. Ridicule kills. Nothing kills better than ridicule. It did Hitler a lot of harm, I'm telling you."

I didn't know exactly what to say to this since Hitler had survived the ridicule and gone on to greater things and only been stopped by forty million men under arms. All in all it seemed a bad precedent for trying to do people in by ridicule.

A stewardess went past us walking forward toward the pilot's cabin, followed closely by a man in a business suit grasping the waistband of her skirt and holding a pistol to the back of her head. I couldn't see the face of either of them. Only a few feet behind came a second stewardess and a second man in a business suit, same grip on the waistband, same pistol to head. Both pairs walked forward steadily and entered the pilot's cabin.

In the First Class cabin was silence, the faint humming of the jets and the slipstream. Some heads turned. There was a small stir. Faces were more expectant than shocked.

"What?" said Sandor. "What are they doing?"

"You tell me," I said.

"They're hijacking?" said Sandor in amazement. "They're hijacking us? Who are they? Where are they taking us?"

Omar's face, anxious, appeared over the back of his seat.

"What's going on?" he said.

"Why us?" said Sandor. "What have they got against us?"

Mouna rose and without turning her head walked swiftly

forward toward the pilot's cabin. Omar, facing back at us, didn't even see her go at first and when he did he twisted around all off balance, reaching out with his arms.

"Mouna!" he cried. "Come back! Where are you going?"

She didn't seem to hear him and entered the pilot's cabin in her turn.

The plane flew along, jets droning. Clouds passed below us. No noise came from the pilot's cabin. No stewardess's screams.

"What did Mouna go in there for?" pleaded Omar. "What's she got to do with this?"

Me he asks.

"Mouna," he mumbled and slumped down in his seat, crushed. "Maybe she's gone to interpret. Maybe she's gone to mediate. Maybe she's gone to offer her services."

"Maybe she's gone to take a dump," I said. "Shut up."

Five extra people had gone into the pilot's cabin now. It must be getting crowded in there. But you couldn't tell anything from the closed door, which was mute, neutral. A woman's voice came over the public address system in excited Arabic, glubble, glubble, glubble, who knows, and then in English: *Down with Saddam Hussein the murderer! This is the Shaela Gazaleh commando. We demand freedom for our brethren imprisoned and tortured in Iraq by the murderer Saddam Hussein! This plane has now been renamed "The Light of Dawn." If our demands are not granted by the murderer Hussein the plane and crew and passengers will all be destroyed. We are ready to give our lives so that Palestine shall live!*

It was Mouna's voice.

"Mouna," murmured Omar. I couldn't see his face.

"Iraq?" whispered Sandor as if awed. "What's she talking?"

The door to the pilot's cabin opened and one of the men in business suits emerged and blandly pointed a pistol in the direction of the First Class cabin at large, not aiming at anyone in particular, his eyes with a strange vacant look.

"Be calm!" he called out. "We are your friends!"

He was one of the young Latin Americans I'd seen standing with Mouna at the hotel in Teheran. He stood waving his pistol at us, aiming now here, now there, as if it was a hose and he was watering the front lawn. No one else came out of the cabin. The plane flew on. The cabin door was closed. Where would they fly us now, I wondered, but didn't feel like asking, or doing anything else that would make me conspicuous. The pistol the Latin American was waving at us had been one of the weapons in my suitcase. The water-polo player I'd delivered the suitcase to hadn't come to the front of the plane yet but I assumed he was stationed in the back somewhere, keeping down the lower orders in Economy Class.

Well, you'll never know what an interesting feeling it was to have labored anonymously in the vineyards of the Lord and to have brought forth this grape juice without even knowing it. I was a little stunned. These were Palestinians for the love of Mike. I'd been helping these *exaltado* Palestinians. I didn't even know what side I was on. I was a witless tool. KUBARK was using me. Here I was acting out of pure patriotism and they were using me. And Mouna. Gack. I didn't agree with this at all. She'd hoodwinked me, I guess. She was smarter than I thought. She'd hoodwinked somebody. How had she conned them into it? Mouna just wasn't the kind of woman you should entrust a dangerous weapon to. Why didn't they ask me? It was all a terrible mistake. As for the politics of the thing don't ask me to explain. I'd given up trying to figure out these Arab feuds. There was bad blood between Palestinians and Iraqis. Now that I thought of it I remembered hearing of joint Libyan-Palestinian assassination squads leaving Tripoli for Baghdad to knock off people. How was I supposed to remember all that? I had films to write. And would Baghdad be susceptible to indirect pressure from threats against innocent third parties? Was Baghdad worried about world opinion? This might all be very ill-advised. And what was in it for ODYOKE? Ingratiating ourselves with these Palestinians? Sowing dissension among the Arabs in general? It was hard to figure out unless you knew everything. And who knew everything? Where would we be flying now? Damascus, I supposed, another four-five hundred miles. I didn't believe it that she'd blow us all up.

The cabin door opened and the two captured stewardesses came stumbling out tearfully and scurried toward the back of the plane as fast as they could go. Mouna appeared in their place, her face haggard, sunglasses gone, a grenade in one hand and a pistol in the other.

"Mouna!" cried Omar, rising, stretching his arms toward her.

A look of panic crossed Mouna's face and she raised her gun arm in a spasm as if fearing attack. Omar started edging into the aisle as if planning to approach her, embrace her, something crazy. "Omar, sit down!" I said and grabbed at him but he beat me off, wriggling away. I clutched him by the back of his collar and finally dragged him down. "She can't do this," he muttered to himself. "She doesn't mean it." Mouna had a wild, hunted-fox look in her eyes. If Omar had gone forward I think she'd have shot him. "I never thought it would come to this," moaned Omar. "What will the Iraqis think?"

Mouna was speaking in Arabic now, her voice raised, shrill. Her partner, the Latin American, waited for the translation, his face blank, his pistol wandering over the audience, but there was no translation. She just stopped. Ideology made curious national bedfellows, a Palestinian hijacking team made up of a woman, a male Latin American who didn't understand Arabic, a second man still in the pilot's cabin who was probably the other Latin American this one had said *vamanos* to at the hotel in Teheran, and my water-polo player in back who'd passed out the weapons, the only male Palestinian in the lot. At least there were no Japanese. Mouna was speaking Arabic again, very high-pitched, her face flushed, the veins in her throat standing out. The muscles at the back of her neck were contracting, giving the effect of her head being tugged back by someone standing behind her. Still there was no translation. She seemed to have lost her English. Her partner's face, no longer blank, was beginning to look apprehensive. I poked my head forward between the two seats in front of me and asked Omar what she was saying.

"She never listens to me," he blurted.

"What's she saying though?"

Omar didn't answer. I tapped him on the arm. His eyes finally became photosensitive and he glanced furtively from one side to the other.

"What was she yelling about?"

"Down with Iraq," he said with an abstracted air. "Very excessive."

The Latin American had disappeared inside the pilot's cabin and soon the other hijacker came out, scowling. He didn't look Latin American after all and seemed distinctly Arab. There were two male Arabs then, one Latin American. Mouna's voice was rising again, staccato, glottal, her eyes wild. She was making some kind of exciting speech but I had a feeling she might not be exactly toeing the party line. Her fellow Palestinian spoke to her sharply in Arabic. She didn't answer. She didn't turn her head. Her partner placed his left hand calmly on her shoulder, and she responded by raising her voice again, almost shrieking, her head jerking back as if to make the words fly higher, to break out, rip out.

"What's she saying now?" I asked Omar in a hushed voice.

"Crazy stuff," he said mournfully. "Very out of place."

"We do not agree with this lady," said Mouna's partner in some embarrassment. "We want only freedom for Palestinian national homeland."

"What in God's name was she saying?" I asked Omar insistently.

Omar didn't speak but laid his full hand across his forehead as if seeing if he had a fever, taking his own temperature.

I poked his arm.

"Duh," he shuddered quietly as if he'd eaten something that tasted very bad, then shook his head despairingly.

I nudged him again, more softly.

"She wants Saddam Hussein's blood," he said dismally. "Vengeance for their martyrs. She wants blood to flow."

"Whose?"

"Saddam Hussein's. The whole Iraqi government." Omar was disgusted. "How do I know? Innocent martyrs' blood has been spilled. Blood for blood. It's excessive as hell."

"Saddam Hussein's supposed to voluntarily commit suicide to save *us*?"

"And not a thought for the movie," said Omar bitterly. "Can you imagine the kind of reception we're going to get in Iraq now?"

I could see it from the Palestinian point of view too. Mouna was absolutely ruining things. Here they'd had it all worked out to give themselves a reasonable image, establishing sensible, limited goals for their operation, and suddenly this crazy erupts in their midst, exactly the kind of person that gives terrorism a bad name. She was addressing the passengers in fits and starts now, grenade in one hand, pistol in the other, while her erstwhile partner eyed her in alarm, a pistol in his hand also. What could he do? Shoot her? It would look harsh. Mouna was shrieking now, her neck muscles contracting strongly as if she was having convulsions. Her head kept jerking back, eyelids flickering. She was hysterical. Her fellow Palestinian edged the grenade out of her hand and stuffed it into the side pocket of his jacket with the pin still safely in place, then soothingly reached for her pistol. Mouna, her face now all white and weak-looking, let him take it. He signaled to a first-row passenger to vacate his seat and, when the place was empty, eased Mouna toward it. Suddenly the wind went all out of Mouna and she almost fell into the seat and sat there limp, lifeless, her arm trailing down over the armrest.

The man who'd given up his seat for Mouna turned from

side to side as if wondering what to do with himself now, where to put himself, hesitating indecisively, Mouna's accomplice now bending over Mouna. Whereupon the displaced passenger swiftly drew a pistol of his own and dealt the Palestinian a crushing blow to the back of the head. He pitched forward into Mouna's lap, rolled off, lay twitching in the aisle. Another man rose in the front of the cabin. I didn't even see from exactly where. He moved intently to the fallen Palestinian, kneeled, disarmed him with quick, practiced movements, operating in grim silence. Standing again he trained a pistol toward the back of the plane, breathing heavily. These two both had quite dark complexions, unquestionably Arabs, Iraqi sky marshals. There was no cry of relief from the stewardesses yet because the hardest was yet to come. But with no hesitation the marshal who had laid out the Palestinian now turned and approached the door to the pilot's cabin with his weapon at the ready, threw the door open, fired once, disappeared. There was the sound of one more shot within. I didn't think they were supposed to fire when planes were in flight. In a moment the sky marshal edged backwards to the doorway again, glancing back over his shoulder, signaled to his teammate. The marshal who had remained in the First Class compartment with us now turned all his attention to the back of the plane, pistol steady, eyes glaring, no doubt planning to deal with the last Palestinian back there. I hoped to hell they weren't going to shoot it out. What the hell did they think this was, the O.K. Corral?

"Get down!" I said to Sandor. "Get ready to get down."

Crouched as I was, ready to hit the deck, I saw slowly, with languid unreality, a man come walking from the rear through the entrance to the First Class section carrying a Kalashnikov submachine gun. The Iraqi sky marshal with the drawn pistol didn't shoot him. This new man didn't shoot the marshal. He proceeded up the aisle with such relaxed, everyday informality that it almost seemed he'd come to peddle used machine guns. He was a machine gun peddler. He stepped over the body of the man lying unconscious in the aisle and arrived at the front of the compartment, turned and trained his weapon loosely back at us all. It was the Palestinian I'd given the suitcase to. My water-polo player. The Kalashnikov had been one of the prize weapons in the suitcase. The two men nodded to each other, mumbled something, stood side by side training their weapons on us amiably, on Mouna still slumped in her seat, on the body lying in the aisle, on the rest of us, benignly, just to ensure order. The man with the pistol broke off and entered the pilot's cabin. A male voice came over the public address system.

This airplane is taken over by the Kurdish National Liberation under the commandment of General Barzani to demonstrate to the world our grievance against the tyrannical despotism of Iraq government which is denying our people its national rights in the most tyrannical way. This is the Mustapha Barzani commando. All passengers will be treated kindly in case they behave themselves. Long live Kurdistan.

The Palestinian wasn't a Palestinian he was a Kurd. And the sky marshals weren't sky marshals they were Kurds. They were all Kurds. How was I supposed to know? They only told me to give the suitcase to who I gave it to. How did I know what he was? There was a whole new cast of characters now. The Kurd with my Kalashnikov stood there with it trained in our direction. His face was calm.

I was stunned again. I was even more stunned than the first time. Two hijackings on the same flight. This was ridiculous. This was the height of ridiculousness. And they were both against Iraq. Couldn't they get together? Couldn't they cooperate? Wasn't there wasted effort? I was very stunned. Kurds. It's too complicated to explain. Kurds were this other group. I wasn't such a witless tool. I was a witting tool. I knew more or less what was going on. These were my Kurds. It's a little complicated to explain. Gack. These were the good guys, and *those* were the bad guys. Lucky I didn't say anything. If the Palestinians had some grudges against the Iraqis, the Kurds really hated them and were fighting a terrific guerrilla war against them up in the hills and were a plucky lot, I thought. This hijacking made more sense than the other hijacking.

It seemed to me we should be banking and changing course and heading back east to Iran where the Kurds had friends, or north to Kurdistan, and I could almost feel the stick in my hands, but nothing so far. I had a safety factor the other passengers didn't know about in that if hijackers killed the pilot and copilot in some policy disagreement I'd have a decent chance of saving the plane. I'd never flown a Boeing 737 but I'd do better than these stewardesses. Unless the Kurds set off a grenade and blew a huge hole in the side and air pressure went to zilch and the plane crashed and everyone was killed, in which case it would be goodbye Omar. I was starting to feel begrudgingly exhilarated, in that can-do kind of way, sensing that I was playing my part in big things, that it wasn't just another hijacking but maybe a hijacking for oil and national survival, a brilliant conceptual breakthrough, the first Kurdish hijacking. It would cause nothing but trouble for Iraq, which was really the big bad place, pro-Soviet, and anti-ODYOKE on oil, weren't they, and enemies of our friends the Iranians, who were also anti-ODYOKE on oil but a whole lot friendlier on other things. The Iranians would love this; they hated Iraq. I was working this out on the basis of informed speculation.

I was warming to this thing. I was all a-tingle now, and excited, and relaxed, I can't tell you how relaxed, with the adrenalin all relaxing me, calming my nerves. And who would think we had anything to do with it? ODYOKE involved in a hijacking? The deniability of the operation was fantastic. The deniability of the Palestinian hijacking would have been fantastic too. I mean the whole thing was really terrible, a great moral nation forced to descend to the lowest depths of lawlessness, and I was basically an abused, well-meaning tool of those bastards in KUBARK. Still as an operation it had pizzazz.

We were banking around to the right, right wing low. I watched the sun coming in the windows slowly moving around. We changed course about ninety degrees. By the sun we seemed to be flying north, probably to Kurdistan, wherever that was. Did they have airfields in Kurdistan? Flat stretches that could serve as landing strips? The Kurd who'd made the announcement over the public address system came back into the First Class compartment, knelt by the Palestinian who was still lying groggily in the aisle, and efficiently tied his hands behind his back with electrical wire, leaving him lying there. He gave Mouna a long, wary look, then made her stand up and turn around while he wired her hands together too. She gazed back at us vacantly, her eyes unknowing, the jacket of her pants suit rumpled. When she sat again her crossed hands in the small of her back prevented her from leaning back and she sat with her shoulders angled, head slumped forward. By my count there must be a dead Latin American in the pilot's cabin but I assume he wasn't taking up too much room. Well, a whole new team had taken over. The chief Kurd was doubtless keeping the pilot and copilot under control up front. The faces of the two Kurds in the First Class compartment with us softened now into half-smiles and they held their weapons more easily. I couldn't have told them from Arabs. They both had this coppery skin color, dark hair; both were in their twenties. The one carrying a pistol had a high forehead and wide-set eyes. With a change of coloring he could even have been Dutch or German. The features of my waterpolo player with the Kalashnikov were more Levantine, the nose aquiline. Relaxed now, their faces seemed quite civilized.

"Do not panic. Do not be fearful," said the one with the pistol, smiling. "We will not hurt anyone. We do this only for our Kurdistan homeland."

He skirted the body in the aisle and stepped forward to address a passenger in the middle of the compartment, a man in his fifties, gray suit, plump.

"You, sir. What nation are you?" the Kurd asked him graciously.

The man looked as if he didn't particularly want to own

up to being any nation, but finally murmured, "German. *Bundesdeutsch.*"

"Now, sir," said the Kurd. "If Germany was bossed around by a tyrannical foreign nation, and you hadn't your own schools, and even no school books in German, only the hated foreign tyrant language, wouldn't you feel this is injustice? Wouldn't you be oppressed? Wouldn't you fight for freedom of beloved German homeland? This is all we want, we Kurds. Freedom for Kurd people like freedom for German people. Freedom for beloved homeland of all peoples."

This felt peculiar; I don't know why. Perhaps it was that we'd just had the Palestinian homeland and here we were on to the Kurdish homeland with no intermission. The world was filled with suppressed homelands. The German was clearing his throat.

"I don't know much about politics in this part of the world," he said tentatively, in good English, grateful for the gentle technique. "Perhaps your grievances should be given consideration."

It didn't commit him to much but the Kurd continued on his goodwill tour, smiling, courteous, very friendly. If you were Swedish he said wouldn't you fight for the beloved Swedish homeland? If you were French he said freedom for the Kurd and French peoples. It went over really quite well with the Europeans. What he said to the Arabs I don't know since it was in Arabic. That part didn't seem to go so well. There were strained looks.

The Kurd completed his tour of First Class and went into the pilot's cabin to confer with their leader, leaving my water-polo player behind to keep us under surveillance, still training his Kalashnikov in our direction. I'd given it to him myself but it was a weapon for which I could claim no great fondness, I must admit, as there was nothing more undiscriminating than a submachine gun. It sprayed slugs over everything at the slightest pretext, critics, innocuous onlookers, well-wishers. Firing with it you couldn't hit a barn door at a hundred yards, and at close quarters if an adversary gave a quick blow to deflect the muzzle and got inside you were in real trouble. When it was pointing at me I liked it even less. The man behind the Kalashnikov gave me no sign of recognition. We had never met. The Kurds' leader came out of the pilot's cabin and conferred with the machine gunner in what I assumed was Kurdish, then returned to the cabin, and the goodwill expert reappeared. Pistol tucked into his belt now, he decided to proceed with the task at hand.

"We present our lives to Free Kurdistan," he offered with an engaging smile to the First Class passengers as he made his way through the compartment to continue his proselytizing in Economy Class.

"Where are they taking us?" whispered Sandor.

"I don't know," I said. "Some desert?"

"And then what happens? They blow up the plane?"

"They just might," I said.

"But they let us get out first?"

"Oh, sure. What would they want to blow us up for?"

"How you know they let us out?" said Sandor, suspicious.

"Well, what's he giving us the glad-hand treatment for if he's going to blow us up?"

I tapped Omar on the elbow and he moved his head lifelessly toward me. His eyes were dull.

"How you bearing up?" I said as a mild sound of scuffling reached us from the Economy Class compartment.

The Kurd with the Kalashnikov rushed down the aisle with his weapon at the ready, his face tensed, and just as he left the First Class compartment an Arab I'd hardly even noticed in a back corner rose with a drawn pistol, took aim at the retreating Kurd, and fired. It sounded harmless, like an air rifle. The man fired again, peered carefully after the Kurd for an instant, then swung around swiftly and aimed at the door of the pilot's cabin as if he expected it to fly open instantly. It didn't and the sound of more air-rifle firing came to us from Economy Class. Pop, pop, pop. Half a dozen rounds from a BB gun. Three or four more rounds. How many people were they shooting back there? I certainly hoped none of the bullets were going to pierce the skin of

336

the plane. In a minute, two more Arabs with drawn pistols erupted from the back into First Class, out of breath but faces empty, strangely expressionless. They had been reloading their pistols and checked them once more as the other man continued to cover the door of the pilot's cabin. Glancing back down the aisle into Economy Class, I saw two bodies lying face down on the floor. The plane flew on. The chief hijacker in the pilot's cabin might not even have heard the sound of shooting with the low-pressure, low-noise pistols. Most passengers sat motionless with shock as the three Arabs prepared themselves for what unless I missed my guess looked like it was going to be another military assault on the pilot's cabin.

"Hey, what is this, a shooting gallery?" whispered Sandor, outraged. "They're not supposed to do this! What if they blow up the plane? What if we all get killed?"

"Get down," I said. "Get down on the floor."

I reached forward and grabbed Omar by the elbow.

"Get down," I warned him. "There's going to be shooting."

At a last glance, all three Arabs were moving forward toward the pilot's cabin and I crouched as low as I could between the seats, doubling up on the floor. The plane flew on, droning like a great vacuum cleaner. I could see only green carpeting, a vanity case Mouna had left by her seat. A faint thud sounded, like a side of meat thumping against a wall. Then pop, pop, pop, air rifles firing. A shout. Another shout. Silence. The seconds passed. Suddenly the whole plane pitched forward and we were diving. There was the old sick-making stomach heave and hateful floating and now terror. Had the pilot and copilot both been killed? I pulled myself down the aisle, clutching at seats. *I'm a pilot!* I shouted to a man with a pistol who was bracing himself in the doorway to the pilot's cabin. He rasped something to me in Arabic, waving me away with his gun hand, his face threatening. Mind my own business. He didn't seem too worried. We were losing altitude at a terrific rate but the plane appeared under control. The pilot must be taking us down to prevent a pressure blowout; a bullet might have cracked one of the windows. We were diving less steeply and I managed to get back to my seat and belt myself in and, sure enough, at about a thousand feet we leveled out, then banked, swinging around, changing course to the left. I saw huge, geometrical beige fields directly out the left-hand windows. Then we steadied on course, scudding along over straw-colored countryside.

The cabin air pressure hadn't dropped and the passengers were all looking at each other dazedly, some of them feeling their heads, rotating wrenched shoulders. Stewardesses ran up and down the aisle. Omar was sitting completely blotto. Despite my warning I don't think he'd even sheltered himself from stray bullets but had just sat there. FASTEN YOUR SAFETY BELTS the sign said now that the action was over. Two of the men who'd taken the pilot's cabin by assault were carrying out a body, half the face a mass of blood. They opened the door to one of the First Class toilets and pitched the body in, closing the door again, surveying the passengers. I sat very still. The third man joined them and there they stood, three Arabs in business suits with the air of having done a job well, but their faces stern, no smiles, no talk of a Druze or Maronite homeland. They were the real sky marshals this time. These were the Iraqi guards. One took off his blue suit coat and, underarm holster and straps conspicuous now on his white shirt, lifted up the Palestinian who'd been lying in the aisle all this time and threw him into the First Class toilet too. *Was he dead? I thought he'd been alive the last time I'd looked at him.* Two of the guards set off to drag away the bodies of the two Kurds that were still lying in the aisle back in Economy Class and stuff them in a toilet compartment back in the tail. There was still one body missing, it seemed to me. What happened to the Latin American? I never found out. I didn't want to appear too interested in all this, acting detached, looking out the window. We were flying at such low altitude you could see people working in the fields.

Out of the corner of my eye I saw that the guards were standing in front of Mouna now, their faces set. She stood up and turned, her eyes dead, while they checked the fastenings around her wrists. When she was seated again, hunched forward, they tied her into her place, standing back to stare somberly at their handiwork. I could just see one of Mouna's shoulders now and the back of her head from an angle. A guard with an unfocused, blurred look seemed to be gathering up a handful of Mouna's hair at the top of her head. He suddenly drove the head back against the seat, lunged at her with his right arm, pulling something crossways, then changed his stance and bore in again with his weight. He stood back, his hand bright red. Mouna's head pitched forward. A man sitting in the seat directly behind her gave a moaning sound and turned his head back in our direction, his eyes frenzied. Mouna had just had her throat cut.

In a few minutes the guards untied her from her seat and one of them, dragging her by her hair, pulled her the full length of the plane to stuff her into a toilet compartment in the tail. Horrified at the thought of a yawning gash under Mouna's throat, I looked away as the guard dragged her corpse by, catching only a glimpse of red. Her sagging, dead-weight body had lost one shoe. Sandor gagged as if he was throwing up and I felt sick to my stomach myself. I didn't look to see how Omar was taking it. I didn't really want to know how Omar was taking it. I just sat with my safety belt on, seeing as little as possible, moving as little as possible, hoping this was the end of it. We were in the same group as Mouna. Would the guards hold us responsible in some way? If they had no hard feelings against us I was willing to have no hard feelings against them. Baghdad. Who the hell wanted to go to Baghdad?

The next thing I remember clearly was the stewardess's announcement: *We apologize to our passengers for any inconvenience during our flight.*

"Champagne?" asked a stewardess a few minutes later.

We were celebrating the triumph of law and order. They broke out champagne for all hands, even in Economy Class, free champagne. The guards were smiling, a job well done. Moslems drinking an alcoholic beverage, imagine that. I didn't want to be conspicuous and took a glass. There was a festive atmosphere aboard. We'd defeated two separate teams of hijackers. The bodies were neatly stuffed in the toilets. Everybody was chatting with everybody else. Except us, our little group, Omar, Sandor, and me. We were less chatty.

"The poor kid," said Sandor with tears in his eyes. "She was under a lot of pressure. A poor, innocent, *zaftig* kid like that gets caught up in all this *mishegaas*."

I couldn't agree with that all along the line of course, but, well, you know. I didn't say anything.

"A tragedy," said Sandor emotionally. "A terrible tragedy."

Omar had drawn into himself with a desolate look and seemed as if he didn't want to have any conversation with anybody and was mourning Mouna sincerely. It must have been a quarter of an hour before he glanced around and our eyes met.

"It's the end of the movie," he said.

"Don't be discouraged, Ome," I said. I felt I should cheer him up. "We'll fix it up somehow. *Inshallah*."

It seemed funny flying along at such low altitude. It was a completely different landscape now, rivers, green fields. We were getting ready for our landing run at Baghdad, banking for our approach to the runway. In the run we lowered our flaps and there was a great roaring, whistling noise and I thought they were right; one of those bullets had pierced something. But the pilot got us down all right. Our wheels touched, and he reversed engines and gradually we slowed and he reduced thrust and we were taxiing. When we finally rolled to a halt everybody was dancing in the aisles as if we'd just won a big football game, Iraqi stewardesses and Western businessmen and Arabs and Europeans and everybody, hand in hand, hopping up and down and yipping, just from the delight of having survived the experience. And you could understand their point of view. I mean what the hell. Who wants to die.

26

IT WAS SAD. I was the first one to admit it was sad. Mouna and those plucky Kurds, and that poor Venezuelan or whatever he turned out to be, all acting out of such idealistic motives. The Palestinian was probably very idealistic too. It was really terrible, stuff like this. You know, innocent parties suffered. In this case the parties who suffered weren't exactly innocent, at least of hijacking, but still their hearts were pure. You know what I mean. It was still tragic. Sandor was right. It was part of the tragedy of life, the rich, human, tragic fabric of the human condition, brave individuals who go forward, willing to sacrifice themselves so that the rest of us can live in peace and freedom. Not you and me, actually, because we're living in peace and freedom already, but their fellow Kurds, Venezuelans, Palestinians, or whatever. At times like this there is a unity to all mankind I think. I weep for them all, really, regardless of faith, creed, or color. I don't mean tears actually came to my eyes. But something inside was weeping.

"You *momzer!*" said Sandor. "Don't you have any human feelings!"

All just because I said Mouna was lucky to die a martyr and that she'd be happy now if she could know. This was back in Teheran. I got out of Iraq fast. I wasn't hanging around there.

So I wasn't emotional. What did I have to do, break down

341

and sob? I had human feelings. What the hell. But you had
to be fair. You had to be objective. Mouna had been a volun-
teer after all. She'd cracked up. Whose fault was that?
She'd said some indiscreet things, screaming for the blood
of Saddam Hussein, for example, their strong man. You
couldn't expect the Iraqis to like that. They were very mean
with her, of course, but they were mean people. Anyway it
wasn't me who'd killed her, but her Arab brothers for Christsake. So why *momzer*? Was it worth ruining a friendship
over because I didn't go to pieces and cry? Would it have
done Mouna any good? I'd always thought Sandor was too
emotional and that he might go soft when you needed him.
A guy like that should stay in the world of fine sentiments.
He'd feel better about things given a little time though. I'd
send him a postcard in a couple of months.

So what do you think, the clown now stands unmasked
before you as a heartless brute? And if we were only saintly
enough the Third World, which like Iran has such high
moral standards, would seek to emulate our shining virtue?
And the rule of peace would come upon earth? And the KGB
would lie down with the lamb? Fuck that. The Russians and
everybody else ran Special Ops, and so did we. I'm not going
to apologize for that. I was the first to grant that this particular incident was sad, that it hadn't been successful. But
you had to keep a sense of proportion. Okay, things could
have been better. I'd go that far. But it was just an episode.
It was just one of those episodes. It ended on a sour note.
Okay, it ended on a sour note.

And look at what happened to the rest of the poor Kurds
right while we were still there in Teheran. The Shah threw
them to the dogs. He'd incited them to rebel to begin with.
He'd supplied them, egged them on, sent weapons, muni-
tions, artillery. Then when he got his favorable border settle-
ment from Iraq, that was it. He just dumped the poor
bastards, cut off all support, and gave Kurdish refugees
two weeks to get across the Iranian border. He'd suckered
them completely. The Iraqis were tipped off ahead of time

naturally and the day after the pact with Iran they launched a full-scale offensive up in the mountains. The brave Kurdish rebellion: thirty-five thousand Kurds dead for nothing. There was a real tragedy. Two hundred thousand refugees. They were streaming across the border in rags even as we talked about it in Teheran. The U.S. did the least little thing and people were screaming at us: we were callous, we were cynical, we were faithless, we didn't stick by our friends, we were external fascists. And the Shah of Iran sold the Kurds down the river and nobody even gave it a thought, the world press ignored it. Actually the Shah was a shit. Actually we were supposed to guarantee the operation to the Kurds or they would never have stuck their neck out, but all our support was going in over the Iranian border. What could we do when the Shah pulled the plug? The dancing Shah was a shit.

Well, we were sitting around the shop talking about the Shah and I told them about Janie Holt from Wilmette, Illinois, because I kept them filled in on things like that in a routine sort of way. And amid the to and fro of intellectual discussion a concept emerged that was so sophisticated you'll never understand it. All I'll say is that even when sexual entrapment operations work people don't like you for it. There's ill will. They have a tendency to think people who set up operations like that are pretty vile people. They take it as a sign of malevolence. They think you shouldn't do that to friends. Well, now. What if we set up the Shah and got pictures of him and Janie Holt from Wilmette, Illinois, and then whapped them into Iran in such a way as to make the Shah think the Russians did it? We'd gotten Russian arms for the Kurds; we could certainly get pictures of the Shah and Janie into Iran through what looked like a Russian channel. There was no chance whatever the Shah was going to knuckle under to the Russians on a thing like that; he'd just get furious at them. But it would keep him honest, you know? I mean that goddamn Shah owed us everything from 1953, with Allen Dulles, Kermit Roosevelt and company

343

saving his ass from Mossadegh, but was the son of a bitch grateful? Ever since the big oil-price rises in 1974 he'd gotten real delusions of grandeur, dreaming he was Cyrus the Great, more imperious every day, pushing for a rise in oil prices every time you turned around, forgetting his true friends. This would remind him of what kind of people the Russians were. Actually whichever way it went it would give us leverage, get the Shah's feet back on the ground, do him good really. Who was he to forbid us access to the opposition, too dumb to let us keep him in power? And if he didn't like little tricks, let him give up the tango.

But now the sophisticated part. You can have all the monster computers in the world, and all the electronic monitoring networks, and all the satellite scanning systems, and nothing will ever replace that spark of creative imagination. Just because the Shah danced the tango with Janie in his dressing gown didn't mean he was crazy. You obviously couldn't set him up in his own palace in Teheran. And Zermatt in Switzerland where he took his skiing holidays would be tough too, crawling with security. But remember the lights were going to be infrared and the print quality would be fuzzy. We weren't going to win any Academy Award for photography. Suppose we got a guy who just looked kind of like the Shah. *But with this real bang of the Shah's.* So even the Shah thought it was the Shah! Stun him as to where we had the camera! Daring, huh? Prudent and intrepid at the same time. The Shah had this very distinctive nose and hairline. We could fake it easy. WANTED. TRIM MIDDLE-EASTERNER FOR ARTISTIC POSES. HIGH PAY. EASY WORK. I'd do it myself but I thought Janie wouldn't swallow it. *Darling, why are you wearing that wig and funny nose?* Just give me a cozy little KUBARK safe house. I'd cast, direct, choreograph, put on make-up. You could call it my vengeance for the Kurds.

Well, boarding the plane for Paris I realized it was finally the end of *Mohammed Superstar*, which I still think would have brought a lot of peace and understanding in the world. Sandor had gone back to Hollywood, where despite his age he was really the king of second-unit directors. There was nobody who could burn Atlanta, or take Vicksburg, or Omaha Beach, or Carthage, or anyplace like Sandor. And you should see his work on Westerns. Anything with horses. Omar was holding up all right. He was back in L.A., already reconciled with his Mormon. He was only bankrupt in a manner of speaking, I should explain. It was only his Liechtenstein company that was bankrupt. He had his producer's fee and his director's fee from *Mohammed Superstar*, which he'd paid to himself in advance privately. In fact it turned out he'd been siphoning money out of the production all along, stealing it you might say, and he was soon set up in Hollywood as the producer of low-budget knock-offs of earlier hits, *Star Schlock, The Schlock Strikes Back, Raiders of the Lost Schlock, Land of the Living Schlock*, movies like that, with a new house in Holmby Hills. I think maybe he wasn't an idealist after all. I think he was less of an idealist than Moustapha Akkad, who got tied in with the John Carpenter movies. At least they're dedicated to the proposition that we live in a vicious universe where something out there is trying to get us, which is really a healthier idea and also serves the national interest.

For me it was a temporary financial step downward, I must admit. "THE LAST TANGO IN ZERMATT" STARRING SHAH MOHAMMED PAHLEVI OF IRAN AND A CAST OF ONE. IN GLORIOUS INFRARED. It had its illicit glamor though. And if the Shah was to fall, it could never be said that I had not done my best to save him from himself. Actually I was the idealist. I thought about it all on the flight up to Paris as we flew over the Alps. All white. Very beautiful.

Janie met me at the airport at Roissy, looking divine, just perfect for the role. And I took her to dinner that night at *l'Ange Bleu*, which she thought was absolutely the right kind of place. The conversation was the usual Gemini-Capricorn routine but all through the evening I looked into those glowing blue Illinois eyes and thought, *You're a patriot, sweetie. Service to your country is one of the noblest activities known to man.* That's what I said to myself. I didn't tell her.